Bad To The Bone

Tony J Forder

ONE

It didn't look much like a corpse. Other than the skull, of course. That was a bit of a giveaway. The bones themselves, clumps of moist soil clinging to them like leeches, looked more like an array of dead branches and twigs than the remains of a human being. In the end, thought Detective Inspector James Bliss, a person doesn't amount to much.

He dragged his gaze from the body, taking in both the immediate crime scene and the surrounding area. Bliss was reasonably familiar with this part of Bretton Woods, which lay to the north of Peterborough city centre. He'd watched a few games of football on the adjoining fields, the woods looming over shabby changing rooms as if preparing to pounce on the players as they emerged. Neither large nor dense, the wooded area was nonetheless well populated with elderly birch and oak and wild clumps of ragged undergrowth. The local township of Bretton had been built around it little more than thirty years ago, developers keen to preserve an echo of the past.

Bliss began to feel like an intruder, quenching a voyeuristic thirst on someone else's misery. He shook off the feeling, reminding himself that emotions could only hamper the investigation that was about to begin.

'You think it's a bit late to consider CPR?' he asked, glancing to his right.

Detective Constable Penny Chandler shook her head and grinned. 'You could try. I bet you've jumped bones with less life in them.'

Bliss chuckled and nodded, turning his attention to the body once more. Twenty-three years in the job, two decades of which were spent in the Met, had inured him against such sights. He recalled his first dead body, an almost mummified male held together by ragged strips of cloth. It had been discovered in a dank Hackney basement after a neighbour had complained about the stench coming from the house next door. Bliss had just knelt down next to the corpse when its chest began to stir. Horror-stricken, he had immediately reared back, falling on his arse, eyes unable to turn from the pulsating series of movements. The stark image of a slime-covered creature erupting from John Hurt's body in the movie *Alien* flashed through his mind. But that was swiftly eradicated when, in an eruption of clothing and petrified flesh, a huge rat burst out of the corpse's ribcage. To this day, Bliss swore that rodent had taken a long, contemptuous glance in his direction before scuttling away.

There had been many corpses since.

Too many.

Not all of them murder victims, but increasingly that was becoming the rule rather than the exception. It was a sign of the times.

Bliss found it curious that the body hadn't been buried further away from one of the many winding tracks that spider-webbed the wood. It seemed to him that if you were going to take the trouble of burying someone, you might as well do the job properly. Even so, he realised it may have lain hidden forever had a couple of ten-year-old lads not decided to bury a time-capsule (in reality a large biscuit tin containing a newspaper, a few coins, a dog-eared copy of *Playboy* purloined from an elder brother's hidden stash, and an audio tape the boys had recorded the previous day).

Bliss filled his lungs. The smell of burning leaves hung heavy in the late autumn air, but beyond it he thought he could detect the promise of a winter encroaching all too quickly. When he exhaled, his breath formed a cloud before his eyes – a stark reminder, if he needed one, that life was better than the alternative.

Hunkered down on the edge of the burial site, Bliss played his torch over the scene, the light bright and steady. Mounds of loose soil enveloped the carcass, tossed away casually by eager, excited fingers. Small footprints embossed in flattened patches of earth suggested a frenzied dig. Odd. Or was it? These were young boys, after all. And even though he sometimes felt as old as the dirt now beneath his feet, Bliss could well imagine the thrill those lads had experienced. It would have been intoxicating.

'How long d'you suppose she's been here?' he asked, rubbing a small clod of earth between his gloved fingers.

'She?' Chandler queried, a ridge forming just above her nose.

'I reckon so, yes.'

Bliss stood fully upright He put two hands to the small of his back and stretched, letting out a gentle groan.

'You sure? I mean, how can you tell?'

'The skull mainly. Females have more oval-shaped heads, the nasal cavities are quite different, and men's eye sockets are more rectangular. I haven't clapped eyes on the hips so far, but I'm certain they'll be the child-bearing kind.'

'I had no idea you were such an expert.'

'It's called reading, Constable. You should try it some time.'

Chandler poked her tongue out at him and blew a soggy raspberry. She leaned forward, head now directly over the tangle of bones. Several strands of hair had escaped the clutches of one of her grips, and now hung like curtains across her face.

'Well, whoever this poor woman is, I'd say she's been here for a few years.'

'Why do you think that?'

'The colour of the bones. They're very dark – they certainly don't look fresh.' She straightened and pulled a face at his look of scepticism. 'You're not the only one who knows their job, sir.'

Bliss studied her face for a moment. A breeze caught the folds of his overcoat, flapping them around his knees as if they were being pawed at by playful puppies. He smiled at the look of challenge in the DC's eyes.

'You're guessing, aren't you?' he said.

'I might be.' A smile touched the corners of her mouth.

'I knew it.'

'You know nothing.'

'I know you. Too bloody well for my own good. But as it happens, Penny, I have a feeling you could be right. I think this poor woman has been here for some time.'

They both peered cheerlessly down into the grave one last time, and then Bliss snapped the torch off with a flick of his thumb. The little remaining natural light fringed the area, as if reluctant to trespass upon this place of death. He pulled off his latex gloves, gripping them in a tight fist as he thrust both hands deep into his coat pockets. Already ideas were forming in his mind, arranging themselves in neat blocks. He and Chandler had responded to the call less than half an hour ago, and were still waiting for forensics to arrive from Huntingdon. The scene of crime officers and a doctor had also yet to arrive.

A uniformed officer stood about ten feet or so away. It was he who had responded to the emergency summons. He was from the local nick, and Bliss didn't know him. A young black officer, who had introduced himself as Carl Simmonds, he appeared both earnest and eager to please. Bliss motioned for the constable to join them.

'Simmonds. You did a fine job keeping the scene secure here. Making sure we had a clear path in and out was good thinking. Are you on duty tomorrow?'

'Yes, sir.'

'Good. I want you to interview the boys. Get them to go over the whole thing again: why they were here, what they saw, whether they'd seen anyone here in recent days. You know the drill.'

'Of course, sir. Should I arrange some counselling for them?'

'Counselling?'

'The boys found human remains, sir. They may be affected by what they saw.' A hint of the Caribbean mixed with the flat vowel sound of the Fenlands gave the policeman's voice a curiously upbeat edge.

Bliss sniffed. 'Constable Simmonds. Having unearthed a human skeleton, the boys did not run screaming out of the woods, did they? No. They calmly found the nearest phone box, called us, and then waited around to show you what they'd uncovered. Does that strike you as the behaviour of lads who have been mentally unbalanced by their discovery?'

'No, sir. But... well, there could be a delayed reaction.'

'And?'

'Sir?'

'You want to add something else, PC Simmonds. Go ahead, spit it out.'

'Well, sir. It's just... it's procedure. The boys are both minors.'

Bliss paused only for a moment before clapping the officer on the upper arm. 'You're right, of course. We must follow procedure at all costs. Make the call only after you've interviewed them, Simmonds. Get yourself off back to your station. And well done.'

As the uniform walked away, Bliss hoped he hadn't come across as overly patronising. Or sarcastic, for that matter. But he couldn't help thinking that if he had unearthed a skeleton at the ripe old age of ten, he would have considered it the best adventure of his young life. He would have gloried in it, relished telling all his friends and family, hoping the event might turn a young girl's head his way. A mouldering corpse might have been too gory, but finding a skeleton simply had to be the coolest thing a young boy could do. These days, however, it seemed you had to feel either guilty or psychologically scarred when presented with the merest hint of adventure.

'With a bit of luck,' he said to Chandler, trying to inject a bit of levity into his voice, 'these bones will be ancient and we won't have to worry about them at all.'

'Ancient?'

'Well, old enough for us not to have to get involved.'

'Hmm.'

'What?'

'Well, I was wondering if this might be something the Bone Woman could help us with.'

The Bone Woman was Emily Grant, a renowned anthropologist currently based at the nearby historically significant Flag Fen Bronze Age site. Bliss remembered her well. He and Chandler had met Grant a while back when she delivered a training course relating to stages of human decomposition. The topic of insect invasion had been a particular eye-opener for the vast majority of attending police officers, and, to his recollection, Grant had appeared to revel in her role as tutor. Throughout the demonstrations she'd handled human bones as if they were made of glass, her long fingers seeming to caress rather than grip.

Shifting his weight from foot to foot, Bliss blew out his cheeks, considering Chandler's suggestion. 'She might be of some help. But if the doc can't nail down the details we need, we could have someone official here within a day or two.'

'For the *official* report, yes. But it would be nice to know a little bit more before that. Right?'

He had to agree. Information was the lifeblood of any case. And it would be no hardship seeing the Bone Woman again.

'I'll give Emily a bell now. See if she'll help.'

'Oh, so it's Emily, huh? I knew you two had hit it off at the training course, but I didn't realise it was quite so intimate.'

'Don't push your luck, Penny.' Bliss did his best to look stern, but failed miserably.

'And I'll bet you just happen to have her mobile number programmed into yours, right?'

'I got it off her card. I thought I might need it one day.'

'Of course, sir.'

He grinned and turned away, stepping out into a small clearing where he hoped to raise a signal for the Nokia he'd pulled from the inside pocket of his suit jacket. It was true that he found Emily Grant attractive, and had enjoyed her company when they chatted both during lunch and after the course, but he would never admit as much to Penny. Ever since they had worked a murder case together six months ago, his DC had been trying to fix him up with her friends and other female police officers. Each time he had resisted with as much good grace as he could muster. Penny's heart was in the right place, and he appreciated her concern. It had simply never occurred to her that, at the age of forty-three, he could cope with life on his own.

Glancing at the digital time readout on his phone, Bliss selected Emily Grant's number. It was gone six, and he wondered if she might have already left work. 'I'm on my way home now,' she confirmed moments later.

'I trust you're using a hands-free set in your car.'

'Naturally. Would you arrest me if I weren't?'

'Well, we could be talking handcuffs.'

'Now that does sound exciting.'

'Yeah, it does. But it'll have to wait, I'm afraid.'

'You sound a little odd, Inspector. Have you caught a nasty case?'

'A nasty case of what?'

She laughed. 'You know what I mean.'

'Yeah. And it does look that way. But this one is different. Actually, I'm calling because you might be able to help.'

'Really? Me? In what way?' Emily sounded faintly amused by the idea.

'I'll tell you when you get here. Or rather, hopefully you'll tell me.'

Bliss gave her directions and snapped his phone shut. When he looked up he saw Chandler standing close by. She was grinning at him.

He hiked his shoulders. 'What?'

'I've never heard you flirt like that before, boss.'

'And you're unlikely to ever again.'

'You want to watch yourself,' she warned. 'People might start to think you're human.'

Even the best laid plans can crumble to dust when trampled all over by the full weight of reality. By the time Emily Grant killed the engine of her Citroen, the cavalry had arrived and the crime scene was in full swing. Uniformed officers kept local residents at bay, and one eye on a whole flotilla of official vehicles, including a black unmarked mortuary van. The normally quiet and peaceful area was a riot of movement and sound. As they worked in well-practised unison beneath a bank of floodlights powered by a petrol generator, Bliss watched SOCO and the forensics team probing and searching the cordoned-off area around the remains, which were now concealed by a large canvas tent. Trace evidence was being collected and recorded, every inch of the scene photographed and videoed, all the while leaving the remains in situ. Paths to and from the shallow grave were now being outlined with luminous strips of tape, helping to protect the crime scene from being tainted.

Bliss was waiting for Grant when she arrived, and he felt a momentary sense of heightened anticipation as she climbed from her vehicle. The dark auburn curls of her hair spilled out over the shoulders of a red knee-length coat, beneath which she wore grey trousers. She looked every bit as good as he remembered. Bliss was suddenly glad he had called.

'Good to see you again, Inspector Bliss,' Grant said, smiling warmly and extending a gloved hand.

They shook, eyes locking for a moment. Bliss returned the smile as she slipped the strap of a bag over her shoulder and used the remote on her key fob to lock the car.

'Please, call me Jimmy,' he said. 'I think we can afford to be a bit less formal, seeing as you've given up your time to lend a hand.'

'Jimmy it is, then.'

'Good.' He led her through the protective wall of uniforms. 'I was hoping to smuggle you in and out before this place became a circus,' he explained as they walked along a rutted, uneven path. 'But unfortunately, the troops descended just a few minutes after I called you, and now everything goes by the book. Even so, I've managed to persuade SOCO to let you have a brief visual inspection of our mystery victim.'

'Well, that's something, at least.'

'I'm sorry it's not more, and I feel like I've dragged you out here for nothing, but until the doctor turns up and releases the remains to us, I'm afraid a physical examination is out of the question.'

'A doctor?' Grant seemed surprised. Her mouth crinkled a little. 'Isn't it a bit late for that?'

'I know what you mean. It's procedure, I'm afraid. We mere mortals can't officially confirm that these bones are human. Or dead, for that matter. Anyhow, take a quick shufti.'

He swept back some undergrowth with his hand to allow Emily through to the scene. As she brushed by him, Bliss caught her scent in the frigid air. He felt his flesh tingle.

Grant spent exactly ten minutes at the grave site. Then, while the various teams continued about their business, she, Bliss and Chandler gathered together by the mobile catering trailer, drinking tea, eating bacon rolls, and stamping their feet to ward off the bitter chill. The night had grown much colder, and the mist closing in around the woods was laden with frost.

'I must say I'm quite looking forward to this,' Grant told them. Forty in less than a month, she was a tall, elegant woman with large green eyes, prominent cheekbones, and hair that looked as if it took an age to maintain, yet Bliss sensed that was of little or no concern to her. Though she dressed casually, Bliss thought she did so with a certain style and elegance. Her educated voice made her sound a great deal more stuffy than she actually was.

'I'm surprised you're not asked to do this sort of thing all the time,' Chandler said. 'We have our own people, of course, but we have to call them in from all areas of the country, and the whole process takes up valuable time. The local hospital helps out occasionally, but it depends on the staff available and their existing workload.'

Grant nodded. She used her teeth to remove a leather glove from her left hand, grasping her hot roll more easily afterwards.

'Well, my real expertise is in anthropology, of course. So I'm much more up to speed with bones from a bygone age. That said, I think I'll be able to point you in the right direction.'

'Let's hope so,' said Bliss. Despite the nature of the crime scene, he was enjoying having Emily around.

'Well, even though I obviously need to inspect the remains more fully, I can tell you one thing from my initial observation.'

'You can? Let's hear it.'

'This is not the only time that body has been buried.'

Bliss looked across at the floodlit scene, quickly glanced at Chandler, then back at Emily Grant. 'How d'you mean?' he asked her.

'The body has been reinterred at least once before.'

'It has? How can you tell?'

'That's easy enough. I'm sure you both noticed without giving weight to what you saw. The thing is, when a body decomposes the flesh simply rots away leaving the skeletal framework very much as it was before. The remains we have here are not in any recognisable form – that is, the structure is not that of a human shape.'

Grant used her hands when she spoke, as if making an invisible model of what she was describing.

'Animals?' Chandler suggested. 'The bones could have been disturbed by scavengers.'

'They probably have been. But not to the extent I saw. Large pieces of the skeleton still form limbs, such as the legs, feet, arms and hands, and the ribcage seems to be reasonably intact. The problem is that the limbs are positioned incorrectly, all jumbled up on top of each other. What I saw suggests to me that they were dumped in a pile. I've seen this sort of thing many times, and my instinct tells me that your remains were dug up and then reburied.'

Bliss was taken aback. A shudder scuttled along his spine. An interesting case had just become intriguing. 'But who on earth would do such a thing?' he asked. 'And why?'

Grant laughed and shook her head. She bit into her roll and, around a mouthful of bacon, said, 'That's certainly not my field of expertise. I rather thought it might be yours.'

TWO

When DS Hogg, the senior scene of crime officer, announced that the doctor had been indefinitely delayed at a serious RTA in the city centre, Bliss reluctantly decided to call time on this particular waiting game.

'It's nights like this that make me wonder why we do this bloody job,' Bliss groaned to Hogg.

The tall, slightly stooped DS, cheeks reddened by the cold, gave a knowing nod before he spoke. 'Times have changed, Inspector. No more blundering all over crime scenes. These days it's all about protecting the evidence.'

Hogg sounded about as irritated by the delay as Bliss felt. Police procedure had its own pace, starting at slow and working its way down. With the duty doctor busy, Bliss decided there was no point in everyone hanging around kicking their heels while the night exhaled fresh layers of frost, coating them all with its chilling indifference.

'Give me a call on my mobile if you come up with anything significant,' he told Hogg. 'Leave a message if it's switched off. Oh, and I'd get a few more holes dug in this area if I were you, Charlie.'

'More holes. Why?'

Bliss glanced around at the busy scene, his gaze finally coming to rest on the tent erected over the shallow grave. He raised his eyebrows and said, 'Who knows if the corpse those boys found is the only one out here?'

The DS winced. 'Shit! You think there could be more?'

'To be honest, I doubt it very much, but for all we know right now this could be some psycho's favourite burial plot.'

'Fuck! Thanks a bunch. You just made a bad night even worse. Have we dropped a bollock here already, Jimmy? Allowing everyone to run their size tens all over the bloody woods, I mean.'

'I don't think so. We sealed off the primary scene, and that's all we needed to do. But let's cover our arses now, eh?'

Hogg stomped away, muttering to himself and barking an order at some unfortunate soul who crossed his path at precisely the wrong moment. Bliss started to grin, but his face hardened as it occurred to him that he might actually be right about there being more bodies. It was a sobering thought.

When he rejoined Chandler and Grant, Bliss offered an apologetic shrug. 'Thanks for coming out here, Emily. I'm sorry to have wasted your time.'

'It's not a problem,' Grant said quickly, shaking her head. She had pulled a scarf up around her chin, but her cheeks were flushed, nose tipped with red. 'And far from being a waste of time, it's actually been a fascinating experience.'

'What, standing out in a dark wood freezing your... well, freezing?'

'No, no, no. This hive of activity going on around us might be common practice for you and Penny, something to yawn over when you're sitting down to breakfast tomorrow morning, but it's all new to me. And what's more, it's extremely interesting for a civilian to observe.'

'Well, I'm glad you see it that way.'

'Honestly, it's been fascinating watching your people go about their business in such a methodical, painstaking manner. It reminds me so much of the way my team and I carry out our own work.'

Bliss nodded, acknowledging the observation. He estimated that the activity around the SOC would continue throughout the night and for the best part of the following day. Perhaps even another twenty-four hours would be requested by SOCO after that. Running a crime scene was a laborious task, yet one that often yielded vital evidence. He and Hogg had bemoaned the delay in a moment of frustration, yet both knew the reasoning behind it was sound.

'It's a shame you weren't able to examine the remains more closely tonight before this lot steamed in mob-handed,' Bliss said. 'Still, what you told us could be very helpful.'

Grant spread her gloved hands, black leather now slick with bacon grease. 'I'd still like to help. If you want me to, that is. Just because I can't study the remains immediately doesn't mean they won't be available to me tomorrow.'

She had a point. And it would be good to get a jump start on this, Bliss reflected, even if it was to rule it out as an active inquiry. He looked at her and nodded.

'If you're sure. I suppose I could give the doctor your telephone number and have him contact you when he's finished here and the remains have been shipped on to the mortuary.'

'I'd like that.' Emily grinned and breathed out a plume of frigid air. 'I love my work, but it can get a little samey. This will make for a nice change of pace.'

DC Chandler had been listening to the exchange, and now gave a short, humourless laugh as they started walking towards their vehicles.

'A change of pace? I can think of better ways to spend the day than probing the remains of a human being.'

'Oh, so can I, believe me. But bones are my meat and drink.'

'Speaking of which,' said Bliss, wondering if he'd imagined the slight pause and glance in his direction before Grant had spoken. 'I'm going to grab myself a swift pint before heading home. You two want to join me?'

'I'm game,' Chandler said immediately.

'That's an understatement.' He angled his head towards Grant. 'How about you, Emily? Let me repay you for keeping you standing around twiddling your thumbs on a bitter night like this.'

'Go on, then. You've twisted my arm.' She looked between them and gave a warm smile. Bliss decided he liked it.

***

In the days when horse-drawn wagons and coaches were the only forms of transport for goods and people alike, a road staggered from London all the way up to Lincoln. London Road, by far the longer stretch, slid like a needle into Peterborough's dark underbelly and emerged on the other side as the imaginatively named Lincoln Road. At the point where its narrow, built-up throughway bloomed to become dual carriageway flanked by industrial estates, it also gave home to the Paul Pry pub and restaurant.

Set back off the southbound side of Lincoln Road, the Paul Pry was a typical example of corporate-style design and decor, the food following a set menu found all across the country, the beer not allowing for local-brewed real ale or lager imports beyond the range determined by the chain. Normally, Bliss would have run a mile from such a characterless place, but it was close to the scene and pleasantly warm on such a bitter night. Despite its size the pub was surprisingly cosy, with little noise other than a low hubbub of voices and the meaningless chatter of a single fruit machine. Bliss bought the drinks and carried them across to a corner booth close by the exit. The three of them shed their coats and began to relax and thaw out. Not necessarily in that order.

'Cheers,' he said, tilting the glass once in their direction before taking several long swallows. He cuffed his lips, then regarded Grant closely. 'I would never have taken you for a beer girl.'

'First of all, I'm no longer a girl,' she replied, before taking a second sip from her own glass. 'And secondly, what's wrong with me putting away a pint of bitter?'

Shaking his head, Bliss raised his hands defensively, palms out. 'Not a thing in my book. But there are some men out there who regard it as... less than feminine?' The last word formed more of a question than a statement, unconvinced as he was by his own argument.

'Well, firstly, if they consider me less than feminine, they are very much mistaken. And secondly, I would not wish to know such moronic men.' Her tone suggested the matter was closed.

'I wish I could take to it,' Chandler admitted. Her elbow rested on the table, chin cupped in one palm, fingers trailing up her cheek like plump pink ivy climbing a wall. 'Whenever I see someone sink their first gulp, they always look so completely satisfied. It's as though just that one drink has slaked an incredible thirst. I've tried it a couple of times but can't stand the stuff. I'll stick to my vodka, thanks very much.'

Emily set her glass down on a table sticky with the residue of drinks spilled by previous customers. With one hand she unconsciously swept back her fringe, tucking a few strands of hair behind her left ear. She wore a black sweater, and Bliss noticed that the gold pendant hanging from a thin chain around her neck matched her earrings. The attention to detail didn't surprise him. That he had noticed came as a bit of a shock, though.

'You have to acquire a taste for beer,' the Bone Woman told Penny. 'It takes a while. I don't think anyone actually likes it the first time or two. Not even men.' Her eyes drew Bliss into the statement.

'You're probably right. I'm a Guinness man these days. It's almost always my first choice.'

'Do you drink it because you like it? Or because it's the cool thing to be seen drinking?'

'You think I'm that shallow?'

'As a worm's grave. But all men are, and you can't help your gender.'

'A pint drinker and a man-hater.' Bliss smiled and glanced across at Chandler. 'Who would have guessed?'

The DC laughed. 'Well, she's certainly got you pegged, boss.'

'He probably adds those two things together and comes up with lesbian,' said Grant, her smile widening.

Bliss looked between them. 'Hey, I am here you know. I do have feelings. I can be hurt.'

Chandler and Grant laughed. Bliss smiled and began to unwind. It had been a slow day until the Bretton Woods shout came in, but as soon as he had laid eyes on the skeleton he had begun mentally preparing himself for any eventuality. Now he loosened the knot of his tie and pulled open the top button of his shirt. The stiff collar had been chaffing his neck all day.

'That's enough fun at my expense,' he said. 'Now, can we move the subject on? I'm beginning to regret ever asking you two here for a drink.'

Emily Grant put a hand on his arm. 'Don't mind me. I tend to use direct humour as a mask to cover my chronic shyness.'

He didn't know whether to believe her, but when Bliss raised his eyebrows he continued to grin. 'If that's an apology, I accept. However,' he looked pointedly now at his DC, 'I would have expected more loyalty from my subordinate.'

'Why would I start now?' Chandler asked.

A loud cheer went up moments after the fruit machine began a scatter-gun distribution of coins. Someone had won a jackpot by the sound of it. Laughter rattled around the bar.

'Lucky sod,' said Bliss, without looking up at the winner. 'I bet he puts it all back before the night is out.'

Grant glanced across at him, her head tilted to one side. 'Now that is a surprise. I didn't have you down as a pessimist, Jimmy.'

'I'm not. I'm a realist. And speaking of realism, I want to return to a question I posed earlier this evening: why would someone dig up a body and then bury it again?'

Pushing her empty glass aside to create a path, Chandler leaned forward and said, 'Perhaps whoever initially buried the body realised later on that they'd left behind something incriminating.'

Bliss nodded. 'That's a decent theory. Assuming that's what they did. Bury the body in Bretton Woods, dig it up and then bury it again, I mean.'

Grant looked bewildered. 'I don't follow.'

'Well, I'm wondering if the body was moved for some reason.'

'Why would anyone do such a thing?'

The notion had only just occurred to him, and Bliss hadn't yet had time to follow it through. 'I have no idea. Penny may well be right, and we'll certainly check it out, but we can't allow ourselves to get bogged down with one train of thought. To my way of thinking, if someone is going to dig up a body and then rebury it, moving it is as good a reason as any.'

Chandler caught the other woman's curious eye. 'The boss likes to think about what's around a corner before he gets to it. To us mere mortals, it's the body we look to for answers. DI Bliss, on the other hand, will seek answers in the why, not the what.'

He had to agree, despite the mocking undertones. 'That's because the body is only the result of what our murderer does. The end. The best way to find that person is to discover what drove them to such an act in the first place. The beginning. Motive, DC Chandler. You recall the word during training down at Hendon, yes? This is slightly different, I grant you, but the principle remains the same. I want to know what drove this person to disturb a dead body. A skeletal body.'

'Well, here's another thought,' Chandler offered. 'What if the whole notion is wrong? What if it was the two kids? Maybe they got excited enough to actually pull the bones up out of the grave. Then, when they realised they had to report it, they bricked it and shoved the remains back where they found them.'

'The boys did say they hadn't disturbed the remains once they'd uncovered them, but I suppose it's not out of the question.'

'Young boys telling lies to keep out of trouble – what are the chances? And they didn't exactly stop digging when they realised what they had, did they? The whole skeleton was exposed when we got there.'

Bliss leaned back in his seat and thought about what he might have done in their place. Once he'd become aware of what they were, would he have continued touching the bones? Probed the unearthed treasure with his fingers? Probably. But perhaps just the skull, running a tremulous hand around its curves, maybe pushing a stuttering finger into an eye socket or between the open jaws.

The frenzied nature of the dig had seemed a little odd to him earlier, but at their tender age the sheer excitement, fuelled by an adrenaline rush, had probably ignited their eagerness. Yet did that necessarily mean they would then have started yanking the bones out of the ground? Bliss had his doubts, but he nodded anyway.

'We have to check it out. It's a vital issue, and you were right to raise it, Penny. The lads are being spoken to in the morning anyway, so I'll make sure whoever does the interview knows what to ask.'

'I may be able to point you in the right direction,' Grant said, taking another pull from her glass, getting down to the dregs now.

'You really think you can get anything from those bones?' Chandler asked her.

Grant's nod was firm. 'All remains tell a story. You just have to know how to read between the lines and ask the right questions in order to get to the truth.'

'How about facial reconstructions? Do you do those? You know the sort of thing: taking a cast of the skull and forming the face from clay.'

'I've done several, actually. But we use laptops and software these days. A hundred times as fast and just as effective. You know, in many ways, I think it must be very much like being a detective.'

Bliss regarded her thoughtfully, eyes narrowing. Emily appeared a much more confident person than the one she had seemed earlier. And there was no doubt that she was extremely pleasant. Her eagerness bothered him a little, though. Involving amateurs in a murder case, no matter how enthusiastic and knowledgeable they might be, carried an element of risk. Experts in crime-related cases learned to look beyond the obvious, but that came only with experience. He hoped he hadn't made an error in asking Emily Grant to look at the remains for them. Bliss made a mental note to request an official inspection from a Home Office-approved expert. And to find out if the local hospital had anyone available in the short term. Just to be on the safe side.

'Well, I'm beat,' he admitted, stifling a yawn. 'You're both excellent company, but I'm off to grab some beauty sleep.'

'Much needed it is, too,' Chandler muttered.

'Oh, I don't know,' Grant said, chin now resting on steepled fingers. When she'd snared their attention, she added with a teasing smile, 'Compared to what we saw in that shallow grave earlier, he's not so bad.'

***

They said their goodbyes in the pub car park, handshakes all round. As she nosed her Ford Focus out of its space, Chandler glanced across at Bliss sitting quietly in the passenger seat. 'I quite like the Bone Woman,' she said. 'I think she'll do us proud.'

Bliss made no mention of his concerns. Though Penny had made the initial suggestion, it had been his decision to call Emily in, and if her presence caused problems he would be the one to carry the can. 'Let's hope so, Pen. Best-case scenario is that our victim has been dead since Plato was a lad. If she's recent, we may have a tough one on our hands.'

Ten minutes later, Chandler had dropped him off outside his front door and he was being greeted by his two Labradors, Bonnie and Clyde. The two dogs were all over him in seconds, and he welcomed the playful intrusion, succumbing to their insistence, rolling around the kitchen floor like a child as they pretended to savage him unmercifully. The only danger he was actually in was from being beaten to death by furiously wagging tails.

Bliss lived in a relatively affluent part of the city called Orton Waterville. The house was on a private estate, and was the first and only place he'd looked at when he moved up to Peterborough from London a little over three years ago. Bliss liked the house well enough, but it was not much more than a roof over his head. The apparent peace and quiet of the estate was the first thing he had noticed, and this was of far greater appeal that the bricks and mortar themselves. It was a home in name only, though Bonnie and Clyde made it a warm place to come back to every night.

After ten or fifteen minutes of unwinding and protecting his face from lapping tongues, Bliss fetched the dogs some food and water, and while they were tucking in he absently checked his post. Idly scanning an offer from a book club, having already discarded one from a credit card company, he noticed a red light winking on his wall-mounted kitchen telephone. Someone had left a message. When he played it back, thinking it would be from his parents, he was surprised to hear the deep, resonant voice of a fellow DI who'd transferred out of Peterborough a couple of months after Bliss had arrived.

'Jimmy? Jimmy Bliss? Uh, it's Bernard Weller here. DI Weller. I don't know if you remember me, Jimmy, but we worked the Werrington Post Office raid together a few years back. Look, I wondered if we could meet up. I'm coming to Peterborough tomorrow and I want to see you about something. I hope to be there around noon. Let's meet in the café we used on that first day together. Wait as long as you can. Cheers.'

Bliss stared at the phone as if it had grown a mouth and spoken directly to him. What the hell was all that about? he wondered. He remembered the case Weller had referred to, but it was the only time they had worked together. The robbery had left one person in hospital with gunshot wounds, and two more severely traumatised. Weller was the senior investigating officer, and Bliss recalled being impressed by the older man's energy and determination. Less than seventy-two hours later, two men were in custody. Both were now serving prison sentences for their part in the raid. The evidence had been irrefutable, and the suspects had eventually pleaded guilty, so Bliss couldn't imagine why Weller wanted to see him now, after all this time. It surely couldn't have anything to do with the investigation. His mind followed the message through, finally settling on the proposed location for the meeting. Bliss played that part of the message back one more time. It was an anomaly. Small, but there all the same. He couldn't understand why Weller hadn't mentioned the café by name. It had been his favourite, used almost on a daily basis over a period of several years. To Bliss, saying the name of the café would have been natural. Not doing so was odd. He shook his head. Perhaps the phone call sounded more clandestine than Weller had intended, but Bliss remained intrigued all the same.

He pictured the large, brooding Cumbrian. A huge, meaty face, leathery and worn. Eyes always seeming sorrowful. Friendly enough, but reserved. When Weller was working a case he had no time for anything else. Bliss had felt a sense of kindred spirits gathering around the investigation, though he considered his own resolve and sense of purpose as a weakness rather than a strength. He could no longer count the number of times he had wished himself able to release the valve, to embrace something other than work. Being driven was not the same as driving something forward.

Anxious now, his good mood ruined, Bliss let go a heavy sigh and swore. The sound echoed around the kitchen, striking a discordant note. There were times when he hated being him, trapped inside his own desolate mind. Everything he saw was filtered through dark tones, everything he felt became tainted by despair. Always suspicious, expecting the very worst life had to offer. Take the bones tonight: many people would have dismissed them as old and requiring only a decent reburial, at least until the evidence revealed otherwise. But not him. No, despite calling in Emily Grant in the hope that the remains would prove to be more worthy of her attention than his own, he was convinced that a more recent crime was responsible. Life was just like that. And what of the Bone Woman herself? Attractive, funny, good company, and still his mind was filled with doubts about her eagerness to please. Now, as the day drew to a close, Bernie Weller. A call out of the blue, the poor bloke probably just visiting the area and wanting to catch up and maybe get a whiff of the old job again in his nostrils. Bliss was unable to leave it at that, though. To him there had to be something furtive beyond the words, beyond the proposed meeting. Never taking anything at face value could have been his specialist subject on *Mastermind*.

It comes with the job, Bliss reminded himself sharply. That instinctive lack of trust, the constant suspicion. They were a package deal. He cursed again. He'd fed himself that same line so many times he was actually starting to believe his own bullshit.

Bliss shook it off. Allowing this ritual self-flagellation to continue would serve no useful purpose. During up times he felt he had a healthy outlook on life, if somewhat pragmatic. But when the down times came, they blew in hard and fast and could be devastating. Over a period they took their toll. In the USA, it was times like these that saw many a police officer bite down hard on the barrel of his or her service weapon. Taking your own life was harder in the UK, and there were times when Bliss was grateful for that. He didn't believe he ever had or ever would reach the point where suicide became a realistic choice, but a pragmatist like him could never rule it out altogether. Being lonely and miserable and, he had to admit to himself, still mourning the loss of his wife, the way ahead seemed dark and distant, paved with thorns.

He fetched himself a Guinness from the fridge. Popped the ring pull and drank straight from the can. Belched loudly because there was no one around to rebuke him. The fresh impetus of alcohol felt good as it slipped through his bloodstream. He nuked some Chinese noodles in the microwave, went into the lounge, threw his jacket on the floor, put on a Joe Satriani CD, and made himself comfortable on the sofa. He worked his way uneasily through the food and ale; disparate thoughts tossed around inside his head. Bliss wanted to give more attention to the inquiry in hand, but every time he set his mind to the human remains lying over in Bretton Woods, he kept coming back to the phone call and DI Weller.

Two more drinks and another CD later, Bliss started to make his way upstairs to bed, more in hope of sleep than expectation. Some nights he managed to force his way up there, other times he made do with the sofa.

Tonight, if his dead wife waited for him up there, he would welcome her.

THREE

Peterborough District Hospital was winding down in preparation for moving to new accommodation away from the city centre. As the local population had increased, so the hospital capacity became stretched to breaking point. Bliss had lived and worked in the city for around three years now, yet was still surprisingly unfamiliar with many of its buildings. He simply wasn't interested enough to care. The one place he knew well, however, was the hospital mortuary. He'd only had cause to visit it on four previous occasions, but once experienced, it could never be forgotten.

All the usual clichés applied: the mortuary suite was located in the hospital basement, its rooms and corridors dark and dank when compared to the rest of the hospital, each carrying a stench no one who entered them would ever fail to recognise in the future. The mix of chemicals and death was a heady concoction, a cocktail of odours no human was ever supposed to be subjected to. The mortuary, in which the Post Mortem Suite was located, seemed more like a Gothic laboratory wrought from the mind of Mary Shelley than a modern medical facility. It was even managed by an oddball who had no idea why his name, Norman Bates, caused everyone to whom he introduced himself to do a double take. His squat, rotund form made the mental image even more of a challenge.

Bliss and Chandler arrived shortly before 8.30 a.m. to be informed by Doctor Bates's assistant that her boss had already gone home. 'He worked pretty much through the night,' she explained defensively, peering up at them from her desk.

'Him and a vast army of police officers,' Bliss remarked, staring right back.

Behind the woman, printed on white card set into a small black frame, was a Kipling poem that read: *I keep six honest serving men. They taught me all I knew. Their names are What and Why and When. And How and Where and Who.* Bliss had always meant to ask for a copy for his own office, but had never got around to it. He shared Bates's credo, but was a little peeved that the doctor had not waited around in order to provide a verbal report at the very least. Long, unsociable hours went with the territory.

Anne Barker gave a weary smile, unfazed by Bliss's abrupt manner. She had been Bates's assistant for a number of years, and Bliss was familiar with her laconic style. A cheery, somewhat plain woman in her mid-thirties, Barker habitually wore short black skirts beneath her unbuttoned white lab coat, and was rumoured to favour stockings in winter. Every time he was in her company, Bliss pleaded with himself to keep his gaze fixed firmly on her face, and every time those pleas fell on deaf ears. Aside from having great legs, Anne Barker also had an uncanny knack of catching him out whenever his eyes strayed.

As they just had.

Stockings.

Definitely.

'Did Psycho leave anything for us?' he asked more amiably.

The smile flickered. 'Don't let him catch you calling him that. I'll only have to explain it to him.'

'Fair enough. But did he leave us anything?'

She jabbed a finger in the direction of the main pathology lab. 'Indeed he did. He left you two bodies.'

'Did you say *two* bodies?'

'Uh-huh. And just for a change, one of them has a pulse.'

Puzzled, Bliss strode across to the double doors leading to the PM suite and, using a hand to ward off any glare, peered through a rectangle of toughened glass. At one of two stainless steel tables located in the centre of the room, Emily Grant stood leaning over the dark strips of bone now forming the outline of a human being once more. Bliss rapped his knuckles on the window, which had become slightly fogged by his breath. Grant turned, looked up, smiled with her eyes. Held up a hand. She wore no mask, and he saw her mouth the words: 'Give me a minute'.

'It's Emily,' he told Chandler. 'She'll honour us with her presence in a moment.'

Chandler must have caught the tone. 'What's wrong, boss? You sound as though you don't approve.'

He glanced over his shoulder before taking a couple of steps back towards her, leaning in, voice lowered as he said, 'It's just that I don't remember sanctioning this. I know Emily wanted to carry on helping us out, and I recall saying it sounded like a decent idea, but I'm not sure I told her to go ahead with an examination.'

'If I remember correctly, you mentioned something about arranging for the doc to give her a bell once the body had cleared the SOC.'

'Yeah, only I didn't speak to him about it. I forgot. So how come she's here?'

'I have no idea. Is it a problem?'

'Not exactly. I just feel she's taken it a bit for granted.'

'Well, we did call her in, boss. We did ask for her help in the first place.'

Bliss raised a hand in submission. 'I know. Forget it. Just me being protective, I suppose.'

'And there was me thinking I'd sensed a little chemistry between you two last night.'

Bliss had thought the same thing. And if Penny noticed, maybe they were both right. 'Chemicals maybe,' he said, shaking his head. 'Plenty of those in the beer.'

Chandler looked across at the lab doors. 'You could do worse, boss.'

'Stop trying to pair me up with every eligible woman I meet. I'm fine as I am, thanks very much.'

'Really? Whose arms did you go home to last night?'

Bliss unconsciously fingered his wedding band – an automatic response. The answer to Penny's question was no one. Not last night, nor any other night these past three and a half years. Not unless you counted the clumsy embrace of two crazy Labradors.

'And you?' Bliss countered, meeting her stubborn gaze.

'Actually, I'm seeing a priest.'

'Your love life's so bad you turned to God?'

'Very funny. No, I'm dating a priest.'

'I thought they weren't allowed to date.'

'Yeah, well, if that's the case then this one is breaking a few rules.'

'I bet the Catholic Church is thrilled about that.'

She flapped a hand. 'Frankly, the fact that he's not humping a thirteen-year-old boy ought to make them happy.'

He laughed out loud. 'You're really dating a priest?'

'Well, we've seen each other a couple of times. Had coffee together. He's going through a crisis of faith.'

'And you're showing him the way to a life of purgatory.'

Chandler punched his arm. 'That's harsh. But seriously, boss, there are reasons why you and I have both spent so much time on our own, and they're understandable. But those reasons are in the past. You need to look forward. We both do.'

He knew exactly what she meant. Following a disastrous relationship in her teens that resulted in the birth of a baby girl, Chandler's daughter had been abducted by the father and removed from the country back to his native home in Turkey. Two years on and Penny was still using private investigators and the reluctant Turkish police to hunt for her child, who was now almost five. Bliss sympathised with Penny's reasons for having a less than hectic social life, her pain akin to grief. As for his own misery, he didn't want to go there. Not now. Not in this place. He shook the smile from his face and turned away from his DC, just as Emily Grant emerged from the lab. She was wearing green surgical scrubs, hands encased in blue latex gloves.

'Do you want to come and see for yourselves what we have?' she asked.

'Do we need to wear protective clothing?' This from Chandler.

'Not now. Not with this body. There's nothing to contaminate.'

Despite its outward appearance, the suite was filled with all mod cons. Though there were no windows, the room was starkly bright. An air extractor worked overtime to pump out the odours resulting from post mortems, and there was a surgical feel to the whole place. Drain gutters ran around the perimeter of the tiled floor, which was spotlessly clean. Ranged along one wall there were a variety of different sized jars filled with liquids and floating specimens. Bliss was reminded of a mad scientist's laboratory once more, and half expected a hunchback to come hobbling in from an adjoining room.

A complete gleaming white skeleton hung from a purpose-built stand in one corner of the room. A training aid, Bliss guessed. The bones laid out on the autopsy table looked alien by comparison. Emily Grant spread her hands as if presenting something she had created.

Here's one I made earlier.

'Not much to show for a life, is it?' she said on a sigh.

'No,' Bliss agreed, shaking his head. The only thing he saw that looked remotely human was the skull, and even that now appeared shrunken.

'I'm done for the time being,' Grant told them as she walked around to the other side of the table. She stretched her arms above her head, yawning. Blinked a couple of times and gave a weary grin. 'I'll need to run some further tests, do some additional analysis, but right now I'm beat.'

'Yeah, you look ropey,' Chandler muttered beneath her breath.

Bliss couldn't help but smile; Emily was stunning even in baggy scrubs and rubber boots, and actually looked as if she'd enjoyed a full eight hours' sleep. Which was more than he could say for his DC.

Grant looked at Bliss and gave an exhausted groan. 'I'm not sure how much help I can provide at this stage, but I do have several items of interest for you.'

'We were actually expecting to find the doc here,' he said. There was no edge to his voice, but Emily seemed to have made herself rather too comfortable for his liking.

'I hope you don't mind, but Doctor Bates and I agreed that I would fill you in. He could see I was keen to get on with my own examination, and there didn't seem any point in him hanging around.'

'He's not usually so accommodating.'

'Really?' She raised her eyebrows. 'Seemed like a pussycat to me.'

'Now that is hard to believe. So how come you're here? I forgot to liaise with the duty doctor last night, so I know he didn't contact you.'

'Hmm, this is where I show how much of an anorak I am. I went home after the pub, but couldn't get my mind off what I'd seen. I knew I wouldn't be able to sleep, so I made a few calls here and was eventually put through to Doctor Bates. It was he who called me when the remains came in. I told him you and I had arranged for me to examine the body. I hope that was all right?'

Bliss wasn't at all sure that it was all right, but he told Grant it was anyway.

'Good. Anyhow, I have the information for you, and should be able to answer any questions you might have in Doctor Bates's absence.'

'Well, that's why we're here.'

'Oh, and I thought it was to see little old me.'

'That, too.' Bliss took a step closer to the table and peered down at the skeletal framework. 'So, what stories does she have to tell us?'

'What makes you think we have a female here?'

'The boss said he knew back at the scene,' Chandler informed her.

Grant raised an eyebrow, appraising him. 'Tell me why.'

'The skull mainly,' Bliss said, quietly confident in his understanding of the human bone structure. 'The forehead is almost vertical, the eye sockets are fairly circular, and the nasal cavity is somewhat pear-shaped. All of those suggest female. Add a broad pelvis with triangular holes, and I'd lay odds on it being a woman.'

'And you'd be right. I'm impressed.'

He smiled. 'As I tried telling Penny last night, it's a basic observation.'

'Still, it's more difficult when you don't have a male skeleton to compare it with. You did well.'

'Not bad for an amateur. But that's as much as I can tell you. Now it's your turn.'

'Very well.' She nodded and drew a deep breath. 'First of all, I can confirm that, as suspected, the body was definitely reinterred.'

'That was a good catch, Emily,' Chandler remarked. 'Any idea how long she'd been there?'

Grant folded her arms beneath her breasts. Her long wavy hair was tied back now and fastened with a clip. The look took a few years off, drawing weight from her face. 'An idea, yes. Within reasonable limits. And I'm sorry to say that you have a criminal investigation on your hands.'

Bliss blew out some pent-up air. He shrugged, licking his lips. 'I think a part of me already guessed that.'

'Well, let's see what I can tell you. For a start, your victim was probably aged between twenty and twenty-five when she died.'

'Now it's my turn to be impressed. How can you tell?'

'There are lots of clues, really.' She swept her hand down and indicated the hip bones. 'A major sign is here, at the crest. It only becomes united at around the age of twenty-two to twenty-five. This is almost there, but not quite fully formed, hence my estimation.'

'It's good to have an approximate age to work with. Cuts the search range down considerably.'

'She's also obviously Caucasian.'

'Skull shape again, yes?' Chandler suggested.

'Among other things. So, a white female in her early to mid-twenties. The size and density of the bones suggest she was slight of build, and I'd estimate her height to be approximately five-two.'

'Not a bad start,' said Bliss. He smiled at Emily, noting the gleam of excitement in her eyes. She was on a roll. He admired her confidence, given her admission of shyness the night before. 'And I can tell just by looking at you that you have more for us.'

'Indeed I do, Inspector. Plenty.' She cleared her throat, popped her chain and pendant behind the sweeping neck of the green scrubs jacket. 'In my opinion, and I must stress that full forensic testing will have to be carried out to absolutely confirm anything I tell you, your victim was in the ground over at Bretton for around three to five years. Prior to that, she spent a considerable time close to the lake over at old Fletton, somewhere near the site of the London brick works.'

Bliss felt his mouth fall open and could not prevent his eyes from widening. He felt like a cartoon figure caught in a moment of characteristic amazement. He glanced at Penny, who blinked back at him, then he locked eyes with Emily once more.

'I don't suppose you can give us map coordinates, can you?'

Grant laughed and leaned back against the smooth stainless steel roll around the edge of the table, crossing one leg over the other. 'Actually, if I had a couple of months out there with my probes, I'd probably be able to do just that. I know my bones, Bliss, but I know my soil, too.'

'Of course.' The anthropology in tandem with archaeology. Bones and soil – the perfect combination in this case. He was starting to think he'd made a wise choice after all. 'So, how on earth do you know these specific details?'

'Well, obviously I carried out the essential chemical analyses, and the levels of nitrogen became a guideline, if somewhat inexact. UV tests revealed a slight pale blue glow to the bones, which again narrowed things down for me. A few scraps of partially rotted material were discovered by Doctor Bates, some of which we thought might be some form of sacking cloth, the rest clothing. We'll know more on that within a day or two, but whatever they are they're not old and are man-made. Once I'd worked through the top layers of decay on several sample bones, it became obvious to me that the remains had at some point been immersed in clay. Now, as you probably know, Peterborough is riddled with Oxford clay soil, but you may not be aware that Bretton Woods is one of the few areas that has a high level of limestone as well. The samples I looked at confirm this. However, the brick works used a particular density of clay that was required for their type of brick, and this was what I found.'

'But there used to be a major brick works out by Hampton and Yaxley,' Chandler pointed out. 'Same company made them, so it must have been the same clay.'

Grant nodded and wagged a finger at her. 'True. So I had to narrow it down further. That was more difficult, but I was able to detect a good deal of moisture in the bones at around the time they would have initially been buried. The level of moisture could not have come from rainfall alone, so I had to check on other sources. The lake at old Fletton is the only major source I can think of in such close proximity to the specific type of clay soil.'

Bliss put his head back and exhaled deeply. 'That's damned fine work, Emily. Really, that's fantastic. So now I suppose the big question is – when was she killed?'

'My estimation is she's been dead for between twelve to sixteen years.'

He ran the figures. 'So, she may have been buried in old Fletton sometime between nineteen ninety and ninety-four.'

'Maybe eighty-nine at the outside, but I doubt it.'

'And then exhumed and reburied around, say, two thousand and one to two thousand and three.'

'Around then, yes. Give me more time and I'll probably be able to firm up on those estimates.'

Bliss nodded. 'But you think you're close?'

'Close enough to put my name to.'

His mouth felt dry. A familiar anticipation lurked inside his stomach. Like pangs of hunger, it gnawed at him. Churning. 'So last night we knew nothing. Now, just a few hours later, we could run a search for an IC1 woman in her early to mid-twenties, who went missing between nineteen ninety and ninety-three. Jesus! That certainly helps us narrow things down. This is terrific news, Emily. Better than I could have hoped for.'

She beamed, strength suddenly renewed. 'I have even more,' she said eagerly.

'Like her name and address?' Chandler ventured, a wry grin on her face.

'Not quite that good. Informative, though. Some of the smaller bones are absent. Assuming your people did their job properly, the missing bones may have been scavenged by animals, or more probably left behind at the original burial site.'

'That's interesting. We can check back through the system to see if any bones have been discovered by the lake and reported.' Chandler turned her eyes to Bliss. 'We can also get a search team out there, yes?'

'I'd like to think so.' Bliss thought about how such a request might be viewed by the bean counters, given the amount of human resources required for such a job. He nodded towards Grant. 'Go on, Emily. What else?'

'I found no evidence of grooving on the pelvis, so I'd say she'd never given birth. We'll come back to that, however. Oh, and this is something I think you are going to like very much: some time in her late teens, this young woman's right leg had been broken pretty badly.'

'Bad enough to cause immobility?' Bliss asked, his mind racing ahead to connect with all kinds of possibilities. He felt his chest tighten.

'For a time. Certainly bad enough for her to require surgery and extensive physiotherapy. And the insertion of a strengthening rod and some bolts.'

Bliss leaned forward, reached out a hand and clamped it over one of hers. He looked down, unable now to contain himself. 'You found them? They were with the remains?'

'Doctor Bates found them, yes. Still in position. He removed them and put them in a plastic evidence bag for you.' She nodded towards a low table by the doors, the bag lying between a foam model of a brain and a hollowed-out skull that was being used as a pen holder. 'If the rod and bolts were fitted here in the UK they'll be stamped with a serial number. If you're lucky it will have been done locally, and you may be able to trace the rod from its number. Otherwise, you'll face a hard slog trying to run a national search.'

'Well, let's think positive thoughts, eh? It could be just what we need to get an ID.'

Grant smiled, pointing to the right fibula, a gloved finger alighting softly in several areas. 'Removing the rod and bolts did cause a little bit of damage, but it was a nice, clean job, so preservation was good. Despite some excellent healing, it's obvious to me that her shin bone had been shattered, probably no more than five years before she died.'

It was a better result than Bliss could have dreamed of. If their victim was a local woman, the hospital would almost certainly have records of such a major operation, even if they were not able to trace the steel rod to a specific patient. Bliss puffed out his cheeks and spread his hands.

'I don't know what to say. You're a diamond, Emily. You're a bloody diamond.'

She flapped away the compliment, but he could tell she was delighted. Her cheeks shone beneath the harsh bank of powerful lights overhead. Then her face grew serious. She rested her hands on her hips.

'So now we all know that I'm good at what I do. But I must say, you two, I'm disappointed at your level of competence.'

Bliss was taken aback. 'You are? Why do you say that?'

'You've not even asked how she was killed.'

'You know that as well?' This from Penny Chandler.

'Of course.'

'That's amazing.'

Emily grinned. 'Not really. The good doctor told me.'

Bliss chuckled. 'I would have got around to asking,' he assured her. 'I was more interested in everything else you were telling us. So, what's the SP from Bates, then?'

Grant gave a curiously vulnerable sigh, her mood darkening in an instant. 'The poor girl was strangled.'

'Strangled. No doubts?'

'None at all. It was brutal enough to snap more than cartilage. The small hyoid bone, just above the thyroid, was broken. That's usually a sign of strangulation, most probably by hand rather than ligature. However, she was killed only after suffering a prior trauma, mostly to the lower half of her body. Damage and slight stress fractures to both thighs suggest that, shortly before she was murdered, your victim was probably struck by a vehicle.'

Chandler whistled softly, her eyes drawn to the remains once more. 'Not her lucky day, then?'

Emily Grant also returned her gaze to the bones lying on the darkly reflective table. She shook her head. 'Far from it, I'm afraid.'

'Would the injuries have been incapacitating?'

'I doubt it. She will have been in pain, but probably able to move and walk unaided. But if that weren't enough, I have one final thing to tell you if you can bear to hear it after all that.'

'More?' Bliss shook his head in wonder. 'You're a mine of information.'

He saw all traces of humour flee from Grant's eyes. And when she told them what she knew, Bliss understood why.

FOUR

Due to the chaotic nature of the parking arrangements in and around the hospital, Bliss and Chandler had to walk more than half a mile to his two-year-old Vauxhall Vectra. He'd ended up leaving his car in a residents' parking bay outside a block of narrow terraced houses squashed together anxiously like London commuters during rush hour. Bliss buckled up, turned the engine over, but made no move to pull away. An LCD display on the dashboard told him the temperature had barely touched five degrees. He tried to recalculate what that might be in the more familiar Fahrenheit. Closest he got was around forty. Bloody nippy, in other words.

Outside the relative comfort of the roomy vehicle, blustery weather scattered leaves across the streets and pavements, where they fled like frightened creatures ahead of the forceful wind, before finally huddling together in the gutter. A bleak sky seemed to press down against the rooftops, the narrow street becoming almost claustrophobic. Winter conditions already, with autumn yet to bid its farewell. Bliss shuddered once, and a shiver ran between his shoulder blades and continued down the knobs of his spine. Whether prompted by the cold or by all he and Chandler had seen and heard back in the mortuary, the shudder made him feel uncomfortable. He switched on the heating and waited for warm air to waft over them.

Mulling over the information they'd gleaned from Emily Grant, Bliss married it together with the impression he'd got from visiting the scene itself. Not the scene of crime, apparently, which would further complicate matters. He knew the lake over at Fletton fairly well, having walked the dogs there on several occasions. Now he wondered if those pleasant surroundings had been the scene of a murder. He recalled the winding paths he and the Labs had taken, fishermen he'd chatted with, carp basking near the surface of sun-drenched waters. It felt odd to think that a young woman might once have lost her life and been buried there.

Penny Chandler sat in the Vectra's passenger seat alongside him, completing her notes on a spiral-bound writing pad. She'd been quiet since leaving the mortuary, but Bliss needed to move beyond his own thoughts.

'So, what do you think?' he asked her, shifting sideways to look at the young officer.

The DC gave his question some thought, tapping the half-chewed blunt end of a biro against her teeth. 'If the Bone Woman is even close to being right, and we have no reason to doubt Emily's findings, then I'd say we've got one crappy job ahead of us. Frankly, I'm beginning to wish someone else had caught the shout last night.'

He nodded his understanding. Chandler had a healthy attitude to work and the people she met during the course of her duty, and was often forthright in her opinions. She could spout the politically correct doctrine when it was needed around superiors who cared about that sort of thing, but out in the job she worked the real world around her. It hadn't taken Bliss long to realise they thought along the same lines. There were a lot of politically correct young coppers in the job these days, but Penny Chandler wasn't one of them. So far it had made for a good working partnership, and Bliss believed a firm, relaxed friendship had been established. Her being easy on the eye was a pleasant bonus, not that he'd ever take that line of thought any further.

He said, 'I think you should see this case as a challenge rather than a chore, Penny. It's not going to be your average job, that's for sure. There'll be several new experiences for all of us, I'm certain.'

'A learning curve, eh?'

'Exactly. These kinds of jobs have a lot to teach us.'

A young kid drew up alongside the car, straddling a Raleigh mountain bike. He had a shaved head and wore sunglasses despite the day's gloom, his jaw working furiously on some gum. His Manchester United team shirt and baggy camouflage trousers were being savaged by the wind, and Bliss had to wonder how the boy was managing to remain on his bicycle. The lad rapped on the side window with his knuckles. He was all of eight, going on twenty. Bliss powered down the glass and peered up at him.

'Want your wheels looking after, mister?' the boy asked.

'Why would I want you to do that?'

'If you're going into the hospital I can make sure no one nicks your motor.'

Bliss shook his head, playing along. 'We've just come out of the place,' he said. 'And if you weren't aware of that, maybe you're not as good at protection as you think you are.'

'I'm the best there is. I was busy, that's all.'

'Even so, my motor didn't seem to come to any harm while we were in the hospital.'

The kid did some quick thinking. 'That's because I was looking after it.'

Laughing, Bliss said, 'Good try, but I don't think so, son.'

'How about next time? You could be one of my regulars.'

This forced another chortle. 'I think we'll be okay no matter where we park.'

Bliss felt the weight of the boy's close scrutiny for a few seconds. Then the kid nodded. 'Oh, I get it. You lot reckon you're better than everyone else.'

'Us lot?' Bliss touched a hand to his chest.

'Yeah. The filth.' The boy shook his head, removed the shades and peered into the car. A dusting of freckles decorated his nose and cheeks. He looked both angelic and demonic at the same time. He winked at Chandler and flashed a smile. 'I should've spotted it right away. Must be losing my touch. I can smell you now, though.'

Bliss exchanged grins with his DC. He rearranged his features into something resembling serious before looking back at the boy. 'Smell us? Where do you get all this stuff? Not Sesame Street, that's for sure.'

'Fuck off, pig,' the kid snarled before riding away, leaving behind his contempt for them to chew on.

'Well, he's certainly not short on confidence,' Bliss remarked, powering the side window back up. The car was buffeted by a sudden blast of wind, and a few people walking by had to lean into the gust to stay upright.

'Little shithead. No respect, and way too old before his time.' Chandler chuckled, craning her neck to follow the youngster who was about to disappear around a street corner.

'I think most of them are in places like this. If you're not streetwise you're not anything.'

'You sound as though you're speaking from experience, boss.'

Bliss nodded. 'I grew up in similar circumstances. Always looking for an edge.'

'And you turned out all right.'

'Just about, Penny. Just about. It could just as easily have gone the other way. Difference is, in my day the worst you got on the streets was a good hiding, a few clumps, some bruises. Badges of honour, really. Today you get a blade pulled on you for looking at someone the wrong way. Sometimes just for being on the same street.'

'That's a pleasant thought.'

'Yeah. Sorry. I'm in a "glass is half empty" mood today.'

'I don't suppose what the Bone Woman had to say cheered you up much.'

Bliss shook his head, sighed. Knew he'd been doing too much of that lately. 'You're not wrong there. Our Jane Doe was one unlucky woman.'

'Do you think the fact that she was pregnant might be significant?'

'It's a real possibility.'

Emily Grant's final revelation had been to tell them that a smaller skeletal form had also been found amongst the main victim's. A child, nowhere near fully formed, definitely unborn.

He sighed. Another one. Ran both hands down his face. 'Come on, Penny. Let's get out of here. That bloody place is still inside my nostrils.'

As he nosed the Vectra away from the kerb, Bliss's thoughts slipped from Jane Doe back to the message left on his answer machine by DI Weller. There were puzzles everywhere. It was now time to focus.

***

Thorpe Wood, the area police headquarters, was located towards the north-west edge of the city. In line with the majority of structures erected in Peterborough during the late seventies, the two-storey building was bland, grey and featureless. Impenetrable tinted windows gave the impression of secrecy, perhaps even a sense of foreboding. A dour edifice to match a grim setting. The underground car park used by Thorpe Wood staff was bursting at the seams, and it took Bliss a few minutes of circling around to find a space. He grumbled about it as he and Chandler made their way up to the rear main entrance, where she tapped in the door code to let them both inside.

Bliss was still muttering to himself when they wandered into the open-plan CID area, where his office sat tucked away in the far corner, one of four set aside for officers at DI level. Out in the main room, between twenty and thirty detectives went about their business, phones cupped to their ears, fingers tapping away at keyboards, a hubbub of voices bouncing off the walls.

'I'll be glad when the new overflow place is ready,' Bliss said. 'That way we might not be lumped together like lab rats and it might take less than an hour to get parked.'

Moving part of the HQ operation to Bretton had been approved by the Cambridgeshire Police Authority, but the much-needed expansion was still some way off. Meanwhile, the simple act of finding a space for his car was enough to irritate Bliss beyond all reason.

'Maybe they'll put us all on bicycles,' Chandler replied, grinning.

'Don't say that within earshot of the bosses. They'd probably take you up on it.'

'Yeah. I can see it now, you and me on our bikes chasing after a souped-up Aston Martin. Listen, I'm going to get myself a drink. You want something?'

Bliss thought about suggesting they take a break in the canteen, but decided he could do with a few minutes alone to pull himself together before getting stuck into the procedure of setting up a major inquiry.

'A cup of tea would be nice,' he said.

Penny nodded. 'I'll get it from the canteen. The stuff that vending machine spews out is toxic.'

The office Bliss had inherited from a DI who'd been struck down by bowel cancer was a basic partition structure that formed a flimsy barrier between him and those working at the desks in the main outer area. Nothing fancy, but a haven all the same. Bliss hung his coat and jacket up on a hook protruding from the back of the office door, before almost falling into a leather-look swivel chair at his desk. The padded cushioned seat was moulded to the shape of his backside, and he knew he would pine when the day came to throw it out.

Towers of folders, files and paper perched precariously on and around the desk, but he insisted his administrative methods were a controlled kind of chaos, that he could lay his hands on anything within a few minutes. So far no one had tested his claim, but Bliss knew the day would come. He also knew he'd be found wanting.

Stretching out his legs and resting the back of his head in the palms of his hands, Bliss closed his eyes and took a few deep breaths. After a minute or so he loosened his tie and unbuttoned the top button of his shirt. He was feeling hot and a little light-headed, his eyes bouncing around like rubber balls beneath the lids. He thought ahead to the hospital appointment he had arranged for the following morning. Wondered if the recent searing headaches and the sense of imbalance were connected. Stress, his GP had insisted, but had referred him to ENT anyway. Bliss pushed the thought aside, moved beyond it. There was enough to worry about here and now.

Chandler joined him a few minutes later and handed over the mug of tea he'd asked for. It was still hot, but he took several small swallows, savouring the taste on his tongue. 'Christ! I needed that,' he said. 'I was as dry as a bone. No pun intended.'

Bliss watched Chandler sip rather more demurely from a bottle of mineral water. He saw her eyes flit to the wall behind him, her mouth curling into a smile. He didn't have to turn to know what she was looking at. Within a month of Bliss arriving from the Met, some wag had stuck up a sheet of cardboard on which was drawn a circle, with a rough arrowed pointer pinned to the centre. Written in black marker on the top was the title: The Bliss Pissed-Ometer. It ranged from 'Mild' to 'Ballistic'. He'd never caught the person responsible, but the pointer was in a different position every day, sometimes actually matching his mood. He had swiftly gained a reputation for having a temper every bit as quick as his mind, and the chart was the squad's response. Being a moody bugger hadn't helped, either.

'What does it read today?' he asked her.

'Steaming.'

Bliss nodded. 'That's about right. The murder of a young woman is inclined to piss me off.' He looked out into the main office, working areas sectioned off by waist-high carpeted baffles. There was some movement out there, but no one was looking their way. No furtive grins. He'd catch the bastard responsible one day.

Chandler perched on the edge of his desk, crossing one leg over the other while removing her suit jacket. The Thorpe Wood building was an enigma – no air conditioning in the warmer months, and a heating system that seemed to have only one setting: blast furnace. Once you were inside, you got rid of as much clothing as was decent. Penny's white blouse clung to a flat stomach, and Bliss could make out the mottled form of a lacy bra beneath the silk. The skirt rose high on her thighs, and he had a fleeting mental image of Dr Bates's assistant. Penny Chandler was attractive without it being obvious – not striking, exactly, but quietly eye-catching.

Bliss averted his gaze before she noticed. He'd already been caught out once today. He placed his mug on top of a blue folder, whose cover bore the scars of many other drinks.

'I'll see what kind of resources I can drum up for this one, Pen. It might be hard work, though. Particularly with regard to putting a search team over at Fletton lake. Cold cases are not exactly flavour of the month around here, but I think we'll need a decent team around us.'

Bliss got to his feet and walked across to a window sorely in need of cleaning. He peered out at the Lloyds TSB office buildings opposite, the offices there appearing every bit as anonymous as his own, and then across to the steady stream of traffic hissing by on the parkway. As tyres rumbled across joins in the road surface at high speed, they created a noise that to Bliss sounded like distant gunshots. He checked his watch. It was ten thirty, the day dribbling away from them. Every officer with even a modicum of experience knew that the first six to ten hours in a missing persons case were crucial. Beyond that and the chances of a successful outcome were dramatically reduced. Jane Doe had been missing for a dozen years at least.

'Tell me,' Bliss said, turning back to his DC, 'what's the skinny on me these days?'

'What d'you mean?' Chandler looked up at him, her bottle of water stalled part way to her lips.

'I mean, what are my colleagues saying about me? Behind my back. Let's face it, Penny, I fucked up big time on our last murder case. Too many people were killed, and I still have a suicide on my conscience.' He raised a hand to ward off a protest. The memory of his failure six months earlier still scalded his mind. 'No, I'm coming to terms with it, Pen. And I'll have to carry on dealing with the guilt. But I need to know that I still have support out there. If I'm going to stand up and deliver this briefing, I have to be confident that the team are behind me.'

'Then you can be.' Her eyes insisted he believe her. 'There are no whispers behind your back. And the only member of the team who blames you for the outcome of that case is you. Shit happens, boss, and everyone I've spoken to about it has nothing but sympathy for your situation. You did your best. It's all anyone can expect of us.'

His best. Bliss wondered if that were true. The investigation had got out of hand, had spiralled out of control. But it was a fact that he had received enormous support and encouragement from many of his fellow detectives in the long months that followed. Perhaps now was more about retrieving some self-belief and accepting things at face value. Bliss looked at Chandler and gave a nod, touched by her assurances.

'Okay, then. Penny, I want you to set up a Major Incident Room and try to round up some suits and uniforms, about half a dozen of each to start with. Have the team assemble at...' He glanced down at his watch again. 'One thirty. I have to be somewhere at noon, but I'll make it back in time.'

Chandler nodded. She recapped her bottle and moved away from the desk, hooking her jacket over one shoulder. About to walk away, she paused and fixed her eyes on him.

'Are you okay, boss?' she asked.

'In what way?'

'I mean, do you feel all right? You look a little bit... peaky.'

Bliss shooed her away with his fingers. 'I'm fine. Tired, that's all. Go ahead, and I'll catch up with you back here five minutes before the briefing.'

Peaky? Bliss thought as Penny left the office, quietly closing the door behind her. Peaky? If only she knew. Peaky didn't begin to cover it. But it's just stress, he told himself. His GP had assured him of that. The stress that comes with the job. Bliss blew out his cheeks. Though some people scoffed at the idea, stress was real enough. He knew that better than most. And a pile of unexplained human remains wasn't about to help.

FIVE

Bliss drove into the city centre and found an empty bay on the third floor of the market car park. It was dark and the spaces were narrow, but it was much easier to find somewhere to park here than over at the main multistoreys by the bus station. He paid and displayed, resenting the fee. Still feeling a little unsteady on his feet, he took the lift down to the ground floor, emerging into the cold and heavily overcast day.

If open air markets sold everything he wanted or needed, Bliss would never even enter a shopping mall. He found such places devoid of character, charmless pods containing overpriced goods sold by underpaid, poorly trained and unenthusiastic staff. Markets, on the other hand, had substance, throbbing with life and vitality. Livelihoods were on display, and there was true competition.

The Wednesday market was in full swing, garish displays of bright colours, discordant sounds, and a variety of smells emerging from stalls, providing an all-out assault on the senses. Protected from the elements by a vast steel and corrugated plastic roof, traders and customers went about their business seemingly without a care.

Though the cacophony of voices was music to Bliss's ears, the largely Asian population of stallholders were nowhere near as vocal as the traders he had both known and worked with in London. Petticoat Lane, Islington's Chapel Street, Roman Road, all great markets in their time, bursting at the seams with loud, gregarious characters, each with a hundred stories to tell. In his early teens, Bliss had earned a few quid every Sunday morning at Petticoat Lane in Whitechapel, first helping to pull the stalls out and dress them, and then selling fruit and veg alongside a friend of the family he'd always known as 'Uncle Reg'. It was only when Uncle Reg pulled a twelve-year stretch in Brixton prison for armed robbery that Bliss learned of the man's shady lifestyle. It had come as quite a shock, given that Bliss's father was a desk sergeant at the local nick in Stepney. This revelation led Bliss to understanding that, while half his father's pals were colleagues, the other half were villains.

Uncle Reg and a miscellany of assorted family friends had been uppermost in his thoughts earlier when he'd told Penny that his life could have gone either way. At that age it had been a close call, and though in later years he would come to understand that boys tend to rebel against their fathers, it was on his fifteenth birthday that Bliss decided he wanted to become a police officer. His father's expression told him he'd made the right choice.

Mixing with villains didn't mean his father was bent. Bliss had somehow understood this. His own fondness for Uncle Reg had not diminished merely because the man was banged up in jail. Carrying out a robbery was wrong, of that Bliss was certain. Being armed when doing so was even worse, and the punishment was suitably severe. Uncle Reg was a convicted criminal, but not a bad man. Not in Bliss's eyes. And this acceptance of a person's darker side was, he believed, the reason he had been successful in his dealings with all types of criminals. The simple fact was, he empathised with them. Had come close to being one of them.

A cry from one stallholder to another brought Bliss out of his reverie. He smiled at the fleeting memory, wondering exactly how close he'd come to choosing the dark side. Not that it mattered. Not now.

On the corner of the market square, opposite a minor Tesco store, was the Tasty-Bite café. A business run by the same family for more than two decades, they prepared food fit for any builder, cabbie, lorry driver, or market trader. Praise didn't come much higher. As Bliss entered the warm, somewhat clammy interior, he recalled the day he and DI Weller had first enjoyed breakfast there together. It was late afternoon by the time they'd managed to free themselves from the scene of the Post Office raid, but at the Tasty-Bite, breakfast started at six in the morning and went on right through to closing time. They hadn't spoken a great deal around their food and milky tea, not even to discuss the case, but Bliss had taken a shine to the DI all the same. Bernard Weller was a good copper and a thoroughly decent man.

Checking his watch, Bliss saw that it was now five to twelve, and Weller was not one of the café's dozen or so patrons. Bliss ordered and paid for a coffee and a bacon sandwich, then tucked himself behind a two-seater table so that he could face the door and the busy market beyond the steam-painted glass. While he waited, his mind flitted between the current murder case and the reasons Bernard Weller wanted to meet with him. Bliss had been suspended as a result of how his last murder investigation ended and, having made an enemy of his superintendent at the same time, he'd been happy enough to keep his head down these past six months or so. He was currently investigating about a dozen cases, but they were mostly forlorn hopes, and murder was always the trump card. Despite Penny's earlier assurances regarding how other colleagues felt about him, doubts swarmed like angry bees inside his head. The only saving grace was that this inquiry was unlikely to be as high profile as the one he had so badly fucked up.

Figuring out Weller's intentions was a much tougher proposition. Bliss could only assume it had something to do with the case they'd worked together, but had no idea why the man would go to all this trouble over something so cut and dried. The two men serving time for the raid were guilty, of that Bliss was certain. What else was there to discuss? Unless it simply was a matter of wanting to keep in touch.

His sandwich and drink was brought to the table by a young girl whose cheeks looked as if they would sizzle if touched. Her limp blonde hair was tied back in a ponytail, and sweat filmed her acne-scarred forehead. Huge hooped earrings hung from her lobes, and her jaw seemed to be working overtime on some gum.

'Busy day?' he asked, offering a sympathetic smile.

A roll of the eyes was her only response as she turned and walked away. Bliss gave a stifled laugh and shook his head; right now the art of conversation was turning in its grave. She'd probably dismissed him as a middle-aged letch, when all he'd sought to offer was common courtesy. Dismissing the waitress from his mind, Bliss ate quickly, feeling hungrier now the smell of bacon was right beneath his nose. The coffee was milky, though he'd ordered black. It didn't seem worth making a fuss over.

By twenty past he was done, and already he felt eyes upon him as café staff waited to free up his table. Hyenas set to pounce on the straggler within the herd. He considered ordering another coffee, but if he did so he would have to mention the fact that they had got his order wrong first time around. Normally he would enjoy a debate where he might get the opportunity to lambaste the entire free world, but today he wasn't in the mood. Perhaps it was because he wasn't feeling at his best, or could the thought of the imminent briefing be getting to him? Either was possible. But maybe, just maybe, he was maturing. Smiling at the thought, Bliss tore a sheet from his notebook and wrote: *Cheer up or get another job!* He folded the sheet twice and left the note wedged beneath his plate, then got to his feet. As he yanked open the door, he glanced over his shoulder and called out to the waitress, 'Bye, sweetheart. I've left you a tip.'

Bliss turned up his coat collar, crossed over the road and stood outside the entrance to Tesco, hands buried deep inside his pockets. The wind had got up again, and the dreary sky was threatening yet more rain. From this vantage point he could see anyone approaching and entering the café, and only now did he realise that when Weller finally arrived, Bliss would either have to disappoint the man or return to the café and face the wrath of a waitress scorned. Jump off that bridge when you get to it, he told himself. He stamped his feet a couple of times and hunched further into his coat, wishing he'd ordered that second coffee after all.

***

By the time Bliss got back to Thorpe Wood, DC Chandler had set up the Major Inquiry Room and was waiting for him in his office. 'Anything to report?' he asked her, stripping off his coat, flapping rainwater from it before hanging it on the door.

'Not really, boss. I've managed to cobble together a small team, but more bodies are promised. Sykes was prowling around looking for you, and if he doesn't make the tail end of the briefing, he wants to see you in his office immediately afterwards.'

Bliss groaned. Stuart Sykes was the superintendent he'd made an enemy of. A slick political animal, Sykes had been destined for the very top, but as the officer in overall charge at the time the previous murder case went tits up, Sykes had been pushed onto his sword by way of punishment. There would be no further promotions, so the whisper around the station went, and in the man's mind there was only one person to blame. It was usually the case that a DI would report to a Detective Chief Inspector, but Bliss was still on some half-arsed form of probation, and therefore had to suffer the ignominy of being supervised by the superintendent instead.

'I'll see if I can find a way to avoid that pleasure as long as possible,' Bliss told her. He rubbed a finger over a small, jagged scar on his forehead. It looked like the Nike logo in reverse. A legacy from a youthful prank that went wrong, the tiny nub of hard skin was like a magnet for his hands whenever he felt under pressure.

Chandler sniggered. 'I'm sure you will. Oh, I forgot to mention, the two boys who unearthed our Jane Doe have been questioned and they both tell the same story: they did not move the bones. One of them admitted to putting a hand on the skull, but that's all.'

Bliss recalled thinking how he would have done exactly the same thing in their shoes. 'Fair enough. I didn't think that would go anywhere.'

'Enjoy your lunch?' Chandler asked. It was no casual throwaway question.

He smiled. 'For your information I was on my own. And no, I didn't enjoy it.'

He'd waited around until just after one, but Weller hadn't shown. By then Bliss was cold, wet, tired and miserable, and even the thought of the briefing didn't seem quite so bad. He'd also been propositioned twice, once by a skanky-looking young woman offering a hand job for twenty quid, and then by a large male of eastern European extraction who offered some crack for the same figure. Bliss reacted the same way both times: told them he'd rather burn the money, suggested they both get proper jobs, then flashed his warrant card and insisted they fuck off away from him.

'Maybe you should ask the Bone Woman to lunch next time,' Chandler said, snagging back his attention.

Bliss jabbed a finger at her. 'Don't even go there, Penny. Just don't. And now, I think it may be time to get back on the horse.'

***

Recent renovations to part of the CID floor had created a new state-of-the-art Major Incident Room. A cluster of powerful computers sat ranged along one wall in a recessed bay, each connected to every national police database and information service. A data projector hung suspended from the ceiling, its lens focused on an interactive whiteboard, which was connected to a sleek laptop computer. The new system allowed a huge amount of case information to be stored on the local network rather than be erased each time the boards became full. Bliss had yet to have the pleasure of using it, but a half-day training session had left him feeling reasonably confident. Whilst he had by no means fully embraced the age of the microchip, neither was he a technophobe. Or a techno*tard, as Penny liked to call him when he cursed at his own laptop.*

Bliss stood before the huge whiteboard now, facing a team of four detectives and three uniformed officers. One of the standard template pages contained a checklist.

Approach
Point of Entry
Activities Within
Exit
Transfer of Evidence
Number of Perpetrators
Contact Trace
Type of Crime

Of the eight items listed, notations had been made against only two. All they had so far was the type of crime and the activities carried out within the SOC. Meagre pickings, Bliss thought. But perhaps quality was going to prove better than quantity at this stage.

'Thanks for making this initial briefing,' he said, taking a moment to make eye contact with everyone. 'Let me start by laying out what we're looking at here.'

He turned side on, navigated to a second page and jabbed a finger at a series of notations made earlier by Chandler. 'Yesterday evening, human remains were discovered in Bretton Woods by two young lads. This morning it was confirmed that the remains are of a young IC1 female, possibly approaching her mid-twenties. The victim has been dead for approximately twelve to sixteen years, and this team has been designated a murder squad because the hospital doctor confirmed cause of death as strangulation. Tragically, our victim was also in the early stages of pregnancy when she was murdered, so I guess you could say there are actually two victims to consider. Now then, because we have had the services of an additional expert in these matters, we find ourselves in the unusual position of having quite a bit of information to work with at this relatively early stage.'

Bliss used the electronic pen to pull up a menu from which he selected a third stored page of information. He spent the next few minutes relating the details provided by Emily Grant at the mortuary that morning. As he was nearing the end of his summary, one of the uniforms raised himself off the edge of a desk and said, 'How reliable is this info, sir? I mean, it sounds like a lot of guesswork to me.'

Fixing the young officer with a tight glare, Bliss snapped off his response. 'This is the first time you've worked with me, Constable, so I'll allow you this one life. Please note for future reference that I prefer to complete my briefing without interruption. You can ask as many questions as you like when I'm finished, but while I'm talking I want you to listen and make mental notes. However, as you *have* asked, I will give you an answer. The information we received from Miss Grant should be viewed as inquiry guidelines based on educated deduction. That is to say, we follow the path as far as it will go and treat it as if it had come from a pathologist or forensic scientist.'

He nodded and smiled at the officer, whose cheeks were by now inflamed. 'Don't worry about it, Constable...?'

'Redpath, sir.'

'You'll learn as you go on, Redpath. Each of us SIOs has our own way of working, and they're important to us when we're under pressure. Just at this moment you may consider me an anal-retentive prick, but as the buck stops with me I'm entitled to a few quirks.' Bliss paused to allow a few nervous laughs to echo around the room.

'Anyhow, as you will all see from the evidence board here, we will be working on the assumption that our Jane Doe was strangled to death shortly after being knocked down by a vehicle, and then buried somewhere near the Fletton lake where the old brick pits used to be. Her remains were then dug up and reburied over at Bretton Woods about three to four years ago.

'So, we need to know who she is, and when exactly she was murdered. The steel rod in her leg may lead us to a name, at least, but let's not count any chickens at this stage. The fact that her body was moved elsewhere after so many years suggests to me that the reason behind it is significant. Needless to say, we will look to focus on that. I intend to split the team into two, one working from the time of death forwards, the other working from the time of reburial backwards. Hopefully we'll all meet in the middle and shake hands.'

This raised a further gentle ripple of laughter. Bliss held up a hand to quieten them down again. He'd turned the valve just enough for a small measure of relief. Looking around at the squad he was pleased to see attentive faces, eyes narrowed in concentration. Still, it wouldn't hurt to remind them of their commitment.

'Okay, listen up. Just because we're dealing with skeletal remains rather than a flesh-covered corpse, doesn't mean we shouldn't do everything we can to find the killer. And that's exactly what our prey is: a killer. I've heard some officers calling these people the 'unsub', the unknown subject, but that's all American TV and FBI fiction bollocks. Our target is a vicious, murdering bastard. You may call him a VMB for short if you like.

'When this briefing is over, DC Chandler will allocate actions for you all. Other officers will join this squad over the next day or two. For the moment, DC Chandler will supervise this office and you will report any findings to her. We have a civilian administrator coming in to handle all the paperwork and databases, so no need to concern yourselves with that side of things. Just get out there and get digging… no pun intended. Now, any questions?'

Fifteen minutes later, Bliss left the room, asking Chandler to join him out in the corridor for a moment. In her eyes he could see both surprise and excitement at being asked to supervise. He leaned back against a wall, hands in pockets.

'That seemed to go well.'

She nodded. 'I thought so.'

'I didn't even fuck up on the new system. And thanks for getting all that set up, by the way.'

'No problem, boss. I'm nothing if not organised.'

'And maybe just a little bit scared right now?'

Chandler's mouth curled and twisted in mock agony. 'Maybe a smidgen.'

Bliss was content with what he saw in her eyes. 'Do your best, Penny. I'll see if I can get a DS in tomorrow to take over, because I will want you with me. But you know what's needed here. Use this opportunity to make a name for yourself. I want someone going back through MisPer reports during the time period our victim would have gone missing, I want someone to get us an ordnance survey map of the two SOC areas as they were during the relevant time periods, and I want you to catch up with Emily and see if she has anything else for us.'

Chandler gave a confident nod. 'Will do, boss. What about organising a search over at the lake?'

'Not yet. Too much manpower required for my level of authority. I'll have to run it by Sykes when he catches up with me.'

'Okay. Is that it, boss?'

Bliss nodded. 'I think so. Are you up for it, Penny?'

'Yes.'

'Sure?'

'Positive.'

'Good. Then knock them dead.'

'I will. Where will you be?'

'Avoiding Sykes,' Bliss replied. And walked swiftly away.

SIX

Penny Chandler couldn't believe how nervous she felt. The DI was right: she knew what had to be done, the procedures to follow, and was acquainted with most of the officers involved. Even so, this was the first time she had been given the huge responsibility for running a Major Inquiry Room and issuing actions. Actions were essentially instructions for furthering the investigation, and as such they were crucial. It wasn't merely a case of handing them out to anyone, either; you had to try and select the right people for the right job. Some officers were better with the public, while other strengths lay in research or close observation, even interviews. Choices and decisions made at this stage of a case could make or break it.

After Bliss had left her alone with her thoughts, Chandler walked swiftly along the corridor and slipped into the toilet, grateful to find it empty. In the soap-spotted mirror, her own inquiring gaze regarded the person the team would see. Dull eyes, ringed by neglect and lack of sleep. Too many deep ridges on her forehead for someone her age, and it looked as if crows had been tap-dancing in the make-up around her mouth. Not a pretty sight if she was readying herself for a night out, Chandler decided, but here in this place the look would work in her favour. The face staring back at her now was mature and responsible. It was a take charge face. She could only hope the brain was as prepared.

Before returning to the room, she fetched herself a cup of tea from the canteen, the desire for a prop outweighing any need to quench a thirst. When she rejoined the squad, Chandler felt the eyes of every officer upon her. Several minutes had passed since she and Bliss had left the room, and tongues would not have been idle. Affecting a warm smile, she strode briskly across to the whiteboard, projecting a great deal more confidence than she felt. She took a sip from the mug, composing herself before looking up.

'As DI Bliss informed you,' Chandler began after clearing her throat, 'we'll be forming two teams. Team A will start by tracking down all unresolved female MisPer reports made between ninety and ninety-three. Narrow the search down to an age range of eighteen to thirty. Oh, and only IC1, as well. You'll need to go through both computer and paper records...'

'Which of us are in Team A?' one of the suits asked.

Chandler swallowed quickly, her hands starting to sweat, an anxious fluttering developing in her stomach. Here was the first test. Bliss had earlier made it clear about his dislike of being interrupted when in full flow, but Chandler was not the senior investigating officer for this case, and as such she was seen as fair game. Now was as good a time as any to put down a marker. Eyeballing her colleague, Penny Chandler added steel to her gaze.

'Does that sound like an interesting line of investigation to you, DC Coleman?' she asked.

'It does, yes.'

'Well, I believe Team A will need patience in abundance, and as you seem to be lacking that particular virtue, I think Team B might be better suited. Okay?'

Chandler maintained eye contact. She and Coleman were equal in rank, but she'd been handed the helm and it was her arse on the line. The squad had to know she was serious. 'Coleman?' she prompted.

The DC gave a reluctant nod of the head.

'Good. Right then, it's like this: we have a single investigation split into two separate strands, so at this early stage I want you all to know about each action, while it's still manageable, just in case you get shipped across to the other team. Now, once you have a list from the MisPer angle, let's see if you can track down any reports relating to an incident where an RTA was called in on the same day, specifically one where no victim was subsequently discovered. Clutching at straws there, I realise, but it's worth checking out. Another avenue once you have relevant names and dates is to have someone look through the local newspaper archives. Make a note of the fact that our victim had major surgery on her leg – this may come up somewhere in a report. Finally, and I know this is reaching further still, cross-check the dates with any reports relating to the lake over at Fletton. Any reported accident in the same vicinity will obviously be of major interest.'

Overlooking something at this juncture might prove crucial, and Chandler didn't want to blow this opportunity, so she mentally checked off the list inside her head. She swallowed some more tea to buy some time, took a breath and continued.

'Team B will be working backwards, so your area of focus will be the two thousand and three to two thousand and four period relating to any reported incidents over at Bretton Woods and at Fletton lake. Anything from both on the same night and I'll eat my hat, but find me or DI Bliss any time of the day or night if you do get a hit that good. I also want someone concentrating on why the remains were moved – what happened over at the lake during that period? What might spur someone into such a drastic act?'

While outlining the formal actions, Chandler was running through the possible permutations of officers. Their faces gave each of them away: overall interest in the case, eagerness to be involved, or lack of either. As in any job, some people were here for the salary and pension, content to lurk in the shadows and do just enough to get by. But even they had their uses, she reflected. By the time she was done talking, she thought she had the balance about right. Without pause for second-guessing herself, she assigned the officers and gave out the assignments. There were no questions and everyone seemed satisfied. When it was over, Chandler blew out a sigh of relief and dismissed the squad. As they began to file out of the door, she made a note on the board of the actions and the names of everyone who had been in attendance.

A few minutes later she was back at her own desk in the main CID area, assessing her moment in the spotlight, eventually deciding she was happy enough with her performance. It wasn't a perfect ten, perhaps, but neither had she screwed the pooch. From the corner of her eye she could see faces turned her way, conversations taking place. Close colleagues were aware that she had been given an opportunity to take a step forward. She found herself listening for sniggers, but none came. Self-doubt was her main weakness, but she was working on it. The boss's confidence in her was a major boost.

Relieved and able to relax for the first time that day, Penny Chandler's thoughts turned to Bliss. He didn't look at all well lately. He seemed drawn, had lost a little weight, and appeared distracted. During his suspension from duty he had considered leaving the job, but she had done her best to convince him he was needed. After a while he seemed to come to terms with what had happened, and when he returned to work he was much more outgoing and relaxed than before. The past month or so, however, had seen a change come over him once again. Chandler thought Bliss might be depressed, but so far had resisted raising the issue with him. Last week she thought she had seen him stumble slightly a couple of times, and briefly wondered if he had been drinking more heavily than usual. Yet that just wasn't him. He'd never allow anything to affect the way he did his job. Jimmy wasn't one to gush and express his feelings, but the two of them had made a connection and she believed he would tell her in his own time if anything was wrong.

Bliss wasn't the only one to have been affected by that rotten case, either. One DI had transferred out, Detective Superintendent Sykes had withdrawn into himself upon realising that his career ambitions were in tatters, and she herself had felt empty inside for several weeks.

That damned investigation.

Two separate cases had eventually merged into one, something the media had afterwards dubbed the 'Fascist Assassin' inquiry, during which the vile mind of a right-wing fanatic had been responsible for the murder of a whole string of people, including a young boy. The boy's father, having initially been a suspect, and who was then used by Bliss to trap the killer, manoeuvred himself into a situation where he was able to end both his own life and that of the man who had murdered his son. No one involved had emerged from the case unscathed, but life went on. And so did crime. She'd worked on one murder inquiry since, but this was her first back in the saddle with Bliss.

Jimmy was her boss, and he had put a lot of faith and trust in her, but she would have to keep a wary eye on him all the same. Chandler thought that one more failure might push him right over the edge.

***

Despite his best attempts at evasion, Bliss had finally found himself cornered by Stuart Sykes, and was instructed to join the superintendent in his office. Bliss refused to be cowed in the super's presence, but their working relationship was becoming almost impossible to negotiate. Every word the man uttered seemed prolonged and drenched with bile, his contempt for Bliss all too obvious. They each understood that Sykes would seek to undermine Bliss every chance he got and that, in turn, Bliss would continue to overcome all obstacles in order to solve the cases he worked. From Sykes there was true loathing, from Bliss only disdain. The only thing they had in common was a loathing for the other. Bliss had long since decided he could live with that. He wondered if Sykes felt the same.

'In your absence earlier today, DC Chandler and I managed to have a chat,' Sykes said tonelessly.

His eyes were large behind rimless spectacles, blinking rapidly as if affected by a tic. He had a long, narrow face shaped like a rugby ball, cheeks hollow in the shadow of prominent bones. Bliss thought Sykes looked malnourished, the downturn of his mouth suggesting discontent. The man had aged six years in as many months, and while some might pity his fall from grace, in Bliss's opinion the super's quest for self-advancement had ultimately been his own undoing. There was such a thing as too much ambition.

'Chandler informed me that you would like a large team working on this,' Sykes continued. 'Is that correct?'

'That's right,' Bliss nodded. 'It's a major inquiry in my opinion.'

'But a large team for a murder that may be as much as fifteen or sixteen years old? Given budgetary constraints right now, is that really necessary?'

The two men sat either side of Sykes's huge glass-topped desk, the super rigid, Bliss slouched. He nodded and said, 'It's the very nature of this particular case that warrants a large team. At least in the early stages.'

'I'll have to consider the numbers.'

'I'd also like a search team out around the perimeter of Fletton lake. It's possible that some bones got left behind when the body was moved.'

Sykes shook his head dismissively. 'Out of the question.'

Bliss conceded defeat. He'd not expected anything other than refusal.

'You can have a week on this,' Sykes said.

'A week?' Bliss pulled himself upright. 'That's no time at all.'

'This is hardly a priority case, Inspector. And you know as well as I do how unlikely you are to get a satisfactory resolution.'

Bliss felt aggrieved. Seven days simply wasn't enough. 'What if we turn up some solid leads in that first week? Do I get an extension?'

Sykes gave a drawn-out sigh. 'We'll see.'

'But I do get a decent team, right? Everything is so vague at the moment, with no definite dates to go on. We need the manpower to get us started.'

Sykes linked hands and leaned forward to rest them on his desk. Bliss could see his own features reflected in the super's glasses. He didn't like what he saw there. Prematurely grey hair cut close to the scalp, receding rapidly. A fleshy face with a doughy complexion, eyes set deep above prominent cheekbones. A stranger in familiar clothes.

'Which brings me to your use of a civilian in this matter,' Sykes said beneath a disapproving frown. 'Exactly how reliable is this woman from Flag Fen?'

'As reliable as any in her field, I should think. Emily Grant is an expert in both anthropology and archaeology.'

'She'll need to be if you are basing your entire line of investigation on her findings.'

Bliss acknowledged this with a dip of his head and a slight shrug. 'All the usual forensic avenues are also being explored, of course. But these things take time, especially with human remains, and I thought we could do with getting a head start on this one.'

In the small silence that followed, Bliss ran his eyes over the office. Four times the size of his own, it had been redecorated in each of the three years Sykes had occupied it. Two windows peered out over the nearby private golf course, of which Sykes was a member. Subtle lighting illuminated pictures and photographs ranged along one wall. On the desk, next to his telephone, stood a silver-framed photograph of Sykes with his wife and two children. Proof, if ever it was needed, that there was someone for everyone in this life. In one corner of the room, by the door, there were two small leather sofas arranged in the shape of an 'L' around a glass and chrome coffee table. The whole office was neat and spotlessly clean, in stark contrast to Bliss's own. Gloss over substance. Much like the man who used up valuable air in here every day.

'This is your first murder inquiry since your return from suspension, of course,' Sykes then commented, showing he had a bite to match his bark. Now, for the first time, their eyes met and held. 'Are you sure you're up to the task, Inspector?'

'Of course.'

'No doubts? Your ego must have taken quite a bashing. Not easy to get over such a thing.'

Bliss kept both his temper and the level of his voice in check, though he could feel both hands clenching.

'I don't see it that way at all. Other people involved may have considered their ego above all else, whereas my overriding concern was for the innocent victims involved. If there is any residue from that investigation, it's a sense of overwhelming frustration, a good deal of sadness, and more than a little guilt. I wouldn't expect you to understand.'

Sykes sat back in his chair, lips twisting into a mild pout. 'I know what you think of me, Inspector. I know, but I don't care. To me, your opinion is of no consequence. Officers like you should have been put out to pasture years ago. Those who do not wish to move with the times should make way for those who do. Perhaps you ought to consider that.'

'Resigning, you mean?' Bliss smiled and shook his head. Six months ago he had given it careful consideration. If he ever did quit, it would be on his own terms. 'I wouldn't give you the satisfaction. No, if I thought I was unable to do my job, then I'd be out of here as quick as a flash. Nothing would hold me back. I admit it's harder these days, trying to work with one hand tied behind my back with red tape, but provided I can still make a difference I'll stick it out. You're just going to have to accept that.'

'I'll accept nothing where you are concerned.' The man's voice hardened, emerging through tight lips.

'Then you'll have to learn to live with it instead. I can take whatever you choose to dish out.'

'Don't be so sure of that, Inspector.'

Bliss narrowed his gaze. He even managed a thin smile. 'You like doing that, don't you? Reminding me who I am, what rank I have. But I know why you do it.'

'Really? Enlighten me.'

'It's the only way you can feel superior. By reminding me that you are, by rank. But we both know it's by rank only, and that must eat away at your insides.'

Sykes rolled back from his desk, stood and strolled across to peer out of a window, hands clasped behind his back. A grey, swollen mass of clouds seemed to press against the glass. The day was about to get colder and wetter.

'You think you have all the answers,' he said, not bothering to look at Bliss. 'I can assure you, Inspector, you do not. You may have Chief Superintendent Flynn in your corner, but he won't be around forever. There are greener pastures calling him. I wouldn't be in your shoes when he moves on.'

Bliss knew exactly what Sykes was driving at. He felt a surge of undiluted anger, briefly considered quelling it, then decided instead to let it loose.

'Yes, okay, the chief super did support me when I was suspended, and perhaps he does sympathise with my position. But there are just the two of us here and now in this room. One of us is a decent copper, and the other is a complete arsehole. And both of us know which is which.'

Sykes turned this time, eyes narrowed, mouth no more than a dark smudge. 'I will remember each and every one of these insults, Bliss. And every barb will be a nail in the coffin of your career. There will be payback, and I'm a patient man.'

Getting to his feet, Bliss moved towards the office door without being dismissed. 'When did you stop being a copper and start being a petty, vindictive coward?' he asked.

'I *am* a copper,' Sykes snapped, wheeling fully around, outrage etched deep into the folds of his face. 'I'm a modern police officer in a modern police service. You bloody… troglodytes couldn't possibly comprehend that.'

'You want to watch your blood pressure,' Bliss said, pausing at the door. 'Stress can be a killer, so I hear.'

'Get out of here! Go on, get out.'

But he was already alone in the room.

***

On his way down to the ground floor canteen, Bliss stopped off at the main administration office, which was staffed entirely by civilians. The open-plan office was bustling as usual, telephones going off, voices bubbling away in the background. At the counter, a large, matronly woman sat tapping at a computer keyboard.

'Afternoon, Betty,' Bliss said. He flashed a wide grin. The spat with Sykes had perked him up.

'Good afternoon, Inspector,' came the reply. She looked up and smiled back at him. Her blonde hair was cut into a neat bob that curled in at the ends and rested on her shoulders. She dressed in green almost every day, and today the mint-coloured cardigan made him think of mouthwash for some perverse reason. She had a lovely smile that cheered everyone who saw it. 'What can I do for you?'

Bliss frowned. It was a good question. 'I'm not sure, actually. Tell me, Betty, do you keep records here of officers who have moved on? Transferred out, or retired?'

'Within reason, yes. We add their new station to their records if they've transferred, certainly. And if they move when they retire, we also lodge a forwarding address. Beyond that, the full personnel records will be stored at Cambridge, though we do have access to the main personnel database.'

'What about a home address or telephone number for someone who transferred, as opposed to just their new station?'

'Possibly. Who is it you want to track down?'

'DI Weller. He was at Thorpe Wood when I started here around three years ago, moved on shortly afterwards.'

Betty's face beamed. 'Oh, I remember Bernie. Lovely chap. Always had time for a chat and a laugh. Drove him away, did you?' She smiled again, her hamster cheeks puffing out.

'Me? With all my charm?'

'Perish the thought, eh?'

'Exactly. No, I just wondered if I'd still be able to contact him.'

'Well, I can certainly look it up for you.'

'That'll be great. Thanks a lot, Betty.'

'No problem, Inspector Bliss. I'll e-mail you with anything I get.'

As he jogged down the narrow staircase, Bliss almost bumped into the Chief Superintendent. Both men took a step back, affecting the sort of embarrassed grins people tend to adopt after narrowly avoiding a collision.

'Ah, Bliss. How are things going?' Joseph Flynn asked.

'Not bad at all, sir. Thanks for asking.'

'Good. Settling back in, then?'

'Yes, I think so. The team have made it easy on me.'

'And Superintendent Sykes? How easy has he made it?'

Bliss rejected the notion of taking the opportunity to whine and bleat about the way he was being treated. Rumour had it that Flynn's opinion of Sykes was about as positive as Bliss's own, but there was a protocol to uphold here.

'Pretty much as expected,' he allowed, a faint smile twitching his lips. 'I think we both know where we stand.'

'Hmm.' Flynn raised an eyebrow. A man of no great height, the chief super was nonetheless a powerful figure, hard behind an expensive suit that drew attention from the burning intelligence within his eyes. His face wore the scars of service in the front line. 'Very tactful, Bliss. So, I understand you're heading this human remains case. Do you have a sense of it yet?'

There was a point in every case where the investigating officers got a real feeling for how the inquiry might go, where it could lead, the impact it was likely to have. Bliss considered the question and realised he wasn't yet there with Jane Doe. He shook his head.

'Not quite. It's a difficult one, admittedly, but it's also early days. All the relevant information is old and we've got to go trawling for it.'

Flynn was nodding gently. 'Well, if anyone can, you can, Bliss. Your obvious tenacity was the thing I most admired about your record with the Met. Just don't push too hard. Don't make the mistake of thinking you somehow have to make up for what happened last time out. You have no point to prove, at least not to me or, I suspect, members of your team. So don't force it. Don't go trying to ram square pegs into round holes just to get a result. If it's not working, take a step back. If the pressure starts to mount, my door is always open to you. I mean that. If you need to talk, I'm there for you. I'll be following this case with great interest.'

With that he was gone, and all that remained was the echo of his shoes as he made his way up the stairs. It was his way – a few well-chosen words here, a gentle massage of the ego there. Quiet and effective management from a hugely impressive man.

In the far corner of the canteen, Bliss found Chandler sitting alongside Detective Sergeant Bobby Dunne. A huge bear of a man, the sergeant was a good and vastly experienced officer, and Bliss considered him a vital cog in his team. They exchanged greetings before Bliss asked, 'Has Penny filled you in on our Jane Doe?'

'She has, yes. I was just telling her how I overheard a couple of uniforms praising the way she handled herself in the incident room. Handled the actions like a real pro, evidently.' Dunne had a deep growl to his voice, as if he gargled with creosote. It was a pack-a-day voice.

'Good for you, Penny,' Bliss said, grinning at her. She flapped her fingers at him, but he could tell she was pleased. Both with herself and the compliments. 'Any updates?'

Chandler polished off an iced doughnut before responding. 'I spoke with the Bone Woman. She's back at work over at Flag Fen, and said she had nothing to add to what she'd already given us. She's agreed to study any additional findings that arise from forensics, and to liaise with our own experts if necessary.'

Bliss considered the offer. Initially sceptical about Emily Grant's involvement, it now seemed like a good idea to have someone close at hand with her knowledge and understanding of what they were dealing with.

'Maybe she could take a look at the gravesite once SOCO are done with the scene,' he suggested. 'She might be able to give us a little more insight or narrow down the time of burial at Bretton.'

'You want to ask her?' The DC licked icing from her fingers, smacking her lips.

Bliss rolled his eyes. 'You don't give up, do you?'

Dunne looked between them. 'Am I missing something?' he asked.

'The boss has a soft spot for our Miss Grant,' Chandler explained. 'You remember her from that course we went on?'

'Oh, yes. Difficult to forget. A hard spot would be more likely with that one, I'd say.'

'Oh, Bobby,' Chandler groaned, shooting him a look of disgust.

He laughed over the rim of his mug, his big shoulders heaving. He sounded like Frank Bruno munching gravel. 'Sorry, Pen. I couldn't resist. Still, she's quite a looker from what I remember.'

'Listen,' Bliss said, 'I admit I find Emily attractive. She seems like a nice woman, too. But that's it. End of story.'

'Why?'

'What do you mean, why?'

'I mean why is it end of story? You're a single bloke, she's a single woman as I recall. You reckon she's tasty, and there's a slim chance she doesn't find you repulsive. So why not give it a go?'

He'd previously tried to treat the matter lightly, but Bliss realised now that neither of his colleagues were going to let this go without a proper explanation. He decided to tell them how he felt, lowering his voice when he spoke.

'The truth is, my head is not right at the moment. Neither personally nor professionally. I have no problem admitting that, and it's hardly a secret. Maybe I came back too soon. Maybe I should never have come back at all. Time will be the judge of that, I suppose. But until I get myself sorted out, I can't even begin to see someone else. It wouldn't be right. Not for either of us.'

After a thoughtful pause, Chandler gave a nod of agreement. 'I'm sure you're right. Sorry for probing, boss.'

'Yeah, me too,' Dunne muttered.

'No need. I know you're both trying to look out for me, and I appreciate it, but I really am a grown man now. A man who knows his own mind. All I need is time.'

'And a nice, awkward case to get stuck into.'

Bliss nodded. 'You've got that right. Are you available to lend us a hand, Bobby?'

'I'm back in court tomorrow. That bloody ridiculous GBH.'

'Right, the two dealers.'

'Yeah. Couple of fucking maggots. I wished they'd topped each other instead of just trading blows with baseball bats. Anyhow, it looks like tomorrow will be the last day, so if you want me I'm on board as soon as I can get away.'

'Good.' Bliss smiled and winked at his colleague. 'For the time being, I'll have to make do with Penny.'

'Thanks for the vote of confidence,' she protested, feigning hurt.

'Don't want your head getting too big, Pen. One good action briefing doesn't make you a star.'

'You're just worried I'm going to get all the glory.'

'You're welcome to it,' Bliss said, shaking his head. 'This one has disaster written all over it.'

SEVEN

The sky looked as if a dense grey gauze was being dragged across it. Fierce winds hurried clouds along at a tremendous rate, and as Bliss stood gazing up out of his office window, he tried to lose himself in the swirling mass. He wondered what it would be like to be up there now, being tossed around at the will of a force greater than any he had encountered before. The thought was frightening, yet the notion of such unfettered freedom was also thrilling.

Bliss had always considered himself to be an unwilling member of the human race. Too many rules, too many boundaries. Expectations he could never live up to. Dreams and hopes crushed and swept aside like dead leaves. Heart and mind shattered by loss, the encroach of reality a burden he was incapable of carrying. Should such an emotional cripple be given the responsibility of solving a murder? Wallowing in such deep melancholy wasn't unfamiliar to Bliss, nor was it the first time he had asked himself that searching question. But the answer always came back the same: if not him, then who?

Yes, there were other people, excellent officers, Bobby Dunne and Penny Chandler among them. But what if they had similar doubts? What if they walked away in despair? For every Dunne and Chandler there was a Sykes, and those who put themselves and their own agendas above the job, ahead of doing what was right, who set their personal ambitions before the quest for justice, could not be allowed to win. And there was another angle, Bliss had to admit to himself: he didn't know what the hell else he could do.

Peterborough wasn't the kind of place where quests were realised. There was no holy grail to be found here, no golden fleece. A dull, faceless city, whose population had risen beyond its worth, it nevertheless deserved the best he could offer. Bliss was as certain of that as he was about anything.

At four thirty he held a media briefing. In the public relations room Bliss saw representatives from local newspapers and regional TV only – pretty much what he'd expected at this stage – and he didn't envisage much national interest arising in the days to come. If the inquiry had been anything resembling high profile, Sykes would have insisted on running the show, but in this instance, Bliss had been allowed to deliver a pre-prepared statement. He fended off a few follow-up questions, though there seemed little genuine interest. Fresh dead bodies demanded front-page headlines, whereas skeletal remains were buried somewhere near the horoscopes.

Just as he was winding it up, Sheryl Craig, a journalist with the local *Evening Telegraph*, got to her feet. An explosion of blonde curls, she was less than five feet tall, somehow managing to cram several extra pounds and a voluminous chest into a tight two-piece navy business suit without it looking ridiculous. The moment he saw her, Bliss's sphincter tightened.

'Inspector,' Craig said, pouty mouth forming a carnivorous smile. 'How does it feel to be handling a murder investigation again, given how terribly the last one ended up?'

'It feels good to have the confidence of both my peers and superior officers.'

'I'm sure it does, Inspector. But surely you must be a little anxious?'

Bliss glanced across at the press officer sitting by his side. Jump in any time, he thought. End this for me rather than make me do it. But the man sat there looking straight ahead.

'I'm always anxious when investigating a murder,' Bliss replied. 'I don't know any detectives who aren't.'

'So you don't expect a repeat of what happened last time?'

'Of course not. Such a rare combination of circumstances comes along once in a lifetime.'

'And you feel no bitterness towards your employers, given that you were suspended for several months?'

'As I said, I have their confidence. My employers were supportive during that unfortunate period.'

'I'm sure they were. But you took a lot of punishment from the media for the manner in which you conducted that investigation.'

Bliss smiled. 'Yes, mostly from you, as I recall. But is there a question in there somewhere, Miss Craig?'

'My question, Inspector, is do you think you are the right person for the job? In fact, given your recent history, should you even be running a murder inquiry again so soon after the last fiasco?'

She was biting hard. Bliss felt the anger simmering inside, but he took a moment before responding. 'Well, that's two questions, actually. The answer to the first is yes, I do think I'm the right person for the job. I'm a DI. This is what I do. Should I be running a murder inquiry? Again, it's what I do. And I believe I do it well.'

'Even last time?' Craig shook her head in mock astonishment.

'Yes, even then. Despite everything that took place.'

'Really? I'd hate to think what you would consider failure, Inspector.'

He shook his head. 'I didn't say it was successful. Did it turn out as we'd hoped? No. Were errors made? Yes. But did we track down the man responsible for several murders? Yes, we did. Hindsight is a wonderful thing, Miss Craig. But we've learned our lessons. *I* have learned *my* lessons. This is a new case, and it's time for us all to move on.'

'Which is all very well for those who are still around *to* move on.'

Bliss winced. The lowest of all low blows. He shook his head and said, 'I think we're straying from the subject in hand once again, Miss Craig. I'd be happy to discuss that particular case with you another time.'

'I'll hold you to that, Inspector.'

Yeah, I bet you will, he thought. Bitch!

After the briefing he caught up with some paperwork – the curse of modern policing – but by six he and Chandler were booked out and heading away from the city to unwind over a drink.

The village of Yaxley clung to Peterborough like a minnow to a whale, fiercely defending its independence while still seeking to bask in the protective shadow of the city's wealth and popularity. Chandler drove through its centre and pulled into a space directly outside the Woodcutter's Inn.

Bliss peered out through the side window, raising his eyebrows. 'A favourite haunt of yours?' he asked.

The tiny pub appeared run down, almost derelict. Its whitewashed walls were broken away in chunks, like a cake whose icing had been picked at by sweet-toothed children.

'Actually, it's run by a family friend,' Chandler replied.

'Looks like he could use the trade.'

'It's a she. And yes, she could.'

Bliss waited patiently while Chandler and her friend caught up, smiled through the inevitable introductions, and then sighed with pleasure as he sank his first mouthful of Guinness. If anything was going to shake off the bloody headache that had been building up all day, it was this. He glanced around the living-room-sized bar, brass horseshoes tacked to the dark wooden beams, landscape watercolours mounted on nicotine-coated walls. An elderly man sat alone by the unlit fire playing some solo version of dominoes, a greyhound curled up by his feet like the shell of a snail.

Chandler looked weary as she knocked back some of her vodka and orange, stretched out both legs and rolled her neck muscles.

'Bad night?' Bliss asked.

'As usual. If I get five hours I'm lucky.'

'Too much on your mind?'

She managed a weak smile. 'To be honest, I can't remember the last time I was able to switch off.'

'You ought to consider putting in for some compassionate leave. You're being pulled apart by the job and the battle for your kid. Maybe the job can wait.'

'It's not an option, Jimmy. I need the money a promotion to sergeant will get me. I'm already borrowing heavily from my parents.'

Bliss nodded thoughtfully. He sipped some more of his drink. Penny was a proud woman, and she fought her own battles. But there was no shame in accepting help occasionally.

'I can smooth out some of the wrinkles for you, Penny. Financially, I mean.'

'I couldn't let you do that. Why would you, anyway?'

'You *could* let me. I did very well on the housing market when I moved up here, and there's a pile of insurance money I haven't touched. As for why, isn't wanting to help out a friend reason enough?'

'It… it might make things awkward between us.' Penny was finding it hard to meet his eyes.

'I don't see why it should. Call it a loan if you like. Pay me back the interest I'll lose if you want. Pen, I don't mean to embarrass you, I just want you to know that if you need it, it's there. Don't fail to get your daughter back because you're short of money. That's all I'm saying.'

There was a pause, and for a moment Bliss thought he'd offended her. But then Penny nodded her head and gave a wide, genuine smile of gratitude. 'Thank you, Jimmy. You don't know what your offer means to me.'

He chuckled. 'Hey, it's not entirely altruistic. I want your full concentration on the job while you're here.'

'I knew there'd be a catch.'

Bliss gave a satisfied nod. The moment was over. 'I admire your determination. I know it's been hard for you, and I can't even begin to imagine how you must feel. But don't ever worry yourself about the job. You're doing just fine.'

Chandler flashed a grateful smile.

'I take it nothing of interest came in from the troops while I was with our journalist friends,' Bliss said.

'Hardly any reports at all, let alone anything worthwhile. I gave word for either or both of us to be contacted if something does turn up, but otherwise left updates for the morning briefing tomorrow.'

'You told them eight thirty, right?'

'Uh-huh.' She took another sip of her drink, smiling with pleasure this time. Ice rattled in her glass as she placed it back on the table. 'I hope to have a few more bodies available, too.'

'Good. We'll probably need them. Oh, and it's a no on the Fletton lake search. Sykes won't sanction it. Did Emily manage to get over to the gravesite?'

'No. SOCO were still finishing up and hadn't cleared the scene, so she's heading over first thing in the morning. I did consider going with her, but I thought you might want me with you for the briefing.'

Bliss set down his glass, surprised to see two thirds of his drink already gone. 'Actually, I want you to lead the briefing. I have somewhere else to be.'

'Oh. Anywhere interesting?'

He tapped a finger against the side of his nose. 'It's personal. Cover for me, will you?'

'Of course. What do you want me to do with the teams?'

Bliss sensed both reluctance and anticipation in his colleague. Penny was an excellent detective who, despite her competence, was always eager to learn and move on, remaining enthusiastic about the job and her prospects. He had high hopes for her.

'React accordingly to what they have to tell you, to their findings. If there are any. You know what's needed. If they've come up with nothing, get them back in there to carry on where they left off today. If something useful crops up, do what feels right. Take it to the next level.'

She pulled a face as if she had bitten into a lemon, anxious now, he could tell. 'Can I get hold of you if someone comes up with something more than useful?'

'No. Sorry. I'll give you a bell as soon as I'm able, though. Listen, Pen, don't worry about this. You have good instincts. Trust yourself and go with them.'

'And if I screw up?'

Laughing now, Bliss said, 'Then you'll join a large and non-exclusive club whose members include every copper who ever had to make a decision. Mistakes are part of the learning process. Happens to everyone. Even me, believe it or not. You're only a liability if you don't learn from them.'

Chandler nodded. Took a breath. Eased it out slowly. The bar door opened and an elderly couple came inside, complaining bitterly about the weather.

'This place is buzzing now,' Bliss said.

'Yeah, it's a riot. You want to call for backup?'

'I think so. Armed Response and the canine unit.'

They chuckled, letting the nonsense relax them. Chandler drained her glass and said, 'Thanks, boss. For this opportunity at work. Your confidence in me means a lot.'

'You'll do fine. By the way, when are your sergeant's exams?'

'January. I'm hitting the books, but not much of what I read tallies with what I see out there every day.'

Bliss shook his head. 'It wouldn't. There's theory, and then there's reality. Seldom are they the same thing, not in any game. And especially not in ours.'

***

When he got home just before eight, Bliss took Bonnie and Clyde for a short walk over at Ferry Meadows. The park was virtually empty, the emergence of cold and damp weather starting to keep folk indoors of an evening. The only people he encountered were fellow hardy dog walkers, most of whom kept their heads down as they passed by. Darkness changed the whole feel of the place, making it seem smaller and less defined, but considerably more threatening. The air smelled fresh, its chill moist. Bliss's teeth began to chatter, so once around the lake was enough for him, if not the Labs.

Walking back the way they had come, Bliss found himself thinking about Emily Grant. What he'd told Penny and Bobby Dunne was true: he didn't feel right in himself, not about his work, nor about his life, and it would be unfair to begin a relationship with those twin monkeys on his back. It had been a very long time since he'd dated, and maybe he was misreading Emily, sensing signals she wasn't giving off, but he thought he'd detected interest. Even a little bit of flirting.

He found Emily attractive, had admitted as much to his colleagues, but Bliss asked himself if mere attraction was enough. It wasn't as if he was looking to have a woman in his life right now. Perhaps he never would. He missed his wife terribly, and that awful ache expanded in his chest every time he thought about her – which he did several times a day. Her death had left a gaping hole in his heart that still seemed impossible to fill, though more than a thousand days and nights had passed since Hazel was taken from him. She hadn't been merely a part of his life, she had *been* his life. His very essence. What he was left with now was mere existence. Next to Hazel, anyone would pale in comparison. Even someone as beautiful and delightful as Emily Grant.

Back home Bliss fussed over the dogs for a few minutes longer, wondering at the simple pleasure gained from the company of a pet. As a child he'd had the usual goldfish, hamsters and rabbits, but his only dog had been run down and killed by a car when he was just eleven. For a while that had put him off the whole idea of owning an animal, but he couldn't now imagine life without Bonnie and Clyde.

As the night unfolded he ordered himself an Indian curry, then fed the dogs and made sure they had ample water. While he waited for his own meal to be delivered, Bliss changed out of his charcoal grey suit into more comfortable clothing. When he emptied out his trouser pockets, he noticed the contact information Betty from admin had mailed him moments after the media briefing ended. Bliss looked at the sheet of paper he'd printed out, paused only for a moment to consider what he should do, then dialled the telephone number. Earlier that afternoon he had decided to forget all about Weller, annoyed that the man hadn't bothered to turn up for their meeting. But now, almost inevitably when he felt at a loose end, curiosity got the better of him.

After several rings Bliss was about to hang up, but then a female voice answered, 'Hello?'

'Oh, hello,' he said, unsure now how to proceed. 'Is that Mrs Weller?'

'No. This is Sharon Callard, Mrs Weller's sister-in-law.'

'I see. Mrs Callard, my name is Bliss. I'm an ex-colleague of Bernard's. We worked in Peterborough together.'

'Oh, well thanks for calling. Allison is not up to speaking with anyone at the moment. But I'll let her know you called. Bliss, you say?'

'That's right.' He frowned. The woman appeared a little confused. 'DI Bliss. But, actually, I was calling to speak with Bernard, not his wife. Is he not at home?'

There was a brief pause, a total silence that seemed to hum inside his head. Then the woman spoke once more, her voice softer now. 'I'm terribly sorry. I thought you were calling to offer your condolences.'

'Condolences? I don't understand.'

'Bernard was killed earlier today, Mr Bliss. A car accident.'

Now it was his turn to be silent. Weller was dead. Probably killed on his way down to Peterborough. Eventually Bliss found his voice. 'I had no idea. Obviously. Sorry, I must sound like a babbling idiot. Can you tell me what happened?'

'It seems as though he just ran off the road. Killed instantly, we're told.' She sounded doubtful, and was right to be. According to most emergency service people given the terrible job of delivering the worst kind of news to relatives, no one ever died a lingering, painful death. Bliss knew the truth was usually very different.

He was dumbfounded, caught completely unawares by the shocking news. 'I'm so sorry. Please do give my sympathies to his wife. I didn't know Bernard that well, but I liked him. He was a good man.'

'Yes. He was.'

After offering a few words of comfort, Bliss said his goodbyes and hung up. Over what was now a distinctly unappetising chicken balti, he couldn't turn his mind to anything but poor Bernard Weller. More than the untimely death, however, Bliss began to question the coincidence. Weller calls him up out of the blue one night almost three years after their last conversation, arranges a somewhat secretive meeting, and is then killed on his way to that meeting. What were the chances these two incidents were not related? He was thinking like a copper, of course. But then that's what he was. And something about this didn't feel right. Long before he'd shoved the foil dishes and their cooling contents to one side, Bliss knew he wasn't going to let go of it.

***

Alan Dean thought: so this is what the cold steel muzzle of a gun feels like when it's pressed against the back of your neck.

He'd seen guns before, had even stared wide-eyed at one pointed in his direction several years back, but he'd never actually touched one. More importantly, one had never touched him. Standing in the darkened hallway of his own home, he instinctively knew that the gun barrel jammed against his goose-pimpled flesh was the last thing he would ever feel.

The day had started a hell of a lot better than it would end. His last day on the job after almost forty years in the police force. Now a service, of course, because 'force' gave the wrong connotations in a world littered with politically correct fascists. For the past five years he had spent his time at the main criminal courthouse in Milton Keynes, shuffling prisoners from holding cell to courtrooms and back again. There'd been the occasional flutter of excitement when a prisoner tried to escape or threw a hissy-fit when sentenced, but mostly it was a yawn-inducing winding down of a career in which he never rose above the rank of sergeant and had never wanted to.

At the end of today's shift his colleagues had presented him with a Sara Lee chocolate gateau, a lit candle spluttering away like a sparkler in its centre, and a boxed chess set – wooden board with marble pieces. Dean had started a chess club at the courthouse, and playing a game or two while eating chocolate cake had become a popular way of passing time with fellow officers of all ages. The set was a lot nicer than the ebony and ivory one he had at home, and the retirement gift meant a great deal to him. What had almost brought a tear to his eye, however, were the promises of many games awaiting him in the future. He was waving goodbye to his job but not to them, his friends assured him.

A farewell drink in a nearby pub had also been arranged, and Dean hit the whisky harder than he had in many a year. By the time he and a dozen or so of his friends headed across the city centre to an Indian restaurant, he was feeling light-headed and unsteady on his feet. At around midnight his closest friend, Bill Smith, had driven him home heavier by one tandoori mixed grill and several pints of lager.

If only you'd let Bill see you in like he'd offered, Dean thought now. He'd refused, believing he was about to throw up everything he'd eaten and drunk during the day, and not wanting to have his pal witness it. Bill might have been sober enough to sense that something was wrong, however. Then again, maybe driving away with Dean still stumbling on the pavement was the luckiest thing that had ever happened to Bill Smith.

Alan Dean wondered who might find him, hoping no one he knew would have to smell his piss and shit and decaying flesh. Having experienced that for himself a few times, he wouldn't wish it on his worst enemy.

Well, perhaps the man standing behind him right now with his finger on the trigger. Shit! How had he let this prick sneak up behind him in the dark?

'Don't turn around,' the man insisted.

His breath moved around Alan Dean, its odour fetid.

'You could use a mint,' Dean said.

'You could use a miracle. Now, don't turn around.'

'I won't.'

'You're not going to struggle? Not going to plead for your life?'

The voice was calm. Devoid of emotion. It also sounded somewhat familiar. Dean swallowed and said, 'Would it make any difference?'

'It might.'

He wasn't convincing. 'Yeah. Right. I wouldn't give you that satisfaction.'

Halitosis man chuckled in Dean's ear. 'You know why I'm here?'

'I think so.'

'You were expecting me?'

'Someone. At some point. I thought I had a few years yet. Thought I might even get to go all the way.'

'You've been lucky up to now. Unfortunately, your luck has run out.'

Dean closed his eyes and swept his mind back in time. A career to be proud of, spoiled by a single, terrible lapse. Tears squirted down his cheeks, warm and salty on his lips.

'I take it they found her, then?'

'They did.'

'Then maybe this is for the best.'

Silence filled the hallway with its own distinctive menace. Then the gunman said, 'It's nothing personal.'

'Fuck that. Murder is always personal.'

His own voice was the last thing Alan Dean ever heard. By the time the sound of two gunshots bounced off the walls of his hallway, the retired police sergeant was already dead.

EIGHT

On Thursday morning, Bliss called in at Bretton Woods. The forensic investigation was winding down, and he wanted to get an update from SOCO before they pulled the plug. Signing investigators in and out of the scene was a uniformed constable by the name of Morris. He looked up from his clipboard as Bliss approached.

'Morning, Constable,' Bliss said. He blew on his hands to warm them. Though the overnight rain and severe winds had relented, there was still a bite to the air. 'Tell me, did anyone manage to organise the digging of exploratory holes around the gravesite?'

'I've only been on scene since the early hours, sir.' He nodded towards a small mobile trailer. 'We can check it out in the incident office if you like.'

They stepped up into the long, narrow trailer, inside which stood two desks surrounded by a number of boxes. The mobile incident office was a crucial point at which information was both gathered and stored until it could be moved across to Thorpe Wood. It was also the access point for potential witnesses.

Morris checked the case book, flicking through a number of pages which logged the investigation procedures. He looked back up at Bliss and nodded. 'Yes, sir. All clear, it seems.'

Bliss gave a slight hike of his shoulders. He hadn't given serious consideration to the notion that they might have a serial on their hands, but the procedure was worth doing. If only to confirm they had if asked.

'Anything else found in or around the site itself?' Bliss asked. 'More clothing, coins, buckles?'

It took a minute or so of sweeping through the pages before Morris shook his head. 'Nothing, sir. It looks like we got everything first time around.'

As expected. Secretly, Bliss had hoped that an ID of some sort might be discovered, but sharing that with the officer might make him appear desperate. He thanked Morris, walked back to his car, and drove off to make his appointment just a mile or so away on the other side of the Soke parkway where Bretton bordered Westwood.

***

Edith Cavell was a mostly NHS hospital that added to its overall income by allowing facility access for a number of private patients. Bliss had been referred by his GP, and using his own personal health plan rather than go through official channels, he was now lying on his back in a skimpy cotton gown waiting to be inserted into a huge tube. A young female technician in a long white coat had made sure he was comfortable, and was now rubbing something between the palms of her hands.

'Am I getting a massage as well?' Bliss asked, hoping his voice betrayed none of the anxiety he felt.

She smiled as if she'd never been asked the question before. 'No, that's my other job. And I don't come cheap.'

'What are you doing, then?'

'Making your earplugs pliable. They need squeezing and moulding, so that when they expand they fill the ear chamber.'

'Why do I need my ears plugging?'

Raising her eyebrows, she said, 'You didn't read your MRI booklet, I take it, Mr Bliss.'

He gave a guilty shrug. 'No. Sorry. I forgot.'

The technician tutted amiably. 'The MRI machine makes a fairly loud noise each time it rotates, and the sound can add to the overall level of stress for the patient. Once you're inside you need to stay as still as possible, otherwise the readings might not take and you might have to do it all over again.'

'Sounds reasonable. How long will I be in there?'

She laughed. Her eyes twinkled with good humour. A good couple of stone overweight, she was a perfect advert for those who believe all heavy people are jolly. Bliss thought she was sweet, and extremely pretty beneath the excess of flesh.

'You really didn't look at your booklet at all, did you?' she said.

'I'm sorry. I've been busy.'

'Hmm. Well, look, the scan will take around thirty minutes, and during that time I'll be in the control room behind that glass pane.' She pointed towards a large rectangular window set into the rear wall. Other than the MRI scanner and a chair, there was nothing else in the room. 'I can see and hear you from in there. If any panic sets in, just ask me to stop and I will.'

'Panic?'

'Claustrophobia. Even people who don't suffer from it can be affected once they're fully inserted into the scanner. But it's all in the mind, so I'd advise you to close your eyes and shut off until we're done.'

'You're the expert. And thanks for making me feel less concerned.' It's not the scan itself that worries me though, Bliss thought. It's the result.

Little more than half an hour later, it was all over. He was shown back to his cubicle in the small changing area, where he stripped off the hospital gown and got dressed. He slipped his watch and wedding ring back on and went upstairs to wait in the ENT reception for his appointment with the consultant. There he waited for a further twenty anxious minutes.

When he was eventually shown into the consultant's room, she was running her gaze over a series of what looked like X-rays. 'Good morning, Mr Bliss,' she said, smiling pleasantly. Lines neatly bracketed her mouth. 'Nice to see you again. Please sit down. I won't be a moment.'

Captain Judith Scowcroft, an ex-army officer, stood tall and rigid, as though a metal spike ran the length of her spine. She had the kind of bearing that had suggested military to Bliss, even before he'd been made aware of her full title. Close-cropped hair and little make-up implied either a reluctance to conform, or a schedule too busy for anything more than casual preparation. When she eventually turned away from the light box, she came and sat down opposite the chair he had taken, no desk between them. The consultant wheeled herself forward until their knees were almost touching.

'First the good news.' Full beam smile this time. Teeth and all. 'There is no sign of a brain tumour.'

Bliss let go a lungful of air he hadn't realised he'd been holding back. The recent episodes of dizziness, coupled with a series of lancing pains down the right side of his head, had screamed tumour at him despite the consultant's doubts expressed during their previous appointment. At the time of arranging the MRI she had insisted the scan was nothing more than a precautionary measure – more to rule something out than in. Human nature didn't often allow the luxury of thinking only positive thoughts, however, and Bliss had been unable to prevent himself from worrying.

'I can't think of better news right now,' he said, relief clattering against his chest. Emotions highly charged, Bliss suddenly felt close to tears. He took a breath and collected himself before speaking again. 'But I gather there must be some bad news, too.'

Scowcroft inclined her head and pursed her lips. 'Only in that your symptoms remain undiagnosed. That said, I do have a good idea what might be wrong with you. Tell me, how's your hearing?'

'Pardon?' Bliss cupped a hand around his right ear. He grinned and gave a shrug. 'I know, you must get that all the time. Actually, there's still that element of fullness, like a build-up of pressure, as I described to you last time we met. And if pushed I'd say the hearing is a little worse.'

'We may be able to help that with the insertion of a grommet. This will release any build-up of fluids. How about the tinnitus?'

Bliss rolled his eyes. 'Some nights I feel like ripping my ear off. The high-pitched squeal creeps up on me the moment I think all is quiet. And that other sound I described to you last time, like the noise an ultrasound scan makes, that also seems to have got worse.'

The doctor nodded, scribbling something on her chart. 'That may be because you're now acutely aware of the sound, expecting it when there are no other obvious sounds. They say Van Gogh had tinnitus, hence the lopping off of one ear. If true, it's very sad, as actually it would not have resolved the problem. All right, tell me about the other symptoms.'

Bliss took a moment to recall what had happened to him. 'I've had two more attacks of vertigo since I was last here. The first time it lasted only a few minutes. I felt nauseous, but wasn't physically sick. The second attack was more severe, and I dropped to the ground. Fortunately, I was at home both times, but that second one worried me, I must admit.'

'I'm sure it did. How long did this second attack last?'

'The vertigo itself for about half an hour, but I was very dizzy for an hour or so afterwards. And incredibly tired for quite a while after that.'

'No vertigo whilst sitting, is that correct?'

'No. None.'

'Good. You realise if you do get an unannounced attack whilst sitting, you'll have to inform the DVLA. They will probably withdraw your driving licence for an initial three-month period, pending further tests, diagnosis and prognosis.'

Bliss nodded. Losing his licence was the least of his concerns. He glanced down at a tray of stainless steel implements, each of which looked like an instrument of torture. He pondered his condition for a moment, the impact it was starting to have on his life. Fear lurked in the dark corners of every terrible thought.

'The imbalance is a major concern,' he went on. 'I have it every other day or so now. It doesn't last long, but it's unnerving. I feel like I'm stepping off a kerb all the time. It's like walking on sponges. Then, as you warned me might happen last time we spoke, the headaches are constant and intense, and my energy levels are falling away every day. The fatigue is immense. I feel like I'm on the verge of mental and physical exhaustion.'

Saying this out loud made Bliss feel uneasy. Admitting weakness was not something he was used to, and he felt a little embarrassed by it. He'd always been so healthy, believing his physical condition was as much about character and inner strength as it was levels of fitness. Accepting that he was ill at all had been a battle, but now he was wondering how bad it might be.

Captain Scowcroft was making notes on his chart each time Bliss spoke. 'How are your sleeping patterns?' she asked.

'Reasonable with the help of a tablet every night. Without them I have no chance. A pill helps me get to sleep, but if I wake up in the early hours I can't get back off again.'

After a few moments, the consultant set her notes aside and leaned forward, meeting his gaze directly. 'I'll arrange another hearing examination, and also a caloric test.'

'And that is?'

'We look at your balance in closer detail. We attach a number of sensors to your head and then put on a spectacular light display, followed by a few moments of pumping warm water into your ears. Sounds a lot worse than it is, believe me. This will induce severe imbalance, and we'll be able to measure both the extent and the length of time it takes you to respond and recover. By the way, are you aware of the rapid eye movement you now have?'

He was. 'It's worse still when I close them.' He snapped his eyelids together and felt his eyes crawl and swivel beneath. A creepy sensation.

'Very well. I'll get you in for your tests within the next week or so, but I won't let you go today without giving you an idea of the way I see things at the moment. Mr Bliss, have you ever heard of Ménière's Disease, or Ménière's Syndrome?'

'No.' Another flare of mild panic exploded inside his gut. Nothing with disease or syndrome in the title could be good. He swallowed and pulled some saliva into his dry mouth.

'There are four major symptoms, which are vertigo, imbalance, affected hearing, and tinnitus. Although our understanding of the illness is changing and growing all the time, the diagnosis of Ménière's is made when all four symptoms are evident and cannot be explained away by other illnesses. You have all four, plus all recognised resulting effects. The caloric test will tell us more, but I think Ménière's is likely in your case.'

'Okay.' He took a breath, not liking the way this was shaping up. He saw no real concern in Scowcroft's demeanour, but neither did she appear entirely at ease. 'And if you're right?'

'Well, let me first put your mind at rest by saying that Ménière's is not a life-threatening condition. It's not going to kill you, Mr Bliss. However, in anything other than its milder forms, Ménière's is very often life *changing*.'

'In what way?'

'Think of how you have been feeling lately, Mr Bliss. Then think of each of those symptoms becoming more frequent and more intense.'

It didn't take much imagination. Bliss saw himself stumbling, falling, becoming deaf, eventually being unable to drive. Unable to work? The thought caused his stomach to drop away.

'How do we fix it?' he asked. Bliss saw the consultant's face became immediately solemn, and knew it had to be bad news.

'Ménière's has no known cure,' Scowcroft told him. 'However, there are ways we may be able to alleviate some of the symptoms, and long periods of remission are quite common.'

'You mean it could just disappear as quickly as it came?'

'It happens. But I do have to stress that Ménière's is a chronic, progressive disease. That is to say, although it could just wink out, it could just as easily become worse. It's very much a disease of peaks and troughs. Unfortunately, there's more that we don't know about it than we understand. I'm being as blunt as I can be, because I do think it's likely that you have Ménière's in one of its many forms.'

He took a deep breath. 'How did I get it?'

'Impossible to say, I'm afraid.'

Unable to take it all in, Bliss felt on the verge of shock. He could feel his hands shaking, and he quickly clenched his fists in order to stop the jerky movements. The euphoria he'd felt at learning the result of the MRI scan had drained clean away, replaced now by a dread that lay like a rock deep inside his heart. He found it impossible to fully comprehend, with far too many details to consider, and all he wanted to do right now was get out of there and draw some fresh air into his lungs. Despite this, the practical side of his nature compelled him to remain.

'You said there were ways to relieve the symptoms,' Bliss said. He swallowed. 'Tell me more.'

***

Bliss walked out of the hospital at ten fifty. Forty minutes later he was still sitting in the car park. His head was buzzing, and this time the tinnitus was not to blame. It was a peculiar feeling; on the one hand he felt immense relief that his illness was not due to the brain tumour he had feared, and on the other there was the disbelief at what he had learned from Captain Scowcroft.

Ménière's. An illness that could send him tumbling to the floor at will, no apparent cure, yet one that could be gone when he woke up the next morning. The disease revolved around problems with fluid and blood flow within the inner ear, causing the sensory balance system to send out wrong signals. Balance, the consultant had explained, depended on the eyes, ears and brain working in harmony. One of them only had to malfunction slightly for the balance to be thrown completely. In the case of Ménière's, the hearing was also affected, but it was the imbalance and attacks of vertigo that were the main potential physical disabilities.

Scowcroft had given him a letter for his GP, advising a course of tablets designed to help improve the blood flow. In addition he was to watch his salt intake, and set about improving the healthiness of his lifestyle. She had given him a few leaflets, but had also pointed him in the direction of the Ménière's Society, a charity dedicated to the illness, for further information.

'Ménière's Disease is misdiagnosed an awful lot,' she'd admitted. 'And we won't stop trying to nail down possible alternatives. I know it's not exactly scientific, but with this illness we have a similar line to that of Sherlock Holmes: when you remove everything else, what remains is given the label of "Ménière's"'

The irony for Bliss was that he was feeling better today than at any time over the past few weeks. On a purely physical level he didn't feel as if his life had changed in any significant way, but if the captain's diagnosis was correct, then there was every possibility of the main symptoms worsening over a short period of time.

Staring out of his Vectra's windscreen at the dull, lifeless sky, Bliss's mind went back more than five years. He recalled in vivid detail how he and his wife were sitting down to dinner when she dropped a bombshell into the conversation.

'I have a lump,' she told him. 'A small one, on my left breast. I first noticed it a few weeks ago. I checked it again last night, and I'm certain it's got bigger. I saw Doctor Lewis this morning, and she referred me immediately to the clinic. I'm hoping for an appointment within the next fortnight.'

So matter-of-fact. No emotion at all. That was Hazel all over. His wife faced every obstacle, every piece of bad news, with the same strength of character and dignity with which she approached her entire life. Her concern more for him than herself, she'd obviously taken time to prepare and rehearse how she would tell him. During his career, Bliss had been threatened with knives and guns, and had once been shot at. But that day, that gut-shredding moment when Hazel told him about the lump and he realised how much the thought of her being in pain tore at his insides, was the most frightening time of his life. In his head, Bliss knew it could be nothing more than a cyst, but his heart burned the word 'cancer' on the forefront of his mind. The thought of his beautiful wife suffering was more than he could possibly bear.

Ten days later, a cyst was diagnosed and drained away by a syringe. Panic over, move on. But the memory of that day lingered in Bliss's mind.

Today was running it a close second.

NINE

Bliss decided not to return immediately to work, and instead drove straight home from the hospital. His hands on the wheel were shaky, his head muddled and fuzzy as he made his way through light traffic to his house in the quiet, modern cul-de-sac. Bonnie and Clyde were pleased to see him, but the fuss he made in return was at best half-hearted. He toasted a couple of slices of bread, spread boysenberry jam on one. He also made a tall mug of Earl Grey. Less than halfway through his lunch he realised he hadn't tasted a single mouthful, and did not want the rest.

The enormous shock he'd felt at the shattering news presented to him by the ENT consultant was now beginning to wane. The mind made adjustments, Bliss knew. Wrapping itself in a protective cocoon. A coping mechanism he had drawn from many times. Personal fear and concern over his health were replaced now by other thoughts moving insidiously to the forefront of his mind. First came the Bretton Woods human remains, the developing inquiry that had sprung into action as a result of two boys' desire for immortality. This was followed by the nagging realisation that the phone call from DI Weller, and the man's subsequent death, were not issues Bliss could readily leave unresolved. Several things about the situation intrigued him, and he reacted to one now.

He made one short phone call before contacting DS Dunne on his mobile. 'Are you available, Bobby?' Bliss asked.

'Just left Huntingdon and I'm heading back up the A1 as we speak. The court let me go early.'

'If only they knew you. They'd lock you up and throw away the key.'

Dunne laughed. 'And rightly so. What's up, boss?'

'We're going on a trip. A little drive out in the country. You game?'

'Of course.'

Bliss smiled to himself. He liked that about Dunne; the man just went with the flow and seldom questioned colleagues' motives. The attitude of a detective who knew what real coppering was all about.

'I'll pick you up at the Marriot hotel car park in fifteen minutes,' he said to Dunne. 'You can leave your motor there safely without it getting clamped or towed.'

His next call was to Penny Chandler. 'How's it going?' he asked. 'Any good news for me?'

'Not at the moment, boss.' The line was crackly, the aged telecommunications system grinding to a stubborn halt back at Thorpe Wood. 'I've got the Bone Woman coming in to see me after her visit to Bretton Woods, but the team are still hard at it.'

Bliss pictured the smiling face of Emily Grant and wished he could be there. 'Fair enough. How are you? You sound a bit stressed out.'

'Oh, it's nothing. I had a bit of a run-in with Grealish, that's all.'

Sergeant Grealish was a uniform who rarely strayed beyond the confines and relative safety of his HQ desk. Bliss had the man down as an opinionated, bigoted arsehole. 'What happened?' Bliss asked her.

'Don't worry about it, boss. It'll blow over.'

'Tell me.'

Chandler gave a sigh. 'He stopped me in the corridor, you know, all red and sweaty as he usually is. He made a few of his more offensive remarks, yanking on his obviously miniscule dick as he did so. I told him where he could stick it. He gave me some shit about sleeping my way into CID. It was bullshit.'

'But it got you wound up.'

'Yeah. I shouldn't let fuckwits like him worm their way inside my head, but I'd hate to think others share his low opinion of me.'

'They don't,' Bliss assured her. 'Grealish is a knob, but none of his colleagues takes him seriously. Listen, if you meet him in the car park one night after shift, you have my permission to deck him.'

Chandler laughed. 'I wouldn't soil my knuckles.'

Bliss laughed, too. 'Good for you. So, how did the briefing go this morning?'

'Not too bad, actually. There really wasn't much to say other than to put the teams back on the same jobs. How come you're at home?'

He realised his number would have been revealed on her telephone screen. 'I'm not coming back to the office right away, Pen. Something else has cropped up. Something I need to take a quick look at. Listen, do you remember a DI Weller? He was stationed at HQ when I first moved up from London.'

'Vaguely. I hadn't been here long myself, remember. I never worked with him, but our paths crossed on a few occasions. Why d'you ask?'

Bonnie's head appeared between Bliss's legs, forlorn eyes begging him to take the animal for some exercise. The right paw came up and thumped down on his thigh. Bliss rubbed the dog's head and shook his own, saying to Chandler, 'It's just that Weller left a message on my machine the other day, completely out of the blue, asking to meet up with me. That's who I went to see yesterday lunchtime.'

'Oh. So how is he?'

Bliss could tell she was wondering where this was headed. 'He didn't show. I was a bit put out, to be honest, so I didn't give it a lot of thought during the afternoon. But I called his house when I got home last night, only to find out that he'd been killed on his way down to meet me. Drove right off the road.'

'Jesus! That's awful.'

'I know. It's dreadful. The thing is, there was something a bit off about his call. Something in his voice, the way he made the arrangements for us to meet. I can't quite put my finger on it, but it felt odd. After which I find out he died on the way down here.'

'And you're making five out of two and two?'

'Maybe I'm coming up with the correct answer. The fact is, I don't like that kind of coincidence.'

'So what are you going to do?' Chandler asked. 'You said you wanted to take a quick look at it.'

Bonnie padded away back out into the garden. Bliss had an almost overwhelming urge to join her. Play with the dogs, walk them, live in their carefree world rather than his own.

'Boss?'

He'd drifted away for a moment. 'Penny. Yes. I just got off the phone with Weller's wife, actually. I'm travelling up to Lincoln to see her. I need to satisfy myself that there's nothing in this, and up there is the logical place to start.'

'You looking for some company?'

'Already sorted. Bobby's coming with me.'

'Well, we can handle things here for the rest of the day, I'm sure. Is it all right to call this time if something breaks?'

'Of course. And Pen, if you're wondering why I chose Bobby rather than you, I really am between a rock and a hard place. I figured I'd get grief from you if I left you out, but also if I pulled you off the Jane Doe case. In the end I opted for leaving you where you are so you can gain some valuable experience.'

Laughter rattled across the airwaves. 'Me? Give you grief? Wherever did you get that idea? No, I understand, boss. Never crossed my mind to question your decision.'

His smile grew broader still. 'No. I'm sure. Look, I'll come in when I'm done with Mrs Weller.'

'Okay. See you later. Oh, and boss… be careful.'

***

As the modern architectural features of Lincoln University appeared to his right, the spire of the city's cathedral rising up in the distance beyond the scalloped rooftop, Bliss wondered about Penny's warning. Was there something happening here that he needed to be careful of? And where exactly was his mind leading him with this? That Weller's death was no accident? That the man was murdered? And if so, why? Unlikely, Bliss's rational mind insisted. But was it not more improbable that the day after an ex-colleague calls him up out of the blue to arrange a meeting, more than three years after they'd last spoken, that same ex-colleague is killed whilst driving to attend the meeting?

Shit happened, Bliss knew that. The T-shirts and bumper stickers told him so. The most bizarre, chance happenings occurred almost every single day. But not to him. Not like this. It might be nothing, but he felt he owed Bernard Weller the time it would take to find out the truth.

This much he explained to Bobby Dunne as they drove hurriedly, the roads swooshing and sometimes swirling beneath the Vectra's wheels, as rainfall pooled in potholes and collected around unyielding storm drains. The car's wipers duelled with the beads of rain and spray from other vehicles, but the downpour was winning hands down. When Bliss was through talking, the DS nodded sagely.

'Does seem to be stretching coincidence too far,' he agreed. 'On the other hand, I read once about the most incredible coincidence ever recorded. It was about these three ships that sank at different times over a period of a hundred years or so. In each case there was just one survivor, and in each case that man went by the same name.'

Bliss regarded his companion thoughtfully. It was a wild story, but just wild enough to be true. Unless you believed your destiny was already written, then you had to believe in the power of chance. Chance meetings. Chance happenings. Bliss didn't like the idea of a preordained destiny, opting instead to believe that choices shaped futures. Every other day you'd pick up a phone to someone you'd just been intending to call, and how often when you were thinking about a song did it come on the radio? At first these things seem extraordinary. Yet further inspection might cause one to question why such things didn't happen more often. It seemed to Bliss that a belief in fate gave people the opportunity not to take responsibility for their lives. Pro-destiny types took the easy way out, whereas the pro-chance brigade tried to shape their lives as best they could.

'Do you think I'm reaching?' Bliss asked his companion. It was possible. Being human, he made mistakes. 'Seeing something that's not there?'

Dunne ran a hand down the stubble on his chin. 'Maybe. But I'm not seeing any downside in checking it out.'

No arguing with that. Bliss nodded and turned his attention to finding his way, aided by a sweet-voiced satnav woman who occasionally got irritable with him when he didn't do exactly as she'd instructed. The home they eventually parked outside was a pleasant dormer-roofed bungalow in a quiet, tree-lined avenue. Bliss immediately decided it was somewhere he might enjoy his own retirement.

Allison Weller was a much smaller person than her husband had been. A number of years younger, too. She looked to be in her late forties, and would have been attractive with a few more pounds on her slender frame. Pale and glassy-eyed, the woman showed them through into the dining room and out into a large and tasteful conservatory. Dark wood built around a brick structure, a light shade of green on the walls, wicker furniture with olive green padded cushions. The windows and French doors opened up to a long, wide garden, fully developed with obvious care. By now the rain had stopped, and there was more blue than angry grey in the sky.

'I hope you don't mind my colleague joining us,' Bliss said, gazing out at a small water feature made from bamboo. The hypnotic motion fascinated him. 'It's always good to have another pair of eyes and ears around,' he explained.

'No, it's not a problem. Please take a seat. I have the kettle on – can I make you both some tea?'

Bliss accepted her offer, nodding that Bobby should, also. People invariably seemed to open up more over a cup of tea. It was the British way, tea being almost a linctus for the heart and mind. When Mrs Weller came back with a tray of cups, she handed them out, set her own down on a small round metal table, then began watering a number of plants arranged in ceramic pots along one wall. She seemed preoccupied, as well she might.

'Please excuse me,' she apologised. 'But I was part way through this, and I don't want to forget which ones I've done. They were Bernie's pride and joy.'

'No, you carry on. I'm sorry to be bothering you at a time like this,' Bliss told her. 'We won't take up too much of your time, I promise.'

Mrs Weller shook her head. 'Don't worry about that. You've come a long way.'

'It's not so far. You must have lived in Peterborough yourself when Bernard was stationed there.'

She paused, looked up as if to recall. 'Market Deeping, actually. We were there for twelve or thirteen years. I have fond memories of our time there.' Her eyes drifted away for a moment, alighting on a framed photograph that stood on the table beside her cup. The happy couple on their wedding day. Bernard a good deal lighter, Allison Weller striking and confident. When her mind snapped back into focus, she blinked once at Bliss and asked, 'Did you know my husband well, Inspector?'

'Sadly not, as I explained to your sister-in-law. We worked only one case together, shortly after I moved into the area. It was long enough for me to realise that he was a good detective, though, and I very much enjoyed his company.'

'Yes. Me, too.' She smiled. Cleared her throat hurriedly and looked away. She finished with the plants and sat down in a chair opposite the two police officers.

'I knew Bernie quite well,' Dunne offered. He took a sip of his drink, eyes distant now. 'He was a popular chap. Very good at his job. My name is Bobby Dunne, perhaps he mentioned me.'

She shook her head, cheeks flushing a little. 'There were so many names. I'm sure he did if you'd worked together.'

'There were a few cases. The odd drink after work. This has all come as a bit of a shock.'

'Yes. Yes, it has.' She smiled and nodded expectantly. 'So, tell me why you've come here today. I'm intrigued.'

'I can well imagine. I share your sense of intrigue, Mrs Weller,' Bliss told her.

'Please, call me Allison.'

'Thank you. Allison, did you know Bernard was on his way to see me yesterday?'

'When he was…?' Mrs Weller frowned, shook her head. 'No, I had no idea. When the police asked me where he was going, I told them I didn't have a clue. I couldn't imagine why he was on the A16, though I did know the road went all the way down to Peterborough. Why was he coming to see you?'

Bliss drank some of his tea before proceeding. Used the pause to process his thoughts. 'That's just it. I don't know. He called me the night before last, left a message on my machine at home. I was surprised to hear from him, even more so when he said he wanted to meet. It sounded to me as if he didn't want to give too much away before we caught up.'

'How odd.' Her frown deepened. 'You know, he was acting strangely the other night. He'd been his usual self all day, and then later on that evening he seemed… I don't know, preoccupied. Anxious, even.'

'And you have no clue as to why?' Bliss's curiosity deepened. His instincts were right on this one, he could feel that all the more now.

'No. It was a usual evening for us, as far as I can recall.'

'Did anyone pop round? Were there any phone calls?'

Allison Weller thought about that for a few moments. She wore a navy pleated knee-length dress over flat-heeled boots. Into the dress was tucked a linen blouse, buttoned fully to the neck. Her hair looked clean, but she'd applied no make-up. A neat, orderly woman, even in mourning.

She shook her head. 'No one came round, I'm certain about that. As for the phone, I'm almost as sure that there were no calls. Certainly not before his mood changed.'

'Thinking about it now, can you pinpoint anything that might have upset your husband?'

'Inspector, I'm not sure where this is all leading. What exactly are you suggesting?'

Bliss edged forward on the chair, softening his eager gaze. 'Allison, I'm just trying to make sense of why Bernard called me. I can't help but wonder what it was he wanted to say.'

'Do you think it's important? Could it have been on his mind when he… when the accident occurred?'

'It's possible. But it seems strange to me that he would make the call out of the blue the way he did, seemingly without anything prompting the change in him.'

Her eyes went blank for a while. Bliss could tell she was struggling to remember the last evening she and her husband had spent together. He said nothing, hoping she could fill in a serious void. Eventually she nodded.

'We were watching the news after dinner. The national news switched to regional, and Bernie was annoyed that we'd got the wrong one again. Sometimes we get the London version, but this time it was the Anglia region. I was doing the crossword in my newspaper, leaving Bernie to chunter through the features as he usually does.' She paused, smiling gently. 'He always had an opinion on something. The only thing that strikes me as odd now is that he went quiet for a while. Next time I glanced up he was marching out of the room. Now that I think about it, his face was quite stern.'

Bliss frowned. What on earth could Bernard Weller have seen on the news that would have upset him so much and driven him to make...

His mind cut the thought off in mid-flow. Bliss felt a shiver work its way down his arms and across the back of his neck, tiny hairs rising in its wake. He knew exactly what item would have been on the regional news that night. Tuesday night. And now Bliss was more intrigued than ever.

***

On their way back down south, Bliss had Bobby Dunne make a few calls on his mobile to find out which unit had responded to the accident in which Weller had died. The stretch of A16 just north of Spalding was on the wrong side of the Cambridgeshire/Lincolnshire border for Bliss's liking, but having ascertained that at least one member of the responding team was currently on duty at the Spalding station, he drove straight there.

'What do you think now?' he asked Dunne. Allison Weller hadn't been able to give them a great deal more information, but her impression regarding her husband's state of mind had been extremely revealing. And once back in the car, Bliss had revealed his own line of thinking: that maybe the news item Weller had seen was the one featuring the remains discovered in Bretton Woods.

'I think it's more than interesting, boss. Interesting would have been him having something important enough to tell you that it got him nudged off the road. But if what he had to say was connected with your Jane Doe, then we have something very tasty on our hands.'

Roads, hedgerow, fields and ditches fled by in a seamless blur, courtesy of Bliss's advanced police driver training. He was out of practice and his card had elapsed a few years ago, but he retained a few old tricks and maintained a decent speed throughout the journey.

'Unless it's another extraordinary coincidence, I think it's the only logical conclusion.' Bliss shrugged, keeping both hands resting gently on the steering wheel. 'But I can't imagine what it was he needed to discuss that couldn't have been said over the phone.'

They arrived in Spalding shortly after three thirty. Sergeant Eddie Glazier was waiting for them in the rest room, his own curiosity obviously kept on the boil since being asked to remain in the station for their arrival. Glazier was as wide as Bobby Dunne, but was a good foot shorter. A pocket powerhouse was the term that came to most people's minds when they met him for the first time. He wore tinted spectacles, and sported a three-day growth of stubble that had all the makings of a goatee. Bliss hoped the man changed his mind; goatee beards didn't work on men above a certain age. They spanked of desperation, of rebellion quelled by life; a compromise on the midlife-crisis Harley.

The rest room comprised a row of tables and chairs, and a TV hanging off a steel arm high up in one corner. The box was on, but the sound had been muted. There was no one else in the room, which adjoined a small and grubby-looking canteen.

The three men shook hands and Bliss got right to it. 'Tell me what you found,' he said, once he'd explained his interest.

'Mr Weller's vehicle was on its roof some way off the road on a sloping hillside with a pretty steep incline,' Glazier told them, his voice a deep Yorkshire growl. 'Both sides of the car were battered, as was its roof. It was obvious that it had flipped over a few times on its way down the hill. Mr Weller was still in the vehicle, being held in place by his seat belt. The driver's airbag had deployed, but the front offside and the offside door panels were crushed in on him. He was dead when we arrived on scene.'

Bliss nodded, trying to picture it. 'Was there any doubt in your mind about it being a single vehicle accident?'

Glazier raked his nails through the mild growth of hair between his ear and chin. 'It didn't seem likely that another vehicle had been involved, no. The marks on the road surface seemed to suggest that Weller's vehicle had moved off-line, the brakes were applied, but the severity of the movement caused the vehicle to spin and tumble off the road. The incline and gravity did the rest. We found no evidence of another vehicle, and I think we would, had someone else been involved.'

Bliss knew these guys were experts at weighing up accident scenes, but still he pushed on. 'Did your accident investigation team agree with your initial findings?'

'Completely. The fact is, all car debris found at the scene belonged to Weller's vehicle. One set of tyre marks. One car down the hill.'

During the drive down from Lincoln, Bliss had all but convinced himself that Weller's car had been rammed off the road. Clearly the evidence did not support his line of thinking, and he now began to doubt his theory that Weller's death was suspicious. Perhaps it was nothing more than a coincidence after all.

'I take it no witnesses have come forward?' Bliss asked.

Glazier shook his head. His eyes became fixed. 'That's about the only odd thing regarding this accident. And very odd at that, now that I think about it a little more. The A16 is a well-used road in both directions, and it must be a rare occasion indeed when a car could have a shunt like that and there be no traffic moving either way along any stretch of it. It's a first for me, that's for sure.'

And now there it was again. Yet another oddity, something out of kilter. Bliss pursed his lips and gave a long, puzzled sigh. 'But in your opinion it's not possible that another vehicle was responsible for Weller's car ending up off the road?'

Here, Glazier shook his head. Folded his arms. 'I didn't say it was impossible. Unlikely. Improbable, even. But it could be done if the other driver knew what he was about. If it was deliberate.'

Bliss felt his heartbeat quicken. The door hadn't completely slammed in his face. He glanced at Bobby, flashing a thin smile. Dunne gave an encouraging nod.

'Tell me how that might be done,' Bliss asked Glazier.

TEN

Having arrived back in Peterborough shortly before five, Bliss first dropped Dunne off in the hotel car park to collect his Rover, then drove directly to Thorpe Wood HQ. On his way through from the car park, he bumped into Sergeant Grealish, the uniform who had given Penny a hard time. They were both using the short corridor between areas. The man was every bit as red and sweaty and Penny had described, and judging by the ripe aroma around him, Grealish had only a nodding acquaintance with deodorant.

'Can I have a word?' Bliss asked.

Grealish brought his bulk to a juddering halt. His stomach continued to move after the rest of him. He nodded. 'What's up?'

The two men stood like gunslingers waiting for the other to draw.

'That depends. We may have a problem, but I think it can be resolved.'

'Oh? What problem is that, then?'

'You gave my DC a hard time this morning. Chandler is a good officer, and she doesn't need that kind of shit. Not from you, not from anyone. She's got a lot on her plate right now, and I want you to back off.'

'She come running to you, did she? What, she can't fight her own battles?'

Bliss narrowed his gaze. 'She likes to tough it out with people her own size. She'd have to put on two hundred pounds to do that with you.'

Grealish started to turn away. 'Yeah, whatever you...'

Bliss put his arm out, blocking the man's way. 'I mean it. You give her a hard time again and I'll come looking for you.'

The sergeant took a step back, his face splitting into a wide grin. His tongue snaked out to moisten his lips. 'Is that right? What's up, Bliss?' He formed an 'O' with the thumb and forefinger of his left hand, and began slipping the middle finger of his other hand in and out of it. 'You sticking it to her?'

When Bliss hit the man he did so without warning. The punch jabbed out only from the hip, but it was powerful and caught Grealish just beneath the ribs. He doubled up as if cut in two, his breath emerging in one loud explosion of escaped air. Bliss put a hand on the man's back, leaned down to speak.

'You're just winded, Grealish. You'll be fine in a couple of minutes. Just suck in some air when you can, and straighten slowly. I'll be going now, but if you want to discuss this matter again, you come and find me. If not, keep away from Penny Chandler and you and me won't have any more problems.'

Bliss patted Grealish on the shoulder and walked away, heading up to CID.

Chandler was nowhere to be found, and the incident room was empty of all but two civilian administrators. Both looked up at Bliss and waved a greeting, which he returned. Already the room looked as if it had been taken over by savages, with plastic sandwich containers, open biscuit packets and chocolate bar wrappers spread all over the desks and floor. Cigarette smoke hung like strips of unwashed linen in the air, and the ashtrays looked as if they were stuffed with the cremated remains of several fat people. As a rule, Thorpe Wood was a non-smoking working environment, but incident rooms were considered a special case. Just popping his head in caused Bliss's eyes to water and sting.

In his office, Bliss checked through his written and e-mailed messages, but none of the subject headings were interesting enough to snag his full attention. If it was important, people would get back to him. There were several mails from Sykes, who was chasing him for an update, but Bliss deleted the messages.

There had been no memos in his pigeonhole, and there were no new post-it notes stuck to his desk or laptop monitor. Two days into the investigation and information was proving hard to come by.

As he sat at his desk and pondered the next move, Bliss was feeling a little guilty, wondering if he had given Jane Doe the attention she deserved. It was unlike him to go running off to chase down something which, at the time he'd made the decision, was entirely unconnected with the murder investigation in hand. Lacking focus at this relatively early stage was not a good sign. With the guilt came the inevitable second-guessing, and the usual doubts began to seep back beneath the thin veneer of optimism he'd built up.

Even so, there did now seem to be a connection after all. Bliss was convinced that Bernard Weller had seen a news item featuring the discovery of the remains over at Bretton Woods, and that the unearthing of Jane Doe had prompted both a change in the man's mood and the subsequent phone call requesting a meeting. Whatever information Weller had decided to share with Bliss had probably died with him, though there was a chance that a search of Weller's home might reveal something useful.

Bliss's mind tracked back to the possibilities Sergeant Glazier had outlined to him and Bobby Dunne: that a trained driver could nudge someone off the road without causing a lot of damage to their own vehicle. Many highway patrol officers in the USA used the technique to end car chases. It was all about getting the angles right rather than adopting a method that relied on brute force, Glazier explained, and while the sergeant didn't believe such an incident was responsible for Weller's death, he could not rule out the possibility. That was enough for Bliss to latch on to. Keen to develop more leads, he took a slip of paper from his pocket and called Allison Weller's number.

'Mrs Weller? It's DI Bliss. Sorry to bother you again, but I was wondering if your husband owned a mobile phone.'

'Yes. Yes, he did.'

'Would it be all right by you if I had the number and the name of his service provider?'

Allison Weller gave him the information. 'What's this all about, Inspector? I may be grieving at the moment, but I still have my wits about me. I noticed unspoken messages passing between you and Sergeant Dunne. Something is going on and I'd like to know what it is.'

Bliss paused. There was a need to be guarded, but Weller's widow was owed some sort of explanation. Besides, he wanted to search through her husband's possessions and needed her on his side.

'I'm not exactly sure,' he replied gently. 'The fact is, I'm concerned about Bernard's accident. I'd prefer it if you kept this to yourself for the time being, Allison, but I'm wondering if there was more to it than simply running off the road. There are a few too many coincidences for my liking.'

'Are you saying you think another vehicle may have been involved?'

'Possibly, yes.'

'And that Bernie's death may have been… deliberate?'

'It's only supposition at this stage, Allison.'

There was a brief moment of silence. Then Allison Weller asked, 'But why would anyone want my husband dead, Inspector? He's been retired for more than a year.'

'I wouldn't want to speculate at this stage. Some criminals have long memories, of course, but I can assure you that I'm going to look into this. For a number of reasons, I can't make it official at this stage, but I will be spending time searching for answers.'

'I… I'm shocked by this, Inspector.' Her voice sounded weak, and Bliss felt responsible for a grief renewed. He pictured her fragile features. 'I'm still coming to terms with losing Bernie, and now you're telling me he may have been murdered.'

The alarm in her voice made Bliss wish he'd said nothing. He had to calm her down. 'Allison, please understand that I'm by no means certain about any of this, and I have absolutely no proof of anything untoward. This is just me, the opinion of one man, and at the moment it's based on nothing more than pure instinct.'

'A gut feeling? Yes, Bernie put great store in those.' He heard the reflection in her voice, the sense of loss. At some stage it was going to hit her that she would never share moments with her husband again. Bliss thought that point was still some way off.

'It's a policeman's lot, I'm afraid. We're suspicious by nature. And I could still be completely wrong.'

There was a pause long enough for Bliss to grow concerned. But when she spoke again, Allison Weller's voice was much softer. 'I'm sure you'll do what's best for my husband, Inspector Bliss. You'll keep me informed, won't you?'

'Of course.'

'How will this affect the procedure? I had hoped Bernie's body would be released to me within a day or two, but if you now believe there may be suspicious circumstances…'

Bliss hadn't considered this aspect. Allison Weller was right. Yet Bliss remained convinced that it would be a mistake to make his suspicions formal at this juncture. This was a decision he would have to live with.

'You don't have to worry about that,' he assured her. 'You must carry on as if you and I never spoke. One more thing – is there any chance that I or another officer could come up and have a look through Bernard's personal things? There may be something, anything, that might help us find out more about what happened to him.'

'Yes, of course. If you think you need to. He had his own study, but I really have no idea what you hope to find.'

'Probably nothing,' Bliss told her. 'But maybe everything we need.'

He ended the call with a promise to contact her with further news, and immediately got to his feet, intending to head back to the incident room. As Bliss rose, however, his head seemed to lurch from side to side, and the room swam in and out of focus, walls and ceiling closing in on him. He felt a warm, tingling sensation in his right ear, a piercing high-pitched shriek filling his head, and his knees buckled slightly. Bliss reached out a hand and placed it palm down on the desk to steady himself, spreading his fingers to their widest span, drawing in a deep breath at the same time. The sensation was similar to that of a panic attack, he'd been told.

'Are you okay, boss?'

Looking up, he saw Chandler standing in the doorway, concern creasing her face. He nodded and straightened immediately, raising a hand. 'I'm fine. My fault. I've not had a thing to eat all day. Bit of a head-rush, that's all.'

His DC said nothing, but she didn't look at all convinced.

'Let's not get into it right now,' he said, more abruptly than he'd intended. 'Do you have something for me?'

The smile that formed never touched her eyes. 'A break, hopefully. One night in June nineteen ninety, two separate emergency calls were made regarding an accident. Both callers said they had heard a vehicle revving hard, followed by squealing brakes, moments before striking something or someone. One of the callers claims to have seen a body lying on the side of the road immediately afterwards, a car idling close by. They made the call, but by the time they got outside, there was no sign of either the body or the car.'

Bliss felt himself nodding excitedly. The possibilities raged inside his mind. This was more like it. 'Where was this?' he asked.

Chandler's smile grew wider. 'High Street, Fletton.'

Getting better all the time. Less than half a mile from the lake where Jane Doe had most likely been buried first time around.

'The team are putting together all relevant information as we speak,' Chandler pressed on. 'I've asked them to have a report prepared for an eight thirty briefing tomorrow morning.'

'Excellent news, Pen,' he said, scarcely able to contain his enthusiasm. Bliss wanted that information now, wanted to press on with the case, but Penny had made the call and, despite his frustration, he refused to alter her decision. Patience was not one of his few virtues, but loyalty was. 'Did you keep the other team working on the reverse chronology tracking?'

She nodded. 'Normal hours for them. Unless they come up with anything useful, of course.'

Bliss reflected on his earlier concerns. Delegation did not come easy to him, and he still had regrets over leaving Penny to fend for herself all day, but she had done a good job in his absence. He'd not been missed.

'Well done,' he said, finding her eyes with his. 'Look, I'm sorry if you felt abandoned today. I shouldn't have gone off on a tangent this afternoon, but I was just sucked in by the odd coincidences surrounding DI Weller's death. No excuses. I was wrong to leave you hanging in the wind. You did a great job, but I shouldn't have gone off like that.'

Chandler shrugged, allowed herself another smile. 'I'm glad you did. I needed something like this to give me a kick start. Those sergeant's exams have been hanging around me like a bad smell, but today has given me fresh impetus. I'm encouraged by how I handled things.'

He grinned. 'Well, good for you. All part of my master plan, of course.'

'Of course. So, did you find what you were looking for at Weller's place?'

'I'm not entirely sure. Probably, but I want to turn it over a few times in my mind and make sure I have it straight before I run it by you.'

'Sounds reasonable. Anyway, I forgot to ask earlier, but how did you get on this morning?'

'This morning?' For a moment he wondered if he'd slipped up and said something he'd rather have kept to himself.

'You had something on the go, but you didn't say what. Anything I need to know about?'

She was fishing. He knew it, and she knew he knew. But Penny being Penny, she didn't care.

'No. Thanks for asking, though. Nothing you need to concern yourself with. It was a personal matter, as I think I mentioned.'

'Did you? I'd forgotten.' She paused, then fixed her gaze on him. 'You'd better get some food inside you, boss. Can't have you fainting like a big girl.'

Bliss laughed. As they moved to leave his office together, Chandler turned her head towards him and leaned in. It was the slightest of movements, but Bliss noticed, and for one awkward moment he thought she was going to kiss him. Instead he saw her nostrils flare, her head dart back.

'What was that?' he asked. He stopped walking and stared at her.

'What was what?'

His mind raced. What exactly had she done? Sniffed the air? Sniffed him? Did he smell? Did he have bad breath? His thoughts finally came to rest on what she may have seen when she entered his office.

His frown deepened. 'Were you smelling my breath?'

He heard her suck in some air. 'Sir, I…'

'Do you think I've been drinking? Is that what you thought when you saw me sway, Penny?'

Bliss saw Chandler wrestling with her emotions. Her first instinct would be to back off, but her true nature would plough ahead regardless of the consequences. It was one of the things he most admired about her.

'Sir, I'm worried about you,' she admitted finally. 'You're pale, you look weaker than I've ever seen you, and today is not the first time I've seen you stagger.'

'And all that adds up to my having a problem with booze, right?'

'Not necessarily, no. You may not be eating right. You said yourself that you hadn't had a meal today.'

'Yes, but clearly you didn't believe me. You think I'm hitting the bottle.'

'You've had a bad time recently. You wouldn't be the first cop to…'

'Stop,' Bliss snapped, raising a finger. He left it there in front of her face. 'Just stop right there. I'm grateful for your concern, but frankly I'm very disappointed that you see me as the sort of bloke who'd get pissed while on duty. You know a great deal about my life, Penny. Far more than anyone else, and I mean *anyone*. You've seen me drunk exactly once, and I couldn't have been more off duty than I was that night.'

The memory of waking up in her spare bedroom still burned inside his mind. He'd gone on a drinking binge after a bout of depression. Fortunately for Bliss, a barman had recognised him and had called Penny. She had rescued him from his moment of weakness, and had never mentioned it since.

'I'm not saying I think you've been drunk on duty,' Chandler argued.

'Then what are you saying?'

She couldn't answer him. Bliss didn't accept for one moment that she actually thought he would be drinking on duty, but dark thoughts of him and the demon drink had formed inside her mind and those thoughts had not been fully explored. Perhaps he ought to have explained his illness, but Bliss believed he was entitled to a little privacy. That she had dared try and capture the smell of alcohol on his breath hurt him a little. And that was the overriding feeling right now.

'I'll see you at briefing tomorrow,' he said eventually. His tone suggested their conversation was at an end. 'Please try not to think the worst of me if I happen to smell of mints.'

ELEVEN

Suitably ashamed, Bliss later chastised himself for that final cheap shot at Penny. He would make a point of apologising before the morning briefing, and she would forgive him; in fact, she probably already had. In her own way, Penny was looking out for him, and her concern should have been welcomed rather than rejected in such a mean-spirited manner. He'd acted like a jerk. He knew it wouldn't be the last time.

After work he hadn't felt in the mood to join his colleagues for a drink, so instead Bliss treated himself to a poor three-course meal at a pub close to his home, washing down the tasteless food with a pint of IPA. At best it was fuel, at worst a culinary disgrace. As he pushed his dessert plate aside and drained his glass, Bliss caught sight of his reflection in a window and briefly saw himself through the eyes of other patrons in the pub: some poor, pathetic loser eating alone, a Billy-no-mates with less life than a dog's pelt.

It was this thought that led Bliss to calling his parents the moment he returned home. They had moved to Spain many years ago, taking over a small bar and restaurant in a mountain village twenty miles north of Marbella. On hearing the news, Bliss had joked with his father that they were only moving out there in order that he could meet up with all the villains who had skipped bail to live abroad. According to subsequent letters and phone calls, he'd not been far wrong.

It was his mother who answered the phone. Bliss could hear the pleasure in her voice as they exchanged greetings, but it wasn't long before the maternal instinct kicked in.

'How are you doing, Jimmy?' she asked, the question much more than casual.

'I'm fine. Bonnie and Clyde send their love.'

She laughed. 'I'm sure they do. Seriously, though, how are you?'

'Seriously, though, I'm fine. Why wouldn't I be?'

'I could always tell when you were lying, Jimmy.'

'Really. How?'

'Your lips were moving.'

Now it was his turn to laugh. 'How's the old man?'

The sigh that rattled down the line was born of frustration. 'Oh, that bloody old fool. We brought in that new manager so your dad could take a back seat, and he spends more time there now than he ever did before. Says he doesn't trust the manager to run the place properly.'

Bliss shook his head. That was typical of his father. 'You tell him to take a breather. It's time the both of you started enjoying your money.'

'What money?'

'Don't plead poverty, Mum, we both know you're rolling in it. Anyway, I'm thinking of coming out there for Christmas,' he told her. He wasn't sure if he meant it, but it had been something to say.

'Really? That's smashing. We'd love to see you. Anyone coming with you?'

Subtlety wasn't one of his mother's strengths. 'I doubt it, Mum.' Bliss thought about Emily Grant, but made no further comment.

They batted some small talk back and forth for a further ten minutes or so. When eventually he told her he had to go, his mother gave it one last shot. 'You would tell me if anything was wrong, wouldn't you, Jimmy?'

A layer of guilt settled on him when he thought about the news Captain Scowcroft had given him that morning. But he couldn't see what good it would do anyone to upset his parents right now. They'd had enough of that, Bliss thought.

'All right,' he said. 'I give in. I confess. Mum, I'm gay.'

'Thank goodness, love. For a moment I thought you were going to tell me you'd found God.'

Relieved that the conversation had ended on a real belly laugh, Bliss decided that in future he would call his parents only when he was feeling at his best. His mother's radar was simply too good. She'd be great in a room interviewing suspects.

After walking Bonnie and Clyde over by Orton Mere, Bliss spent some time surfing the Internet, having entered the keywords 'Ménière's Disease' into the Google search engine. He found a lot of websites dedicated to the disease, along with several online forums. One of the sites in particular seemed to have a wealth of interesting material, so he set it as one of his favourites and also saved some of the more informative pages to his computer's hard drive. Bliss believed the Internet to consist mostly of porn or useless information, but at times like this he appreciated its usefulness. On the forums he discovered people with the same fears, the same lack of comprehension, and knowing there were other sufferers somehow made him feel a little better.

When his patience for surfing was exhausted, Bliss watched the movie *K-Pax* on DVD, wondering as he had after each previous viewing whether the character played by Kevin Spacey was, as he'd claimed, visiting from another planet, or if the Jeff Bridges character had been correct in his diagnosis of mental instability caused by harrowing family murders. Bliss enjoyed films that made him think about them long after they were over. They reminded him of life and all its absurdities. The movie *Crash* had the same effect, the unfolding story revealing how critical the impact people have on each other can be. Bliss had considered those possibilities long after the haunting Bird York song had died away and the credits stopped rolling.

After the DVD he'd tried to sleep, but the night would not release him. Neither would the investigation, thought of which kicked aside both his illness and the speculation relating to the movie. Recognising the familiar signs of insomnia, and not wanting the effects of a late sleeping pill to muddle his thinking during the morning briefing, Bliss decided to go for a drive to see if he could make himself drowsy.

It was only when driving either through or around the city that Bliss realised how little it felt like home. Having always considered it characterless, in recent times he had come to think of Peterborough as a place without soul. Its inhabitants seemed to drift through it like balls of tumbleweed, occasionally bumping into each other and creating a minor tangle, but leaving no lasting impression on each other. The word he could best use to describe it was ordinary, and perhaps that meant he did belong after all.

An aerial shot of Peterborough at night could never be confused with one of Las Vegas. The only real illumination was the cathedral, and while the building itself was magnificent, it could hardly be called a Mecca for tourists. A dull amber sodium lighting cast a sombre glow over the parkways that ringed the city, but the centre itself was dimly lit and gloomy. Having lured in both sizeable businesses and a more metropolitan public than it was used to, Peterborough had spent the last quarter of a century wondering how to deal with the influx. That it had promised more than it delivered was not in doubt, and the signs of ageing were gathering like carrion crows around road kill.

Bliss drove over to Bretton, pulling up as close to the woods as he could, not far from where he had parked on Tuesday evening following the shout. A flat-roofed, two-storey secondary school huddled in the moonlit darkness to his right, while to his left lay a wide single-track path that led to a large playing field and the woods themselves. This was the most likely parking spot for whoever had buried Jane Doe a few hundred yards away. A bit of a struggle with a corpse, but easy enough with a sackful of human remains and a spade. Not a lot of bulk, and even less weight. Few houses close by had a good view of the path entrance, and just a dozen or so yards along it became entirely obscured by trees. The person responsible for digging that shallow grave would not have been hurried.

So why not go further off the path and deeper into the woods? Bliss wondered, remembering his initial thoughts when first surveying the scene. If he was going to bury someone he would do it as far off the beaten track as possible. Perhaps their quarry had been disturbed after all. Someone walking a dog? A couple seeking intimate contact away from prying eyes? Bliss shook off the questions, the answers to which, he guessed, would probably never reveal themselves.

As he sat quite still in the car and reflected on the way the investigation had panned out so far, Bliss's thoughts strayed once more to his hospital visit. The news he'd received earlier in the day just might account for the insomnia. He would spend time finding out more about this bloody Ménière's thing, but it would have to wait. If the disease allowed him to. The scariest thing about it was the control it seemed to have over the individual sufferer. It was all very well intending to fight it, looking to make it into work each day and focus on the job, but what if the symptoms became so bad he couldn't move without fear of falling over? What if he couldn't even climb out of bed? Another bridge to jump off when he got to it, he supposed. At this rate he'd need a bungee cord around his waist.

He shrugged the negative thoughts aside and brought Emily Grant to mind. It would have been nice to see Emily earlier, and he'd forgotten to ask Penny about her. The two of them had been due to meet at Thorpe Wood, and Bliss wondered if Emily had managed to discover anything else of interest. Absurdly, he also found himself speculating as to whether Emily had mentioned him. Bliss laughed at himself and shook his head. At the age of forty-three, it was time he grew up.

He gunned the Vectra's engine and drove off. One of the oldest parts of Peterborough, Fletton was all the way across the other side of the city, but at this time of night it took less than ten minutes to get there. The High Street was a long, narrow road that ran between Fletton and Woodston. Bliss drove along it both ways, passing darkened houses, cars jammed close together on both sides of the street. Pausing briefly on a deserted corner, engine idling with a gentle, well-tuned purr, Bliss wondered what further news would be revealed later that morning. Where on this road had the reported incident taken place? Who had made those calls? Had anyone else heard or seen something that night but not bothered to call? How in-depth had the official reports been, considering no body was discovered? How well would those involved remember the incident now? Would they even still be around? These were all questions the murder squad could and should be able to answer over the next couple of days.

The incident as reported by at least one person seemed to match the investigation team's line of thinking: that Jane Doe had been struck by a vehicle shortly before her death. Bliss wondered if they were looking at a true accident here, some drunk driver perhaps, who had been sober enough to cover his or her tracks afterwards, or had Jane Doe been run down deliberately? Bliss could see it in his mind; the driver checks the body, discovers she's still breathing and, aware that the commotion would have been overheard and probably reported, pulls her into the vehicle and speeds off. Either scenario was possible, and both would be fully explored. Whichever proved to be the truth, the ultimate act had been one of murder.

Still not in the least bit tired, Bliss's last port of call was to drive past the lake. No roads led directly to it, though fishermen and dog walkers like himself knew where to park in order to get close enough to make the lake a worthwhile choice for a little relaxation.

But at a price.

The city had once reeked of sugar beet being processed in a huge factory along Oundle Road, but when the production side closed down, the local population realised that it had merely been disguising the awful stench pouring out of the Pedigree Pet Foods factory. On a warm day, the combination of that in addition to the landfill upon which the Hampton township had been built brought tears to the eyes.

From up on the parkway, the still water of the lake looked black and forbidding, visible now thanks only to a cloudless sky and low moon. Also visible, Peterborough's own version of Spaghetti Junction, a bizarre new series of intersections that looked like the web of a drunken spider. Bliss continued westbound past the lake, slipped off the parkway and headed back the way he had come towards the city centre once more. It was as he drove past a large sign and his eyes followed a new road leading to a huge, low building, that the reason behind the removal of Jane Doe's remains came to him in a single clear thought.

TWELVE

It was just after eight on Friday morning. Bliss caught up with Chandler at her desk as the DC was finger pecking the keyboard of her computer. He set a cup of coffee down on a spiral-bound notepad, then placed an iced doughnut alongside her drink. Bliss waited for her to look up. She made him wait just long enough to make a point, but after a brief glance at the peace offering, Penny eventually turned her attention to him. She said nothing, but Bliss saw understanding in her eyes.

'No, the breakfast is not my way of apologising,' he said. 'I can do that for myself. I'm really very sorry, Pen. I was totally out of order yesterday, my rant was a complete overreaction, and I hope you accept my apology.'

Chandler took a pull from her cup and a bite out of the doughnut before responding with a tentative smile. 'You're forgiven,' she told him. 'And for what it's worth, I'm sorry for doubting you.'

'Good. That's that done with then.'

'Not quite.' Her eyes widened expectantly. Clearly she wanted to know what was causing his apparent imbalance if booze was not the culprit.

'Now is not the right time,' he told her. 'We'll have a chat over lunch or a drink after work.'

'How d'you know I don't have a date?'

'Since when do you date?'

'Remember the priest?'

Bliss grinned. 'Oh, him. I thought he was imaginary.'

She pulled a face and blew a raspberry. A familiar reaction. She stood and they started walking together towards the incident room.

'I'm keen to know what the team has to tell us this morning,' she said. 'It sounded as if these triple-nine calls could be a valuable lead.'

'They're our only lead,' Bliss remarked, shaking his head. Then, injecting a little more nonchalance than he felt, he went on, 'By the way, how was your meeting with Emily? I was wondering if she came up with anything from the Bretton site.'

'I did manage to find a half hour with her. Unfortunately she had nothing to add to what she'd already given us. She did some tests on the soil, but doesn't believe it'll throw up any surprises. She volunteered to study the remains in more detail and take a look at the results of the tests she carried out that were sent for analysis. I told her I thought the official forensic people would probably become involved at this point, but that her insight into local conditions might still prove useful.'

Nodding, Bliss said, 'Good. For the benefit of Sykes we will have to run things by the book, but there's no harm in having Emily in our pockets as well. See if you can hook her up with forensics and get them in the same room when analysis is complete. Also, it'd be good to have a written report confirming everything she's told us so far.'

'I'll do my best. We should really offer some payment.'

'That's fine. I'll authorise it.'

'You think those bones still have something to tell us?'

'I hope we don't have to rely on that, but I'm not ruling out the possibility.'

'She asked about you. Wondered how you were. We chatted for a while. I think you should call her.'

'Who? Jane Doe?'

'You know who I mean.'

Bliss felt himself flush, feeling ridiculously pleased with himself. 'Oh, give it a rest, Pen. Anyway, she's probably got a partner.'

'Partner, eh? So you noticed the lack of a wedding ring?'

'I'm a detective. And if she's as interested in me as you seem to think she is, DC Chandler, she will have noticed that I *do* wear a ring.'

'True. But you're no longer married.'

He shook his head. 'Yes, but she doesn't know that.'

'Maybe she does.'

'You told her?' Bliss didn't know whether to be annoyed or pleased. He decided it wasn't worth making a fuss over.

'I might've said something along those lines,' Chandler admitted. Her expression became serious. 'But only the basics. No details. I wouldn't ever go that far.'

For that, at least, he was grateful. Penny was one of only three people who knew all the squalid details surrounding his wife's murder, but those secrets were locked away in a dark place he had no desire to revisit right now.

'It really doesn't matter, anyway. I'm too busy for a relationship,' Bliss said, ending the conversation as the doors to the Major Inquiry Room loomed up on their left.

The room was full of suits and uniforms mingling together, and the hubbub of chatter died away as Bliss and Chandler entered. Smoke coiled loosely up towards the ceiling, creating a dense fug. Some of the team were munching on their breakfast or sipping hot drinks. Bliss saw tired faces that were nonetheless eager and expectant. It was what he'd hoped to see.

He began the briefing by informing the team of his early morning insight. 'We've been looking for a good enough reason for someone to dig up human remains and relocate them. The best reason of all is that their original location might have become compromised. Ruling out chance discovery, we had to consider something more organised. I happened to drive by the lake over at Fletton last night, and something obvious leapt right out at me. I think news that the area was being redeveloped in order to site the IKEA storage and distribution warehouse might just have be reason enough.'

'Of course,' one of the female uniforms said, snapping her fingers. 'I knew there was something about that area. That IKEA warehouse being built was the bane of my life with all the traffic jams it caused. The timing is spot on as well, I would think.'

Bliss nodded. 'It is. We can figure some time between the announcement at which the redevelopment of the land was made public, which was late in two thousand and one, to the time when work first began the following year. Still a considerable window of opportunity, but narrowed down all the same from where we began. Now, I understand someone has information for us about a reported accident in Fletton.'

It was DC Mia Strong who got to her feet. Called into the team late yesterday, it was she who had first latched on to the details. Small, thin, blonde and busty, Strong was known around the squad as 'Cuffs and Baton Barbie'. Few fellow officers had the courage to call her that to her face, and those who dared were usually ridiculed unmercifully in return. Like Penny Chandler she was slight of build, but unlike her colleague, Mia was a ticking time bomb in a Marks & Spencer suit. A good, intelligent officer, Mia was pushing Chandler all the way in their personal duel for promotion. Today her hair was tied up and clipped neatly in place, causing her, Bliss thought, to look like some porn-seeker's ultimate librarian or schoolteacher fantasy. Not that he knew anything about that sort of thing, of course.

'We have everything related to the incident now, boss,' Strong said, offering her usual warm smile. She waved a handful of A4 sheets in the air.

Standing to one side, Bliss said, 'Well, come up here and reveal all, DC Strong. Broad strokes only at first, please.'

She did so, accompanied by a few muted whistles and cheers. Mia turned and faced the squad, her confidence impressing Bliss. 'At nine thirty-seven p.m. on Tuesday twenty-sixth of June, nineteen ninety, the first call was logged. A Mr Malcolm Twist reported hearing an accident close to his home in Garrick Walk. He gave few other details. A minute later, Mr Gordon McAndrew called in a similar report, only he described hearing a fast-moving vehicle brake hard and then strike something, followed by a cry or a scream. He was living in hostel accommodation along the High Street on the corner of Fleet Way, and when he looked out of the window he saw a car slewed across the street, and the body of what he thought was a woman lying in the gutter.

'Officers arriving at the scene found no sign of an accident, but Mr McAndrew was waiting for them. In his statement he says that having made the triple-nine call, he went immediately downstairs and out to the road. He found no car and no victim. The officers inspected the scene, but found no obvious indicators. A report in the case file suggests that Mr McAndrew had been drinking, and that either he didn't actually see what he reported, or that the accident wasn't as bad as it had appeared to the witness. The officers did spend a little bit of time door-to-door canvassing, but there were no further witnesses. The log and crime file were left open for a week or so, and then closed due to lack of information.'

Strong lowered the sheets of printed paper she had been reading from. Bliss blew out some air and nodded. It seemed to him that the case had been closed a little too quickly, but he wasn't about to second-guess the investigating officers at this stage. He made a mental note to come back to it.

'Thanks for that, DC Strong.' Bliss switched his attention back to the teams. 'Only two witnesses to an accident at shortly after nine thirty on a summer's night. Why so few?'

'That was covered in an accompanying note from an attending officer,' one of the suits replied. 'England were playing Belgium that night in the football World Cup. The game went into extra time, so the streets would have been deserted. That's probably also why other residents didn't hear it. Mr McAndrew, a Scot, had no interest in the game and had been lying in his room reading a newspaper and putting away a few cans of Special Brew.'

Bliss ran a hand across his chin. His shave that morning had been cursory. There had been no spins upon waking, but he had felt a little unsteady for several minutes. 'All right. Does anyone here think this report is coincidental? That the attending officers were correct in their assumption?'

No hands were raised, nothing was said. Bliss ran his gaze over the squad.

'We know the victim wasn't killed by her injuries, and Jane Doe's condition suggests the blow from being struck by a vehicle wasn't about to become life threatening. However, it may have been more than enough to temporarily disable her. If we follow this theory through, we can assume that in the time it took Mr McAndrew to place his call and then get outside, whoever ran our victim down managed to scoop her up and force her into the car before driving off. It wouldn't have taken long.'

'Sounds about right, boss,' Strong said, smoothing down the pleats of her skirt. Dunne and Chandler, flanking Bliss, nodded their agreement.

Bliss took a moment. His gaze flitted across to the room's largest window, beads of rain drumming gently against the tinted glass. He shivered once, chilled by the sight. Yet warmth touched the pit of his stomach, because for the first time he felt as if the squad was getting a grip on the inquiry.

'Okay,' he said, nodding and managing to find a thin smile. 'So, I can see four clear lines of investigation to pursue: one, assuming our victim was taken directly to where she was killed and buried, where is the closest access point from the original scene? Two, let's wind in those MisPer reports to cover two weeks either side of June twenty-sixth. Let's not assume Jane Doe only went missing the night she was killed. Widen the search by a week either side if you need to and keep on going until you get something positive. Three, let's try and contact both Mr Twist and Mr McAndrew, our two witnesses. Finally, a word with the attending officers wouldn't go amiss. I know it was a long time ago, but who knows what they might recall?'

'McAndrew was living in a hostel at the time,' one of the team reminded him.

'Correct. So there's every chance he got a council or housing association place sometime afterwards. Check with the hostel first, and then the council.'

'I'll get the actions written up as soon as I can,' Chandler chipped in. She looked across at him. 'Do you want to put all our efforts into this, or do you still want a team working on the Bretton backwards angle?'

He gave that some thought. It would be too easy to have everyone chasing down the same line that might yet lead them nowhere. Against that, having everyone working on the fresh actions would cut down on time. But after so many years, would a few hours or a few days matter?

'Trim the other team back to four officers,' he said eventually. 'Everyone else works on new items. Is that everything, Mia?'

DC Strong nodded. 'Yes, boss.'

'Then let's get cracking, everybody. Mia, let me have your notes before you go.'

She handed them to him and rejoined the team. As everyone in the room broke into a cacophony of renewed enthusiasm, Bliss ran his eye over the sheets of paper. Mia hadn't missed anything salient. When he came to the final entry, a list of further details relating to the incident report, his breath caught in his throat and he felt as if his legs might buckle.

'Jesus,' he whispered.

Penny Chandler, still standing close by as she wrote on one of the boards, peered hard at him. 'Boss?'

In a quiet voice he said, 'We'll discuss it in my office.'

'Discuss what?'

'Bide your time.'

She grinned and said, 'Ooh, a surprise. I like surprises.'

Bliss shook his head. 'Not this one you won't.'

THIRTEEN

They sat facing each other across his desk, office door closed, blinds pulled on the windows. The Pissed-Ometer was set to 'Grumpy'. Whoever the joker was, they'd guessed wrong today. Bliss's mood was up a notch or two from that.

'Come on, boss,' Chandler implored him. 'You've kept me in suspense long enough. Tell me what's wrong.'

Bliss tapped a finger on the report DC Strong had given him. 'Two officers attended the scene of the reported accident that night in June nineteen ninety.'

'I know. That much Mia told us.'

'One of those officers was Bernard Weller.'

Chandler's eyes grew wide. She said nothing, simply sucked in some air through clenched teeth.

'Yeah. That was my first reaction.' Bliss shook his head. 'But you don't know the half of it.'

He spent the next ten minutes filling Chandler in on everything he and Dunne had discovered during their visit to Lincoln and Spalding. Even as he related the events piece by piece, so Bliss was growing increasingly uncomfortable with how it was panning out. All at once he felt old and weary.

'So Bernard Weller sees the item on the news, and shortly afterwards calls you to set up a meeting,' Chandler said. She shrugged expansively. 'He obviously knew something relevant relating to Jane Doe.'

'Not obviously,' Bliss cautioned. 'But extremely likely, that's for sure. And then the next day his car is found overturned in a field, Weller dead inside it. What does that suggest to you?'

'That someone didn't want him to make that meeting. That someone silenced him.' Chandler gave a worried shake of the head. 'But the RTA crew say it was an accident, yes?'

'They do, but the first officer on the scene, Glazier, he did think it was odd that there had been no witnesses on such a busy road. With me and Bobby there posing difficult questions, he began to ponder whether Weller had been helped off the road at the most opportune moment. He's going to arrange a second inspection of the wreckage and the scene, see if there's anything they might have missed.'

'You say it's not obvious that Weller knew something about Jane Doe, and I can understand why you thought that initially. But now?' she leaned forward and spread the fingers of her left hand over the report sheets. 'Now that you know Weller was one of the officers who attended the scene of the accident in Fletton, surely you no longer have any doubts?'

'Alleged accident,' Bliss reminded her, waggling a raised finger. 'You're forgetting everything I've taught you. Remember, we don't just look at this from our angle, we have to see it with regard to obtaining a prosecution. For a moment, forget what we suspect, and concentrate on hard evidence.'

'That's easy enough,' Chandler scoffed. 'There is none.'

'Precisely. Everything is circumstantial at the moment. That's something we have to address.' Bliss looked hard at her, hoping she would see in his eyes where he was headed.

It took only a moment before Penny put back her head and groaned. 'You're not going to make this official, are you?'

'No. Not at the moment.'

'But you know you have to. With the greatest respect, boss, your suspicions should be reported right now.'

Bliss thought back to Tuesday evening, the sight of Jane Doe's remains lying in a heap. A life discarded so casually. Bernard Weller had known something about it. Had wanted to tell Bliss. Now he was no longer around to tell anyone anything. Police officer involvement. The phrase screamed at Bliss, who knew exactly what it might mean. Not just for him, but for everyone involved with the investigation. Bliss pulled himself back to what Penny had just said, feeling a weight starting to press down on his shoulders.

'Of course my suspicions should be reported, Penny.' Bliss rubbed the heel of his hand across his scar. 'I don't need reminding of that. But I'm not going to shift any wheels into gear until I know exactly in which direction they're pointed. And, perhaps more importantly, where they'll end up.'

'I don't understand.'

Bliss leaned in, lowering his voice despite them being alone in the room. 'Penny, Bernard Weller wasn't the only officer who attended the scene of that reported accident. He wasn't the only officer involved with the investigation. And if, as we suspect, Weller was murdered in order to prevent him telling me something about our Jane Doe, don't you think it would be wise for us to find out more about what we're dealing with before we plunge in head first?'

The startled look on her face told him his words had struck home. It hadn't occurred to her that they themselves might become targets because of what they knew and suspected. Or that whoever had them in their cross hairs might be working in the same job. Perhaps even the same station, Bliss thought then, licking lips that were suddenly very dry.

'If Weller can get hit, what's to stop us being next?' Chandler said in a hushed tone. 'That's what you're telling me.'

'It is, yes.'

'So what do you propose to do?'

Bliss studied his DC. She looked wary now, possibly frightened. He didn't like being the one to have put that fear in place, but neither would it have been right to have let her remain unaware of the possibilities he was seeing.

'I want to have Weller's phone records checked out. He called me. Maybe he called someone else.'

'Is that likely? I mean, you said his manner was... secretive.'

'It was. But if I'm right about this, about what happened to Weller, then someone else knew he was going to be driving down to Peterborough. And when.'

Chandler shook her head, puffing out her cheeks. 'I don't like this, boss. I don't like anything about it. It's going to be tough keeping this to ourselves. Maybe even impossible.'

Bliss met her frank and even gaze once more. He'd asked a lot of her in the past, and now he was doing it again. Playing with her career. He would take the blame if it all got bent out of shape, but if Penny was caught withholding evidence that might be viewed as pertinent, even vital to their ongoing case, it would hurt her. He came to a swift decision.

'Look, I'm sorry, Penny,' he said softly. 'This has already got way out of hand. Let's agree that this conversation never took place. In fact, no conversation relating to DI Weller took place between us. You carry on with the official investigation as part of the squad, working with the facts as the squad has them. Whatever's on the boards will be your game plan. I'll be working it, too. Only I'll be working with what's not on those boards. I'm going to get Bobby involved in your place. He'll be safe if the brown stuff hits the fan, and he has no career ambitions.'

Her face took on all kinds of creases. 'Why?'

'I need some help with this, Pen. Bobby's the next best thing to you.'

She shook her head abruptly. 'No, I mean why are you dumping me in favour of him?'

'I'm not dumping you. I'm shifting you out of harm's way.'

'Again, why?'

'Because, as you rightly pointed out, it will be difficult to investigate this angle without it becoming common knowledge. If it all goes off, I don't want you harmed by any fallout.'

'Isn't that my choice? We're a team. You and me, I mean. You confided in me, and I'm big enough to decide for myself whether or not to get involved.'

Bliss smiled, as impressed with her now as he had been earlier by Mia Strong. 'I know you are. But it's because we're a team that it's unfair. Your loyalty alone would prevent you from going over my head to report this matter.'

'Which I still could,' Chandler argued. 'Just because these conversations never took place, doesn't mean I didn't hear them.'

Bliss raised a hand. He shifted uneasily in his chair, uncomfortable now. 'Hold on a second. Why are we having a row about this? I'm offering you a way out.'

'And I don't want to take it.' Penny crossed her legs at the ankles and folded her arms. Indignant. Bliss smiled once more. She was every bit as determined, pig-headed and stubborn as he had once been and probably still was.

'Okay,' he said, relenting. He got to his feet and stretched his legs. He waited for any sign of imbalance, but he felt fine. 'But Bobby is already part of this and I want him to carry on with it as well. We could actually do with one more body. Any ideas?'

'Mia,' Chandler answered without pause. 'She's low-key, and will keep this as quiet as it needs to be.'

'You do know what you'll be asking her to take on? You do understand that if Weller was somehow involved with what happened to our Jane Doe, no matter how peripherally, we're going to have to look at every other investigating officer as well. Particularly…' He came back to his desk, eyes quickly scanning the sheet of notes. 'PC Hendry, who attended the scene with Weller.'

'She'll be as fine with it as I am.' Chandler gave a confident nod. 'We're mates, and I know her very well. We have similar ideals. But you know, maybe we're getting worked up over nothing. DI Weller, Sergeant Weller as he was at the time, attended the scene of a reported incident. That just means he was around at the time. Maybe he was going to talk to you about our Jane Doe, but perhaps the information he was going to give you had nothing to do with what happened to her afterwards.'

Bliss peered sceptically at her. 'You don't honestly believe that. I know you better, Penny.'

'Perhaps I don't believe it. And I know you don't. That doesn't make it a lie.'

Nodding, he dropped his eyes to the list of officers whose names had come up in relation to the incident. 'So we know what became of Weller. Any idea about his partner that night, Ian Hendry?'

'Doesn't ring a bell.'

'So that's one name to chase down. That just leaves us with the duty officer they reported to after attending the scene, PC Clive Rhodes.' Bliss's eyes narrowed into thin slits. 'Rhodes? Isn't he still based at Bridge Street Central?'

A rapid nod. 'Yep. A sergeant now.'

'All right. See if he's on duty. If not, get his address and we'll pay him a visit. Oh, and see if you can also locate PC Hendry.'

When Chandler had gone, Bliss sat down and eased back in his chair. He rolled his neck, hoping to ease some of the tension building there, but the motion made him feel a little dizzy. The buzzing in his ears suddenly increased in both timbre and loudness, and a machine-like sound pulsed with each beat of his heart. From a website he had learned that one of the Ménière's triggers was stress, and stressful just about summed up the notion that he might soon be investigating one or more of his own colleagues.

But it was Friday, and a quiet weekend would ease the strain, provided he could force himself to relax – not an inconsiderable matter. A few hours with Bonnie and Clyde over by the Ferry Meadows lakes would soften the edges at least. He was neither on duty nor on call for the next two days, so there would be an opportunity to switch off.

Bliss coughed a harsh laugh at himself. Switch off? Sure. Easy enough. All he had to do was break the habits of a lifetime. He shook his head and read the report in his hand one more time.

***

Over the next few hours, trickles of information began to leak in. Mia Strong reported that Malcolm Twist, the witness who made the first emergency call, now lived in Chicago.

'Do you want me to have him traced, boss?' she asked Bliss.

'Of course. I know it's a long time ago, and it seems like he had the least to report the night it happened, but who knows what tumblers might fall into place if he's asked to recall exactly what he heard.'

'All right. I'll get it actioned.'

'Any news on McAndrew?'

Mia shook her head. Smiled. Cute smile to match her high-cheeked, flawless features. Bliss knew that many of her male colleagues had tried it on and, given that her personality matched her looks and physique, he understood why. Yet from what he had learned from the rumour mill, Mia avoided work-based romances like the plague and was living happily with a secondary school teacher.

'We can't find out anything from the hostel directly,' she told him. 'So we're working on the council.'

'Hmm. That'll be like pulling teeth.'

Mia laughed. 'I'll try and charm them if I have to.'

'I'm sure you can.' Bliss first smiled, and then became serious once more. 'Does that bother you, Mia? Using your looks to gain an advantage, I mean.'

'Does it bother me personally?'

'No, professionally. Does it piss you off that someone will open up to you more because of what you look like than who and what you are?'

Strong thought about it for a moment. Then shook her head. 'Swings and roundabouts, really. I can get some blokes eating out of my hands, but women tend to clam right up.'

'I think you probably intimidate them.'

'I suppose so. Still, like I say, I win some and lose some. As for it bothering me, I think it would if my superiors thought the same way.'

Bliss nodded. 'I hope you know I don't. I'm not saying I would never use your appearance to our advantage, but with me your abilities come first.'

'I can live with that, boss,' Strong told him.

He was writing up his notes when a call came in from Technical Services. The head of the department was a civilian, an intense, earnest individual called Vic Tallow.

'I've pulled the records on Bernard Weller's phones, Inspector. It wasn't too difficult. On the night in question there was no activity on his mobile, but on the landline there were two calls. One made, one received.'

Bliss knew the made call had been to him, which left the one received. 'Which occurred first?' he asked.

'About a quarter of an hour before Weller phoned you, one came in from a mobile.'

'And you can trace it, yes?' Bliss felt a jab of excitement.

'Um, yes and no. Yes, we traced it. But no, I can't give you a name. The number can't be located and matched against an owner. My guess is they must be using a fake SIM card.'

'Damn.' Bliss felt as if ice-cold water had been poured over his genitals. 'So it's a dead end, right? You can't take it any further?'

'Sorry, no.'

'Is it possible to tell me how long the call lasted?'

'That I can do. Uh, just shy of four minutes.'

'Okay. Thanks, Vic. You did your best.' It was hard not to sound disappointed.

Having Tech Services run Weller's records had been a judgement call. Bliss had no wish to advertise Weller's name, but he needed information. Bliss's request would be logged, but because the technicians were civilians they would respond only to requests, so Tallow would simply move on to the next one without giving it a second thought.

When Chandler returned to his office, she had both bad and even worse news for Bliss. 'Sergeant Rhodes is on sick leave and can't be reached on his home number,' she told him. 'And as for Hendry, he left the job in ninety-two and joined the Air Force.'

Bliss let go a lengthy, frustrated sigh. He thumbed the small scar on his brow. This was not going anywhere near as well as he'd hoped. What had started out as a cold case likely to remain unsolved was fast becoming the stuff of nightmares.

'Okay. Have someone keep trying Rhodes, and in the meanwhile see if you can find out where Hendry is based. Let's just hope it's not bloody Iraq.'

Laughing, Chandler said, 'No, we'll get lucky, I'm sure. Cheer up, boss. We've taken a big step forward today.'

He wasn't quite so certain, but Bliss nodded anyway. 'I suppose we have. Let's hope it's not followed by two larger ones backwards.'

FOURTEEN

On Saturday morning, Bliss took time over his breakfast of scrambled eggs and toast, idly scanning the pages of the *Daily Mail* in between bites. Aside from the sports section and the adverts, every other page screamed bad news, and there was a sour, desperate slant to the editorial style. Bliss wondered if it was time to cancel the paper and try TV news for a change. Either that or forget about the outside world altogether.

He'd managed to get away from work shortly after six the previous evening, having endured the dubious twin pleasures of delivering a second media briefing, followed by twenty minutes stuck in a room with Superintendent Sykes. Press attendance was down fifty per cent already; old bones were fast becoming old news. A wise man had once said that today's headlines were tomorrow's fish and chips wrapper. These days they no longer used newspaper to wrap food, but the fish were just as dead and they didn't give a damn. To those who bothered to attend the briefing, Bliss fed the bare essentials, omitting any of the leads that had not led to direct contact so far. He concluded the briefing by promising more updates on Monday, and could almost taste their apathy. Sheryl Craig, the rag-doll lookalike who worked for the *Evening Telegraph*, attempted to hijack the briefing again, but she was not subtle about it and Bliss cut her short. He wasn't playing her games anymore.

In a hurry to get away for the weekend, Sykes was unusually civil. Though his attention seemed to be focused elsewhere, he asked to be brought up to date with the case. Bliss briefly outlined everything they had, leaving aside the path that led to Weller. The super seemed satisfied, if as unenthusiastic as the press, with the way things were going. The conversation was all business, mostly courteous. They traded a couple of mild insults, but it was pretty innocuous. Sykes demanded he be kept in the loop, and Bliss agreed to do so. They both knew he would do no such thing. The lack of genuine interest was evident in the super's demeanour.

Cold case. Dead fish.

Bliss spent much of Friday evening watching *Aliens* and *Blade Runner*. He'd seen both movies so many times that every scene was branded upon his mind, each piece of dialogue pre-empted by his own lips. It didn't matter that no surprises lay in store; for him, being absorbed by the storylines and characters was more than enough. Bliss loved the genre. He'd heard that Peterborough had its own sci-fi association, and, though mildly interested in what they might have to offer a man of his tastes, he had imagined it to be populated by nervous, sweaty men who could speak Klingon better than they could English. He wasn't one for clubs, anyway.

When the movies were over, Bliss still wasn't in the least bit tired, but he had no intention of taking another sleeping pill. For an hour or so he sat playing his guitar, headphones plugged into the amplifier so as not to annoy the neighbours. As with everything else in his life, music had taken a back seat following his wife's death, but during his suspension from work he'd taken the Ibanez out of mothballs and got his fingers loose once more. He worked his way through familiar numbers, closing his mind off to everything except the chords and scales. It felt good to lose himself in something so heartfelt.

In bed before midnight for the first time in many weeks, feeling relaxed and clear of thought, Bliss knew nothing more until he woke shortly before seven. It was the first decent night's sleep he'd had in months. Strange that it had come now, at a time of such heightened stress in both his personal and professional life. The weekend opened up before him.

His eggs now devoured, half-eaten cold toast scraped into the bin, Bliss was washing the dishes when the phone rang. He looked at it coldly before answering its summons. It had to be work, and that could only mean either a breakthrough on the case or trouble.

He was wrong.

'I've been waiting for you to call me,' said Emily Grant without preamble.

Bliss searched his mind rapidly. Couldn't recall arranging anything of the kind. 'Sorry. I've been busy with the investigation, as you might imagine. Remind me why I was supposed to call.'

'It's not that you were supposed to. More, I was hoping you would.'

A breath caught in his chest. 'Oh. I see.'

'Don't sound so wary, Jimmy. I don't bite. Not in a bad way, at least.'

He chuckled. Emily Grant had an admirably direct way about her. Even stretching so far as to make the first move, it seemed. After a moment's pause, Bliss pushed caution aside.

'I'm glad to hear it. Look, Emily, I was just about to head out for a walk. Would you like to meet Bonnie and Clyde?'

He heard her laugh, and could immediately picture Emily's beaming face. It was a pleasant image. 'Who could resist such an intriguing offer?' she asked.

They arranged to meet at Orton Mere. Emily wore a dark blue puffa jacket to ward off both the chill and the threatened rain if it fell. Beneath the jacket she had on a black sweater and dark blue jeans. She looked good. Smelled good, too, a light, citrus fragrance that hung in the cold air around her. Emily made a fuss over the Labs, who repaid her interest with plenty of huffing and lapping tongues. When the dogs finally lost interest, Bliss and Emily strode side by side towards the mere.

'Is this how you usually spend your days off?' she asked him.

Bliss nodded. 'As often as I can. The dogs are good company. How about you? What do you get up to in your spare time?'

'Oh, I'm a lot lazier than you. My only real hobby is painting, and I rarely get around to that these days. I read a lot, and I like my music.'

'Sounds like a decent way to pass the time. Let me guess: Danielle Steel and classical?'

Emily turned to him and smiled. 'You're way off with the books. I'm a crime and thriller buff. Patricia Cornwell, Nelson DeMille, that sort of thing. You got the music right, though.'

Bliss admitted his liking for sci-fi, and confessed that his musical tastes tended to revolve around AOR; elevator music.

'Please tell me you're not a Trekkie,' she said, frowning.

'No. I'm not. More *Star Wars* than *Star Trek*.'

'I'm not sure that's an improvement, actually.'

On Osier Lake to their left, a couple of men stood on a narrow wooden jetty with remote control devices in their hands, guiding small power boats over the calm surface, disturbing the wildlife. Bliss didn't care for the noise they made, the high-pitched racket sounding like duelling lawnmowers. Ducks and geese ran amok around the perimeter of the lake, leaving behind a trail of feathers and crap.

Away in the distance, a flock of crows emerged in a black, restless cloud from a tall oak tree, bursting into the murky grey sky like an exploding firework. The trees, hedgerow and foliage were starting to look barren, and the parkland was taking on a completely different guise as autumn waved goodbye. The naked, skeletal appearance of winter was looming and, as he did every year, Bliss envied bears their hibernation period.

At a leisurely pace they followed a sign for Thorpe Meadows, cut across the Nene Valley railway line, and made their way towards the river. Bliss walked the dogs here often, so the route was familiar to him and the Labs. Right now he was feeling more than a little bit awkward, tongue-tied like a pimply-faced juvenile, yet at the same time eager to fill every silence with words, no matter how inane. When they emerged through an overgrown section of path, two distinctive sounds hit them at the same time: river water gushing through the mere, and parkway traffic thundering across the flyover that spanned the river and the railway line.

As he and Emily approached the mere and lock, a couple of young men in full protective wetsuits slipped their canoes down the swirling, surging water – a six-foot drop in two levels – the mini white-water rapids providing a few seconds of adrenaline rush. Bliss watched them work, circling and shifting between slalom strips hung from thin wire attached to rust-tipped poles on either side of the river. The water tried to trick them and suck their vessels under, churning wildly. It was hardly Niagara Falls, so they made it easily.

Standing on the grass and gravel bank of the river, Bliss pointed out a fleet of boats moored alongside a long row of summer houses, the rapid flow of the Nene river urging the wooden and fibreglass hulls this way and that. He inclined his head towards them.

'Listen,' he said. 'Tune out the sound of the mere and you can hear the mooring posts creak and groan as they bear the strain. Such a peaceful sound, I always think. Close your eyes and you could be anywhere.'

The paintwork applied to newer boats somehow managed to gleam in the meagre sunlight, and a few flags hung limp against their poles, stirred occasionally by a light breeze. To Bliss they looked like wounded birds making vain attempts to fly.

'Do you like the water?' he asked Emily.

She shrugged and pulled her jacket tight around her. 'From a distance. I love the sound it makes, and I enjoy the sight of waves crashing in to shore, or even the stillness of a lake, but water itself frightens me.'

'Me, too. I can swim, and I don't mind splashing around in a pool. But I panic if my head goes beneath the water.'

Emily nodded, giving a mock shudder. 'The very thought terrifies me.'

They continued across a narrow steel bridge, the river pulsing beneath their feet. On the far bank they turned left past a line of leaning fence posts whose strands of rusty barbed wire no longer formed a threatening barrier. Together they cut along a well-worn track known as the Nene Way, which first expanded to a wide stretch of open ground that formed part of the Thorpe Wood gold course, before narrowing so much that only one person at a time could make their way through. To their right along the trail lay some tall, dense undergrowth that grew deeper still as it reached a substantial thicket into which Bonnie and Clyde had long since disappeared.

'Are you glad I called?' Emily asked him, fastening her jacket zipper and pulling it halfway up. The temperature had dropped a couple of degrees in the last twenty minutes.

Bliss didn't even have to think. 'Yes. Yes, I am.'

'Are you sure? You seem a bit uncomfortable.'

He was unhappy at being so obvious, but grateful to Emily for raising the issue. He felt awkward, and was glad of the opportunity to speak about it.

'I suppose I am. It's been a long time since I did anything like this.'

'Penny wasn't at all certain how you'd react. Apparently you have a lot on your mind.'

'Well, that's true enough. But I do get some time to sit back and relax.'

'Hmm. She said you'd say that, but doesn't believe you're capable of switching off. She also said you may not be ready to see anyone just yet.'

'Penny says too much.'

'Ah, but is she right?'

'Perhaps,' he acknowledged with a slight dip of the head.

The truth was, he couldn't be sure. He hadn't been looking for a relationship with anyone, no matter how short term, but this one had sought him out. And while he didn't expect anything substantial to come of it, right now he was feeling good about being with someone again.

Emily hooked an arm through his. 'Is this okay?' she asked, and when he nodded she gave a broad grin. 'You know, Jimmy, I'm a patient woman, so I'm willing to give you time. You might just be worth it. But I'm a really good listener, and I do want to get to know you better. I can sense your anxiety, and I understand that you have issues. I suppose what I'm saying is… give me a chance.'

The dogs came racing back, hair extended, tongues flapping. 'They do this all the time,' Bliss explained, as they sped off again. 'They come and check on me every few minutes. I've never quite worked out whether they're concerned about me, or worried that I might've buggered off and left them.'

'I would think it's a bit of both. How long have you had them?'

'Since they were pups. Five years now.'

'They're sweet. A bit crazy, though.'

'As nutty as squirrel shit.'

She laughed. 'Did you and your wife choose them together?'

His heart skipped a beat or two. Bliss actually felt the lurch. It felt peculiar talking about his wife while walking arm in arm with another woman. In his mind he pictured the day Bonnie and Clyde had first entered his life.

'No, Hazel got them from the RSPCA when I was at work one day. It was one of those impetuous moments, you know? She saw them, they were cute. It was madness because we both had full-time jobs, but I think they were meant to be our surrogate children.'

They stopped walking, stood for a while by the river's edge, gazing upstream as the flowing water slipped by just below their feet. Bliss peered at a grey sky that seemed to be lowering with each passing minute, pale light being squeezed from it. The day was cold, chilled by the wind, but for the moment it was keeping the rain at bay. Not for much longer, he feared.

He waved a hand at a clutch of boats moored opposite. 'Do you like the blue one?' he asked.

Emily nodded. 'It's very nice. It looks quite old.'

'It is.' The fifteen-year-old, sixteen-foot cruiser bobbed in unison with the other vessels around it. Its fibreglass hull had lost its lustre, but the royal blue paintwork stood out from its close neighbours. 'I bought it because it's my team's colours. Chelsea colours.'

'It's yours?' Her voice contained both excitement and surprise. She laughed and shook her head. 'Somehow I didn't imagine you to be a sailor.'

'I'm not. I saw it a few months back when I was walking the dogs, and the next day the owner was on board. We got chatting, he told me she was up for sale, I made an offer, he accepted. It was as easy as that. I've never moved it away from its berth. I hope to one day, but for now it's just a place to get away from it all.'

Emily's hand tightened around his arm. 'From what exactly? The job? The past?'

'From both, probably.'

'Maybe you'll take me out on your maiden voyage.'

'Maybe I will. Let's hope it does better than the Titanic.'

'I don't imagine there are too many icebergs around here.'

'No.' Bliss tried to inject some levity into his voice, but his thoughts had unravelled once more.

'Hey, what's up?' Emily asked, squinting up at him. 'You were relaxed a moment ago, now you're wound tight again.'

'Sorry. My fault. Stupid really, but *Titanic* was Hazel's favourite film.'

Bliss shrugged. He knew he lived his life with one foot in the present, the other dragging its heel in the past, making it difficult to ever consider stepping into the future. But the mind had an uncanny habit of throwing up unbidden memories when you least expected them, and sometimes even chance remarks had the capacity to inflict an ageing wound.

Emily was nodding. The breeze had reddened her cheeks and the tip of her nose. 'I felt you tense up when I asked the question about your wife earlier. It's obviously still very much a raw nerve with you. If you don't mind me saying, though, three years is an unusually long period of mourning.'

Bliss peered at her, eyebrows arched. 'You are direct, aren't you?'

She hiked her shoulders. 'I find it cuts through any awkwardness.'

'I think it's probably the way she was taken from me,' he said eventually. For a moment he was drawn back, seeing himself returning home late from work, creeping up the stairs, taking care around suspect floorboards, moving silently into the bedroom, trying not to waken Hazel, managing to climb out of his clothes without stumbling, unconsciously wondering at the odd odour permeating the air around him, and then his bare feet slipping in his wife's blood…

'Penny told me your wife was murdered.' Emily shook her head. 'I can't imagine how you must have felt.'

'Particularly when I was the prime suspect for quite some time afterwards.'

'My God!' A hand shot to her mouth. 'How awful.'

'It's the nature of the beast. The "Detecting for Dummies" guide tells us to always suspect the husband or boyfriend first. If you happen to be one of those *and* you claim to have found the body, well…'

'But they caught this man, yes? The man who murdered your wife?'

He shook his head. 'It's complicated, Emily. Not something I like discussing. My wife was murdered by someone she knew. Someone we both knew. Once I realised who was responsible, it was obvious to me that he would never be charged. And he never has been.'

Bliss felt Emily's fingers dig into the meat of his arm. 'No wonder it won't let go of you,' she said.

'No. *I* won't let go of *it*. I know my wife is gone, and I accept the fact that she's never coming back. But pushing Hazel to the back of my mind would be an insult to her memory. That may sound stupid after all this time, but it's the way I feel.'

'It doesn't sound stupid at all. You two obviously had something very special together. I'm sorry, Jimmy. I should never have brought it up.'

He took her hands in his. 'Hey, listen. You've met Bonnie and Clyde, we're out here together, I'm having a good time, and that's a promising start, right?'

Emily took a breath. 'Absolutely. Look, Jimmy, about your wife and this whole situation. Penny warned me I might have to walk on eggshells, but I truly had no idea how deep this ran with you. It was crass of me to have brought it up so soon. God, we barely know each other and here I am rooting around in your misery. I won't ask about it anymore, I won't push. In fact, if you'd rather I left you alone, I'll walk away now with no hard feelings whatsoever.'

Bliss closed his eyes for a moment. Slithering through Hazel's blood had been only the start of the horror. It was something he would carry with him for the rest of his life. But while forgetting was not an option, moving on had to be. He stepped forward and drew Emily close.

'I don't want you to leave,' Bliss told her. He heard the tremor in his voice. 'You're right, we don't know each other well. But I'd like to see what we can do about that. I can't promise you all of me, Emily. Not right now. But I can promise you trust and honesty.'

The light returned to her eyes. She nodded. 'Who knows where this might lead, Jimmy? It may be nothing, but it may be something we can enjoy, even if only for a short while. But despite my insensitivity, at least we seem to have taken a step in the right direction.'

'I'm glad we did,' Bliss told her. 'And I'm very glad you called.'

It felt good to say the words. Better still to mean them.

FIFTEEN

The Peterborough United football stadium was located in the centre of the city, a couple of hundred yards from the Nene river. While its pitch in the nineteen sixties had once been favourably compared with the famous Wembley turf of that era, the ground itself was basic and functional and several decades out of date, little more than tin sheds hunched over lush green grass. As a Chelsea supporter since the age of eight, and an all-round fan of the game, Bliss knew enough about the Peterborough club to understand that they were in decline. He was unsurprised, therefore, to find the place like a graveyard even on match day. When he pulled into the car park, he yanked on the handbrake and sat for a few moments to reflect on how the day was panning out.

Less than half an hour earlier, he and Emily had been making their way back to their vehicles when his mobile interrupted what had become a pleasant day laced with all kinds of possibilities. It was Mia Strong, one of the few detectives assigned to Saturday duty.

'Sorry to bother you on your day off, boss,' she said, her voice as perky as ever. 'Only I thought you'd want to know that we've tracked down Gordon McAndrew.'

McAndrew. Bliss ran the name through his internal databanks. The second person to dial triple nine the night Jane Doe was murdered. *Probably* murdered, he had to remind himself. So far everything they had was circumstantial. What they lacked was clear, hard evidence. Perhaps this was their opportunity to obtain some.

'Good job,' he told her. 'Has anyone spoken to him yet?'

'No, boss. He's at work. He's a groundsman at Peterborough United, and he'll be there until after the match this evening.

I'm duty officer here, so I can't up and leave just for a witness interview, and we haven't got anyone else available today.'

He heard the unasked question. Didn't blame her for trying it on. Agreeing to see the witness himself, Bliss killed the line and made his apologies to Emily. She smiled at him and raised a placatory hand.

'I understand. A policeman's lot and all that.'

'It could wait,' he admitted. 'But I'd rather it was out of the way come the Monday morning briefing.'

'Really, Jimmy. It's all right. Honestly. I watch *Frost* and *Morse*. I know you policemen have little or no private lives.'

'And you're still interested?'

'I am.' Emily nodded enthusiastically. 'Very much so.'

Bliss was still grinning to himself as he climbed out of the car and headed towards the main stadium doors. He had to admit that, despite many initial misgivings, spending time with the Bone Woman had been a pleasurable experience. They'd agreed to him calling her later, perhaps arranging a Sunday dinner somewhere. Work permitting, of course. After waving her goodbye, he'd dumped the Labs back home and then sped towards the city centre.

He found himself in a surprisingly smart reception, and flashed his ID to an Asian woman who sat behind a sweeping limed-oak counter. There were several large photos arranged neatly on the walls in the entrance area, teams and managers going back decades. Bliss thought the trophy room was likely to be smaller than his own toilet at home. The receptionist directed him out onto the pitch, where Gordon McAndrew stood forking the turf around one of the penalty areas, in preparation for an expected deluge later in the afternoon. Bliss marched over, the pitch sucking at his shoes, and held out his warrant card as the man glanced up.

'Police?' McAndrew said in obvious disgust, throwing his head back as if in physical pain. His face screwed up into a tight scowl. A knot of veins in his neck appeared from nowhere. 'Not again. What did I do this time, pal? Fuck your dog?'

'Well, if you did,' Bliss replied casually, 'the other one will be very jealous and you'll have to apologise. If you ask him nicely he might let you get away with licking his balls.'

McAndrew took a step backwards, eyes narrowing. 'What kind of filth are you?' His voice was pure Gorbals: harsh and almost unintelligible.

'One who'd rather be sitting in the Shed at Stamford Bridge than standing out here in the cold with you. Now, can I ask the questions I came here to ask?'

Wiry and flame haired, the Scotsman was all taut muscle and barely controlled aggression. So pale he was almost blue, the man's thick nose glowed red from both the cold and, Bliss guessed, a fondness for alcohol. McAndrew jabbed the soil with his fork.

'I didn't do nothing,' he snarled, turning away. 'That's all I have to say.'

'"Anything". You didn't do *anything*. Mr McAndrew, I hate double negatives almost as much as I hate you fucking Sweaties. Now, I'm not here to question you about any crime you may have been involved in. I'm here to ask you about something you were a witness to.'

'A witness?' The man shook his head. 'I didn't see nothing, either.'

Bliss gave an exasperated sigh and kicked at the turf. A few yards away, ground staff were fitting a net to the goalposts, and in the stands other staff were making running repairs to seating. There was something sad about a stadium bereft of supporters. He focused once more on the witness.

'Sixteen years ago you were living in a hostel in Fletton. You phoned to report someone being hit by a car.'

This time McAndrew left the fork standing upright in the turf. He turned to face Bliss, brow creased into horizontal furrows. 'Bloody Hell! Who are you, the fucking ghost of Christmas past?'

Bliss had to concentrate hard to understand what the man was saying. People like McAndrew ought to come with subtitles, he thought.

'I'm just here to ask you about what you saw that night, Mr McAndrew. Please don't make this a pain in the arse for me, or instead of treating you like a witness I'll start treating you like a suspect. Police brutality is still very popular in this city. Particularly with me.'

'Suspect? For what? Fuck all happened. Aye, I remember that night, and I did my bit by phoning you lot.'

'Yes. You did, and we're grateful. You took the time. You bothered. So take some time and be bothered now.'

The Scotsman gave a stifled moan. 'All right. But there's fuck all I can tell you now that I didn't tell your pals at the time. I heard the car, heard something being hit, saw something in the gutter and the car spread across the road.'

'The car was askew, but on its correct side of the road. Yes?'

'Aye.'

'Was the vehicle facing the pavement or the centre of the road?'

The man chewed on his lower lip. Harsh acne scarring dominated both cheeks. 'Pavement, I think. Your pals didn't ask that one.'

'Just now you said that when you first looked out of the window you saw something in the gutter. Sixteen years ago when you made that call you seemed certain it was a body.'

'Och, I was bladdered. It was all a blur. Your pals found fuck all on the road, and then when they smelled the booze on me…' He shrugged.

Bliss thought about that for a moment. Recalled the case notes. 'Tell me, who suggested you might be too drunk to recall the incident clearly? Did you tell the officers, or did they tell you?'

The man's eyes switched away. 'It was a long time ago, pal.'

'I know that. But I really would appreciate your help, Mr McAndrew.' He wondered about the witness's reluctance to assist, guessing it might be more than an aversion to the law and its enforcers.

The groundsman breathed heavily through a nose that looked to have been broken on more than one occasion. He seemed to struggle with his memory for a few seconds. Then he nodded and wagged a finger.

'Oh, aye. That's right. It wasn't that night. All they did was take a few notes and then left me to go on and search the road. It was a few days later that one of them came back and spoke to me again.'

'Really?' To Bliss's recollection a second interview was not recorded in the case notes. At least, not on the printout that Mia Strong had pulled up. 'Can you remember what was said?'

'No.' Again the eyes focused on something in the distance.

Bliss didn't believe him. There was something evasive and shifty about the man. 'It was sixteen years ago, McAndrew. Whatever was said then is water under the bridge. If someone leaned on you, they're no longer a threat. It's me you're answerable to now, and I don't let go of things easily.'

This time the man's gaze found his. He had the eyes of a trapped animal that knows its time has come. He nodded once.

'Aye. All right. The copper told me nothing had been reported, that if there had ever been an accident, no one had been hurt, and that if I didn't change my story they'd have a shitload of paperwork to do all for nothing. Your pal made it clear that I was going to suffer for that. He said all I had to do was make another statement saying I must have been out of my head on something. I dinnae want any trouble, you know?'

Bliss nodded. 'I think I do. And the officers, they were the same two who investigated your initial emergency call?'

'Well, one of them stayed in the car while the other one did all the talking. But aye, they were the same ones I spoke to that night.'

'Can you remember the officer's name? The one you spoke with that second time?'

'No. No chance. But he was a Glaswegian like me.'

***

So Weller and Hendry had made a point of visiting McAndrew again. Only this time, Weller had remained in the car while Hendry applied pressure to have McAndrew change his version of events. As Bliss negotiated his way out of the car park and back onto London Road, he worked it through, trying to see the pieces being slotted together, the various strands being traced back to a single act. It seemed likely that Weller and Hendry had attended the scene genuinely following the emergency calls, but on finding no sign of an accident, and certainly no evidence that someone had been struck by a vehicle, they had approached the incident with little enthusiasm. Shortly afterwards, however, someone had got to them. Someone who wanted to make sure the incident was forgotten about altogether.

Bliss sat in traffic built up ahead of some road works on Oundle Road. He switched on the radio which was tuned to the local station, Hereward FM. Traffic updates featured regularly, particularly on Saturdays when the city centre was at its busiest. A Coldplay cut was fast approaching its keyboard outro, so Bliss kept one ear open for the end.

He thought about what to do next. McAndrew's information hadn't given the inquiry the injection of pace he'd hoped for, but the subtle nuances related to the way Weller and Hendry had handled things suggested either a lack of professional integrity or a cover-up of some description. Bliss couldn't see Bernard Weller dumping an inquiry for no good reason, though it was possible that he'd been persuaded. But why, and by whom? Those questions remained unanswered.

Bliss considered driving across to Thorpe Wood and pulling out all the case notes again, but Mia Strong would look to get involved and he wasn't sure he wanted to bring her in on this just yet. For the time being he didn't want Weller's involvement even known of let alone discussed, because it was the single strand that he was determined to keep flying on its own. Bliss was becoming more and more convinced that the line he, Bobby and Penny were following was the one that would ultimately lead them to the place they needed to go.

Whether they would like it once they got there was another matter entirely.

SIXTEEN

Everyone has their secrets. Even policemen. For some it is a reliance upon either drink or drugs, whichever one makes them forget. Others are on the take, or run up huge debts that spiral out of control. Some make use of the prostitutes they deal with, or remove stolen goods for themselves during a raid on known fences. Jimmy Bliss had an acquaintance with booze that was still recent enough to recall in vivid detail, but he had never touched drugs. He'd never taken a pay off in his life, either, though a few had been offered.

But Bliss did have secrets. Secrets seared into his very soul. Like the fact that he and his wife had been sexual swingers for the final year of their marriage. Hardly something you discuss in the staff canteen, or chat about over a cosy beer after a hard day's coppering. As secrets go, it was a big one. As intimate as they come. Squalid, perhaps. Deadly, too. Because ultimately this lifestyle choice had led to Hazel's murder.

Bliss thought about this as he sat in the smoky lounge of a bar tucked away beneath a small baker's shop in an alley that ran between two of the main pedestrianised roads in the city centre. He sat alone at a perfunctory table, working on a pint of Old Peculiar, while he waited for the evening's musical attraction to appear on a tiny stage wedged into the corner of the subterranean bar. The band covered work by a number of guitarists Bliss admired, and he'd been looking forward to this evening for a number of weeks. Whilst waiting for the set to get going, his thoughts had become introspective. He wondered why he hadn't called Emily and asked her to join him. The obvious and immediate answer caused further reflection: these were the sort of moments he had once shared with his wife, and Bliss had no idea how he might react with someone else alongside him.

Though their musical tastes had been a little different, Bliss had appreciated Hazel's commitment to sharing that part of his life. Music was in his soul, and she had often sat in their living room listening to him play his guitar. Many dim-lit evenings had seen the pair of them curled up together on a sofa, while his CDs played softly in the background. It was almost impossible for him now not to hear a piece of music without associating it with his wife. Perhaps this evening had been a bad idea after all, he thought.

Mood somewhat soured, Bliss could then think of nothing else but Hazel, and the course of events that had led him to this solitary existence. He and his wife had become friendly with a couple Hazel worked with at a central London advertising agency. Their friendship with Darren and Lucy Martin had entered its sixth month when Hazel came home one night and told Bliss about their friends' alternative lifestyle. At first Bliss had laughed it off, but had also fleetingly imagined what it would be like to see Lucy spread eagled on a bed with her clothes off. Even screwing her. The imagination was a powerful thing, almost entirely without conscience.

At first there was no real encouragement to join in, but when Bliss and Hazel were enjoying dinner one evening at their friends' house, Darren showed them both a photograph of him and Lucy posing naked with another couple. There was nothing sordid or unsavoury about it, and all four seemed perfectly relaxed and at ease with what they were doing. Later that night as Bliss and his wife lay together in bed, Hazel suggested going to the next swingers' night. Just to watch, at first. But to join in if they felt like it. They agreed that if either of them felt it was wrong, they would stop and never talk of it again.

Though astounded by the suggestion, Bliss was also excited by the prospect. There was no jealousy; it was only sex, after all. Not love, not a relationship. It quickly went on to become a significant part of their lives. Once every few weeks they joined other couples in losing their inhibitions, exploring possibilities, pushing sexual boundaries. Then one night as they lay on the living room sofa together, Hazel told him she wanted to stop. Bliss remembered being both surprised and relieved, realising for the first time that he had been on the verge of suggesting the very same thing. They never discussed it again.

Less than a month later, Hazel was torn from his life.

It was five days after her death that Bliss discovered his wife's reason for wanting to quit the swingers' club. Lucy Martin called him up unexpectedly and told him that one of the men Hazel had been having sex with had become obsessed with her, and that he had been pestering Hazel to change her mind and continue attending the events. He then tried to persuade her to have an affair with him outside the swingers' environment, something she had refused to do. Less than a week before she was murdered, Hazel told Lucy Martin that the man's pursuit of her was becoming aggressive, and that she feared him.

The day after Lucy's tearful confession, Bliss used his contacts within the swingers' community to track the man down, only to learn that he was a Detective Inspector stationed in Croydon. By now entirely convinced that the DI had killed Hazel, Bliss waited patiently for several days until he was able to confront the man alone and on neutral territory.

A burst of applause plucked Bliss from his reverie. He blinked a couple of times, and through the smoke-filled gloom saw the band wandering onstage and hoisting their instruments. His own hands now almost frozen around his pint glass, the hubbub of low voices becoming obscured once more by the past, Bliss dragged his thoughts away from the present and back to that night of violent confrontation.

'My name is Jimmy Bliss,' he'd told the man, whose eyes gave him away in an instant. Bliss knew then, without even asking, that this fellow policeman had murdered Hazel.

To his recollection, Bliss had only ever wanted to take the lives of two men: the first was a paedophile who walked free from court due to a break in the chain of evidence, having raped and tortured several children between the ages of eleven months and seven years. The second was the man who had ended the life of the only woman Bliss had ever loved.

But there was a difference between wanting to kill, and doing so. Wanting to was, perhaps, a very human reaction to extreme behaviour bordering on evil. Doing so was to take that final step across a line where morality and justice merged to form a smudged and indistinct boundary.

The fierce beating he administered was a release of rage and grief – something he had never once regretted. Neither did he regret leaving the man alive, though beaten badly enough to require an extensive stay in hospital. The killer had already taken away the most precious thing in his life. Bliss wasn't going to allow the man to remove what remained.

Bliss brought himself back into the bar lounge, released a deep breath and cuffed a stray tear from his eye. He'd come out this evening to enjoy himself, to relax and blow away some cobwebs, but had instead allowed melancholy to prevail. A solemn end to what had been a pretty good day. He'd spent the afternoon chilling out in front of the TV watching sports. First a decent game of rugby between the Leicester Tigers and Northampton Saints, and then Sky Sports News for the latest football news. Chelsea beat Everton convincingly, Peterborough lost for the fourth game in a row. He'd then called Emily and made arrangements for the following day, feeling like an awkward teenager once more. At that point the promise of a pleasurable evening lay ahead of him.

The band launched into 'Room 335', a Larry Carlton cut that Bliss had been trying to learn recently. He nodded in time with the beat, tapped a hand on the table, moved the fingers of his left hand as if fingering notes on a fret board. He did his best to immerse himself in the music, trying to let it seep in through his pores, but the damage was already done. After only two more songs, Bliss drained his glass and left the bar.

His head was buzzing as he drove home, but that was the after-effects of the smoky lounge and the plague of terrible memories. Nothing to do with his disease this time. Not even that had managed to force its way through today.

So here he was, about to sob uncontrollably and blind himself to the dark streets. More than three years on and still every time he thought about his wife, the tragedy of her death, it reduced him to tears and a sense that gathering black clouds of doom would circle above him for the rest of his life.

The lyrics from the chorus to a track by Dream Theatre came to mind:

Once the stone you're crawling under
Is lifted off your shoulders
Once the cloud that's raining over your head disappears
The noise that you'll hear is the crashing down of hollow years.

It was a beautiful song, insisting that a state of utmost misery could be emerged from, but thinking of it now made Bliss realise how hollow and alone he felt, cast adrift from the kind of happiness other people took for granted. Viewing life from a distance rather than experiencing it for himself.

Not for the first time, Bliss succumbed to the weight of misery heaping itself upon him. Warm tears leaked from his eyes, and a low, rumbling moan emerged from somewhere deep inside his chest.

In a perverse way, Bliss welcomed these moments. Though other, better times might lie ahead, for the time being, it was sometimes enough to be reminded that he was still alive.

If not exactly living.

SEVENTEEN

Walking Bonnie and Clyde was the first thing on Sunday's agenda. Instead of taking them over to the mere, he walked the Labs down to the Ferry Meadows country park and once around the largest of the lakes. He'd set out with the intention of walking further, but his body didn't feel up to it. Weariness enfolded him, sapping his energy in a swift and merciless fashion, and there was nothing he could do about it. Fatigue being a major factor with Ménière's, Bliss realised this was an aspect he would have to work on. Mentally as well as physically.

As he showered and then dressed in preparation for his lunch date with Emily, Bliss's mind drifted back to the night before. Speaking with Emily earlier in the day about his wife had drawn Hazel close to the forefront of his thoughts for the first time in a while. The evening at the bar had been a washout, a huge disappointment. His mood upon returning home had become increasingly morose, and instead of watching something from his vast DVD collection, he'd wallowed in memories stirred by music from the past couple of decades. Sitting in his living room, with the curtains drawn and the stereo on low, was like being trapped inside a time machine. Close your eyes and you were taken back, remembering where you were when you first heard a particular song. Who you were with. Favourites shared.

He was certain he would dream about Hazel, and knew it wouldn't be a pleasant experience.

Each time it was the same. Bliss found himself looking up through his wife's eyes, his body hers, seeing the man raping her, yet at the same time feeling the penetration; seeing the man come at her with a knife taken from their own kitchen drawer, feeling the pain of each attack; seeing the gleam of excitement in the man's eyes, feeling the life ebb away from her; seeing himself in place of the man responsible for Hazel's murder, feeling his wife's sense of betrayal.

Bliss woke in a cold sweat. Panting. Not like they do in movies where people sit up abruptly, but with his head pressed back into the pillow, weighed down by fear and outrage. He wept for a few minutes, the horror of it all too much to bear, yet unable to stop himself from remembering. On the night of Hazel's murder he'd realised what his bare feet were slipping in long before he saw the dark, slick pool of blood. He'd known what he would find on the floor by the bed long before his eyes came to rest on his wife's open eyes and terribly abused body. He'd recognised the shrill sound of the scream rising up from the very centre of his being long before it emerged from his lips.

He'd reacted as a husband, not as a policeman. A policeman would have secured the scene, protected the evidence. The husband collected up the empty husk of his wife and held her bloody body close, sat that way for very nearly an hour before picking up the phone and making the call. Not once did it cross his mind that he would be called to account over those details: the blood on his clothes, the delay in calling for help. Nothing else had entered his thoughts. His wife was dead. Murdered. Bloody and broken. That's all there was, then, and for a very long time afterwards. Even now.

As Bliss checked his pockets and prepared to leave, he realised that the previous night's mood had gone, had been consigned to the past like so many before it. He had no intention of dwelling on it. There would be more such evenings, and he would handle them in the same way. Accept them for what they were, and move on.

***

At one thirty he met Emily at the Windmill Tavern, just a few minutes' walk from his house. A conservatory-style extension had been added to the old stone building, which was adorned with a lush thatched roof, providing a restaurant that served wholesome, reasonably priced food. Emily was wearing a vivid turquoise sweater and black pinstriped trousers. She looked gorgeous, and today smelled of oranges. They ordered and settled in, Bliss trying to think of the situation as more of a meal with a colleague than a date. That way he might be able to remain calm.

While they waited for their first course, Emily spent a few minutes telling Bliss about her background: bright kid, shy and somewhat lonely, happy, affluent family, decent degree, a love of anthropology, a good deal of time spent studying and working in many countries spread across five continents, culminating in her job at the Flag Fen Bronze Age site.

'Have you been to see the exhibit?' she asked him, just as their food was served.

'No. Sorry. It's just not a subject that interests me.' No sooner were the words out of his mouth than Bliss was cursing himself. It wasn't the best of starts.

Emily appeared unfazed. 'Don't apologise. It's a vocation that seems dull to most people, but the site is an important one. Perhaps the most important of its kind in Europe. But if it keeps drying out we'll lose much of it, I'm afraid.'

'I don't even know how old it would be.'

'Oh, only about three thousand years.'

Bliss was taken aback. 'Really? I had no idea. It must be fascinating if you're into that sort of thing. But isn't it more of interest to archaeologists?'

She nodded, forking some chicken into her mouth. She chewed and swallowed before answering. 'Of course, but that's also my area of interest. They pretty much go hand in hand. Flag Fen itself interests me because of the heritage aspect, but I dare say I'll move on when a good old bone dig crops up.'

'Do you find it easy to do that? Just up sticks and move on, I mean.'

'It's one of the plus points of living on my own.' Emily took a sip of wine.

'You have family though, right? Parents? Don't they miss you?'

'They live in Canada, so we only get to see each other once or twice a year anyway. It means I can move around at will without that emotional pull.'

'Have you ever tied the knot?' Bliss asked, downing some of his own house red.

'Yes. It was a disaster, I'm afraid. As much my fault as his. Married and divorced all within three years.'

'I'm sorry. That must have been tough.'

'Not really. The end was fairly amicable. There's no baggage.'

'I wish I could say the same.'

Emily looked at him, her eyes glistening. 'From just those few brief details you gave me yesterday, I can only say I wouldn't wish such an end on anyone. The fact that it still hurts so much tells me how strong your love was for her.'

Bliss nodded. 'Our life together was everything I'd ever wanted. Well, almost. Having a child, despite what happened to Hazel, would have made it perfect.'

'You decided not to start a family?'

'We couldn't.' The regret was thick in his voice.

'Your wife couldn't have children? How terrible for you both.'

Bliss shook his head slowly. 'No, it's me who can't have children.'

Emily groaned and rolled her eyes. 'Would you excuse me for a moment? I have to go and have both feet surgically removed from my mouth.'

Chuckling, Bliss raised a hand and said, 'Don't worry about it. I came to terms with that situation a long time ago, and you weren't to know.'

'That's kind of you, Jimmy. I must say, though, you don't appear to have had much luck when it comes to your personal life.'

Bliss put away some of his lasagne before responding. It tasted creamy and fresh. 'I have looked at it that way before. Many times, I must confess. But you know, I consider myself lucky to have spent so many happy years with my wife. Thirteen, to be precise. So that's the other side of the coin. The one I prefer to see these days.'

'That's a great outlook to have. I'm a positive person myself, but then I don't think I've been tested in quite the way you have.'

He drained his glass. 'I won't kid you it's been easy. The night it happened, and for so many days afterwards, I didn't think I would ever emerge from the despair. I wouldn't say I wallowed in it, exactly, but it almost sucked me under. Hazel's death changed me, that much I do know. Something like that can't fail to change a person. And three years on I'm different again. I'm becoming whole once more. But you don't forget something like that. You never forget.'

He pushed out a long breath of air, head down, staring at nothing for a while. Still it had the power to overwhelm him. Moments later he felt Emily's hand on his, her fingers moving between his own, interlaced. He looked up into her warm and sad eyes.

'I hope one day we'll be close enough for you to tell me it all,' she said. 'In the meantime, let's enjoy the beginning of what might just be a beautiful friendship.'

'I think I've heard that line before. Something like it, at least.'

'Are you a movie fan?' Emily asked him.

He thought of his large collection of DVDs and smiled. 'You might say that.'

'Maybe we can go and see one together.'

'I'd like that.'

'What sort of thing do you prefer?'

'I have a wide range of tastes. I'm a bit of a sci-fi nerd, as you know, but I love comedies and good drama. Thrillers, too.'

'Then we'll go,' she said. Nodded, as if that made the agreement more firm.

'We will. And soon.'

***

A quick kiss on the cheek was all they exchanged when they went their separate ways after dinner. Bliss drove home and sat in the garden for a while, playing with the dogs. It was a cold day and the air was damp, but he kept his jacket on and paid no attention to the weather. Until the rain came, that is, lashing down with a vengeance in heavy sheets, as if making up for being delayed. Bonnie and Clyde drifted into the dining room where their beds were, leaving Bliss to sit alone in the kitchen, staring out at nature doing its work.

While openly admitting to hating the brutal chill of winter, he loved the rain. For many years as a child he had lived on the seventeenth floor of a tower block in the heart of London's East End, and a balcony had run outside the length of his bedroom. When rain fell, the sound of it slapping off the balcony rail was like a rare form of music, a discordant harmony that both lulled and excited him. Watching the thick droplets mottle the kitchen window now, Bliss was reminded that he had yet to purchase something that had been recommended to him by the RNID – a device much like a clock radio, but instead of music it played a selection of natural sounds designed to help obscure the din of tinnitus. Rainfall was one of the default sounds.

Bliss nursed a tall bottle of IPA beer. There was a time when he'd been capable of putting away several pints an hour in a binge session that might easily last half a day. Hazel had weaned him off the booze, to a point where he could now take it or leave it. He still enjoyed a drink, but never again would he allow it to dominate his life. In the months following Hazel's murder, it would have been the easiest thing in the world to succumb. But the thought of her looking down at him had helped him to steer clear. Virtually. The bottle in his hand was now almost warm, and he tossed the dregs away into the sink.

Around seven thirty he made himself a sandwich and a mug of black Earl Grey tea. He'd just finished both when the phone rang. He thought it might be his mother, perhaps even Emily, but as usual it was work. Only this time the call was welcome.

'I just got a call from DC Gillings,' Penny told him, almost breathlessly. 'Record Archives came up trumps.'

'In what way?' Bliss asked.

'In the best way possible. We know who Jane Doe is.'

EIGHTEEN

The semi-detached house was set in a quiet avenue of similar homes built in the nineteen thirties. Like many of its neighbours it had undergone a few cosmetic changes, but structurally it was pretty much as its architects had set out on their blueprint. Modest and unassuming, the house blended in with its surroundings and seemed content with that.

At just after nine on Monday morning, the avenue's pavements were pretty much empty beneath another dull, overcast sky that had become gradually darker and filled with swollen clouds. It was the kind of weather that made people think twice about venturing outdoors for no good reason.

Bliss gathered his thoughts outside the house while his car's engine cooled. His day had started at seven thirty; he had woken to several minutes of imbalance and dizziness, before the world righted itself just as he stepped into the shower. As a consequence, his mind was still all over the place. At Thorpe Wood, Chandler had confirmed that the name revealed by a missing persons record in archives matched that of one held by the NHS database regarding a steel rod inserted into a female patient's right leg following a motorcycle accident in Norwich.

Since calling Bliss on Sunday evening, Chandler had run the name through their own database and had come up with two hits: one for prostitution and one for a class A drugs offence. The mugshot Bliss had seen in the incident room less than an hour ago revealed a pale young woman with sunken cheeks and hollow eyes, hair thin and lifeless, skin breaking out all over. Bliss could see that with only a minor makeover the girl would be attractive. Even pretty, if the hard edges were smoothed over, though he got

162

a sense that those edges had been hewn on misery and neglect, and would have taken a lifetime to smooth out. He looked at the face for some while, thought of the skull he had seen in the mortuary. His mind morphed the two images, and he suddenly felt weary with sadness.

There was a lot of satisfaction amongst the squad in knowing they had put a name to their victim, but for Bliss this was tempered somewhat by the sensation of light-headedness, of walking through cotton wool. His thoughts were fuzzy, and this was no time for distractions. He'd drawn his attention back to the MisPer statement, and volunteered to interview the person who had made that report.

After a couple of minutes sitting outside the house, Bliss climbed out of his car, walked swiftly up the cracked concrete path and rang the doorbell. Moments later it was answered by a tall woman in her late forties, head peeking around the door. Her eyes looked a decade older than the face they were set in.

'Connie Rawlings?' he asked, holding out his ID out for her inspection.

The woman rolled her eyes when she saw who and what he was. 'It's just a massage parlour,' she said. 'Nothing else. No extras.'

Bliss shook his head. 'I'm a DI, Connie. I don't get involved with taking down knocking shops. It's not why I'm here.'

She'd been around long enough to see the sense in that. 'You here for a freebie, then, love?'

'No. Though I'm sure I'd enjoy every minute. Actually, I'm here to ask you a few questions, that's all.'

'What about?'

He nodded beyond her shoulders. 'Inside would be better, Connie.'

With obvious reluctance she showed him into a small, neat lounge that was spotlessly clean and smelled of berries. Good quality carpet, hi-tech electronics and luxurious furnishings. Providing massages was obviously a decent living. Rawlings wore a cream silk dressing gown and, he guessed, very little beneath. Her ample bosom pushed the shiny fabric almost to bursting point. As she took a seat opposite, the gown rose up to reveal strong, healthy legs, good calf muscles. She was in good shape.

'What's this all about?' Connie Rawlings asked. Her manner was brusque, though not unpleasant. All business.

'Jodie Maybanks,' he told her, checking her face for signs of recognition. Seeing it immediately in those dead eyes.

Rawlings sucked through her teeth. 'Now there's a blast from the past. It's been a while since I thought about her.'

'More than sixteen years since you last saw her,' Bliss pointed out.

She shook her head, eyes scouring the ceiling. Raked a painted fingernail along the groove of her chin. 'Really? That long? Yes, I suppose it must be.' Her gaze drifted back to Bliss. 'What about her?'

'She's dead, Connie.'

Rawlings clasped her hands together and hooked them around her knee, gently swinging her leg back and forth. 'I can't say I'm surprised. She had one hell of a habit. I'm amazed she lasted this long.'

Bliss had been watching the striking woman closely. Her reaction came across as perfectly natural. He had debated how much to reveal during this initial interview, but he decided to lay it all out for her.

'Oh, she didn't last this long. In fact, by the time you reported her missing, Jodie was already dead.'

For the first time, something approaching emotion touched the woman's face. The metronomic movement of her leg stalled. 'Poor cow. It's odd that I didn't get to hear about it, though. News like that usually spreads like wildfire in my… circle of friends.'

'Actually, Connie, we've only just found her. The remains discovered over at Bretton Woods. You may have seen it on the news.'

'Read it in the *Telegraph*, actually. So that was poor Jodie. Shame. She was a lovely kid when she wasn't buzzing.'

As the national press were not on this, Bliss assumed Rawlings had been referring to the local newspaper, the *Evening Telegraph*.

A mobile on a nearby coffee table warbled, vibrating across the slick ash-veneered surface. 'D'you mind?' Connie asked. 'Probably an over-eager punter.'

Bliss shook his head and waved a hand.

Connie pushed a button on the phone and greeted the caller. She listened for a moment before speaking again, the lightness in her voice never touching her eyes. 'Yes, sweetie. It's sixty for thirty minutes, a hundred for a full hour. That's a body-to-body massage, some O without, and a full personal. Yes, ten thirty will be fine. We have a mature woman or a teenager, both with stunning bodies, both busty. Mature? That's fine then, sweetie. We're in Stanground.' She gave out the address.

'Thanks,' she said to Bliss, ending the call. 'I don't like to miss out on a bit of business.'

'No problem. Tell me, though, what exactly *is* body-to-body massage?'

She laughed, easing the harshness of her features. 'We spread oil over our boobs and rub them all over the punter. Bit of a tit-roll, you know?'

'And O without?'

'Oral without a condom.'

'And the full personal would be…?'

'Intercourse, yes.' She laughed once more. 'Fancy that freebie now, do you?'

He ignored the question. 'I take it you're the mature woman?'

'Well, I'm not the bloody teenager, darling.'

Bliss felt himself becoming uncomfortably aroused. Connie Rawlings was a sexy woman, and the thought of what was lying there beneath such a thin layer of material was exciting to him. There were many coppers who would take advantage of their situation, and though he'd been tempted once or twice in the past, it wasn't in his nature. He'd never quite worked out whether that made him a gentleman or a coward.

'So tell me about Jodie,' he said, getting them back on track.

'Well, we were street girls back then, of course. None of this luxury.' She glanced around the room. 'I took Jodie under my wing, that's all. Not much else to tell. How did you track me down, by the way?'

'Fortunately for us you're still at the address we have on record for you. From the last time you were nicked.'

Again a roll of her eyes. Clearly she believed the police ought to be doing something else with their time other than pulling in easy targets such as prostitutes. Bliss thought she had a point.

'Jodie arrived out of the blue one day. Scared shitless, guilty about selling her body, but desperate to feed her habit. I felt sorry for her. Back then I wasn't exactly old and wrinkly myself, but she was still a child in many ways. She told me she'd run away from home when she was sixteen. Never did know where from.'

'Actually it was Downham Market. I suppose if she wanted to run away to a big city not too far from home, it was either here or Norwich.'

Rawlings nodded. 'I could tell the accent was fairly local. She was a real nice girl. Sweet. Kind. Not hard faced or skanky like some of them. Like I said, I took care of her.'

'So you were worried when she went missing?'

'Of course. The way she talked about her home life, I knew she'd never have gone back to her parents. I checked at her bedsit, but she wasn't there. After a few days, me and the other girls decided I should report Jodie as missing.'

Bliss gave a gentle smile. 'I can imagine how that went down at the time. Her being a brass.'

'Yeah. One missing whore being reported by another whore. The cops went through the motions. We weren't expecting much, but we thought we owed it to her to do what we could.'

Bliss pulled a photograph out of his inside jacket pocket. Held it up for Rawlings to see. 'Is this Jodie?' he asked.

The woman nodded once before turning away.

'So when she disappeared off the scene, what did you think might have happened to her?' Bliss asked.

'Street work can be rough. Dangerous.' Her eyes clouded over, almost drawing back protectively into their sockets. Bliss imagined she had some horror stories to tell.

'Didn't you have a pimp?'

'Yeah, but in name only. He took his cut, but did fuck all for us.'

'I'll need that name.'

'Don't bother, he's long dead. Got glassed one night in a club fight and bled out on the floor before the ambulance got to him. Can't say any of us were disappointed on hearing that news. It was then that we all went our separate ways.'

Bliss thought it through. There were really only a couple more avenues to explore. 'Did Jodie have a boyfriend?' he asked.

'No. She was disgusted by herself and what she did. She once told me no one would ever love her. I tried convincing her she was wrong, that if she got herself cleaned up… But those bastard drugs had her completely fucked up.'

'How about regular punters, Connie? Did Jodie ever speak about, or can you think of anyone, who might have wanted to harm her?'

He caught a familiar eye movement. Evasive. Bliss leaned forward, forcing her to meet his gaze. 'Connie, did you know she was pregnant?'

'Jodie?' She shook her head. As she moved, her breasts jiggled beneath her gown. 'I had no idea. How far gone was she?'

'We're not certain. Enough to show, I would've thought.'

'I didn't notice. Honestly, Inspector. She might have bound herself up. Some girls did that when they were in the early stages. Didn't want to put the punters off, you know?'

Nodding, Bliss said, 'Thing is, if she had unprotected sex with a regular punter, and maybe then told the punter about the baby…' He let her fill in the blanks for herself.

Connie sighed and closed her eyes for a moment. 'There were a lot of regulars. Jodie had a fabulous body, even with her habit.

Plus she didn't mind letting them do it without a condom. A lot of blokes got off on that, with AIDS still being seen mostly as the "gay plague" in them days. But there was a man, someone she mentioned more than most. See, he gave her a false name, of course, but she saw his photo one day in a free magazine that came with the *ET*. Turned out he was a top bloke at Jenkins Engineering.'

The engineering company was one of Peterborough's biggest employers, doing business with countries all over the world. Anything stamped with the Jenkins Engineering logo was a respected sign of quality. Someone with such a high profile might well have some sway with one or two influential people.

'Do you remember his name?' Bliss asked, careful not to show his eagerness.

'Yeah. Palmer. Simon, I think. Maybe Stephen. But definitely Palmer. I remember me and Jodie making jokes about it, you know, sort of a play on him jerking off.' Her face clouded over at the memory.

'Okay. We'll look into it. How was Jodie in the days leading up to her disappearance? Did she seem scared, anxious? Was there anything bothering her? Anything on her mind?'

Rawlings barked a harsh laugh. 'You just described the way every prostitute out on the streets feels every hour of every day. I know what you're asking, Inspector, but I didn't even know she was pregnant and I was the closest thing she had to a friend.'

Bliss heard the sadness in her voice. If this woman lacked anything, it certainly wasn't compassion. 'Is there anything else you can think of that might help us, Connie? Anything at all that sticks in your mind about Jodie, her punters, the time she went missing?'

'No. I don't think so. It was such a long time ago.'

For a moment Bliss thought he saw that earlier evasiveness reappear, but when he looked harder her eyes revealed nothing. If there had been a glimmer, they were cold, hard blanks again now.

'Did you know the name of Jodie's dealer?'

'You think she might've fallen out with him?'

It had only just occurred to him, but it seemed like a decent enough theory. 'It's a possibility,' Bliss admitted. 'Any ideas? Could be important.'

'I can't be certain, but I did see her a couple of times with a pusher who was known on the streets as Snake. I don't know if that was coincidence, see Jodie never wanted to talk about that side of her life, but I did see them together.'

The name was unfamiliar to Bliss. 'You still see him around? I know you're not on the streets anymore, but I guess you still go into town shopping occasionally.'

But this time Rawlings shook her head. 'Haven't laid eyes on him for a good few years now.'

It wasn't a problem. He'd run the name past the drugs squad back at HQ. Bliss thanked the woman for her time and got to his feet. There was nothing else he could think of asking. Nothing relevant to the inquiry, at least.

'How young is the teenager, Connie?' he asked as they moved back into the short and narrow hallway, recalling the call she had taken.

'She's twenty-three, but looks eighteen. I'm not into pervs, Inspector Bliss.'

'Aren't they all pervs?'

She frowned. Her disappointment in him obvious. 'I'm surprised at you.'

He held up a hand. 'Sorry. You're right, I do know better. I have nothing against what you do, Connie. Nor the men who visit you.'

'Really?' She folded her arms beneath her breasts, pushing them up, exposing some cleavage. 'Have you ever visited one of us?'

'No.'

'You'd rather use your hand?'

Bliss grinned and waggled his left hand before her eyes, showing her his wedding ring.

'Married men have more need than most,' she said, scoffing at him. 'Twenty years humping the same woman? Some men are looking for something younger, firmer, bigger tits maybe, or even just different. I've had more than one punter tell me that after years of trying to please the wife by making love to her, all they really wanted to do was fuck. To just please themselves. Anyway, Inspector, I think that ring is just camouflage.'

Bliss squinted at her, stunned by her perception. 'What makes you say that?'

'You just don't strike me as a man who has a wife to take care of him. I can't put my finger on it, but you have that air about you.'

He turned the latch and pulled the front door open. 'Well, anyway. I'm sorry if I came across just like all the other arseholes. I really don't have a problem with what you do.'

Connie Rawlings winked at him and smiled. 'I should hope not. And do you really think I didn't notice you shift your legs back in the living room?' She stared blatantly at his crotch. 'Getting a bit perky, was he?'

Bliss had to grin. 'You're a fine-looking woman, Connie. Sue me for being human.'

'Well, give me a bell if you're ever at a loose end, sweetie. I might be nearing my sell-by date, but I'm still better than your own hand any day.'

The heavens had opened up during the past twenty minutes or so, and on a stiff breeze the rain clattered into the house. On the doorstep, Connie Rawlings grew serious. 'I hope you find the bastard who killed Jodie, Inspector. Don't matter what she was or what she did. She didn't deserve that.'

'No.' Bliss took a deep breath. Shook his head. 'I don't suppose she did.'

NINETEEN

While Jimmy Bliss was thinking lustful thoughts about Connie Rawlings, DC Chandler and DS Dunne were interviewing Jodie Maybanks's mother. Now in her late fifties, the woman lived in Norfolk with a man some ten years her junior. The couple worked for a businessman who travelled all over the world, though he had never resided anywhere other than the tiny village of Denver. Nora Maybanks took care of the household, while her partner drove the boss to and from airports and his company's HQ in London's Docklands. They appeared to have an unexacting life in a beautiful setting.

Seated in the main house's grand hand-crafted oak kitchen, Mrs Maybanks dabbed at her eyes with a balled-up tissue and tried to stem the flow of tears. 'I suppose a part of me wondered whether Jodie might be dead,' she admitted, sniffing and wiping her nose with the same wad of Kleenex. 'It was awful when she first left, not knowing what had become of her, but after a while you just accept the fact that she's gone and is hopefully out there somewhere, getting on with the new life she's made for herself.'

Chandler gave her best sympathetic smile. It was well practised, but in this case genuine. 'I realise this must be difficult for you, Mrs Maybanks. I'm sorry to have brought you such bad news.'

And it's just about to get worse, she thought, not relishing having to tell this proud woman that her only daughter had been both a junkie and a prostitute.

As it turned out, she didn't have to.

'Me and her dad did our best for Jodie,' Mrs Maybanks insisted. More tear mopping. 'But she went off the rails when she turned sixteen. It was as if someone flicked a switch inside her head. I mean, she went through the usual teenage troubles, but she was never a bad kid. I think she took up with the wrong sort. Before we knew it, our little Jodie was out of her head on drugs and selling her body to pay for it.'

'Did you force Jodie to leave home, or did she run away?' Bobby Dunne asked.

The woman looked at him defensively. 'Derek, my husband, couldn't live with what she'd become. We both found it very difficult to cope with. There were a lot of arguments, obviously. It was a terrible, terrible time. Derek gave her an ultimatum, and then one day when we got home from work, Jodes was gone. Instead of leaving her friends and kicking her bad habits, she packed up all that she could stuff into a bag and left our lives for good. I think that was the beginning of the end for Derek and me.'

'You say your daughter left your lives for good, Mrs Maybanks,' Chandler said, wondering about this aspect. 'Did you really never hear from her again? No phone call? Not even a letter or postcard?'

'No, nothing.' She put back her head and shook it, a tiny grief-laden breath escaping her lips. 'It was as if she'd vanished off the face of the earth.'

Dunne checked his notes. 'Your husband reported your daughter missing. Did he, or you for that matter, have any idea where Jodie might have gone at that time?'

'All her friends were local to where we lived. Few of them were willing to talk to us, but those who wanted to help thought she'd probably gone down to London.'

Chandler nodded. Many teenage runaways headed for the bright lights of the capital, looking for a life in more exotic surroundings. Mostly what they found was dirt and squalor, pain and misery. She and Dunne spent another twenty minutes covering the basics, but it was clear that when Jodie Maybanks walked out on her parents, she had cut herself off from them completely.

'What happens now?' Mrs Maybanks asked when Chandler told her they were done.

'We need to hold on to Jodie for a while longer. The coroner will eventually make an official announcement and then her remains will be released to you.'

The woman nodded. Dabbed her puffy eyes. 'I hope it's soon. I'd like to bury my daughter.'

I think she's had more than enough of that, Chandler thought but did not say.

When they were through in Denver, Dunne and Chandler visited Jodie's father, who now ran his own mini-cab firm in King's Lynn. Having taken the news of his daughter's murder in stoical fashion, he pretty much related the same tale of woe to them. Had the same answers to the same questions. It was only at the end, as the two detectives were walking out of the tiny office from which Derek Maybanks ran his business empire, that the man broke down.

'I knew it would end this way for her,' he said through a terrible wail, mucus streaming from his nose. 'These fucking wankers who want to legalise drugs should be made to experience something like this, I tell you.'

Thinking of the life Jodie Maybanks had endured, Chandler couldn't bring herself to argue.

***

On his way back to Thorpe Wood from Stanground, Bliss's mind was caught in a whirl he found impossible to control. The information Connie Rawlings had provided was useful, but as his Vectra fought its way through traffic, Bliss found his thoughts wandering from the crime itself.

Nineteen ninety was the year he had met Hazel. On their second date he'd taken her to see Julia Roberts in *Pretty Woman*, a chick flick he'd not been looking forward to yet had enjoyed despite himself. The only other movie he recalled from that year was *The Krays*, a bizarre attempt to dramatise the lives of the violent gangsters by using the Kemp brothers from Spandau

Ballet to play the lead roles. When looking at the cinema screen the eyes saw sharp suits and attitude, but the mind could not veer from silk blouses and mullets. As for the portrayal of the vicious thugs and East End gangland life in general, Bliss had seen more violent things splattered on pub toilet floors.

As the decade began finding its feet, the B52s were extolling the virtues of a 'Love Shack', while Del Amitri were bemoaning the fact that 'Nothing Ever Happens'. In Bliss's mind, the Scottish band were both completely wrong and absolutely spot on at the same time. Hazel had mocked his liking for reflective lyrics, while her love for B52s' version of paradise had simply washed over him. They were compatible in so many ways, but their taste in music had not started off that way.

Nudging the Vauxhall off the parkway and taking the first left off the roundabout, Bliss now shook his head at the clear memories. It was almost as if his life had truly begun that year, that unlike the tortured soul in the U2 song, he *had* found what he was looking for. The eighties had fixated on people finding their inner selves, but Bliss hadn't needed to find himself at all; he'd needed to find someone else, someone with whom he could share his life. Within a month of meeting Hazel, he'd known she was the one.

Back then the cynical Bliss had wondered how no one else saw the irony of celebrating Nelson Mandela's release from prison in the same year that the slaying of Tory MP Ian Gow by an IRA bomb was so roundly condemned. Were acts of terrorism acceptable if your cause was just, Bliss had asked his colleagues at work. Now, he reflected, we have a peace agreement keeping the Irish bombers at bay, while radical Muslims seek to blow the entire western world to pieces. Del Amitri could never have known how right they were.

As Bliss approached HQ, he suddenly smiled at another fleeting glimpse of the past. In his mind he saw his wife's beaming face, in his ears he could hear her laughter as the two of them had almost wet themselves upon learning that Glasgow had become the cultural city of Europe. They'd reflected on the notion that in years to come, Parisians would be seen sitting outside cafés tucking into deep-fried Mars bars, Romans knocking back can after can of Special Brew, and the Swiss swapping their army knives for cut-throat razors.

The swirling mass of his mind turning to darker thoughts, Bliss recalled Hazel's horror at Iraq's invasion of Kuwait, her assertion that Armageddon's origins would be from the Middle East. While politicians applied trade embargos, there were deep rumblings concerning a Gulf war.

Bliss's final thought before pulling into the Thorpe Wood car park was: God, those Del Amitri people were good.

***

The Major Incident Room was thrumming with excitement. While he waited for everyone to assemble, Bliss listened to the sounds, the textures of conversation, ran a studious gaze over faces and, in particular, eyes. There was a moment in every major investigation when something clicked into gear, something that gave the team a pulse all of its own. A single vision, one heart. And here it was again, he thought. Every breath we take from this point on is unified.

'Let's do it then, ladies and gents,' he said, rapping a hand on the desk that sat closest to the incident board. 'We'll begin by presenting everything we know so far. DC Strong?'

Mia was leaning casually against the electronic whiteboard, to which she now referred. 'Just to confirm for those of you on late shift, Jane Doe has now officially been identified as Jodie Maybanks, just twenty years old when she was murdered. A MisPer report from June nineteen ninety was pulled from archives. The report listed Jodie as a street prostitute, who ran away from home when she was sixteen. Subsequent national MisPer requests were made and we came up with a report made by Jodie's parents back in eighty-six. To confirm that Jane Doe and Jodie Maybanks were one and the same, we put some pressure on hospital records and they came up trumps. The rod discovered in Jane Doe's leg was identified as the one inserted into Jodie Maybanks's leg following a serious road accident when she was fifteen.'

'Thanks, Mia,' Bliss said, trying to match her own exuberant smile. 'DS Dunne, what do you have for us?'

Dunne coughed into his hand before speaking. Uneasy in front of an audience, the sergeant nonetheless took it in his stride.

'Mrs Maybanks confirmed information acquired from the boss's source that Jodie ran away from home when she was sixteen and never set foot back there again. Never once contacted her parents, either. Mrs Maybanks puts a lot of blame on her husband for the way he was constantly getting on at Jodie, but did admit that her daughter was out of control. Drugs, drink, boys, stealing. Though obviously distressed, I got the impression she'd been expecting our visit for the past few years. Jodie's parents are now separated, but for my money they're both out of the picture regarding the murder of their daughter. I don't think either parent can take us further with this.'

Bliss nodded. 'Okay. Cheers, Bobby. Now it's my turn. The nineteen ninety MisPer was reported by a Connie Rawlings, street brass, and mother hen to our Jodie. Connie is still plying her trade, though in the far more salubrious surroundings of her own home. According to her, Jodie Maybanks did what she had to do in order to survive the life she'd become accustomed to. That is, getting a fix on a regular basis. Rawlings claims not to have known that Jodie was pregnant, and I believed her.

'Now, we do have a couple of potential leads. Firstly, Connie Rawlings believes Jodie used a pusher who went by the street name Snake. There's no obvious motive here, but as we all know, the drugs business can be fractious. I want this man traced and interviewed. According to Rawlings, Jodie did not have a boyfriend. So, it's not much of a reach to imagine a punter being responsible for the bun in Jodie's oven. This brings us to the second potential lead: Jodie had several regulars by all accounts, but only one name that really stuck and came through. Simon

Palmer, then a high-flying manager at Jenkins Engineering. I checked him out. He's now a director at the same company.'

'I know him, sir,' Mia Strong said. She gave a small shrug. 'Well, of him. He's also head of the Peterborough Chamber of Trade and Industry.'

'Well, whatever he is, he's not above getting a visit from us. I'll handle that one myself. Now then, DC Chandler, please bring us right up to date with the finer details of this investigation.'

'Yes, boss.' Chandler took a step back from the board, taking in the timeline, the incidents, the acquired knowledge. When she looked back around at the team, they were rapt.

'Okay, this is what we believe happened: Jodie Maybanks was run down by a vehicle in June nineteen ninety, but was not badly hurt. She was then dragged into that vehicle and driven the short distance to the lake at Fletton, where she was strangled to death and then buried. Many years later, shortly before the IKEA factory was built, Jodie's remains were exhumed and reinterred in Bretton Woods. We have to assume that the reason for doing so was fear of the body being discovered when the factory and new road system were being constructed. Going back to the murder, the most likely motive is that Jodie was pregnant and had made the mistake of telling the punter responsible. Possibly even blackmailed him.

'So, where do we go from here? Well, for the time being we still have a list of officers who need to be interviewed to see if they can throw any more light on what happened the night Jodie was murdered. We will also cast a wider net for any other reports made that night, just to see if there's any potential connection. And we'll follow up on the drug dealer possibility. But, of course, if our hypothesis is correct, then in Simon Palmer we have a definite suspect.'

'Who is very high profile,' Bobby Dunne pointed out.

Bliss nodded. Felt eyes upon him. Just what he needed when climbing back on the horse. Last time around he'd ended the flourishing career of the head of the local council, a woman gunning to be the city's MP. It wasn't Bliss's fault that her campaign manager had also happened to be a volatile extremist responsible for a whole series of racially motivated murders. Not Bliss's fault, but as the senior investigating officer, his actions had been investigated and called to account by several more senior officers. Only Detective Chief Superintendent Flynn had set aside lofty ambitions and reviewed the case without any form of prejudice. Though ultimately cleared of all but a few minor indiscretions, Bliss now felt the pressure moving in from all sides once more.

'High profile or not,' Bliss said with great deliberation. 'Mr Palmer will be interviewed as a witness who might also be considered a suspect. I'll make sure of that. Meanwhile, DC Chandler will again draw up some actions. I want all remaining interviews completed. I want someone to get me a list of officers involved with the MisPer report by Connie Rawlings. She claimed it was all cursory, so let's tread lightly there until we know more. I also want someone to look into whoever worked on that IKEA building, in particular those workers who would have been there marking out prior to the diggers coming in. I want to know if anyone noticed anything strange, such as a recently dug up shallow grave. Continue with the door-to-door canvassing around Bretton Woods, because we could still do with getting a clearer idea of when that reinterment happened. And let's chase up some finals from forensics if at all possible.'

Bliss leaned forward over the desk, resting on his fists. So far he had resisted telling the squad about the seven day limit Sykes had insisted on, and he saw no reason to add that kind of pressure now.

'We're getting somewhere, people. Wheels have started turning, and there's momentum behind us at last. Let's rip into this between now and five tomorrow afternoon, tear this case apart. I want tomorrow's p.m. briefing to take us as far forward again.'

***

Bliss spent the rest of the afternoon in his office catching up on paperwork. Sykes was ensnared in a meeting with fellow Detective Superintendents from neighbouring areas, something Bliss was grateful for. It kept the man from interfering, which had to be a good thing for everyone involved.

In addition to a computerised case file which was maintained by the efficient data administrators, Bliss kept two of his own paper-based versions. In the first he wrote detailed notes covering every aspect of the investigation that he would happily present to a senior officer upon request. The second was similar, but contained notes relating to his own suspicions and events best kept separate from the official inquiry. In the hours he spent at his desk, Bliss carefully reviewed all three case files. It soon became obvious that, while good progress had been made, there were still many paths this investigation could take. He felt it all slowly coming together, but also had the uneasy sensation that huge chunks were missing.

Bliss decided to end his working day with a visit to Mepal, hoping to interview Simon Palmer, whose home address had been traced within minutes. As that meant driving almost past Bobby Dunne's front door in Whittlesey, Dunne had invited him over for a bite to eat and a drink. It was an invitation he'd been more than happy to accept, having found a warm welcome in the Dunne household on two previous occasions.

Susan, Dunne's small and dumpy wife, wasn't at all fazed at having to feed another mouth at such short notice. She looked like the kind of woman who only ever felt comfortable at home in her kitchen, taking care of her house, her husband, and three lively children. She welcomed Bliss as if he were a regular visitor, the wide smile plastered across her face entirely genuine.

The food a thick, greasy bacon and egg sandwich, smothered in tomato ketchup. Just what Bliss needed. As they took their first bites, Dunne beckoned him out into the back garden and across to his large, weather-worn shed.

'While the missus finishes up and gets the kids bathed and ready for bed, I thought we'd grab this opportunity,' Dunne said to Bliss, tapping his nose.

'Opportunity?'

The big man grinned and pushed at one of the wooden boards in the shed roof. Something clinked. 'When I put this big bugger of a shed together I left a cavity,' he said, taking down a bottle of brandy. 'So whenever I feel like a nip, I come out here to… work.'

Bliss laughed. 'So you've built your own little haven out here. A world away from the wife and kids, eh. Nice one, Bobby. Susan knows nothing about the booze, I take it?'

Dune shook his head. 'Not a clue. You know, I think all the secrets of the modern world can be found in a man's shed.'

The drink was thirty years old, smooth as a baby's backside, and left Bliss smacking his lips in appreciation. A pleasant warmth settled in his stomach. He nodded at the bottle in Dunne's hand, noting the thin coating of dust.

'It looks like you only pull that one out on special occasions,' he said, raising his glass.

'Like when I want to impress the boss.'

'Your work does that, Bobby. No need for bribery. Your evaluation will be every bit as good as it was last year.'

They clinked glasses. 'That's good to know,' Dunne said, his big ruddy face reddening further still. 'So, what do you make of this case, boss? It's one thing for us to run the investigation down all the obvious avenues as we have been, but it's not sitting right with me keeping what we know about Bernie Weller to ourselves. From what we've seen and heard, his role was probably minor. So why would someone want him dead all these years on?'

'Someone has something to hide, Bobby.' To Bliss it was that simple. He'd been in this grim business long enough to understand that people could and would do absolutely anything to protect themselves. 'Weller's involvement might well have been relatively trivial, but at this stage we can't be certain of that. It's possible that he wanted to dig deeper into the reports relating to that accident, but was warned off. Or persuaded.'

'You mean bought off?'

'That's a possibility we have to consider. Look, you, me and Penny will have to sit down and thrash this thing out. Mia Strong, too, if we decide to rope her in. We need to discuss what exactly our plan of action will be behind the scenes of the official inquiry. We also need to be clear about how far we're all willing to take it.'

'That might depend on where it leads.'

'True. Hopefully it's already led somewhere, because Palmer is a real possibility; he has enough clout to make something like this happen, and may well have had deep enough pockets to pay a few people off.'

'If he did put the Maybanks girl up the spout, it's not something he'd've wanted broadcast, that's for sure. Means and motive, I'd say.'

Bliss agreed. 'Now all I need to figure out is if he had the opportunity. Or paid someone else to create one.'

'You want me to come with you tonight?' Dunne asked. 'See if we can't double up on this creep. Tag team him.'

'No, you're all right, Bobby. You spend some time with your family. We've got a lot of work ahead of us, and many late nights to come I would think. Make the most of an evening off. I've got nothing better to do.'

Dunne tossed back his drink and poured them both another. 'One for the road, then, eh, boss?'

'I'm not sure I should.'

'Why not?' Bobby Dunne laughed. 'You're hardly likely to get breathalysed, are you?'

TWENTY

Bliss carved his way across the Fenlands, driving faster than usual where the roads were long and straight, slipping easily through the gears whenever he had to wind his way through a serpentine route around drainage ditches, fields and tiny hamlets. The flat, open landscape was bleak, yet a surprisingly appealing part of the country, as much of a mystery to him as the people who inhabited it.

Rumours of inbreeding were rife out here in these harsh outlands. Bobby Dunne, himself a Fenlander, had once warned Bliss that if he met a girl in a pub out there and she offered to take him home to meet her father and her brother, they might well turn out to be the same person. Bliss had certainly met a few mouth breathers over the past few years, but he saw nothing wrong in their desire for privacy. Rough around the edges and largely unwelcoming people they might be, but they were also dependable and hard-working and had a humour all of their own. Bliss appreciated the countryside surrounding Peterborough far more than the city itself.

The night was dark and moonless, but it was dry and there was no mist. Bliss drove within himself, but a little speed helped to blow away the cobwebs. Normally he would have the CD player belting out, but tonight he wanted to concentrate on his thoughts.

The interview with Palmer had been both brief and unsatisfying. The moment Bliss mentioned Jodie Maybanks, the senior director within Peterborough's largest engineering company ushered Bliss into an office set off the main hallway of his luxurious modern house that stood in what looked like a few prime acres. The office was relatively small and quiet and well away from Palmer's obviously inquisitive wife.

'Just about business, sweetheart,' Palmer called out. His wife stood in an open doorway that led to the kitchen, a dishcloth in her hands, eyes troubled. 'Something that happened at work recently.'

Mentioning business did the trick. Bliss saw the woman's eyes glaze over as she switched off and went back to whatever she had been doing. Bliss politely refused an offer of tea before he and Palmer got down to the matter in hand.

Unless he was an excellent actor, the man was genuinely surprised to hear of Jodie's fate. In his late forties, of average height, portly and balding, Palmer was hardly an imposing figure. Bliss guessed the man had kissed a lot of arses to attain his lofty position, and now had a genuine fear of seeing it all crumble to pieces around him. And all for the sake of dipping his wick.

'Yes, I saw Jodie on a regular basis,' Palmer confessed. No flush crept into his cheeks, but his eyes found something interesting on the floor. 'My wife lacks passion, Inspector, and has no desire to… experiment.'

'I'm not interested in why you felt the need to see Jodie Maybanks,' Bliss told him. 'Only that you were. So tell me, when did you stop paying her for sex?'

Palmer swallowed and turned his head away, eyes flitting across to the closed door. 'Do you have to put it like that?'

'Is there any other way that wouldn't sound equally squalid?'

Bliss had decided on the drive over that he would be confrontational. He wanted to keep Palmer on the defensive, and not have the man think Bliss approved of what had taken place. No man-to-man nods of acceptance.

'When you put it as bluntly as that, I suppose not, no.' Palmer's face hardened, though his voice took on a sulky edge.

Bliss ignored both. 'So when was the last time?'

'Let me see, I suppose it would be about fifteen or sixteen years ago now.' He frowned, scratched the back of his neck, nodded. 'Yes. That sounds about right.'

'Why did you stop seeing her?'

'She left the area. At least, that's what I assumed. She certainly wasn't on the street anymore.'

'Did you stop using prostitutes altogether after that?'

This time a definite flush crept across Palmer's cheeks. As embarrassed as he was anxious. 'No. But there was no one else who became a regular.'

Bliss was surprised the man hadn't opted for bluster over contrition, but was glad of it all the same. It made his job a whole lot easier.

'Okay, we'll set that aside for the time being. Now then, what's next? Oh, yes, can you tell me where you were on the night of Tuesday, June twenty-sixth, nineteen ninety?'

The noise Palmer made was one of incredulity. Snorting through a closed mouth. 'Are you serious? I'm so busy I couldn't tell you where I was last week without consulting my PDA.'

'I can sympathise. You're a busy, important man. I understand that. Still, give it some thought, eh? June nineteen ninety. The Word Cup was being played in Italy, and that night England...'

Palmer sat upright as if a bolt of electricity had passed through him. He wagged a finger in Bliss's direction. 'Of course. I can tell you exactly where I was. In Japan. Went there in April, came home early October.'

'Japan?'

'Tokyo to be precise. On business. We were merging with an engineering company out there. I did the negotiations and oversaw the opening.'

'And this can be verified through company records?'

'Of course. Plus, I was there with a colleague the whole time.' Palmer's forehead creased. 'What is this all about, Inspector Bliss? You wanted to know about Jodie Maybanks, and now you're asking... Oh, I see. Jodie didn't leave the area at all, did she?'

Bliss shook his head. If the man truly had no idea, Palmer was the best liar he'd ever met. 'No. Jodie Maybanks was murdered that night. She was strangled and buried, and her remains were unearthed in Bretton Woods last Tuesday.'

He made no mention of the lake in Fletton, hoping to see something flare in Palmer's eyes. There was nothing.

'Yes, I saw that on the news.' He gave a slight shudder. 'It's a little unnerving now that I realise I knew the person found. And you thought I might have something to do with it? Jodie had a lot of clients, Inspector. Are you speaking to them all?'

'As many as we can trace.' It was true enough, though Bliss neglected to mention that Palmer's name was the only one that had cropped up so far. 'Mr Palmer, before you left for Japan, did Jodie tell you she was pregnant?'

Palmer reared back as if physically threatened. 'Pregnant? No. She never mentioned it. But why pick on me? She had sex for a living.'

'Yes, but you see, the information we have is that you were one of the very few men who had unprotected sex with Jodie. As a regular, there's a decent chance you were the father. Had you been told, I doubt you'd have been best pleased.'

'Had I been told I would have been apoplectic. Even so, I wouldn't have killed the poor kid.'

'So what would you have done? Brought her home, introduced her to the wife?'

'I would have paid for an abortion.'

'And if she'd not wanted one?'

'I would have persuaded her. Anyway, I'm sure she would have been only too happy. What would a girl like that want with a baby?'

Bliss sat back and gave it a little thought. There were no alarm bells ringing, no hairs raised on the nape of his neck. Palmer neither appeared nor sounded guilty of anything other than visiting prostitutes. Bliss didn't much like the man, but that didn't make him a murderer. Still, he felt Palmer's attitude warranted a little tweak of conscience.

'Did you not consider the risk of having unprotected sex with a prostitute, Mr Palmer? A drug addict, too, for that matter.'

'Somewhat. I assumed she was on the pill, and imagined she would abort any child if that were not the case.'

'I'm talking about health risks, sir. STDs, that sort of thing. Not very pleasant, so I hear. Neither for you nor your wife.'

'My wife and I are both fine, thank you, Inspector Bliss.'

'I'm glad to hear it. Still, I take it you are aware that HIV and AIDS can lie dormant for fifteen years or so?'

Bliss had no idea if that was the case, but he was looking to rattle Palmer before he left. Judging by the man's suddenly pale and waxy face, he guessed he had managed to do so.

'Oh, yes,' Bliss continued, nodding. 'It might be worth getting yourself checked out, sir. I can't imagine what Mrs Palmer would say about it. I do hope you haven't passed it on to your wife. For her sake.'

He concluded the interview by requesting a DNA sample. With a great deal of reluctance, Palmer agreed, provided nothing was mentioned to his wife. Bliss asked Palmer to present himself at Thorpe Wood, and to bring with him the name of the colleague with whom he'd spent six months in Japan, together with any documentary evidence related to the business trip.

'You do believe me, don't you?' Palmer asked, leaning forward in his chair. 'About my innocence, I mean?'

Bliss looked around the room. Small but tasteful, a few nice older pieces of furniture that looked like they might be worth a bob or two. Judging by what he'd seen and heard earlier, the Palmer's didn't have much going on between them. He was the earner, while all her efforts went into making them a nice home. No time for anything other than the appearance of a happy life together. Bliss wondered if Mrs Palmer knew about her husband's proclivities, perhaps even approved of them.

'Innocence?' Bliss said. He gave Palmer a look of both contempt and pity. 'You may not have murdered Jodie, but as for you being innocent… I suppose you'll be your own judge of that in years to come.'

As Bliss now thundered back towards Peterborough along the road that ran alongside the Ramsey 'Forty Foot' drain, he glanced to his left and saw only blackness. Pretty much what Jodie Maybanks had seen for too much of her short life. Bliss knew the river was lurking just a few yards away, but saw only occasional glimmers of light reflecting off the water. He could never remember where the drain's peculiar name originated from, it being neither forty feet wide nor deep, but several signs along the grass verge reminded him that a combination of road and river had claimed numerous lives over the past few years. The camber of the road leaned towards the river, providing good drainage, but it made for an anxious journey, particularly at night. Bliss was thankful when the river angled sharply away and the road followed a different course.

Ahead, Bliss could see nothing coming towards him across the flat lands. He checked his rear-view mirror, but still there was no sign of headlights. He looked up again. Something. Just a flash, but something not quite right. Scarcely had his eyes moved back to the windscreen when he felt the collision.

***

The shunt from behind threw his body forwards, the seatbelt biting into his chest and shoulder, snapping Bliss back again against the seat. Pain flared across his neck and spread instantly across his shoulders. Tiny pinpricks of light danced before his eyes. Whatever had slammed into him had appeared out of the darkness like a shark striking without warning from the murky depths of the ocean.

'Bastard!' Bliss cried. About to stamp on his brakes, he sensed movement and his gaze was drawn to the mirror. Immediately alert to the fact that he was about to be rammed again, Bliss pressed down hard on the accelerator. From behind he heard an engine roar, and fear settled on him like a thin film of sweat. He switched his attention back to the windscreen just in time to manoeuvre across a hump-back bridge, his stomach dropping away as the Vectra seemed to leave the tarmac for a moment. On the other side of the bridge, Bliss shifted down into fourth gear and put more weight behind his right foot.

Seconds later he was blinded by dazzling white lights reflecting off the rear-view mirror. Full beam headlights that were moving closer, growing larger. His mind attempted to wrestle its way through the flood of adrenaline, and Bliss thought about the layout of the roads ahead. Even at this speed he was more than ten minutes away from a built-up area and decent street lighting.

The headlights snapped off again, drawing Bliss's eyes back to the mirror, a curious spectral glow clinging to the periphery of his vision. A halo effect. This time he saw the pursuing vehicle's grille, high up off the road, like a row of gritted teeth. It smashed into him at an angle, propelling the Vauxhall's rear end out and to the right. Bliss snatched the steering wheel back, the car fishtailing, but somehow managing to stay in lane.

'You fucking prick!' he cursed at the top of his voice. What the hell was going on here?

Bliss felt his chest pounding, as if someone inside was hammering a fist against his ribs in a wild bid for escape. A thin trail of sweat trickled down from his brow. Above the roar of blood pounding in his head, Bliss heard the howling whine of his car's engine. Still in fourth. Rev counter approaching four thousand.

He found fifth clumsily, gearbox howling in confusion, accelerator still pressed all the way down, the speedometer nudging ninety. Eyes back on his mirror. This time the chasing vehicle was right on him when its lights blazed once more. Bliss was prepared for the jolt, but at such a high speed his grip was loosened for a second and the wheel almost got away from him. His fingers tightened, but the Vectra was snaking back and forth across the road as it struggled to straighten.

Up ahead, Bliss could see a faint amber glow. A small village. The road he was on cut right through its heart. His mind was filled with desperate possibilities: a pedestrian crossing the road, a car pulling out of a side street, him losing control and careering into someone's house. Something cold seemed to wrap around his heart. He had to do something about this right now.

Without pause to question the sanity of his decision, Bliss stood on his brakes and threw the gears into reverse, the transmission screaming in protest at him now. Eyes on his mirrors he turned the steering wheel sharply and somehow managed to avoid the onrushing vehicle. As it flew by his door he saw that it was a large Mitsubishi four-by-four, a Shogun, the big fat spare wheel clinging like a limpet to the rear panel. Its brake lights flared and the vehicle shuddered to a halt. Bliss turned his wheel all the way now and swung the Vectra right around, ending up facing the way he had come. A quick glance told him the Shogun was doing the same. But he'd gained a few valuable seconds.

Bliss floored it. Back in fourth he steered off to his right and away from the road that led towards the river. The headlights behind him winked out one more time. Fifth now and engine racing. Looking for a wide turnoff that might lead to a farm or even just a field. He had to get out of the car, because whoever was chasing him was so much better at this than he was.

Again his head snapped forward and the Vectra's boot flew open as it was struck from behind for a fourth time. For a moment he thought he had everything under control, but then he felt the rear end slide out and, as he tried to correct it, the car went into a spin. Bliss braked, but not hard, desperate not to flip the car over. Went with the skid. Almost side on now, the Shogun hit the front end this time and the Vauxhall was sent hurtling off the road and down a small embankment. Bliss jammed on the brakes this time, sending the car into one more slide before it came to an abrupt halt in the bottom of a shallow ditch.

Adrenaline still pumping furiously, Bliss took deep breaths so as not to hyperventilate. His chest and shoulders were aflame. He leaned on his door and forced it open, threw off his seatbelt and pulled himself up and out of the car. Leaving the engine running, exhaust fumes pumping out into the chill night air,

Bliss half ran, half crawled along the ditch, moving upwards at a slant like an animal. He threw himself to the ground and peeked over the top of the rise at the road. Expecting to see the big four-by-four parked up, its occupant or occupants moving through the darkness towards him, Bliss was astonished to find the road empty, the Shogun nowhere to be seen.

Bliss rolled over onto his back and took several deep breaths, gulping in some much-needed air, willing his heart to slow down before it burst apart. When he thought he could manage to talk, he made a call and went back to his car to switch the engine and lights off. Twenty minutes later his eyes started to follow the blue-and-whites as they made their way along the Fenland roads towards him.

TWENTY-ONE

'They breathalysed you?' Bobby Dunne said. 'They fucking breathalysed you? Those wankers. Tell me who they are and I'll go and kick their fucking arses.'

Bliss was sitting with Dunne and Chandler in his own living room. It was just after ten thirty, and other than a minor residue of shock and a few bumps and bruises, Bliss was feeling pretty much okay. Having dismissed the pleadings of the ambulance crew to allow them to take him to hospital and have a casualty doctor check for concussion, he persuaded the attending police officers to run him straight home. Bliss had given himself a while to calm down and collect his thoughts before calling both Penny and Bobby, summoning them to a low-level war cabinet at his house.

Six months earlier, Chandler had been the first person to actually visit Bliss's home, which was all red brick and stained hardwood, rooms so small you'd have to cut a cat in two if you wanted to swing it. During that initial visit, Chandler pointed out that Bliss had, a couple of years after moving in, not yet unpacked all his boxes. Half a year on, nothing much had changed.

Bliss was touched by his colleagues' resentment at the way he had been treated, but he held up a hand and firmly shook his head. 'No, leave this one alone, Bobby. Believe me, it's not a fight we need to have. I could see they were building themselves up to do the breath test anyway, but actually I was the one who insisted on it. Pre-emptive strike, as it were.'

'You did? Why?'

'I don't want to give Sykes any ammunition. This way, having them stick to procedure, he can't come at me some time in the future and claim abuse of position.'

Chandler was nodding. 'That makes sense. Especially given the volatile relationship you two have.'

Dunne agreed. 'You probably did the right thing. It stinks, but no harm done I suppose. So, this motor that shunted you off the road. A Shogun, you say?'

'I'm sure of it. Big bastard, and heavy with it. Bull bars, the lot. No number plates, though. Neither front nor back.'

'Actually, that's quite interesting,' Chandler said. 'It suggests the vehicle was owned by the driver. If it had been nicked, surely they'd've just kept the plates on.'

'I had the same thought,' Bliss admitted. 'Not that it gets us very far.'

'Might do later on,' said Dunne. 'You think whoever drove the motor was also responsible for killing poor Bernie Weller?'

Bliss spread his hands. His mind replayed the incident. 'Could be. At one point I'm certain they tried the tactic of angling me sideways, the exact method Glazier described. But you know the weird thing is, I didn't get the impression they were trying to kill me. I think it was more some kind of warning, a threat perhaps. Maybe put me out of action for a while, but not actually kill me.'

'What makes you say that?' Chandler asked, clearly dubious.

'Mainly because they waited until I'd driven past the river. If I'd gone off the road into the Forty Foot, I most probably wouldn't have come out again. But the roads elsewhere are all soft verges and shallow ditches. They had several miles of that road to choose from, but they only made a move just as the drain went one way and I went the other. Also, if they did want me dead, why didn't they stop to finish the job?'

'Good point.' She frowned. 'I wonder if whoever did this only intended to warn Bernie off as well.'

'That's a sobering thought.'

'You could be reading too much into it, boss,' Dunne said, shaking his head. 'Whoever was driving the Shogun might not have wanted to tangle with you close to the drain in case they got it wrong and ended up in there themselves. As for not stopping, if they were on their own they might not have fancied themselves one on one with you.'

Bliss ran a hand across his face. The episode spun a continuous loop inside his head, and he felt goose bumps spread across his arms. Not for the first time that night he asked himself if he had come close to death. While he couldn't be certain of anything, the answer was that he didn't think so.

'What you say is true enough, Bobby, but it still doesn't feel right. I'm not sure I can explain it, but while the driver was persistent, I'm not convinced they intended to kill me.'

'Could it have been Palmer?' Chandler asked.

'I doubt it. After I called you two I phoned Thorpe Wood and had a PNC check run, and the only car the Palmers have registered is a Mazda sports job. The Lexus I saw in their drive is probably a company car. Anyway, Palmer's no longer high on my list of suspects.'

'Because he was in Japan when that kid was murdered?' Dunne scoffed, much as he had when Bliss first told them about the meeting. He screwed up his face. Sniffed contemptuously. 'He could have ordered it. Made sure it coincided with him being away. What better alibi?'

'Yeah, I know. And I'll have someone go through his bank account details for that year if they're available, see if he withdrew a large sum of cash before he left. We'll also have someone check his itinerary and records in full, make sure he didn't forget to tell me about a quick trip back to Blighty. But having spoken with the man, I have to say I don't think it was him. He seemed genuinely shocked, and I don't buy the hired hitman theory, either. Everything that seems to have happened to Jodie Maybanks, the car screaming after her, the strangulation, it suggests something personal. Emotional. Besides, no hitman is going to do it that way.'

'How about Palmer's wife?' Chandler suggested. 'What if she found out what was going on? Or maybe Jodie turned up at the Palmer home and told the wife about being in the family way. That's personal. That's emotional.'

Bliss gave himself a few moments to think about it. Eventually, he shook his head. 'I'm still not convinced. I can just about buy Palmer himself having some influence and being able to get to officers involved with the investigation. But Mrs Palmer? I don't see it, somehow.'

'Maybe she killed Jodie, then panicked and told her husband, who then put the squeeze on.'

Bliss nodded. 'It's a good argument, Pen. No question. But you didn't have the advantage I had of speaking to Palmer. He had no idea. I'm convinced of that.'

'Well, if you're right, that leaves us with the scrote of a dealer Jodie knew.'

'It does. But again, I'm sensing something working in the background of this. Someone maybe pulling a few strings, perhaps taking out Weller as well. And what I don't see is some pusher having that kind of clout.'

'But we'll check him out, yes?'

'Of course we will.'

'But you don't think we'll have any joy.'

'No, I don't. I'm afraid I come back to my original line of thinking: that it's someone far closer to home.'

Dunne snapped his fingers. He shook his head and his eyes became hooded. 'Speaking of which. I got a worrying call earlier tonight from Mia. She told me that an old colleague of mine, Alan Dean, who just happens to be the primary officer involved with the Jodie Maybanks MisPer case, was found shot dead in his home last week. The night of his retirement, actually. Not a suicide, either. Local CID are working along the lines of a burglary gone pear-shaped.'

'Shot dead?' Bliss hissed air between his teeth. 'Another cop involved with this case. How bloody convenient. I'm not buying that line of bull about the burglary, that's for sure. Fuck me, people, first it's Weller, and now we have another of our own murdered as well. This is getting nasty. Someone has decided it's time to shut a few mouths, permanently, and the spur seems to be

Jodie's remains being dug up.' Bliss shot a nervous glance at his two companions. 'This has got to be coming from the inside. You two know it as well as I do.'

Penny Chandler put both hands to her face and drew them slowly down her cheeks. Pale and drawn, she sat alongside Dunne on the living room's only item of furniture – there wasn't even a coffee table to hold their drinks – and Bliss had dragged in a high-backed dining chair from the kitchen, on which he perched uneasily. Chandler gazed across at him now.

'This is fucked up, boss,' she said. 'Seriously fucked up. I think we should turn this over right now. Drop the whole thing in Sykes's lap and see what he makes of it.'

Bliss shook his head. 'I'm not prepared to do that at this stage. If he even suspects that another cop is responsible, he'll drop it like a fresh turd and bury it as deep as he can. Somewhere the stench will never notice. No, I want to know more about this before I make any firm decisions. I want to know who's responsible. Only then will I consider going through the proper channels.'

'I'm with you,' said Dunne. He took a swig from his mug of white coffee, sweetened with three sugars. 'This has got to be handled delicately for now, then passed on to the right man at the right time.'

'But Sykes must be clean,' Chandler argued. 'He wasn't even stationed in Peterborough when all this happened.'

'Sykes is a political beast, Penny,' Bliss reminded her. 'You know that much. I don't want him putting a career ladder in place again on the back of doing a favour for someone higher up. This needs to go to someone who will run with it. But we need to dig deeper ourselves. Are you okay with that, or do you want out?'

He met her gaze. Saw a small glimmer of fear in her eyes. Bliss understood. This was more than a rap on the knuckles or a backward step regarding promotion if it all went tits up. People were being murdered.

'Neither of us will think any less of you, Pen,' he urged softly, hoping she'd walk through the door he'd opened for her, but knowing that wasn't her way. 'I mean that. This has little chance of ending up well. There's no way I'll bring Mia Strong into it now, and if I were you I'd walk away with my head held high.'

Almost as the words were out of his mouth, he knew he'd blown it. Chandler was shaking her head and jabbing a finger at him. 'No. That's just it. You wouldn't walk away. You're not now, and you wouldn't even if you were in my position. And I know why, too.'

She got to her feet. Walked around the centre of the room for a few seconds, nodding her head, fists clenched tighter with each stride. 'You can't walk away from this now,' she said, a look of triumph in her eyes as she swung her head to face Bliss. 'And the reason you can't is because this is much more than a case number to you. More than a cold case. More than a Jane Doe. No, this is Jodie Maybanks. And no matter that it was drug and sex fuelled, it was her life to live and it was far too short. No one had the right to take it away. This investigation has moved on, hooked a place inside you. The truth is, boss, you want justice for Jodie Maybanks.'

For a moment Bliss made no reply. Then he clapped his hands together. 'Very impressive, Penny. Very impressive indeed.'

'But am I right?' she demanded to know.

Bliss was thrilled at the sight of her flushed cheeks, the enthusiasm, commitment and, it had to be acknowledged, emotion and compassion. DC Chandler was going places. But only if he could nurse her through this mess.

'Yes,' he said simply. 'You're right. So what are we going to do about it?'

Chandler came back to her seat alongside Dunne. She shook her head, folding her arms. 'There's one obvious problem: and that's if someone else hooks into the information we have. Mia obviously found out about Alan Dean while she was chasing up records relating to the MisPer report. If she, or anyone else on the squad, gets wind of Weller's death as well, they're going to bring it to our attention. We'll have no choice but to follow it through then.'

Dunne was nodding. 'That's a real possibility. But the fact that both the reported accident involving Jodie and the MisPer report were handled by Bridge Street Central works in our favour. Of all the officers involved, the only one I really knew well was Alan Dean. I probably bumped into the others from time to time, as you do, and I got to know Bernie a little, but then I've only ever been stationed here.'

'How does that work to our advantage?' Chandler wanted to know.

It was Bliss who answered her. 'Because it'll be harder for someone to put the pieces together the way we have without knowing what the finished picture is. Few serving officers currently stationed at Thorpe Wood will have known both Weller and Alan Dean. Certainly not well enough to be aware that both have been recently killed.'

'So it'll buy us some time, at least.'

'It should. And remember, the actions for tracing and interviewing both Weller and Hendry are down to us, so we can write up what we like when we like.'

Dunne raised a finger. 'That's true enough, boss. But what about Hendry? He was at the scene that night with Weller, and according to McAndrew, the witness, it was Hendry who later warned him off. Hendry may also be in danger.'

Bliss nodded. 'You're right, Bobby. Absolutely. My fault for not picking up on that earlier. Of course, we have to assume that Weller was only murdered because he was coming to see me, possibly to confess his part in whatever took place that night. My guess is Hendry is likely to remain safe provided he doesn't contact us.'

'Even so…'

'I know. Whoever's behind this might not take that chance. We hadn't heard from this Alan Dean, either. Okay, we'll attend to it tomorrow. Along with everything else.'

'So what exactly are we all going to be doing?' Chandler asked.

'How about I take Hendry, boss,' Bobby Dunne suggested. 'I can also spend some more time going back through archives.

Seems to me that with the initial mowing down of the poor kid and the subsequent MisPer, we've raised a few different names internally. What would be good now is to turn up one that spreads over both inquiries.'

'Good call, Bobby,' Bliss nodded his approval. Things were coming together fast. He felt his flesh prickle. 'You get on to that first thing after briefing tomorrow. Locate Hendry, have a word, then do some digging. Pen, your reward is to head up to Lincoln and go through Weller's house, particularly his office, see what you can come up with.'

'Okay. It'll be a nice change of scenery. What will you be focusing on?'

Bliss was ready for the question. He had made up his mind about this almost from the moment Bobby had told them about it. 'I'm going to look into this Alan Dean shooting. I think we would all agree this was no burglary gone wrong. And a deliberate shooting might be easier to prove than a deliberate forcing off the road. I have a feeling, just a few raised hairs on the back of my neck, that one of us is going to come up smelling of roses tomorrow.'

'Losers buy drinks and dinner,' Chandler suggested, smiling at them both. 'So you two get your flexible friends ready.'

Bliss laughed. He was grateful to Penny for lightening the mood. 'From anyone else that would have sounded crude.'

'And how did it sound from me?'

'As innocent as Snow White herself.'

He winked at Dunne, who said, 'Yeah, and we all know how she drifted.'

TWENTY-TWO

Once renowned for its field of concrete cows welcoming visitors to the town, Milton Keynes was now better known for being the roundabout capital of England. Bliss lost track of how many he'd navigated through since crossing the M1 and hitting the town's ring road, and even the satnav was finding it hard to cope. The Bradwell area he sought was located in the centre of Milton Keynes, and, after a couple of aborted attempts and three-point turns, Bliss finally pulled up outside Alan Dean's terraced house. Dean's home was a relatively older property in what looked to be a modern township, the so-called progress seeming ugly to Bliss.

He sat and gathered his wits for a few moments. So far the morning had been one to forget; starting with a thirty minute bout of vertigo that took him from nausea to vomiting, resulting in a late team briefing during which he had felt close to being overwhelmed by the symptoms of his disease, and culminating in an arse-puckering near miss in the pool car when a white-van man almost sideswiped him on a dual carriageway. Reflecting on how awful he'd felt when waking up that morning, Bliss began to question how long he'd be able to keep the illness from his employers, particularly if the episodes of vertigo increased in either number or duration. Or worse still, both. The imbalance was a symptom he might be able to adapt to and disguise, fatigue something he would have to somehow push his way through, but attacks of vertigo, such as he'd experienced upon rising from his bed, were completely incapacitating.

Drawing in a good lungful of air, Bliss climbed out of the silver Ford Focus and headed over to the house, outside which a uniform stood like a royal guardsman. Bliss had earlier made a call to Milton Keynes CID, and he now flashed his warrant card and asked if DCI Radcliffe had arrived as arranged. The constable directed Bliss through to the back garden, where two suits stood smoking, despite a steady drizzle misting the air around them.

The DCI and his colleague, DS King, greeted Bliss warmly, but he sensed a wariness in them that he'd half expected and could empathise with. When he'd called moments after ending the squad briefing, he'd given them the cover story that Alan Dean was an ex-colleague, explaining that all he wanted to do was chat about the circumstances of the shooting, perhaps take a look around at the scene while he was there. Like most cops, these two looked uncomfortable at having an outsider on their patch, an interloper who might snoop and seek out errors in the way the investigation was being run. Keen to move beyond their discomfort, the first thing Bliss did was assure them that this was not the reason he had driven over. The moment he saw the two officers visibly relax, he jumped in with both feet.

'This notion of a robbery gone bad,' he said, arching his eyebrows, 'it's a load of bollocks, right? I mean, you two don't look as if you've been fast-tracked straight from university and are now flying by the seat of your pants, cribbing from a text book.'

Radcliffe and King exchanged uneasy glances. After a telling pause, it was the DS who spoke up. 'You're spot on about the last part, but I'm not sure why you think the robbery angle is out of the question.'

Bliss pursed his lips. Shrugged. 'Experience. Law of averages. I've been in the job almost twenty years, fourteen of them suited and booted, and I have never encountered a house breaker shooting someone. I know it has happened on the odd occasion, but I think it's unlikely in this case.'

'So this could be the exception that proves the rule,' Radcliffe suggested. He flicked his cigarette away in a shower of tiny sparks.

The two CID officers were like a couple of junkyard dogs: one all taut and bullish like a Doberman, the other jerky and skittish like a Jack Russell.

Unwilling to reveal the link between Alan Dean and Bernard Weller, Bliss merely gave a wry smile and said nothing. His eyes spoke eloquently and forcefully, however.

'Okay, you're right,' DCI Radcliffe, the Doberman, admitted. 'Everyone who has taken a look at this has come to the same conclusion: a hit. Careless tossing of the place afterwards to make it look like a robbery, but whoever did it had no heart for the deception. They did what they came to do.'

'A hit?' Bliss wasn't prepared for them knocking it out of the ground with the first swipe. He had hoped they would stroke it around a bit first. Now he had to try and finesse this a little. 'You think Alan made an enemy recently?'

Radcliffe frowned. 'Sergeant Dean turned a key in the local courthouse. It's not the kind of place you make enemies.'

'Maybe his troubles kicked off before he moved here,' DS King suggested. He peered at Bliss over his boss's shoulder. 'Back in Peterborough.'

Oh, shit, Bliss thought. This wasn't going at all well. He shook his head forcefully. 'Alan transferred to Milton Keynes six years ago. Who would hold a grudge that long?'

'Someone who's been banged up?' King glanced across at his DCI. 'Perhaps we ought to be looking at who Dean put away before he bailed out to become a jailer.'

It was time to be a little more insistent. 'Wait a minute,' Bliss said. 'Why are you so desperate to move this away from your own patch? You can't possibly have run down all aspects of Dean's life here in just a few days. This shooting could have been over anything.'

Radcliffe picked up on the slip right away. 'Dean? What happened to *Alan*? Just how close were you two, anyway?'

Bliss felt like slapping himself. Such an amateurish mistake. He'd blown this, big time. Blundering in without a plan.

'All right. Alan Dean and I were not actually colleagues. We only got to hear about the shooting yesterday, and one of my DSs had a word with me about it. He and Dean *did* work together. He latched on to the bogus burglary claim right away, and wanted to check it out. But he's tied up today, and anyway we thought I might have a bit more clout.'

'Why the pretence?' Radcliffe wanted to know.

The drizzle was becoming more insistent, droplets tap-tapping on the heavy plastic covering Alan Dean's garden furniture. Bliss hunched deeper into his long jacket.

'I didn't want you to think I was trying to muscle in or pull the case down around you. It seemed easier just to go with the colleagues story.' Bliss gave half a smile and shrugged. 'It wasn't much of a plan.'

'This DS back at your place,' King asked. 'Did he have any ideas about who might want Dean topped?'

Bliss saw an opportunity to pull this around after all. 'No. We talked about it, obviously, and he couldn't think of anything. In fact, he was firm about it. Alan Dean was a uniform, a beat and desk man. Any arrests he made were strictly low-level collars.'

'Was he gay?'

'Gay? Why would you ask that?'

'The man was still single at his age. Lived alone. It's a theory, that's all.'

Bliss shook his head. 'I really don't know anything about his private life. I'm not sure my DS did, either. They were colleagues, not close friends.'

'No rumours? Drugs? Kiddies? We're looking for a motive here, Bliss. Someone went to the trouble of taking him out. There had to be a good reason.'

'And I still think you'll find that reason somewhere here,' Bliss argued. He was starting to feel uncomfortable, but decided to push it anyway. 'From what I can gather, and judging by my sergeant's concern, Alan Dean was well liked and respected. He was good at his job and he did it without ruffling any feathers. So, if we can concentrate on the here and now for the time being, any chance of you telling me what you have so far?'

'Other than suspecting it was a hit?' DCI Radcliffe shook his head. 'Fuck all just about sums it up. Door-to-door came up empty, forensics the same. We've found nothing in Dean's personal possessions or his phone records to lead us anywhere. I've been in touch with a CHIS who would know if there had been any talk, any money changing hands for a local hitman. Nothing.'

Bliss thought about this. CHIS: a Covert Human Intelligence Source – modern parlance for a snout, or an informant. He could not abide this aspect of modern policing. It seemed to him that the top brass were never happier than when they were thinking up new and meaningless acronyms.

Bliss rubbed the scar on his forehead, chewed on his bottom lip for a few seconds. He'd been hoping for a witness or two, someone he could visit in his own time to see what they knew, but this was getting him nowhere. He felt a slight pull of guilt in not telling these two fellow officers what he knew, helping their inquiry rather than focusing solely on his own. But he was convinced that throwing it open to a full investigation at this stage would lead to it being buried beneath a sea of internal bureaucracy. He hadn't known Alan Dean at all and, while he'd worked with Weller only the once, he felt he owed the two murdered men his best efforts.

'You seem to have everything in hand. I won't waste any more of your time. Mind if I look around?' Bliss asked.

'Help yourself,' Radcliffe said. He took a card from his breast pocket and handed it over. 'We've got to shoot off. Give me a call if you want anything else, or if you can think of anything from your end that might help.'

'Yeah, will do. I doubt I'll find anything here, but I said I'd do what I could. I'll check into a few things back home, make sure Dean's past is looked into. That okay by you?'

'Sure. Saves us a job.'

With the heating having been switched off for a few days, it wasn't a great deal warmer inside the house. But it was dry, and there was no wind. Because a murder had been carried out, Bliss knew the search of the house would have been thorough. Even so, he spent some time checking in less obvious locations, though he had no idea what he might find. If this had gone down the way he thought it had, Alan Dean had been given no warning of the hit.

As he picked his way through the minutiae of Alan Dean's life, Bliss grew reflective. There was an emptiness in the murdered man's home that suggested a lack of companionship, an overwhelming sense of loneliness. The fridge held only a few basic items, the cupboards contained a mismatch of plates and bowls, the drainer by the sink a single plate, one cup, one knife and one fork. Bliss couldn't help projecting ahead and seeing himself in Dean's shoes, growing old on his own, retiring in the knowledge that he would live out his years alone.

Alan Dean is not you, Bliss told himself. And you will not be him.

But he wasn't sure he believed the voice inside his head.

Bliss stood for a while in the hallway. According to the SOCO report, Dean had met his death soon after entering his home after a night out with friends. The gunman had been waiting behind the front door. For another victim the shooter might have hidden in one of the rooms, but a good pro would have allowed for a cop's instincts.

Blood, bone and brain matter still stained the wall and floor of the hallway. Samples for forensic examination had been taken of each, but the larger mass decorated the hall like Jackson Pollock's vision of hell. Had Alan Dean known the man who took his life? Bliss asked himself. Had Dean peered into familiar eyes? The gunshots from behind suggested otherwise. Bliss left feeling angry and wondering where this was headed and who might be next on the hitman's list.

***

He was approaching the M1 turnoff when he took a call from Mia Strong. 'I've managed to track down the dealer,' she told

Bliss. 'This Snake gimp. He's actually retired from his upstanding profession and is now – get this – an adviser for a drugs rehab centre in Northampton. You want him pulled in?'

Bliss worked the idea for a few seconds. There was a lot of procedure involved, plus the not inconsiderable matter of human resources, in taking someone off the streets and bringing them into custody. The alternative was to send someone to speak with the former dealer, and Mia was perfectly up to the task. But with the motorway looming up, Bliss knew he could be speaking to the man face to face in less than half an hour.

'Give me the details,' he told Strong. 'I'll pay him a visit myself.'

Gordon Wilson, aka Snake, worked in a community centre near the Park Campus of Northampton's university. Now aged forty, Wilson had been counselling and advising on drugs matters for more than five years. His own rehabilitation had come about during an eighteen-month prison sentence, during which he met the woman who had subsequently become both his mentor and lover.

When Bliss arrived unannounced at Wilson's place of work, the adviser was shut away in a room with a student from the nearby university. Bliss waited patiently outside in the scruffy hallway, his attention snagged by the centre's hall in which a number of youths gathered to play pool. Faces turned his way and immediately hardened, as if sensing who and what he was.

Bliss used the waiting time to think about what Gordon Wilson might be achieving here. Working this closely with addicts might present the perfect opportunity to fall back into familiar ways. It was actually the perfect cover.

Ever the cynic, Bliss chided himself.

The first thing that took Bliss by surprise, when he was finally shown in to see Wilson, was how healthy the man looked. Not all dealers were users, but at the level this man had worked, the chances were good that he had been jabbing his arm every bit as much as his clients. Bliss had been expecting a reed-thin, pallid individual, full of facial tics and nervous sweats. But Wilson was a sturdy man, well-nourished and obviously fit and strong if his handshake was anything to go by. The second surprise was that Wilson welcomed Bliss with a warm smile that seemed genuine.

'Good to meet you, Inspector,' Wilson said. His Lancashire accent was less of a surprise, Mia Strong having fed Bliss as much information as she could over the phone.

'You don't know why I'm here, yet.'

'True, but why should that alter how I feel?'

Bliss looked around the small, yet neat office. 'You've come a long way,' he said.

'In terms of distance, or on the evolutionary scale?' Wilson smiled again, then shook his head. 'Inspector, I know better than anyone what I was and what I did. But that was the old me, and no matter how much I regret the choices I made, I can't undo them. Nothing you say here today will affect that one way or another.'

'Fair enough.' Bliss gave a thoughtful nod. 'Tell me, then, Mr Wilson, what do you recall about your business dealings in Peterborough?'

'You mean was I off my face too much to remember all the gory details?'

'Something like that, yes.' Bliss had to admit, he admired the man's head-on approach.

'Well, the answer to that is no. I used, but not hard. As for your question, ask me something specific and I'll give you a specific answer.'

'That's what I like to hear. Tell me then, does the name Jodie Maybanks mean anything to you?'

Wilson frowned. 'From my time in Peterborough? I'm not sure it does.'

'She was a street girl. Early twenties.'

'I dealt with a lot of those, Inspector. But yes, I do remember a girl called Jodie. I never knew her surname, so I can't tell you if it was the same girl.'

'I don't suppose you got too close to your victims, eh?'

'You don't like me much, do you?' Wilson continued to smile.

Bliss shook his head. 'I don't know you well enough to have an opinion either way. I don't like what you are, that's for sure.'

'What I was, Inspector. What I was.'

'Mr Wilson, you are responsible for untold horrors. The drugs you pushed literally destroyed lives. There are people dead because of you, people ruined for life because of you, people who steal and sell their bodies because of you. Because of your greed, your complete disregard for the misery you caused.'

'You can't know any of that.'

'For certain, no. But in here,' Bliss tapped a hand on his heart. 'I know because I've seen the aftermath, the wreckage your kind leaves behind.'

Wilson's cheeks flushed, the smile faltered. 'But you can see for yourself what I'm doing now. I'm steering young people away from drugs. I'm giving something back.'

Bliss let his gaze harden. 'You think you can ever compensate for the lives you've ruined? You'd have to live a thousand lives of your own.'

'Well, I only have this one, Inspector. And I'm doing the best I can with it now.'

'Do you think you can account for your whereabouts in June nineteen ninety?' Bliss asked, letting it drop and moving back on track.

'Not unless I was either banged up or out of the country. Why? Does this have something to do with this Jodie kid?'

'That's when she was killed. So, yes.'

The adviser sat back in his chair, wary now for the first time since Bliss had started speaking. 'Okay, I think I can see where this is headed. Now let me tell you this, Inspector Bliss, whilst you may think I am responsible for the deaths of users down the years, I have never knowingly murdered someone. Not Jodie. Not anybody. You may be right, in fact you probably are, that I have blood on my hands. But not that way. Not deliberately.'

As much as he didn't want to, Bliss believed the man. Wilson's fierce denial appeared genuine. Still, Bliss figured it couldn't hurt to finish what he'd gone there to do. 'So, were you in jail in June nineteen ninety?' he asked.

The man shook his head. 'No. I was still living in Peterborough, and I'm reasonably certain that I wasn't abroad that summer. I got pulled every few weeks or so, spent a few nights in a cell. But that far back... I can't be positive where I was at any given date or time.'

'So, that hardly removes you from the frame, does it?'

'I suppose not. But like I said, I'm no murderer.'

'We'll see,' Bliss said, abruptly getting to his feet. 'I'll have some checks run on you, Mr Wilson. If I can't come up with anything that provides you with an alibi, we may have to have another chat.'

'Won't that be a pleasure?'

'It's a murder investigation, sir. It's not supposed to be fun.'

'Of course. I'm sorry. It's just that it's such a long, long time ago,' Wilson said, his eyes glazed as if peering back into his past.

'Yes, it is. But not for Jodie Maybanks. Her life ended there and then.'

Bliss turned and left the office without another word.

TWENTY-THREE

It was almost one thirty when Bliss, Chandler and Dunne met up at the Pizza Hut restaurant in the Boongate district of Peterborough. Boongate was home to both new and second-hand car dealerships, large trading estates, DIY stores, and a few fast food places. It was also home to the lunchtime buffet special.

Each of the three detectives took a large plate up to the hot food stand and helped themselves to a variety of pizza slices and pasta. When they were all settled back around their table, it was Bliss who got the ball rolling.

'Milton Keynes was a complete bust,' he told them. 'The Murder Squad seem to have done a good, thorough job so far, but it doesn't look as if they're going to get even a sniff of a lead. No witnesses yet again. For a while I thought they were going to start looking at Alan Dean's time here, but I think I managed to convince them it would be better for me to do any necessary digging around on my own manor.'

Bliss told them more of what he had learned about the murder.

'Whoever took out Weller and Dean were very professional,' Chandler said, sucking some tomato sauce from her fingers.

'So a hitman and not a cop,' Dunne said thoughtfully.

'Why not one and the same?'

'Much more likely to be hits paid for by a cop,' Bliss suggested. 'It's not as if people like that are hard to find in our line of work.'

'True. So how about this born-again do-gooder? Snake, the dealer? What's the story there?'

'I think that's also going to be a dead end,' Bliss admitted. 'I'll run him through the system, and pull him in if I think it's necessary, but I think Wilson's culpability ended with providing Jodie with her regular fix.'

'Which makes him an accessory in my opinion,' Dunne growled.

Bliss nodded. 'Yeah. If only the law saw it that way. I'd have that bastard banged up for life.'

'Well, my trip to Lincoln was equally fruitless,' Chandler told them. 'Weller kept a neat office and tidy records. Nothing came up, no names, no numbers.'

'How was Mrs Weller?' Bliss sipped from a chilled bottle of Stella. In addition to watching his salt intake he was also supposed to cut down on his alcohol consumption. Pizza and beer wasn't quite what his ENT consultant had had in mind. Bliss was feeling much better now, though, the early morning vertigo a distant memory.

'She was fine. Welcoming. Quiet, as you'd expect. Appreciating what we were doing for her and her husband, I think.'

'Did you get the impression she'll keep schtum?'

'You mean will she try going around us to make an official appeal?' Chandler shook her head. 'I think she's shrewd enough to realise that something is not quite right, and that it's better if a lid is kept on it for the time being at least. Certainly I think she'll speak to you first if she decides to go a different way.'

That was as much as Bliss could hope for. He'd got the same impression from talking to Allison Weller on the telephone. He glanced to his left. 'Bobby? How did you get on?'

Taking a moment to fork some pasta into his mouth and chew it down, Dunne finally gave a slow shrug. 'I managed to spend some time with Hendry. He works security over at the Wittering RAF base, and happened to be on duty this morning. I went at him casually, purely as a fellow officer. I asked him about the triple nine, the response and the follow up. A few casual remarks about Weller. I had no sense that his replies were guarded. He pretty much gave me what we read in the reports.'

'He didn't seem anxious, agitated in any way?' Bliss asked.

'Not at all. There was no sign he felt threatened by anyone or anything. If I didn't know better, I'd say his involvement ended with that conversation he had with McAndrew.'

'On the other hand, perhaps he feels safe because he's keeping quiet,' Chandler suggested. 'I mean, we have to assume he was either bought off or frightened off all those years ago.'

Dunne was nodding. 'I didn't feel I could push it. I didn't want him to get a sense of what was going on. As far as Hendry was concerned, I was following up on a minor report, that's all.'

'No, you handled it just right,' Bliss told him. He didn't like to second-guess his close colleagues. 'It doesn't look like Hendry is going anywhere, so he'll keep. If things take off, then we can bring him in and go to work on him. Right now, it's best that he suspects nothing.'

'Tell the truth, he seemed like an okay bloke. I hope his part was as minor as we think Weller's was.'

'I've been giving that some thought,' said Chandler, slashing the air with her knife. Not quite the mark of Zorro, but it was a definite flourish. 'You know, it is possible they had no idea what they were into until it was too late. Maybe they were warned off initially by a more senior officer, a bit of gentle persuasion. It happens all the time – one cop doing someone a favour, bending the rules a little bit. Weller and Hendry could have swallowed some story, and only found out or were told later what they'd helped cover up.'

Bliss looked at her. Smiled. Penny liked to think the best of people. The perfect foil for his own misanthropic views. 'I hope you're right. I really do.'

'Maybe they didn't even know the full extent until the other night, when Jodie Maybanks's remains were found.'

Bliss glanced out of the rain-beaded window. Traffic was building up by the roundabout, and the nearby garage forecourt was overflowing. Drivers in the line of vehicles steamed almost as much as their wheels, and those pumping petrol seemed glad to be out of it, albeit only briefly. He gave Chandler's suggestion some thought, but this time he shook his head.

'You're forgetting one thing. The triple nine they attended was in Fletton. Even if the body had been unearthed there, it would still have been an impossible reach for Weller to tie its discovery in with what happened that night. No, if he knew or even suspected those remains were relevant to that accident report more than sixteen years ago, then he must have known about the cover-up. I'm not saying either he or Hendry had any part in the murder itself, only that Weller, at the very least, knew someone had died that night.'

Chandler nodded. 'You're probably right. I guess I was hoping for Allison Weller's sake that her husband might come out of this clean.'

'Yeah. She seemed like a very nice woman. I'm going to hate having to tell her about this.' Bliss glanced at Dunne, looking to change the subject slightly. 'So, did you get any time down in the catacombs?'

Dunne grimaced. 'Yeah, time and a lungful of dust. Those files are thick with it. Nothing of interest so far, though. I'll be diving back in this afternoon, but I'm not holding my breath.' He chuckled at the pun.

'So a complete waste of a morning,' Bliss complained.

'That's hardly unusual, boss,' Chandler pointed out. 'I wish I had a quid for every hour I've spent chasing my tail.'

He nodded. 'I know. I'm frustrated, that's all. Putting a name to our Jane Doe was a major boost, but this business of us working on our own in the background is a bit more complicated than I thought it would be. Take this morning, for instance, we haven't even discussed what our cover stories will be. Three of us working on three separate lines of investigation, none of which we can report back to the squad. None of which were actioned. Questions will be asked soon, tongues will start to wag. We need to deflect attention away from what we're doing.'

'So let's come up with something credible. Shouldn't be too hard for three major brains like us.'

Dunne continued eating, saying nothing. Bliss ran it through his mind. By later tonight or early tomorrow morning the squad would have everything actioned, witnesses spoken to, and the paperwork well under way. They would need further direction. Not only that, but Sykes would be breathing down his neck, looking to close the case completely.

'We could give the squad Jodie Maybanks and Simon Palmer as their focus. We started the legwork with both, but there's a lot more that could be done along those lines. It's mostly procedure, but frankly if Sykes has his way it'll only be for another couple of days, anyway.'

'And we could trim the squad down,' Dunne suggested, punctuating the air with his drink. 'Sykes will love you for it, but better still it'll suggest we're winding the inquiry down as he wants. Skeleton staff for the basics, while the three of us do the business.'

Nodding eagerly, Bliss said, 'That'd do it. Good thinking, Bobby.'

The big man shrugged. 'It's a gift.'

'And a rare one, at that. I'll also feel better about not wasting the time and talents of so many officers. By and large they have the essentials. The official essentials, that is. We three know what happened, as good as anyway. We know where it happened, and when. We also know how. All that's missing is the who.' He looked across at Chandler. 'Agreed?'

'Yep. Sounds about right to me. If there are any actions still outstanding, we can put a couple of uniforms on them. Have someone chase forensics, and a DC each for the life and times of Jodie Maybanks and Simon Palmer.'

Bliss finished off his lager. Deception was never easy to live with, but he was starting to feel a little better about the situation he found himself in.

***

One by one, the team members stood and informed the assembled group how far they had been able to take their actions. It was five twenty, Bliss and Chandler standing at the front as usual,

Mia Strong beside them making relevant notations on the various whiteboard pages retrieved from the network. Bobby Dunne hovered in the background, as much as a man his size was able to hover. The investigation had been running for a week.

A nervous uniform cleared his throat twice before reading from his notebook. 'The duty officer on the night of the triple nine, Sergeant Rhodes, is still stationed over at the Bridge Street Central nick. He called in sick last week, and then took seven days' holiday. He must have gone away because we can't contact him at home.'

'What day did he call in sick?'

A quick check of the notes. 'Wednesday morning, sir.'

Bliss nodded as if it were of little importance, though it was hugely significant. Rhodes may have either fled or been spirited away. Gone the way of Weller and Dean, perhaps. That would need to be checked out.

He surveyed the team once more. 'Malcolm Twist, anyone?' Twist had made the first emergency call the night Jodie Maybanks was run down.

'Still trying, boss,' DC Wallace replied. 'Chicago PD are tracking him. Details by morning, so they reckon.'

'That just leaves forensics.' He turned to Mia. 'DC Strong?'

'Everything is back with us, boss. Unfortunately, there's nothing we can use at this stage.'

Bliss tugged at his memory. 'There were a few scraps of cloth found with the remains. Anything on that?'

'Sacking and possibly a cotton top. The rest must have rotted away. I figure the remains were carried in the sack when they were moved from Fletton to Bretton Woods. Anything else of value was probably left behind in its original burial plot.'

That seemed a plausible explanation. Bliss gave a nod of appreciation. 'And the steel rod removed from our victim's leg? What do we have from Latents?'

Strong shook her head. 'Not a thing. Smudges only, I'm afraid.'

Bliss sighed. It was disappointing, but not a complete surprise. They had no fresh crime scene to work with. 'Okay,' he said. 'Listen up.'

He told them he was reducing the numbers on the team. There were a few groans of protest, but they all knew it was inevitable. Human resources were stretched to the limit right across the service, and whatever they might feel as a team or as individuals about the injustice of Jodie Maybanks's passing, the fact was they were looking at a sixteen-year-old murder.

As Chandler released some team members back to normal duty and gave out actions to others, Bliss started back to his office with guilt pressing on him like a shadow. He was running the case this way for all the right reasons, but that didn't stop him from feeling miserable about it.

Bliss was stopped by Sykes on his way back to his office. The super appeared harried. 'Are we confident enough about the identity of our remains to go public?' he asked.

They were standing in the main CID area, so the super's manner was cordial.

'Absolutely.'

'And your investigation?'

Bliss thought about what had been discussed earlier. 'Winding down,' he said. 'We've run through our options. There are a few loose ends to tie up before I'll be happy putting it to bed, but essentially, we're just about done.'

'Good. In that case, I'll relieve you of your media duties and make the announcement myself. I'll make it clear that whilst the inquiry is ongoing, we do not expect to conclude it with an arrest.'

'That's certainly the way it appears.' Bliss found it hard to lock eyes with Sykes. The man was enjoying himself, no doubt viewing the winding down of the case as a minor victory over Bliss.

'Free up your team, Inspector. Make sure your... loose ends are bound tight sooner rather than later.'

'Already ordered. It's pretty much a formality from here on.'

'A satisfactory conclusion, then,' Sykes said, smiling and nodding.

'If not being able to arrest and convict a killer can be deemed satisfactory, then yes. If not being able to deliver justice for Jodie Maybanks is satisfactory, then again, yes.' This time Bliss did meet the other man's eyes.

'You know what I meant, Inspector.' Sykes glanced around to see if they were being observed or could be overheard.

Bliss gave a stifled laugh. 'Yes. Unfortunately, I do.'

'This was never going to have a happy ending. Why waste valuable resources on it?'

'Why indeed?' Bliss shook his head and turned to walk away. 'Perhaps we should ask Jodie Maybanks's parents that question.'

TWENTY-FOUR

Bliss knew something was wrong the moment he opened his front door to find Bobby Dunne standing on the doorstep. Rain was falling so hard that Dunne looked soaked through even though his car was parked only yards away on the small drive. So close, in fact, that Bliss could hear the time bomb ticking of the engine as it cooled, steam rising from the bonnet as if from a skillet.

'Got a few minutes, Jimmy?' Dunne asked. As usual his face gave nothing away.

Bliss checked his watch. 'Fifty of them,' he said, stepping to one side and allowing his colleague inside. 'My undivided attention. Then you're on your bike.'

'Seeing the Bone Woman tonight?'

'Actually I am. She's due here at eight, by which time you'll be gone. Fancy a drink?'

Dunne nodded. 'A beer if you have one.'

Bliss jerked his thumb in the direction of the lounge. 'Grab a seat.'

A couple of minutes later he handed his DS a cold bottle of Directors bitter, and then took a seat opposite. Dunne had shed his jacket and was sitting with a bundle of folders on his lap, the buff envelopes fastened together with a thick rubber band. He took a sip of beer, gave the obligatory sigh of satisfaction, and sat back on the sofa. He smiled and shook his head as his eyes devoured the room.

'Three years,' he said. 'Three years you've lived here and still it looks as if you've either just moved in or are about to move out.'

'Penny said pretty much the same thing the other night.'

'I know. This time it's my turn to nag.'

'I'll put my mark on it eventually.' Bliss allowed his own gaze to wander. Beige walls, no photos and no pictures. A few meagre sticks of furniture. Only the TV and hi-fi looked as if they were comfortable here. More at home than he was. Perhaps more than he would ever be.

'Maybe the Bone Woman can help you out there, boss.'

'It's a bit too soon to start thinking along those lines, Bobby. We're taking baby steps at the moment, mate.'

Dunne tipped the neck of his bottle. 'Penny reckons she'll be good for you.'

Bliss rolled his eyes. 'Penny. That young woman wants to take the place of my mother, I swear it.'

The sergeant laughed. The fingers of the hand not clutching the bottle beat a restless tattoo on the stack of folders. Bliss noticed, eyes drawn to the movement, ears to the sound. Dunne's apparent anxiety was unusual.

'So, what brings you here tonight, Bobby? I hope you signed for those records and case notes.'

There was a slight pause. It lasted long enough for Bliss to think, *No, don't tell me, Bobby. Get up and walk away and let's never talk of this. I have a feeling that what we're about to discuss here will change my life forever.*

Dunne blew out some air. His eyes were glazed. 'I've found the link, boss. A link, anyway. The name of one officer who crops up in both the triple nine and the MisPer cases relating to Jodie Maybanks. Crops up in a significant way, too. In a way that's not entirely reflected on the electronic version of our records.'

Bliss eyed him for a few seconds. He remembered sensing something unusual about Bobby Dunne during lunch at the Pizza Hut. 'You found these records this afternoon?'

'No. This morning.'

'So why not mention it while Penny was with us?'

Dunne stared at him. '*Because* Penny was with us.'

'I hope you can explain that, Bobby.'

'I can. Fact is, Jimmy, the same officer signed off all the logs and case notes relating to the accident and the report made by Connie Rawlings.'

Bliss processed that news. Something acidic squirted in his stomach, which seemed to swell and press against his skin. His flesh crawled and prickled. His instincts had been right; this was going to be big.

'Then we must be talking about a senior officer,' he said.

'We are. Even more senior now.'

Swallowing hard and with some degree of difficulty, Bliss began to understand why Dunne had not wanted to involve Penny. 'Who are we talking about, Bobby? Is it someone still stationed in the city?'

Dunne set his bottle down on the carpet. He peeled off the rubber band and spread the folders, fanning them out like a deck of cards. 'It's all in here. The man we now have to look at very closely is Joseph Flynn. Inspector Flynn back then.'

Bliss couldn't have been more shocked if Dunne had told him Martians had been responsible. 'Flynn? Detective Chief Superintendent Flynn?'

Dunne gave a slow, solemn nod. 'It's not just that he's the only officer who is named in both cases, either. I checked the paperwork relating to each incident, and in the triple nine one it was Flynn who made the decision to drop the inquiry at such an early stage, and it was Flynn who suggested that McAndrew may have been intoxicated when he made the call. Flynn also closed the MisPer case, citing Jodie Maybanks's occupation as reason enough to believe that she had simply moved on to another area. Flynn got involved in both, he closed both. These particular records and case notes were buried well away from the ones our team discovered, and according to the signature on the inside flap, Flynn was the last officer to have had them.'

Bliss swallowed, something terrible snagging in his throat. It made sense for a senior officer to be involved, but none at all that the officer in question was Joe Flynn. Bliss knew people, he knew his fellow officers, and Flynn had come across as one of the good guys. Which, Bliss thought, perhaps he was. *Now*. He glanced across at Dunne.

'Surely we're not saying Flynn is also responsible for Weller and Dean? Tell me we're not thinking that, Bobby.'

'We have to think that, boss. We have no choice but to start there.'

Bliss ran a hand across his scar. Beads of sweat had broken out on his forehead. Cold. Clammy. It was possible that Flynn had covered the tracks for someone else, and that the same someone else was responsible for the murders of Weller and Dean. Equally, it was entirely possible that Flynn lived behind a mask and had blood dripping from his hands. Bobby Dunne was right, though. Flynn was in the frame for it all, and everything they did from this point on had to be based on that premise.

'You're certain his is the only name that crops up in both cases?'

Dunne nodded. 'Neither Weller nor Hendry were listed on the MisPer report. PC Rhodes, duty officer the night of the triple nine, may have been on duty at the time of the MisPer, but he's not named.'

Bliss leaned forward, elbows resting on his knees, head dropping into his hands. Not an ounce of his experience or expertise could have led him to this outcome. That Flynn was involved felt like a betrayal. Strands were interlocking at last, but for the first time in his career, Bliss wished he could simply walk away from a crime.

'You were right to keep this from Penny,' he said to Dunne. He wet his lips, feeling a sharp pain building behind the hollows of his eyes. This was going to be a long, dark night. 'I need to think very hard before I involve her any further.'

'What's to involve?' Dunne asked. He'd picked up his beer again and had taken a long swig. 'You'll be dropping this now, right?'

'Dropping it?'

The bottle paused halfway back to Dunne's mouth. His eyes became thin slits. 'Of course. You're not going to continue investigating this? Not now you know who is involved.'

'What else do you suggest I do?'

'Bury it, man. As deep as you possibly can. I'll put these files back where they'll never be found again. Wind the Jodie Maybanks case down, close it like Sykes wants you to, and forget all about it. No one need know a thing.'

'I'll know.'

'So what? Nothing good can come of this now.'

Bliss knew the DS was right. Bad could only now get worse. Still he gave an apologetic shrug. 'I have to pursue this, Bobby.'

Dunne's features took on a look of astonishment. 'With respect, Jimmy, are you crazy? Are you out of your fucking mind? We're talking about Joe Flynn here. The most respected Detective Chief Superintendent in the entire county. He's already earmarked for the next rung on the ladder. He's Mr Goldenballs, and you want to chase him down.'

'I know all that. Damnit, Bobby, I regard him as a personal friend. But if he's our man, I have to do something about it.'

'And what if he's only involved in the Jodie Maybanks murder? What if Weller and Dean are down to someone else? Someone who helped Flynn back then. Or may have been helped by Flynn.'

'Then he's still guilty. Of something. Guilty and still running our nick.'

'I can't believe you want to go digging around in this now you know Flynn is in the frame,' Dunne complained.

Bliss kept his gaze steady and unblinking. 'And I can't believe you don't.'

Bobby Dunne got to his feet, setting the folders aside as he filled the room with his frame. 'But it would be madness, boss. You can't sniff around someone like him without kicking up a shit-storm. If he gets to hear about it he'll crucify you, even if he's done nothing wrong. And if he's guilty of what you think he is, then it may be even worse. You're not just risking your career here, Jimmy. You could be risking your life.'

Dunne was on a roll. Absolutely right in everything he said. From his own bitter experience, Bliss knew that sometimes you broke the rules, broke the very laws you'd vowed to uphold, and he had been guilty of both in the past. But there were also times when you had to confront apparent hypocrisies, ignore the warning voices inside your head, and do what your heart told you. DCS Flynn was everything Bliss thought a senior officer should be; he'd come up through the ranks, had walked a tough beat in the Toxteth area of Liverpool, had led officers stoically despite his personal political beliefs during the miners' strikes, and held the reins of power with the grip of a man who had never forgotten his roots. Flynn had taken a gamble on Bliss when few others had even considered the risk, had looked beyond the sealed records and ill-disguised disdain from the Met, and demonstrated solidarity and compassion once the air had settled after the last major murder inquiry debacle.

Bliss owed Flynn. Big time. But not if the man was a murderer. Bliss felt the same indignation now as he had when speaking to Gordon Wilson, the Snake. It didn't matter what good you did afterwards. Taking a life meant you would always be a killer. It was a badge of dishonour you could never throw away. Bliss looked deep within himself and accepted that a part of him wanted to do exactly as Dunne had suggested, to just turn his back and move on. But the larger part of him demanded he do the right thing.

'I have to do this, Bobby,' he said eventually, hearing the dull tone of disappointment in his own voice. 'I know what the risks are. I'm not asking you to stick with me. I don't expect that from you, would not expect it from anyone. Just promise me you won't do anything to force me to make it official.'

The heavily built sergeant had retaken his seat and now sat on the edge of the cushion with both hands pressed to his temples. He couldn't look small if he tried, but to Bliss he did appear shrunken.

'I'm not sure what I want to do at the moment, boss. Apart from run a mile, that is. Logic tells me to back off, leave you to it, but something else tells me you're going to need some help.'

'Don't do it for me, Bobby.' Bliss shook his head. 'Do what's right for you. I carry my own water.'

'And Penny?'

'That one I'll sleep on.'

'Perhaps I'll do the same.'

'Fair enough. Usual pre-briefing meeting in my office, then?'

DS Dunne let go a huge sigh. It seemed to last minutes. 'I still say you're crazy.'

Bliss barked a short, humourless laugh. 'You may well be right.'

'Sorry I ruined your evening, Jimmy.'

Bliss frowned. Then he realised what Dunne meant. For a few minutes he'd forgotten all about Emily Grant and their night out together. The job again. It had taken over. And from what Bobby Dunne had just told him, it wasn't about to let go any time soon.

TWENTY-FIVE

The movie was excellent. The Pixar people had done it again. The basic premise about a bunch of dysfunctional aliens trying to live as human beings reminded Bliss of the American TV comedy, *3rd Rock from the Sun*. Bliss thought the script was hysterical, way too smart for kids. CGI graphics seemed to have advanced yet again. He loved his sci-fi stuff, but films like *Toy Story*, *Shrek*, *Ice Age* and *The Incredibles* had blown him away. This new one was right up there.

The company had been pretty good, too.

After the film, he and Emily Grant had a couple of drinks in the Windmill, where he had taken her for their meal on Sunday. The bar was small and reeked of old world charm, the original stonework exposed, net curtains up at the tiny windows, sturdy wooden support beams functional rather than aesthetic. The place was a thick fug of smoke, but the atmosphere was pleasant and, best of all, they sold Guinness. Bliss put away the first one quickly, relaxed more over the second.

'You seem to have a lot on your mind,' Emily said, taking Bliss by surprise. He thought he'd managed to keep his concerns at bay, his mind on their date. She'd seen through him, though.

He apologised. 'I don't mean to be distant. I've really enjoyed myself tonight.'

'You haven't been distant. Not exactly. I can just tell.'

He inclined his head. Allowed the observation with a rueful grin. 'With my job it's not always possible to switch off completely. I'm not exactly conscious of my mind wandering, but I know it does.'

'You did seem to be wrapped up in the film, though.' She smiled at him, drank some of her white wine.

'It was a good choice. I'm a sucker for films like that. It surprised me that you were, though.'

Her smile grew broader. 'Yet again my choice of career goes before me. I'm sure you're not the only one who thinks I'm an old fuddy-duddy whose idea of fun is a night in with the cats and a spot of knitting before my pre-bed Horlicks.'

Bliss put down his glass. 'Hey, I don't think anything of the sort. I'm sorry if I…'

Emily was laughing at him now. 'I'm kidding, Jimmy,' she said. 'You're so easy to tease.'

He took a breath. Notched back his shoulders a little. Nodded and smiled. 'Yeah, you had me going there.'

'Really?' Her eyebrows twitched. 'I had no idea I had that effect on you.'

Both coy and flirtatious at the same time. Bliss liked that about her. As their eyes met his mind wound on the clock. Where next? Another peck on the cheek outside in the car park, or coffee back at his place? The anxiety he was feeling now was different from anything related to either work or his illness. Bliss knew his job inside out, backed his judgement every time, and he was coming to terms with the immediate effects of the disease. Both were challenges, but this was different. This was personal and he had no idea how to proceed. It had been such a long time.

As if she had been reading his mind, Emily leaned across the table and took his hand in hers. 'I'll put you out of your misery,' she said. 'I'm not a tease, though I am flirting with you. I like you very much, Jimmy, but I'm not about to jump into bed with you. I'm not the kind of woman who has needs without some kind of emotional bond. I think there's hope for us, and if we get there I can guarantee you a damn good time. But neither of us is ready, so I don't think we're quite there yet. Is that all right by you?'

It was his turn to laugh. 'I don't think I've ever met anyone quite as blunt as you.'

'Is it a trait you approve of?'

Bliss nodded. 'Very much so. And yes, it is all right by me. I like you, too, Emily, and I find you very attractive. But if I'm honest, you're right when you say I'm not ready.'

'And I thought men were always ready.'

He remembered something she had said on the night he'd called her out to Bretton Woods. 'Maybe I'm not quite as shallow as you thought I was.'

Emily took a sip of her drink. 'Oh, I could see that right from the word go, Jimmy. You have an unnatural depth.'

He frowned. 'I'm not sure "unnatural" is a good word to be using.'

'I'm not sure either. Not yet.'

She asked him about the investigation, how it was proceeding. It was a leap away from their discussion, but Bliss was glad of it.

'It's not.' He hated lying to her, but anything else he told her other than the complete truth would not gel with what would be reported in the local media following Sykes's briefing. And there was no way he could reveal what was really going on. Bliss settled for offering the official line.

'That's a shame,' she said. 'Somehow I feel close to this young woman. I suppose because I've spent time with her, handled her bones. It's sad to think that we may never know what happened to her.'

'I agree. But is there much difference between Jodie's remains and those that are, say, a thousand years old?'

'Yes. Because she was murdered during my lifetime. It always makes a difference.'

Bliss couldn't argue with that. 'It's not completely over,' he allowed. 'Who knows what the next couple of days may bring? I've seen cases move from dead to solved within a few hours.'

'She needs to be at peace.'

'If I can help her, I will.' The promise was made as much to himself as Emily.

They settled for parting in the pub car park, but this time it was no peck on the cheek. Emily's lips were warm and soft, their kiss long and gentle. Her fingers brushed his cheek.

'I understand we have more to get past than just your job,' she told him. 'I think what you feel for your wife is something to admire, and it tells me more about you than you might imagine. I told you on Saturday that I would give you time. I meant it then, and I mean it now. If something is intended to happen between us, then it will. If not, I'm sure we'll have some good times and a few laughs. What could be wrong with that?'

'Nothing,' Bliss breathed, the moment almost overwhelming him. 'Nothing at all.'

***

Instead of driving straight home, a journey of no more than a minute or two, Bliss headed out of the city towards the tiny hamlet of Elton. He circled around for a few minutes before finding a secluded spot from which he could observe a particular house. He parked up and killed the engine, switched off his headlights. Bliss settled back into the pool car's seat. For the next hour he watched the illuminated windows of DCS Flynn's home.

Flynn's dark blue VW Passat was parked in the driveway of the detached, comfortable family dwelling that looked to Bliss like a barn conversion. The house backed onto acres of farmland, its closest neighbour more than the length of a football pitch away. In one downstairs room a blueish light flickered, the TV obviously on. Every so often there was a little movement in and around the house, but no one left, no one entered. Bliss had no idea what he'd expected to see. Flynn and his remaining accomplices hatching plots, perhaps.

Bliss sat and thought about Flynn's possible involvement until the air inside the car grew cold enough to cause his breath to become visible. He still couldn't visualise Flynn being responsible for murder. The man he knew, liked and respected could not be capable of such actions. Yet still there were few other conclusions to be drawn from the evidence Dunne had discovered. The windows started to mist, becoming as fogged as Bliss's thoughts.

Disgruntled and angry, he fired up the engine, turned the Ford around and headed back towards the dull sodium glow of the city painting the dark sky ahead. His mind now in a whirl, Bliss knew he was in for yet another sleepless night.

***

Bonnie and Clyde were down for the night. With just his thoughts for company, Bliss made himself busy, tidying up and attempting to sort his CD, DVD and book collections into some sort of order. He found a box of old cassettes, and slipped one marked 'Various' into the player. Just a few bars in he recognised one of his mixed tapes from the eighties. Jimmy Barnes rubbing shoulders with The Cars, 1927 following It Bites. The songs relaxed him, but still his eyes would not grow heavy.

Bliss knew the insomnia had a grip on him, but equally he understood why. A dozen years spent tucked up beside the same warm body created a pattern of sleep based around specific comforts. The additional heat, familiar movements, the sound of Hazel's breath, soft exhalations wafting across his cheek, occasional gentle snoring, and her amusing dream conversations. All that awaited him in bed now was a pillow, one that still smelled of Hazel's perfume, because once a month he sprayed her favourite Eau de Toilette over its cover. For a large part of his life, the simple act of going to bed had been associated with pleasure. Now it felt cold and lonely, and no matter where his mind had led him throughout the day, slipping between the sheets never failed to remind him of his grief. How was it possible to sleep when missing his wife caused an ache that threatened to tear him in two?

Sitting with his spine pressed up against the living room wall, with Steve Perry of Journey wondering who was crying now, Bliss pictured his own sleeping form in the bed above, wondering if anyone would ever lie beside him again. Someone like Emily Grant, maybe. It was nothing more than an idle thought. He liked her a lot, and as he'd told her earlier he found her immensely attractive. But she would never fill the void in his heart. Never soothe that dull ache. Never be able to recapture the part of him that had been torn away the night Hazel was murdered.

Bliss realised he was erecting barriers, closing his mind to any stray notions of future happiness. His wife had been killed. He had failed to protect her. He did not deserve to live his life unbound by heavy chains, and he most certainly was not worthy of ever being blessed by love again.

This was his penance.

The night continued to fight him as usual. What little sleep he managed led to dreams he did not wish to pursue. The alarm was set for six thirty, but he was up, showered and dressed an hour before it went off. Tea and toast for breakfast, some time with Bonnie and Clyde. The angry sky unleashed its cargo shortly before seven. It brought to mind a homily: into each life a little rain must fall.

Fair enough, Bliss thought. He just hadn't expected such a deluge.

TWENTY-SIX

Connie Rawlings used a chipped nail to hook sleep from her eyes, her other hand clutching a thick towelling robe tight around her neck.

'Remember me?' Bliss asked. The smile he gave might not be winning, but it was genuine enough. He held up his open warrant card.

She blinked a couple of times before acknowledging recognition with a single nod of her head. 'You're a bit early if you decided to take me up on my offer of a freebie, love.'

She cracked a smile of her own. He could only guess at its legitimacy.

'I'm just after a chat right now, Connie. Ten minutes of your time is all I ask. I swear.'

She yawned and jerked her head. 'I just made a pot of coffee. Want some?'

'I'd love a cup,' Bliss replied, stepping into the hallway, the warmth of the house immediately enveloping him.

At the kitchen breakfast bar a couple of minutes later, Rawlings sat facing him, two steaming mugs on the counter between them. Her dirty blonde hair was tousled, sculpted into peaks and ridges during the night. Bliss imagined even Rawlings had forgotten its original colour. Without make-up she looked her age, bags tucked up beneath both eyes like a spare set of padded eyelids, deep lines causing her flesh to sag and gather around her neck and mouth. Yet still she was a sexual magnet. Bliss wondered how some women managed to achieve that without even trying.

'Connie,' he said, both hands cupping the warm mug. 'I'm here looking for answers. My investigation has stalled. I desperately want to find Jodie's killer, but time is running out and now is the moment for people to step up and be honest with me. Several people. Including you.'

'The honest hooker?' she said, peering at him over the top of a crooked smirk. Bliss could see interest there, though.

He nodded. 'I'm hoping so, yes.'

'You think I lied to you the other day, Inspector Bliss?'

'No. But I do think you held something back.'

Rawlings sipped some of her coffee. They both took it black, no sugar. It was strong and hit the spot. 'I don't know what you mean,' she said, still blinking sleep from grey eyes that had long since lost their lustre.

Bliss scratched the back of his neck. He wasn't sure himself, but he thought he was on the right track. 'When I asked you about Jodie's regular punters, you gave me Simon Palmer.'

'Uh-huh. Was that useful?'

'More interesting than useful, so I don't think we'll be taking it any further. Palmer admitted seeing Jodie, but I think he was genuinely shocked to hear of her murder. The thing is, Connie, at the time we were discussing Jodie I sensed you were being a bit evasive. Keeping something from me. I've given that some more thought, and I'm pretty sure I know why you weren't keen to open up.'

Setting her mug back down on the counter, Rawlings stared at him. 'You do?'

'Yes, I do. I think it's likely that one or maybe even several of Jodie's regulars were police officers. Now, if that's the case, I can see why you'd want to keep it to yourself. After all, I'm a copper, too, and you have no particular reason to trust me. You don't want any trouble, and I understand that. But you have to understand that I need to know the truth if I'm going to do my job. I need to know if she was taking care of cops. Perhaps one cop in particular.'

Bliss knew by the slight changes in her demeanour that he was right. Rawlings had stiffened, squared her shoulders, hard lines had reappeared on a face softened only moments before by the injection of caffeine. He drank from his own mug before continuing.

'It's difficult for you, I realise that. On the one hand you want to help Jodie, while on the other you want to remain under the radar.'

'I can't help Jodie now,' Rawlings said, her husky voice suddenly quick and loud. 'No one can help her now.'

He nodded. 'That's true enough. As it stands. But what I mean is that you might be able to help nail her killer. To my mind, Jodie would see that as helping her.'

'You never even knew Jodie.' The woman's voice dripped with contempt. Her nostrils flared, and for a moment Connie Rawlings looked disgusted with his presence in her home.

Bliss widened his gaze. 'Oh, but I've known dozens of Jodies. Believe me, I have. Young girls who became part of the currency within their community, and who were then just flushed away like toilet paper. It's hard to find someone who cares, even within their own families. So why should you go out on a limb, right?'

'Right.' A defiant nod. Not matched by the uncertainty in her eyes. 'Why should I?'

'Because I think you're better than those who won't. On the surface you're as hard as nails, you sell your body to anyone who can come up with the right amount of cash, and you go to sleep every night wishing your life had been different. But there's something inside you, Connie. Something I can't define. But I know it's something that will compel you to do the right thing. All I ask is that you do it now. Don't wait until your conscience gets the better of you, until it's too late to be of help to us.'

The room was silent for a minute or two, other than the low hum of the refrigerator. They both drank their coffee, neither meeting the other's eyes. When he heard her take a long, faltering breath, Bliss knew he had her.

'How about if I give you a name?' he prompted, trying to make it easy on her. 'One name. You nod or shake your head. That way you tell me, but you don't tell me. How's that sound?'

'Decent,' she said. Her eyes drilled into him now. Bliss didn't think it was a word she used often.

He nodded. 'Flynn,' he said. 'Joe Flynn.'

After only the slightest pause, Rawlings nodded.

Bliss felt his heart begin to flutter, then start to beat louder and harder. His face grew hot. 'Thank you. I know that wasn't easy for you.'

'Is it the answer you wanted?' she asked him.

'Let's just say it was the one I expected.'

'How did you know I'd tell you? What made you think I had that in me? I certainly didn't. Not right up until the moment I agreed.'

'I think I'm a good judge of character.' Saying it out loud made him think of Flynn and how wrong he'd been about the man. He gave a shrug and a faint smile touched his lips. 'Most of the time, anyway.'

'Was it him? Did this Flynn guy murder Jodie?'

'I don't honestly know. I couldn't tell you even if I was certain, but I'm being up front with you, Connie. All I'm doing at the moment is chasing down the leads.'

'So is this copper still in the job?'

'Very much so. He's my boss.'

She looked at him for a long moment. 'And what if it is him? Will you make it just go away?'

'No. If I didn't intend doing the right thing, I wouldn't be here. I can promise you that, at the very least.'

A silence fell between them for a few seconds. Then Connie seemed to make up her mind about something. She smiled and said, 'For some strange reason, I find myself believing you.'

'Good. I meant every word. Thanks for the coffee,' he said, getting to his feet. 'And for the information.'

She looked up at him and, as he had the other day, Bliss saw vulnerability in Connie's expression. As if suddenly she didn't want to be alone.

'Do you have to go?' she asked him.

Her meaning was clear to them both.

Bliss knew he should have walked away and left her to prepare for her punters. Should have said thanks to the offer, but no thanks. His blossoming relationship with Emily Grant was more than enough to make him question the way he lived his life, without adding to the confusion. In that instant, however, he got caught up in a vulnerability all of his own. Overcome by weakness and need. And instead of saying and doing the right things, he said, 'No. Not yet I don't.'

***

It was still raining when Bliss stepped back outside an hour or so later. The whole winter was yet to come and already he was sick of the inclement weather. He yanked up the collar of his coat and started to run for the pool car which he'd had to park several bays away. Instinct revealed movement around him before he saw the two figures.

'Been visiting relatives, have you, sir?' one of them asked.

Two patrol officers. Gascoigne and Hopley. Luke and Jerry, Bliss thought. Both out of Thorpe Wood. They wore fluorescent yellow waterproof jackets, and were hardly trying to blend in with their surroundings.

'Not quite,' Bliss answered. He gave a brief smile then went to move past them.

Gascoigne stepped to his right to bar the way. 'Been getting our pole greased, have we?' he asked.

Bliss stopped in his tracks, momentarily taken aback by the audacity of the confrontation. Turned his head to face the tall, gangly officer, whose cheeks and forehead were pitted with acne scars.

'I think that's enough, Constable. Now, if you'd step aside, I want to be on my way.'

'I don't think I can do that, sir. I'm sure you're keen to see the law enforced at all times, and I'd be neglecting my duty if I didn't follow up on a potential crime.'

'And what crime would that be?'

Gascoigne folded his arms, smiling, enjoying himself hugely. 'On the scrubber's part, prostitution. On yours, solicitation.' He frowned. 'I would have thought you'd know the law, sir. What with you being a detective, and all.'

'Give me a break. Look, I'm sure you don't want to be standing out here in this bloody awful weather, and I know I don't. So, joke over, and let's just get on with our days, eh?'

'This *is* our day. You've been seen entering and leaving the home of a known prostitute, and you are now suspected of indulging in an illegal act.'

Bliss bit down on an angry retort. Sucked in some air and let it go slowly. 'Is this a hangover from that run-in I had with Grealish the other day?'

Gascoigne shook his head. 'I don't know what you mean, sir. This has nothing to do with *Sergeant* Grealish. It's my understanding that a crime may have just taken place, in that you solicited sex with a known brass.'

Bliss closed his eyes for a second, reeling in his rage. This was neither the time nor the place to lose it. 'Okay, officer. You've had your fun. Now, I'm getting wet, I'm getting cold, and I'm getting extremely pissed off with you. So stand aside and then keep the fuck away from me.'

Without taking his eyes off Bliss, Gascoigne said, 'Did you hear that, Constable Hopley? DI Bliss here just verbally abused me. That's crime number two.' He held up two gloved fingers.

'Want me to go for a third,' Bliss said, adding an edge to his voice, 'and take your fucking head off?' The will to keep a lid on his temper had lasted all of thirty seconds.

His outburst was met with another smile. Then Gascoigne took a step closer, lowering his head. When he spoke, Bliss could feel the officer's warm breath on his face.

'You're coming with us, Inspector Bliss. You can come voluntarily, or you can come in handcuffs. But make no mistake, you are coming.'

'What the fuck is all this about?' Bliss asked, his gaze narrowing. He wiped rainwater from his scalp. 'I was interviewing a witness. End of story.'

'Then you'll be back on the street helping to solve crime by lunchtime.'

'Why are you doing this?' He put back his head, then shook it. 'Why?'

'I'm upholding the law, sir.' The officer's face was solemn now. 'It's what I'm paid to do.'

Outraged, Bliss gave himself a moment. He could push his way past Gascoigne and call the bluff. Only, if it wasn't a bluff, he could find himself arrested. There was a time to fight, and a time to take your licks. He hoped he was wise enough to know the difference.

'Are you going to let me drive myself in?' he asked, biting down on the bitterness he felt.

'Are you asking for favouritism, sir?'

Bliss blew out a sigh. 'You're going to make this as difficult as you can, aren't you, Gascoigne?'

The officer nodded. And winked.

***

When Penny Chandler walked into the interview room, Bliss could tell she was having a hard job keeping a straight face. 'I just wanted to look into the eyes of a real criminal,' she said. She studied him for a moment, then gave a mock shudder. 'It's frightening.'

He didn't feel like playing along. He was angry and confused. 'When am I getting out of here?' Bliss asked. He felt something harsh and acidic churning in his chest.

'Actually, I think you're going down for a long stretch.'

'Penny!' He injected severity into his eyes. 'I'm not bloody well happy with this, so spare me the infantile humour, eh?'

Chandler leaned back against the wall and folded her arms beneath her breasts. 'Oh, come on, boss. You have to see the funny side?'

'No. I don't. I'm fucking furious, if you must know.'

'So do something about it. Get Gascoigne and Hopley in here and demand to be charged or released. Have them swab you and your masseuse and run DNA on you if they try to keep this lunacy going.'

Bliss glanced away. He swallowed. Shook his head. 'I can't do that. If they swab me they'll find her DNA all over me. If they check her sheets they'll find my short and curlies. If they check her bedside bin they'll find a condom with my semen in it.'

Chandler laughed. She pushed herself upright, walked over and sat down at the table opposite him. 'Nice one, boss. See, you do still have your sense of humour.'

'Look at me, Penny,' he said. 'Do I seem as if I'm enjoying this?'

It took a while, but then her eyes widened to almost comic proportions. 'You cannot be serious. Tell me this is the biggest wind up there has ever been.'

'I wish I could.' He looked down at his hands spread out on the narrow table that stood between them. He could not meet her eyes. 'But the fact is, if they decide to push this, I'm fucked.'

He heard her draw breath. 'Jesus H Christ. What were you thinking?'

'I wasn't. I went to ask Connie Rawlings a few questions. We got caught up in a moment. I can't explain it.'

'Fucking hell, Jimmy. You're not a twelve-year-old kid. You can't just shrug this off and say "Sorry, I didn't know what I was doing".'

He looked up at her. She was right. There was no defence. Except perhaps there was. 'Penny, the way it goes is like this: I accept that what I did makes me less of a copper, but not doing so would have made me less human. I'm not sure I'd miss being a copper right now, but I do sometimes miss being part of the human race. What happened between me and Connie Rawlings was the most natural thing in the world.'

'But it was wrong.'

Bliss shook his head. 'I thought so, too. Right up until a few minutes ago.'

After a few seconds' pause, Chandler spread her hands. 'Is she going to back you up?'

'I have no idea. She probably doesn't think we did anything wrong, either. If they ask her if money changed hands, she'll say no. If they ask if we had sex… my guess is she'll be honest.'

'Then let's hope they don't ask.'

'I have no idea what they might do. I'm pretty damned sure they were not parked outside her place when I arrived, and I'd love to know what made them pull me in. Or should I say, who?'

Chandler nodded, slowly, as if it had just dawned on her what might lie behind the incident. 'Look, boss, I'll have another word with the custody sergeant, see if we can speed this up. The main thing is they haven't formally arrested or charged you. The word around the nick is that you had a ruck with Grealish and this is some sort of payback.'

He nodded. 'Yeah, so everyone can have a good laugh at my expense.'

'Is it true? Did you and Grealish get into it?'

'It was nothing. A playground scuffle, that's all.'

'Over me? That's what they're saying. You had words because of how he'd been with me.'

'I'd've done the same for anyone else in my team. Male or female.'

Chandler smiled at him. 'Thank you. I can fight my own battles, but thank you anyway. I'm only sorry it ended up like this.'

'I'm not so sure this has anything to do with Grealish. I think this is another warning. A bit more subtle than trying to shove me off the road, but a warning all the same.'

'Do you know how paranoid that sounds?'

'I know. But I think I'm right. Someone wants to ruffle my feathers, and they've used the Grealish issue as cover.'

She gave a shrug. 'I don't know, boss. I'm not so sure. Look, do you want me to get your union rep down here?'

'Not yet. Let's see how far they decide to push. If I think they're really going to move on this, then I'll throw them a "no comment" and request my legal representation.'

'I don't know what to say. At any other time I suppose I'd be happy that you'd finally got your end away. But with a brass? And how the hell does that sit with what you and Emily have going?'

Bliss had been asking himself the same question. 'I don't know, Pen. I don't exactly know what Emily and I have going, and I don't know how this sits with whatever we do have. To tell the truth, I don't know much about anything anymore.'

Chandler opened her mouth to say something else, but stopped when the door to the interview room opened with a groan and Superintendent Sykes stepped in. His eyes fixed immediately on Bliss as if he were a tasty snack.

'Leave us please, DC Chandler,' he commanded.

'Of course.' She stood. Gave Bliss a swift smile. 'Chin up, boss. I'll see what's happening and get back to you.'

'By rights you ought not to have been in here,' Sykes told her. His voice was clipped. 'You go through proper procedures next time.'

When Chandler had left them, Sykes spent a few seconds positioning himself, looking for just the right pose. Bliss wanted to laugh at him. Or slap him. Or both.

'Well now, Inspector,' Sykes said. 'It would seem we have a bit of a situation here.'

Bliss made no reply. He silently cursed himself for allowing this to happen.

'I'm told your defence is that you were in Stanground this morning obtaining information,' Sykes went on, enjoying the taste of each word. 'Is that correct?'

Bliss thought about throwing his first 'no comment' at Sykes, but decided to see if he could work this out. 'It is, yes. I wanted to speak with Connie Rawlings about Jodie Maybanks.'

'And Ms Rawlings is, I assume, a registered CHIS?'

Bliss shook his head. Saw where this was headed. 'No. She's not an informant, as such.'

'Yet you were seeking information from her?'

'As I've explained.'

'So, if we ignore for now the charge of solicitation, we still need to address the fact that you discussed an ongoing investigation with an unregistered CHIS and did so without permission from a superior.'

Policy and procedure dictated that a meeting with a CHIS had to be approved by a senior officer. That this was seldom upheld did not matter here and now, Bliss realised. It was the stick with which Sykes had chosen to beat him. As it turned out, the super had selected the wrong weapon.

Bliss looked up. 'The problem with your theory,' he said, 'is that I was interviewing Connie Rawlings as a witness, not an informant. I don't need anyone's permission to do that.'

Something pulsed above Sykes's right eye. Clearly he hadn't considered this angle. He took off his glasses to polish them with a square of yellow cloth pulled from his trouser pocket.

'That's one version,' he said. 'We may yet have to decide if it's the truth.'

'There's no decision required. It either is the truth or it isn't. In this case, it is.'

'I stand corrected. Our decision, therefore, is whether or not we believe you, Inspector.'

The whole subject seemed to well up inside Bliss's head and deep within his chest. All at once he didn't care what happened. The only thing that mattered was dictating where it went from this point on. Slowly, without fuss, he got to his feet. His ears were ringing.

'I'm here of my own free will,' he said, drawing the other man's attention. 'And I can leave anytime I choose. I know this because I'm a police officer, and I've had to remind suspects of that so many times in the past it's ingrained in every pore. So, here's what you do. Arrest me. Arrest me, or I walk. Right now.'

'You think I wouldn't?' Sykes asked.

Bliss heard the truth in the man's voice. 'I think you'd like to. I think you'd read my rights to me yourself, if you could remember them – they've changed a little since you last did it. But you know what? I know you're not going to. I know you have nothing on me. And I know this because you're such a piss-poor copper it's written all over your stupid smug face.'

Sykes sprang away from the wall like a cat startled by a tin can clattering to the floor. 'How dare you speak to me like that? How dare you?' Spittle flew from his lips.

Bliss moved close enough that their faces were only inches apart. 'I dare because it's true. You're a joke, Sykes. A joke and a fucking disgrace. Did you arrange this? Did you set me up?'

'I have better things to do with my time, Inspector.'

Shaking his head, Bliss uttered a short laugh. 'No. The sad thing is, you don't. Even so, I do actually believe you. The fact is, you haven't got the imagination to pull a stunt like this.'

Bliss stepped past the super and headed out through the doorway. Sykes put a hand on his shoulder. 'This is not over, Inspector. Not by a long way.'

'Yes, it is,' Bliss told him, shrugging off the hand. 'At least as far as I'm concerned.'

'I'm your superior officer!'

'Then act like it. Arrest me. Do your job. And if you're not prepared to do that, keep the hell away from me.'

With that parting shot, Bliss stepped out of the room without looking back.

TWENTY-SEVEN

The first thing Bliss did after leaving the interview room was to get Connie Rawlings released. She had fared less well than he, having been shoved in a cell upon arrival at Thorpe Wood some twenty minutes after his ignoble entry into the station. With an enraged Sykes wailing in his wake, Bliss instructed a smirking custody sergeant to get word to Gascoigne and Hopley that they were to either charge Rawlings or let her walk. They had ten minutes, he told the uniform, or he was going to call in a solicitor and make a formal complaint. The two officers used up every second of the time he had allowed them, but Bliss was happy to see Rawlings eventually making her way up from the cells into the custody area.

'Let me see you out,' he said, taking her by the arm. Whoever had brought Rawlings in hadn't allowed her to get changed, and her dressing gown was wrapped tight around her body, slippers slapping against bare heels. Bliss was conscious of being watched closely by several uniforms milling around, their amusement obvious now that the rumour grapevine had done its work. He ignored them completely and hoped they'd choke on his contempt.

Connie Rawlings raised her eyebrows at him. Lines bracketed her mouth as her lips curled into a half smile. 'I'm not sure I should. I might get arrested again.'

Bliss laughed. A hollow sound. She was a tough nut to crack. When he spoke he made sure he could be heard by everyone in the area.

'I'm not sure even those two arsewipes would try that again. Arresting a witness once is a mistake, to repeat it would be the work of morons.' He shook his head as he led her up the stairs to the ground floor. 'I'm so sorry, Connie. I had no idea this might happen.'

Her smile became full, genuinely warm. 'It's not you who should be apologising, it's those storm troopers. Why were they so gung-ho? Have you upset someone around here?'

'Several people. You could take your pick.'

'It comes to something when your lot go to these lengths to nail one of their own.'

He nodded. It made him think about the Jodie Maybanks case, how to proceed with investigating Detective Chief Superintendent Flynn. 'Look,' he said. 'If you've lost money being shut up in here, I can help you out.'

'Are you offering to pay for what happened between us?'

'No.' He shook his head firmly. 'That's not what I meant at all.'

They'd reached the outside steps. She stopped walking. Her eyes drew his in. 'Does that mean you weren't thinking of me as a brass at the time?'

Bliss sensed the answer might be important to her. It was to him. 'Anything but, Connie. Not before, during, or after. I wanted to be with you. It's as simple as that.'

'Good.' She gave a nod. 'Then keep your money to yourself. Even us hookers are entitled to a private life.'

He smiled. 'If you wait here a moment, I've arranged for someone to run you home.'

'Thanks. I'd feel a bit out of place getting on the bus dressed like this.' She glanced down at herself and laughed at her own joke. 'Listen, let's get things straight between us. I don't expect you to come calling again. I don't expect anything from you. It was nice, but I'm not stupid enough to think it was anything more than a one-off.'

Connie Rawlings was letting him off the hook. They both knew it.

'By the way,' she said, lowering her voice. 'I've been thinking more about our chat earlier. I don't know if she'll be able to tell you any more than I have, but next to me, Jodie's closest friend was another working girl called Simone Jackson. As far as I know she now runs her own set of girls over at a rented place in Werrington.'

Bliss nodded his appreciation. It was never bad news to have alternative leads. 'Thanks for that, Connie. I'll bear it in mind.'

'It amazes me how many of the old gang are still spreading our legs for a living.' She gave a self-deprecating laugh.

'How long are you going to keep at it?' Bliss asked her. 'I mean, what are your plans?'

'Oh, I'm saving for early retirement. There are a few freaks who like their women old and saggy, but I'm just about worn out.' She chuckled. 'Well, one part of me is, at least. When that day comes you won't see my stilettos and suspenders for dust.'

Bliss smiled and nodded. He admired her enormously. He'd met many prostitutes. They didn't all have a heart of gold, but they were as human as the next person, each with human hopes, needs, and frailties.

'Listen, I have to nip off. I hope things go the way you want them to. Take care of yourself, Connie.'

'You too.' Her eyes narrowed as she looked up at him. 'You know something, Inspector? For a copper, you're not a bad bloke.'

'It's Jimmy,' he told her. 'Jimmy Bliss. And Connie, if vice pay you a visit in the future, give me a call.'

'I told you before, you don't owe me anything.'

'Yes I do,' Bliss said. He touched the back of his fingers to her cheek, ran them around the curve. He felt her tremble. 'More than you'll ever know.'

***

Bliss rode the lift to the first floor and walked straight to his office. A couple of phone calls tracked down Chandler and Dunne, and Bliss asked them to meet him as soon as possible. When they arrived he closed the door behind them and told them both to pull up a chair. He glanced at Dunne before looking directly at DC Chandler.

'Penny,' he said. 'We have some fresh information. I wasn't sure at first if I wanted to share it with you, but we're already running two lines of investigation on the same case, and I don't want a third getting in the way. So, I'm going to tell you something Bobby and I already know. You need to take it on board, make your own decision. Okay?'

She nodded. Frowning. 'Sounds serious,' she said.

'It is. Very much so. Penny, the name of the officer responsible for closing both the triple nine and MisPer inquires relating to Jodie Maybanks is Joe Flynn.'

Bliss felt her eyes bore into his, but she said nothing immediately. He went on. 'Earlier this morning, Connie Rawlings confirmed that among Jodie's customers were a few coppers, and that Joe Flynn was a regular.'

Chandler exhaled slowly. Took her time with it. When she looked up at him once more, Bliss saw genuine fear in her eyes.

'Tell me you're taking this to someone higher up the tree,' she said. Her eyelids fluttered anxiously.

He cleared his throat. 'That's not the way I've decided to go.'

'Boss, I appreciate what you want to do with this case and why, but surely you have to see that we have no choice now.'

'On the contrary, I think it's even more important to keep this to ourselves.'

'Why, for heaven's sake?'

'Because Flynn may just be too big a fish. At the moment we have absolutely no evidence. Yes, we have the case notes and his signature, but they prove nothing. The fact that he was one of Jodie's regulars proves nothing. If those all go up the chain now, someone may decide we can live without the bad publicity, and simply persuade Flynn to take early retirement.'

'What, even if we can link him to the murders of Weller and Dean?'

'*If* we can. And that's exactly my point. Those links are even more tenuous than the one with Jodie.' Bliss shook his head once more. 'I'm sorry, Penny. My mind is made up on this.'

Chandler glanced across at Dunne. 'What's your take, Bobby?'

The big man grunted. 'Not quite the same as yours. I think it's madness to carry on with this investigation, so we're agreed there. But I think we ought to drop the case completely and wind it up. In my opinion we have to let it go, shut the investigation down and walk away.'

She thought about that for a while, then nodded and looked back at Bliss. 'That sounds like a plan, boss. Who cares if it's the coward's way out? At least we'll go on to fight another day. Whichever way you slice it, this is a war we can't win.'

Bliss pushed himself back in his chair and rubbed his eyes, which felt gritty and dry. The pleasures of the weekend seemed like a lifetime ago now.

'There are three ways to go. I've considered Bobby's, and now I've considered yours. Yours is the correct path to follow, Bobby's is probably the most sensible.'

'Then choose correct or sensible,' Chandler pleaded with him. 'Don't go with madness.'

He grinned. 'I have to, Penny. This is not just about Jodie Maybanks anymore. If Flynn is responsible for what happened to Jodie Maybanks, and you have to say it looks likely, then he's also responsible for Weller and Dean, if only indirectly. We can't allow him to get away with those murders as well.'

'Then we go down the route I suggested. Write it up and move it on. Make it someone else's problem.'

'I've already made it clear as to why I don't want to go that way. Penny, my mind is made up. Look, despite his reservations, Bobby is staying in. I need to know if you are, too.'

She spread her hands, shrugging. 'What, no pep talk about how if I quit now neither of you will think the worst of me?'

'No. Not this time. Like you said before, you're big enough and ugly enough to make up your own mind.'

'I don't believe I used the term "ugly".'

Bliss grinned. 'I was paraphrasing.'

'So you want to investigate Chief Superintendent Flynn in the background of the Jodie Maybanks case? You want to pry into his life and career? And you want to do all this while acting as SIO on the murder case?'

'I don't want to. I have no unhealthy desire to put my head on the block. But for me, there's no alternative. And I promise you that if what's left of the team start going down the same road as us, I won't steer them away.'

'It's a fine line, boss,' Dunne commented. 'I mean, we're already holding back crucial information. Isn't that steering them away?'

Bliss considered the question. Bobby was probably right. 'Look,' he said. 'Let's agree that I'm in the wrong here. I feel that as acutely as you two do. It's understood. A given. If push comes to shove I'll make it clear that you two were as much in the dark as anyone else on the squad. We'll need to cover your arses, but we can figure it out. Bobby's in for the time being. So, Penny, that just leaves you to decide if you're along for the ride.'

'Do you have to ask?'

He'd expected as much. Her loyalty to him might take her over the edge one day. Bliss hoped that day wouldn't be soon.

'Good. The main thing now, then, is to decide where we go from here?'

'The pub?' Bobby Dunne suggested.

Chandler glanced down at her watch. 'Seconded,' she said.

'Approved.' Bliss smiled at them. They all deserved a drink right now.

TWENTY-EIGHT

The village of Castor on the western tip of Peterborough was close enough to reach within a few minutes by car, yet far enough away to stand a good chance of not being populated by coppers from Thorpe Wood on their lunch break. With the exception of the three who now sat in the public bar of the Red Lion pub.

As village pubs go, the Red Lion was about as clichéd as you could find. The building was more than four hundred years old and partially listed; heavy thatch laid a thick cover over Collyweston stone, and the interior was criss-crossed by sturdy oak beams. A renovation and extension had been completed sympathetically, and it was hard to tell where the sixteen hundreds began and the nineteen hundreds ended. Old world charm leeched out of every nook and cranny, leaving its patrons with a sense of tranquillity and warmth.

Bliss and Dunne had pints of IPA, Chandler a vodka diluted by sparkling orange. Chicken tikka baguettes were on order, plus a large bowl of house fries. Bliss continued to feel insanely stressed about what had happened to him and Connie Rawlings that morning, and he had to will his hand away from his scar on several occasions. He understood now that stress wasn't good for his medical condition, either, and he could feel heat in both cheeks and a fullness in his ears. Right now, though, all he wanted to concentrate on was Jodie Maybanks and DCS Flynn.

'Okay, here's how I see things,' Bliss began. Other than a ragged mutt lying on a seat in the far corner, they were alone in the bar, so he had no need to whisper. 'In addition to Flynn, there are four main suspects involved one way or another with the Jodie Maybanks murder: Weller and Hendry, Alan Dean who handled the MisPer, and Clive Rhodes, who was on duty when the triple nine came in, and would have been around at the time Jodie Maybanks was reported missing. I never like to assume anything, but with this case I'm afraid that's all we have. It does seem likely that all four officers aided Flynn in some way. Whether they played minor or major roles is what we have to discover. Weller and Dean are obviously of no help to us now, so that leaves Hendry and Rhodes. Let's toss out a few suggestions as to possible involvement.'

Chandler leapt right in. 'If we assume Weller helped with the cover-up, then we must presume Hendry did, too.'

'Not necessarily,' Dunne argued. He took a swallow of beer and shook his head. 'If Weller was Flynn's main ally, perhaps he persuaded Hendry to go along with it without the man knowing what was really going on.'

Bliss nodded. 'Good point. You spoke to him, Bobby. How did Hendry come across to you?'

'Well, I didn't mention Jodie Maybanks or the discovery at all. We only discussed that call-out, and what his feelings were about it.'

'He must have wanted to know where your questions were leading.'

'He did. I told him our thinking was that someone actually might have been hurt that night, but that I couldn't tell him much more. Him being a civilian now.'

'And what was his reaction?'

Dunne shrugged. 'Like I told you yesterday at the Pizza Hut, I didn't see anything there, boss. No alarm, no guilt. No real interest, actually.'

'All right,' Bliss said. 'Maybe we'll come back to Hendry. So that leaves Clive Rhodes. I'm not about to believe that his illness and sudden desire to get away for a winter break is a coincidence, so I'm betting he knows more than is good for him.'

'The question is,' Chandler said, 'has he really taken himself off on holiday, or has he gone the way of Weller and Dean?'

'That *is* the question,' Bliss agreed. 'And it's one we need an answer to today. If we focus on our side of the investigation, we need to reach Rhodes and find out what he knows. He may even put Flynn in the frame for us. We probably ought to push Hendry a bit further, too. And we should also talk to a few of the people Flynn worked with back then. Starting with those no longer in the job.'

'Good idea,' Dunne said, nodding. 'Don't want word getting back to Flynn at this early stage.'

'If Flynn actually is responsible for all this, he must be wondering what's going on. Must be paying close attention, waiting to see if someone is going to piece it all together.'

'I take it he's not spoken to you about the case.'

Bliss shook his head. 'Not as such. We bumped into each other on the stairs last week and he told me his door was open if I had problems working the inquiry. Nothing since then, no request for reports or updates. If he's concerned, he's keeping it in check.'

Chandler swirled her drink around in its glass. 'I can't help but wonder how deeply or otherwise involved all these men were. I mean, right at the start, Flynn could probably have spun both Weller and Hendry a simple story. You know, slight accident, no one hurt, personal problems he'd rather just went away. Asked them to back off. After all, there was no sign of an accident, no sign anyone *had* been hurt.'

'According to their initial report,' Dunne pointed out. 'But yes, you could be right. It could easily have been a simple cover-up at that stage. And then Flynn reacts to the MisPer report by approaching Alan Dean and pushing the same buttons. Maybe Rhodes sniffed out a potential link between the two incidents. But even then, none of them needed to know that Jodie Maybanks was dead. And which of them would even have suspected Flynn at that point?'

'Maybe they never did. Or at least, not until the body was uncovered last week.'

'I have a problem with that,' Bliss told them. He'd listened with growing enthusiasm, but had concerns about the way it was being laid out. About to continue, Bliss paused as the barman came up with their food. They each had a bite to eat while they waited for the man to retreat a safe distance away.

'Go on,' Dunne prompted. 'You were saying.'

Bliss swallowed down some of his baguette, the spicy chicken hitting home. 'I have a problem with it because I'm not convinced that the person who killed Jodie and buried her in Fletton was the same person who later dug up her remains and then reburied them. For the first burial to remain undetected for such a length of time, we have to reckon it was done properly. Deep enough and far enough off the beaten track. The way you would expect. But the grave at Bretton Woods was shallow, and not far away from an arterial pathway. The initial burial implies time and patience, the second suggests panic.'

Dunne and Chandler looked at each other. Shrugged. It made sense, Bliss knew. They would both see it.

'I think Rhodes may now be the key,' he continued. 'Weller and Dean are dead, presumably because they posed a threat. And... now that I think about it, here's an interesting theory: what if Rhodes is behind their murders? Everyone we've mentioned, other than Flynn, was on duty the night Jodie Maybanks was murdered, so he is still looking good for it. But maybe it was Rhodes who panicked and reburied her, and then hit Weller and Dean when Jodie's body was discovered.'

He ran it through his mind one more time. It was certainly possible, and a viable thread. Dunne and Chandler were in immediate agreement.

Chandler said, 'The only thing that keeps us from liking him for the whole shebang is that he was on duty when the triple nine came in. We know he didn't murder Jodie, so...'

But Bliss was shaking his head. Even as Penny had started speaking an idea had come to him. He pushed his plate and glass away and clicked his fingers. 'No, we *believe* he didn't. Couldn't have. But only because of the link between the original emergency calls and Jodie's resulting murder. Throughout this investigation we've tied the two things together and made them all part of the same incident. But we don't actually know how long a gap there was between the two events.'

Bliss paused for a moment, thinking it through one more time. He felt a familiar flutter in his chest. What he'd said was true. They had all been side tracked, steered towards believing the murder had immediately followed the accident. When he continued, his voice was more measured.

'We need to find out when Rhodes knocked off duty that night. There are many variables here, many permutations. So far we've gone with the most likely, maybe even the most logical, but perhaps we were too quick in cutting off other options.'

'That may be the case, but Flynn must have been involved,' Dunne stressed. 'Not only was he one of Jodie's regulars, but he also signed off on those two case files long before they should have been closed. Either way, he's up to his neck in it. We can chase down Rhodes as much as you like, but Flynn is the one to fear.'

'Of course. No argument there, Bobby. But Rhodes may still be the man who did the dirty deed. Let's keep that in mind.'

'Sure. But as things stand we at least have something on Flynn. Not hard evidence, but evidence all the same. We have absolutely nothing on Rhodes, except for the fact that he's been elsewhere since Jodie was discovered.'

'Rhodes needs to be tracked down,' said Chandler. 'And fast. Even if it's only to eliminate him so we can focus elsewhere.'

Bliss glanced around the pub, the bar filling up a little more with, judging by the conversations with bar staff, regulars. Through one of the narrow windows he could see rain starting to fall yet again. Some days he wondered why he bothered getting out of bed.

'You and I need to start on that as soon as we get back, Penny,' Bliss told her. He turned to Dunne. 'Do you fancy having another shot at Hendry? Feed him a bit more, link the two things in his head, see what he gives away.'

Dunne nodded. 'Will do, boss.'

'And if we draw blanks all round, we'll put a list together of anyone else who knew Flynn, and then do a bit of digging. You both okay with that?'

They were.

'Good. Then let's finish this grub. I'm starving.'

***

On the drive back to HQ, Bliss outlined the direction the inquiry would take, making sure they each knew the way they were headed.

'Be as vague as you like about what we're up to when it comes to discussing matters with the rest of the team,' he told them. 'We'll set them some procedural tasks and stall this case as much as possible.' He squinted as rain began lashing against the windscreen.

'What about the case notes and daily records?' Dunne reminded him. 'You can't be vague with them, not when Sykes and maybe even Flynn himself will be looking at them.'

Bliss nodded. 'You're right. So far I've been able to avoid putting anything controversial across Sykes's path, and he's leaving me be for now. But I do need a bit of time to write something up. For all three of us, in fact. Bobby, there's no reason why I can't have you down as working with the team on archives and also include your interview with Hendry. Put something together along those lines yourself, and we'll make sure they correspond.'

'What about me?' Penny asked. 'How do I avoid writing up my trip to Lincoln?'

'Same way I will. We'll lie. How about you and I were checking out Palmer and Gordon Wilson? Then we spent time discussing the information from Connie Rawlings, plus piecing all the strands together. I'm sure we can cobble together something convincing.'

'For Sykes, perhaps. But remember, we're not at all sure exactly what Flynn knows. And if we stray too far from the truth he may start to wonder what we're up to.'

'The crux of that is whether Flynn already believes we're on to him. I can't see it, myself. If it weren't for those hidden records in archives and the confirmation from Rawlings, we'd have no reason to suspect him. Provided we keep schtum about those items of information, I'm sure we'll keep him at bay for a while yet.'

'But what happens when you come to list suspects?' Dunne asked. 'The next stage in the investigation? What do you write or tell them then?'

Taking his time with the question, Bliss switched on his lights as the sky moved from ash grey to murky black. 'It's a matter of keeping all the balls in the air at once,' he said. 'The squad don't know about Weller and Dean, so we can keep well away from having one of our own as a viable suspect. We'll keep Palmer in the frame for as long as we can, maybe even drag his arse in for a formal interview. Same with Wilson. They are both viable suspects, after all. Unless anyone else in the team mentions it, I'll steer away from the issue of Jodie's regular clients. It won't look good, but I'll make it appear as though we're coming up empty.'

'This is going to be a tough one to pull off,' Chandler said on a long exhalation of breath.

Bliss nodded and laughed mirthlessly. 'As tough as they come, Penny. As tough as they come.'

'So when we get back we'll put our heads together and come up with our case notes, yes?'

'Yes,' Bliss said. 'And then we go hunting for Clive Rhodes.'

'And I'll pay Mr Hendry another visit,' said Dunne. He cleared his throat. 'By the way boss, what are you going to do about these rumours involving you and this Rawlings woman?'

Dunne was sitting in the back of the car, and Bliss eyed him now through the rear-view mirror. 'Absolutely nothing. Bobby, I don't give a flying fuck what people think of me. They can laugh at me behind my back all they like, and if they want to get brave enough to do it to my face then I suppose we'll see what happens.'

'That's probably the best way to go. Was she able to give you any more information this morning?'

'Other than confirm that Jodie was seeing Joe Flynn? Not really. But she'll stand her ground if we need her later on. She's a tough one.'

'Was she good? A good witness, I mean?'

Bliss shook his head, smiling. 'Don't even go there, Bobby.'

Dunne chuckled and spread his hands. 'Hey, you can't blame me for trying. There's a decent betting pool on the go.'

'Put a fiver in for me that nothing happened.'

'Not good odds.'

'Really?'

'No. Most people reckon you haven't got it in you to have nailed her.'

If he heard Chandler's stifled laugh, Dunne made no mention of it. But Bliss himself laughed out loud.

As they approached the slip road that would take them to Thorpe Wood, Bliss's mobile sprang to life, emitting two high-pitched tones. He thumbed the button to accept a text. When it came up on screen it carried no message, but instead there was a single photograph. Bliss heard himself let out an audible moan, and fear clutched instantly at his throat.

The image was of Bonnie and Clyde. Both dogs were lying on the dusty floor of what Bliss recognised as his own garage, the two Labs surrounded by a pool of what looked like deep red blood.

TWENTY-NINE

When Bliss threw open the garage door and saw his Labs, a fierce pressure welled up inside his chest. It was so intense that for a moment it stalled his breath, and he felt an ache spread deep within his ribcage. Bonnie and Clyde lay exactly as he had seen them in the photograph, and the sour, cloying odour of blood hung thick in the air.

'Oh, Jesus,' Chandler said behind him, hand raised to her mouth.

What hadn't been evident in the photo was just how much blood was smeared all over the two dogs.

Bliss put his head in his hands, and for a terrible moment thought he was going to see his lunch one more time. A horribly familiar sense of loss, of overwhelming grief, brushed against his heart. My babies, a voice inside his head cried out. *My babies.*

'Jimmy, they're alive,' Dunne said, taking a couple of steps beyond Bliss to stand within a foot or so of the dogs. He pointed, finger sweeping between the two animals. 'Look, you can see them breathing.'

What followed was a barely contained form of panic. The three detectives quickly checked the dogs over and found no obvious wounds. Bliss's mind ran amok, unable to comprehend what was going on. He was too close, too emotionally involved. He felt incapable of cohesive thought, memories of discovering Hazel's mutilated body rushing gleefully in.

'Let's get them to a vet,' Chandler whispered softly in his ear. 'You two carry the dogs, I'll drive.'

The veterinary surgery Bliss used was in Stanground. Chandler drove fast, the parkway melting away beneath their wheels. Though both dogs were about the same size and weight, Clyde looked like a puppy in Dunne's huge arms as they all burst through the door of the tiny side street vet's. Though there were two other people waiting to be seen with their own pets in carry boxes, both they and the female vet behind the reception could clearly see this was an emergency situation.

Terrible recollections continued to flood the ravaged corridors of Bliss's mind as he waited impatiently for news. The harsh imagery of stumbling around in blood was too painful to dwell on, yet still it stabbed at him. Pacing back and forth across the small waiting room floor, blood smeared all over his clothes and hands, Bliss voiced his confusion to his colleagues who stood anxiously by the counter.

'What the hell is happening here? That *was* blood they were lying in, right?'

'Looked like it to me,' Chandler said.

'Smelled like it, too,' Bobby Dunne agreed.

'So if it wasn't their blood, whose was it?' It was an impossible question to answer. Neither Dunne nor Chandler even attempted to.

Bliss rubbed both hands across the top of his head and down his distinctive widow's peak towards his face, painting yet more blood across his own flesh. His mind was bubbling, sparking like a frayed electrical cord. Then a stray thought seemed to leap out at him, snagging his attention. Without a word to either of his colleagues, Bliss yanked open the door and stepped outside onto the pavement. An icy wind ripped into him, but he scarcely noticed it. He used his mobile to call Thorpe Wood, and asked to be put through to Detective Chief Superintendent Flynn's personal assistant. A few seconds later he was speaking with Sonia Freeman, the woman who guarded the DCS's office like a sentinel.

'I might want to grab a few minutes of the boss man's time later today,' he said, having difficulty keeping his voice under control. 'What are my chances?'

'Not looking too good, Inspector Bliss. But that might depend on what you want with him. Is it important?'

'It might be, yes. Damn, I would've popped my head in earlier today, but I heard he was out all morning.'

'You heard wrong, Inspector. DCS Flynn has been in his office since eight thirty as usual, and while he's likely to be there until at least six, he does have several prearranged meetings.'

Bliss didn't care. He closed his eyes for a moment and started reining in his emotions. The notion of grabbing a few minutes with Flynn had been subterfuge. He'd got what he called for: Flynn had been at work all day, therefore he wasn't responsible for whatever had happened to Bonnie and Clyde. Not directly, at least.

Bliss stepped back into the vet's waiting room, a chime announcing his entrance. 'It was Rhodes,' he told his colleagues in a hushed tone. 'Had to be.'

Chandler raised her eyebrows. 'It's not like you to toss accusations around like that, boss.'

'Well, it wasn't Flynn.' He told them about his phone call, the pretext of his conversation.

'That was some pretty quick thinking,' said Dunne, nodding approvingly. 'But that still doesn't mean Rhodes was responsible.'

'Maybe not. But if we consider only the names that have cropped up in this investigation so far, who the hell is left?'

Just then the vet came through the doorway that led out back where the treatment rooms were located. A slim woman who looked to be in her mid-thirties, she wore a look that gave Bliss immediate hope.

'They're going to be just fine,' she told him, and Bliss felt like kissing her. 'Your dogs were drugged with a powerful sedative. It completely knocked them out, and while they're both far too drowsy to be moved right now, I'm confident that whatever was used will cause no long-term harm.'

Bliss let go a long, heavy sigh. 'Thank Christ for that. But what about all the blood? Were they harmed at all?'

'No. Physically they are both fine. We washed them down and searched for lacerations, but found absolutely nothing. My best guess is they were covered in pigs' blood. We can run tests if you like.'

'No.' Bliss shook his head. The news had come as an enormous relief, but there was nothing to be gained by pursuing what had already been done. 'Thanks, but if my Labs are going to be okay, then I don't really care where the blood came from.'

The vet frowned. 'Really? Not even if it's human?'

Bliss smacked a hand against his forehead. 'I'm not thinking straight. You're right, of course. Perhaps you'd better have it tested after all.'

'I was teasing.' She smiled, revealing two rows of straight white teeth. 'I thought you could do with a little light relief. There's a simple test to tell us if we're dealing with an animal's blood. I ran it, and we are.'

'Maybe you ought to be doing my job right now,' Bliss said, managing a weak grin of his own.

The vet shook her head. 'No thanks. Judging by what happened to your dogs, you make some bad enemies in your line of work.'

Bliss didn't tell her how right she was.

***

People who are familiar with the place call it 'Sunny Hunny'. On the north coast of East Anglia, nestling alongside the wash, Hunstanton was a typical British seaside town – all kiss-me-quick hats, lewd postcards, a grubby funfair smelling of warm oil and fried onions, litter-strewn beaches, and pale holidaymakers using the groynes as windbreaks. Any notion of class or substance was obscured by the thirst for tourist cash.

The SeaView Caravan Site stood on grounds whose only landscaping was the explosion of weeds rising up from broken and twisted concrete. Rust spots tainted the holiday homes themselves as if the exteriors had broken out in a rash of freckles. Dirty strips of curtain hung behind dirty panes of glass that served as both windows and air conditioning. The site looked like a place where caravans go to die, a white-goods boneyard. Out of season, not a soul could be found wandering its mini-mart, self-service restaurant or bar. The misted windows and humidity-drenched frosted glass of a particular caravan door, however, revealed that at least one owner was in residence.

Enveloped by shiny faux pine, Sergeant Clive Rhodes sat on a long bench seat staring at the ghosting images transmitted by a portable television. He'd been watching it for half an hour and had not the faintest idea what was going on. His mind was so far away it might as well have been on the other side of the world.

On the periphery of his vision he could see the vague shape of his wife, her hand dipping into a large bowl of cheese corn snacks. The movement, an almost perfectly synchronised motion, irritated him. The sound of her biting into and chewing on the bright orange snacks irritated him. The sweet, suffocating smell of them irritated him. The smacking of her lips irritated him. The snorting of breath through her nose because her mouth was too fucking busy irritated him. The swell of her bloated stomach beneath those fucking ridiculous leggings irritated him. And if she asked just one more stupid question, made one more inane remark, he would have to consider scooping out her eyes with a spoon, throttling her until she turned black, cutting her into tiny bite-size chunks, and burning them on the rain-sodden barbecue.

It wasn't really her fault, of course. You could tell from the state of her mother and two older sisters how she was going to turn out. That genetics would have their day. But at least he could take solace in the certainty that when you looked, smelled and behaved the way she did, his wife was never going to be unfaithful to him. Not without money exchanging hands.

Rhodes checked his watch. Almost two. Less than an hour back inside the van and already cabin fever was setting in. He couldn't take any more. It was time to make the call he'd been dreading. He got to his feet.

'I'm just nipping out for a breath of air,' he told his wife.

Chloe looked up at him as if trying to decipher the meaning of his words. Without turning from the TV and with barely a pause in her ritualistic mastication, she said, 'You've not long been back.'

'I know that. I'm not going to be gone for long this time. I just want to go for a walk.'

'But it's pissing down out there.'

'I know that, too. I have eyes. I have ears.'

'You'll get wet.'

'Really? You think?'

Now she somehow managed to tear herself away from the flickering screen. 'Where do you keep going, Clivey? You said we should have this break away, but you're hardly ever here. You got something going on with some local slapper?'

If only, he thought. 'Don't call me that. Why do you do it? You know I hate it.'

'I do it because you hate it,' she replied with a guile he hadn't known she possessed.

Rhodes shook his head, stood and reached for his waxed jacket. 'Back in ten minutes,' he said.

But she was gone. Off into some reality show where the contestants were every bit as vacuous as its audience.

Emerging from the caravan, Clive Rhodes eyed the road that ran alongside the site and curved away up a hill towards the centre of town. He raised the jacket collar and hunched forward into the thick droplets of rain tossed at him by a steady, stiff breeze. He moved around behind the van and walked far enough away that Chloe wouldn't be able to hear the conversation he was about to have. Not that she'd be interested. All she'd said when he told her they were going to dump the kids with her sister and take off for a week or so was, 'What about me bingo?'

He squinted up into the dirty weather. The view didn't quite live up to the promise of the site's name. You couldn't see the sea, for a start. Not on any day, let alone an ugly one like this. The place was a dump, even at the height of summer. Which probably explained why they'd got the van so cheap, and why the plot rental was so reasonable. Still, all things considered, it had provided an effective safe house.

Punching in the number on his mobile, Rhodes wasn't quite sure if he wanted his call to be answered or not. A large part of him hoped the call would be diverted to voicemail. Sometimes not knowing your fate was the best thing all round. Just as he was about to thumb the 'Call End' button, the ringing suddenly died.

'It's me,' Rhodes said. His voice would be enough.

There was a lengthy pause. Long enough to send a chill scuttling between his shoulder blades. Then: 'So it is. I was wondering if I'd actually get to speak with you.'

'I didn't know if I should call or not. I thought you might be busy. And I wasn't sure how you'd react.'

'What, to the sound of your voice, or you fucking off the moment things got hairy?'

Rhodes swallowed, his throat immediately constricted by fear. He considered cutting short the conversation and tossing the mobile into the sea, but knew deep down it would solve nothing. That it would only delay the inevitable.

'Yeah, I'm sorry about that.'

'Sorry? Sorry? Were you deliberately trying to draw attention to yourself?'

'Look, I called in sick then requested my holiday days owing. No one is going to tie me in, anyway.'

'They already have, you fucking moron. All you had to do was stay calm. If they came to you all you had to do was stick to the story we rehearsed.'

'Like Alan Dean, you mean?' When there was no comeback, Rhodes grew a little more confident. 'Yeah, let's not forget about him, eh?'

'Alan didn't stay calm. Alan wasn't tough enough. I thought you were, Clive.'

'I've not gone far. And I'm not about to spill my guts, either. I'm just… cooling off. Anyway, it's not as though I deserted you. We've kept in touch by text. I've still done everything you asked of me.' Rhodes wiped rain from his balding pate, turning his back to the wind.

'Yes, plus a few of your own ideas thrown in for good measure. But you didn't call me. You didn't have the balls to speak to me until now.'

'Yeah, but I had the balls for everything else. I think I deserve a little bit of credit, a bit of leeway.'

'That's as maybe, but your absence has been noted, Clive. It was foolish. Unnecessary.'

'I said I'm sorry. I'll be back in a couple of days. I'll front it. Don't worry.'

'Oh, I'm not worried. You have as much to lose as I do. But we need a chat before you go back on duty.'

'Fair enough.' Rhodes thought the conversation was becoming calmer. It was a time for clear minds, not anger.

'Okay, then. We're back on track. I need you to do me a favour, though, Clive. You've been stupid, but now I need you to be smart. I also need you to be found.'

Clive Rhodes listened with mounting alarm. By the time he killed the call he couldn't tell if his shivering was caused by the cold rain or trepidation. But he did know he had little choice other than to once more do as he'd been asked. Running away up to Hunstanton was one thing. Going the way of Alan Dean was quite another.

THIRTY

Having cleaned himself up and changed his clothes, Bliss turned his attention to the missing police officer, the man he now believed was responsible for murder. Rhodes lived in Yaxley, in a bland three-bed bungalow set off the main road that cut through from the A1 all the way into the centre of Peterborough. Bliss and Chandler parked up outside on the main road and appraised the place for a while through the rain-mottled side window of the pool car. The home, set back from its neighbours, with a little more front lawn, suffered with water-stained rendered walls and a broken downpipe that gushed rainwater. To Bliss it looked like the kind of place you couldn't ever imagine being full of life.

'What are we waiting for?' Chandler asked, gripping the door handle. 'I don't think this bloody rain is going to let up.'

'Twitchers,' Bliss replied.

Chandler squinted at him. 'Bird watchers?'

'No, curtain twitchers. I'm not expecting anyone to be at home, but I am interested to know if the Rhodes family have curious neighbours.'

She smiled at him. 'That's why you're the boss and I'm a lowly DC.'

He nodded. 'Probably.' Less than a minute later he noticed the movement he'd been waiting for. 'Okay. Let's go.'

While Chandler leaned on the doorbell and used the brass knocker, Bliss made a show of peering through the bay windows. 'Keep it up, Penny,' he said in a hushed voice. 'Won't be long now.'

Sure enough, in a brief lull between the knocking and ringing, an elderly woman stepped out of her own bungalow next door and waved a hand at them. 'They're not in,' she called out. 'And I don't think they'll be back until the weekend at least.'

Bliss winked at Chandler and the two of them moved across to the knee-high wooden fence that separated the two properties. The rain had lessened to a fine mist, though if the heavy cloud cover was an indication, it was merely taking a breather.

'Any idea where they went?' Bliss asked the woman, who looked to be in her late sixties. A pair of spectacles hung on a thin gold chain around her neck, and a tea towel was tossed casually over one shoulder.

'Who are you?' she demanded.

'Oh, sorry.' Bliss gave a chuckle and pulled out his warrant card. 'We're colleagues of Clive's. We need to get hold of him quite urgently.'

The woman frowned, peering inquisitively at him. 'If you're his friends I'm surprised you didn't know he was away.'

Sharper than she looks, Bliss thought. That would teach him to judge someone on appearances. He nodded and said, 'Sorry, but I didn't mean to imply Clive and I were friends. We *are* colleagues, like I said, but we're based at a different station.' He didn't press for the information they needed, not wanting to come across as too eager.

'Ah, I see.' She nodded, easing off on the frown. 'Clive and Chloe went away last week. Sorry, but I don't actually know where they went.'

'That's a shame.' Bliss put some disappointment into his voice. Hung his head for a moment. Shrugged at Chandler and slapped his hands against his sides.

'I did hear him and Chloe talking when they were packing up the car, though.' The woman nodded brightly at him.

I bet you did, Bliss thought. He widened his eyes and nodded encouragement.

'They were going to take their children to her sister's place. So she's bound to know where they are.'

'Oh, right. Well that might be very useful. I don't suppose you know where Chloe's sister lives, do you Mrs…?'

'MacBride. Helen. And yes, it so happens I do. I'm not sure of the number, but I know they live in Orchard Street, over in Woodston.'

'Well, thank you, Mrs MacBride. That's very helpful.'

Her face switched to full beam. 'I'm sure you can find out the number. You being the police.'

'Of course. Though, you could save us a bit of time. Do you happen to know the name of Chloe's sister?'

'Oh, yes. Brenda. Brenda Ward.'

'That's terrific. Well, thanks very much, Mrs MacBride. You've been a great help.'

'Oh, it's no problem, really. I like to keep myself to myself, but anything to help the police.'

***

'Can you imagine her keeping her nose out of anything?' Bliss asked Chandler when they were back in the car. They headed west on London Road, towards the city centre.

'Not for a moment. You were great with her.'

'I let her do what she wanted to do. If I'd pressed her right from the word go, she might've clammed up. You know what it's like when people feel they're being questioned. But she wanted to talk, that much was obvious. She wouldn't have come outside otherwise.'

Chandler put in a call to chase up the address, which came back less than a minute later. Woodston was similar in style to Fletton, it being another of the city's older parts. The houses in Orchard Street were mostly terraced, with side alleyways leading to back gardens. Front doors in these small homes led directly into living rooms, and it was the habit of the older inhabitants to use their back doors more regularly instead.

After a couple of rings on the doorbell, Bliss and Chandler were called round to the back of Brenda Ward's house by a large woman with short, lifeless hair and a huge mole between her upper lip and nose. It was one of those growths you had to struggle to keep your eyes off.

'Mrs Ward?' Bliss asked.

She nodded, spare tyres of flesh bulging out between her chin and neck. 'What can I do for you?' She stood with one hand on her garden gate, eyeing them suspiciously. Clinging to her leg was a small child, little more than a toddler, a pink dummy wedged in the girl's mouth, dried snot caked around her nostrils.

Bliss repeated the same story he'd given Mrs McBride. Brenda Ward shook her head this time, her doubts clearly intensifying.

'I don't know where they went,' she insisted. 'They dropped in unexpectedly and asked me to look after the kids for a while. I think Clive had been feeling rough for a few days and they just wanted a break.'

She was lying. Or at the very least, knew more than she was letting on. Bliss flashed a smile her way. 'Any idea how we can get hold of Clive? I wouldn't ask if it weren't important.'

The woman pouted. 'No. Sorry.'

'Not even an emergency number? Mobile?' Chandler asked. 'I mean, just in case something happened to the children.'

Bliss gave an approving nod. It would have been his next question, but Penny had done well. Brenda Ward moved from foot to foot, uncertain now. She swallowed and said, 'Of course. There is Clive's mobile. But… well, I don't think he'd like me giving the number out. It's a private phone, nothing to do with work.'

'We are colleagues,' Bliss reminded her. 'I'm sure he won't mind.'

'You don't know Clive very well, do you? I understand you're police like he is, but I still don't think he'll want me handing out his private number.'

'How about you give him a call for us, then?' Chandler suggested.

Bliss nodded. 'Yes. Good idea. Give him a bell and tell him DI Bliss would like a word.'

He would want more than a word if Rhodes had been responsible for drugging the Labs. He would want retribution.

Ward made a show of checking her watch, a cheap Seiko. 'I was just on my way out.'

'It'll only take a minute. Clive will be glad you bothered, believe me.'

Bliss stood his ground, his eyes never leaving Brenda Ward's face.

The woman let go a sigh to let them know they were putting her out. 'Fine. What do you want me to tell him?'

'Ask him if it's okay if we have his number. Then we can call him ourselves in our own time. Otherwise, a quick word here and now will probably be good enough.'

Shaking her head and muttering to herself, Ward waddled away back into her house, the toddler trailing after her. Bliss rolled his eyes at Chandler. 'Rhodes has covered his arse, hasn't he?'

She nodded. 'Which is a lot tougher for Brenda Ward to do, it would seem.'

Despite himself, Bliss laughed. Moments later, Mrs Ward was back. She handed over a slip of paper torn from a notebook. 'Here you go. I can't say he was happy being disturbed while on holiday, but he agreed all the same.'

'And we're very grateful,' Bliss assured her. 'To you both.'

She said nothing, but her look as she turned away once more spoke volumes.

Back in the car, Bliss took out his phone, entered the number printed on the scrap of paper and made the call. It took several rings, but eventually it was answered.

'Clive Rhodes.'

Anxious, Bliss thought immediately. Definitely anxious.

'Clive. It's DI Bliss from Thorpe Wood. Thanks for speaking with me.'

'From what my wife's sister said, I'm not sure I had a choice.'

'Well, you did, and I thank you for making the right one. I won't take up too much of your time right now, but something has come up that I think you might be able to help me with. I wonder if you wouldn't mind sparing me a few minutes face to face.'

'Oh, what? I'm on holiday. You know, off duty?'

Bliss glanced at Chandler and shook his head. She could hear only his end of the conversation, but he assumed she was getting the gist of it.

'I know. And I'm sorry to intrude. I wouldn't be calling you if it weren't important.'

'What's it about? What case are you working on?'

'I'd rather discuss that with you when I see you. It may be a little sensitive, and would be better aired in relaxed circumstances. Look, if you take the time now I'll see you get another day off in lieu.'

'You sure we can't we do this over the phone?'

'Not really, Clive. It's only a few questions, but the interview will appear in the case notes, so it would be best if we met up. You know how it goes. Bureaucracy.'

A sigh. 'I suppose so.'

Rhodes told Bliss where to find him.

***

Clive Rhodes slipped quietly through the damp and chilly streets of Hunstanton to his vehicle, a ten-year-old Mitsubishi Shogun. Chloe had nagged at him yet again, complaining about him leaving her. The sound of her voice made him want to reach down her throat and pull out her insides. As he walked away from the caravan with his wife's shrill words echoing in his ears, Rhodes decided that when this was all over, he and Chloe were going to have a major parting of the ways.

When he reached his four-by-four he opened up the rear door and took out what looked like a fishing rod bag, folded in half and bound with thick elastic bands. Rhodes unwrapped the bag, pulled back the zipper and gave the contents the once over. The sawn-off shotgun was oiled and ready for action. After a long, hard look around him to ensure he wasn't being observed, Rhodes fed two shells into the weapon. Then he slammed the vehicle's door shut, gripped the shotgun in one large hand and climbed into the driver's seat.

Clive Rhodes gunned the engine and pulled away from the kerb, the firearm nestled in the seat beside him. As per instructions, he had allowed DI Bliss to make his last call to anyone this side of purgatory.

THIRTY-ONE

It took almost an hour and a half to reach Hunstanton. At the best of times the seaside resort had a half-hearted air about it, as though it could scarcely be bothered to turn out in all its gaudy finery. Now, in the grip of early winter, the town appeared grim and two-dimensional. The pool car's wipers batted rain away from the windscreen, providing a crescent window of vision. Bliss squinted through it as darkness gathered over them, heavy black clouds forcing the daylight away. His mind was working overtime now that they had reached their destination, and his thoughts drifted back to the start of the journey.

'Well, that was easy enough,' Chandler had said as they drove off, settling back into her seat for the long trip ahead.

'Maybe a little too easy.'

She looked over at him. 'What do you mean?'

'I got the feeling Rhodes had been expecting us to get in touch,' Bliss told her. 'Either that or he's completely innocent, and I don't buy that at all.'

'So you think he's got a story prepared for us? Either his own or he's been got at.'

'I would have thought so.'

Chandler shrugged her shoulders. 'Then we'll have to be better than he is.' She took out a packet of gum and offered him one. He popped it into his mouth and chewed hard, his mind unsettled.

The rest of the journey passed by in a blur of mindless conversation, sporadically punctuated by the two detectives setting out their plans for the interview with Rhodes. Only once did the subject of Bonnie and Clyde come up, but after Bliss began to seethe and curse out loud, they agreed it would be better not to discuss the matter again. It was only as they drove past the welcome sign on the edge of town that Bliss wondered if Clive Rhodes might have something in mind other than a well-rehearsed story. Something a little more drastic.

'Why would he allow us to look at him when he tells us lies?' Bliss asked Chandler now.

'Boss?'

'Well, think about it for a moment, Pen. We've spent the past hour or so planning our strategy, thinking of questions to catch Rhodes out, how to play the entire interview. He has been one of us a long time now. He knows as well as you or I that it's a hell of a lot easier to convince someone of something if they're at the other end of a phone line. He's been on our side of the desk many times, he understands the importance of body language, knows to watch the eyes. So why would he let us get this close?'

'Maybe he just wants to get it over with. Better now than when he's back from his break.'

Bliss sniffed, feeding the steering wheel through lazy fingers. 'But it isn't, though. We're disturbing him. He went away for a reason, and now we're intruding. If I'm him, I'd want to delay any such meeting for as long as possible. In fact, I'd be looking for ways to avoid it completely.'

Now Chandler was nodding, the thin curve of her eyebrows moving closer in a deep frown. 'So if he's not going to lie, and we can bet our last pound coin he's not about to cough, what does he want with us?'

Bliss turned his head towards her for a moment, then abruptly snapped it back. 'I'm not sure. But I think we'd better take precautions.'

Chandler was looking at him oddly. He felt her gaze.

'What?'

She snapped her fingers and nodded to herself. 'I knew there was something bothering me about you. Have you done something to your neck? Have you got a problem with it?'

Bliss licked his lips, not liking the direction this conversation was taking. 'What do you mean?'

'I noticed it before, but though it nagged at me I couldn't figure it out. But just lately whenever we've been either walking together or sitting in the car, you rarely look at me when we're talking. Just now you looked, but turned away again quickly. What's up, boss? I know there's something wrong. You're not yourself, and I think you should tell me why.'

Bliss said nothing for a moment. His medical condition, the disease, had the potential to be incapacitating. When standing upright he could drop to the floor at any time, vomit suddenly, lose his balance for no good reason, and the fatigue led to a confused mind known as 'brain fog'. Under normal circumstances, in an ordinary job, Chandler would have no need to know this very personal aspect of his life. But they were a team. They relied on one another. And now, if he was right about Clive Rhodes, that reliance might be tested under severe conditions.

Bliss pulled the Ford off the road and rolled it to a rest in a narrow lay-by. He took a deep breath, turned in his seat and told her. Everything. The onset of the illness, his concerns, the GP's referral to ENT, the worry of an MRI, his consultant's diagnosis, the uncertain prognosis. When he was done he shook his head and lowered his gaze, not wanting to see either pity or anger in Penny's eyes when he spoke again.

'I should have told you before. I realise that now. You need to know if there's a problem that might affect what we do out on the streets. You need to know if I might let you down. I'm sorry.'

For a few seconds only the screech of wipers on dry glass broke the silence. Bliss flicked the stalk to switch them off. He peered out through the windscreen, the black clouds now retreating, a glimmer of weak light bleeding through once more. The car rocked suddenly as Chandler snapped off her seatbelt and climbed out, slamming the door behind her. She walked a few steps away and stood with her back to him, gazing out towards the town's boardwalk and the grey, rolling sea beyond. An elderly couple walked by, arm in arm, beige jackets zipped tight to the neck. Heads down, they smiled and nodded a greeting at Chandler.

Bliss gave it a few moments, allowing her steam to evaporate before joining her. He fastened his coat and stood by Penny's side, hands buried deep into his pockets, saying nothing as he moved unsteadily from foot to foot. Letting her know he was there for her, waiting until she was ready to confront him.

'You think that's what concerns me most?' Chandler said eventually. She hugged herself, warding off the cold breeze. 'That you might let me down? For fuck's sake, Jimmy, we're friends as well as colleagues. I hope the friendship comes first with you, because it damn well does for me. Yes, I'm concerned that you might not be able to get my back if I'm in the shit. I'd be an idiot not to be. But more than that, I'm concerned for you and what you're going through.'

He turned to face her. A fine fringe was being mauled by the wind, and Penny's pale forehead was beaded with a fresh spattering of rain. Her eyes were narrow and intense, chin set firmly.

'Penny,' he said softly. 'You're not just my friend, you're my best friend. Well, other than Bonnie and Clyde, of course.'

She coughed up a stifled laugh and shook her head, mouth breaking into a grin despite her best efforts at solemnity. 'Then why the hell didn't you tell me about this before?'

Bliss hiked his shoulders, hunched into himself a little more. 'Believe it or not, Penny, I needed a bit of time with it myself. To work it through on my own before I spilled my guts to anyone else. I haven't even told my parents.'

'You haven't?'

'No. I needed to wear it for a while, find out how it fits. It's not every day you get told you have a life-changing illness.'

Chandler looked at him now, her eyes reflective. 'I can see that. I can. I'm pissed with you, but I'll get over it. The main focus here is you and this disease. What the hell caused it?'

'They don't know. That's why they find it so difficult to treat. They have plenty of theories, but the fact is that while a lot of people have the disease, few have exactly the same symptoms.

I think it's a bit of a catch-all for anything to do with ear disorders that affect the balance.'

'It must be awful for you.'

Bliss shook his head. 'Not really. Not yet. I hear it can get a lot worse, and probably will. On the other hand, long periods of remission are not unheard of.'

'I suppose you just have to hope for the best.'

'Of course.'

'Maybe even pray for it.'

He gave a low chuckle. 'We both know that's not going to happen.'

'I guess not.'

Bliss's phone rang. It was Tech Support at Thorpe Wood. Shortly after setting off from Peterborough, Chandler had called in the telephone number Rhodes was using, asking for information on it. Bliss hoped they had something worthwhile for him. He listened, asked a couple of questions, nodded at the responses, then killed the line.

'Well, well,' he said, processing what he'd been told. 'The number comes up as bogus. No other calls in or out. Obviously a single use phone. Now, why would a copper with nothing to hide have the need of such an item?'

'Let's ask him to explain that, shall we?'

'We will. I'll lead us up to it.'

'Okay. But getting back to you, what are you going to tell them at work?'

'That,' Bliss said, 'is a very good question.'

She smiled. 'To which the answer is…?'

'I'm fucked if I know.'

It was the truth. Every time he got around to thinking about the dilemma, Bliss manufactured something else to focus on. He didn't want to think that far ahead, about the future. It had a habit of taking care of itself.

***

The plan Rhodes had put forward on the telephone was that he would meet them in the car park of a hotel long since closed down and derelict. Bliss drove by once, scouring the immediate area for signs of shadows where they ought not to be. The only vehicle in the car park was an ancient Escort resting on milk crates where the wheels had once been. Its windscreen had been shattered and, from its open bonnet, cables and hosing overflowed as if a monstrous creature were emerging.

'What do you think?' Bliss asked Chandler. He wasn't convinced that Rhodes would take them on, try and eliminate them both here and now, but he wasn't prepared to dismiss the notion entirely.

She checked her watch. 'We're ten minutes late. He should be here.'

Bliss nodded. 'We're not so late that he would've got fed up waiting. You're right. He should be here.'

Bliss turned the car around when he could and crawled back past the empty hotel once more. Its boarded windows, grey stonework and red brick had been tagged by local graffiti artists. Once upon a time it might have been a majestic building, perhaps even a local landmark. Now it merely looked sad and pathetic, like an abandoned puppy waiting for its owner's return. Tear the wreck down and put something useful in its place, Bliss thought. Like a jail. Better still, a lunatic asylum. Either way, the place would always be full.

'You not going to park up and wait for him?' Chandler asked as they drove by the entrance for a second time.

'There's only one way in or out. I don't like the thought of being hemmed in.'

'Good call.'

They gave it twenty minutes of driving around, slipping by the meeting point every so often. Bliss felt himself growing more and more agitated. The day was slipping away, and this was getting them nowhere. Bliss tried to keep the irritation from his voice when he spoke to Chandler now.

'Rhodes said he and his wife were staying nearby in a caravan. I saw a signpost for one just up the road from where we keep turning round. I say we take a look. Happy with that?'

Chandler was. Bliss turned the Focus around one last time and headed towards the campsite. As they neared the place, Chandler was the first to point out the blue-and-whites flickering ahead and to the right. As the pool car emerged from behind a clutch of hills and jagged walls of wild vegetation, Bliss began to see the commotion for himself.

Several police cars, an ambulance, and two fire tenders huddled around the smouldering wreck of a burnt-out caravan. Bliss glanced across at Chandler, whose eyes were wide and alert. They both shrugged, silently shook their heads. Bliss didn't like the thoughts that were rushing through his mind. Didn't like the conclusions he was already drawing.

He turned in to the site and parked up on a grassy verge, making sure that emergency vehicles could get by. The two of them then stepped out into the unrelenting breeze. They approached the taped off area cautiously, a uniform with a clipboard peering at them as they made their way across the uneven, broken ground. As Bliss reached for his warrant card, Chandler tapped him on the arm and pointed.

Bliss followed her finger. He swallowed once, and knew he'd been right moments earlier. Beyond the emergency vehicles, several yards behind the caravan, stood a Mitsubishi Shogun.

THIRTY-TWO

Bliss and Chandler waited patiently for everyone to do their jobs: fire crews, ambulance service, a DS from the local CID, on-call doctor and, finally, the area pathologist. Smoke lingered in the air long after the inferno had been extinguished, choking lungs and stinging eyes. That the stiff breeze blew ash from dead people around the campsite and beyond was a thought no one needed to dwell upon.

In a mobile incident room, Bliss and Chandler spoke to each relevant member of the emergency team in turn, taking notes as the story unfolded, trying to piece the incident together as best they could given the lack of verifiable evidence. All they knew for a fact was that two bodies were discovered inside the burnt-out shell of the caravan, both unrecognisable, both mercifully dead before the flames reached them – if having a shotgun take your face off could be deemed merciful.

Though Clive and Chloe Rhodes had yet to be formally identified, there was sufficient evidence to presume that they were the deceased couple. The caravan was registered to Clive Rhodes, the Shogun to his wife. A few possessions had been retrieved from the blackened caravan, including a purse inside which Chloe Rhodes's driving licence had been discovered. Both DS Green, who was the SIO on scene, and the pathologist, Professor Graham Thompson, were in full agreement that murder/suicide was the most likely scenario. Clive Rhodes was the registered owner of the shotgun found on the floor of the charcoaled ruins. Investigations by the fire service and SOCO were ongoing, and would be for some time to come, but the scenario fit the bill. It was the most logical conclusion.

Under normal circumstances, Bliss would be insisting that the involvement of a third party ought not to be ruled out. But in this case, he hoped DS Green would go along with the easy option. Professionally irritated, Bliss was personally happy that not all avenues were being explored.

'If you don't mind me asking,' Green said when only the three police officers remained in the mobile incident room, 'what are you two doing all the way out here? I mean, I know you've explained how the Rhodes come to be here out of season, but not why you're here today. Did you just happen to pop by to visit a friend?'

'Not exactly,' Bliss replied, sensing the man's scepticism. 'We were coming to interview Clive Rhodes about his involvement in an ongoing case back in Peterborough.'

'That's interesting, Inspector. Do you suspect his involvement to be serious enough to cause this kind of reaction?' Green jerked his head in the direction of the smouldering ruin still being dampened down by the fire crew.

Bliss regarded the caravan for a few moments before responding, wondering what exactly had taken place in there prior to the blaze.

'That's what we were hoping to find out,' he replied.

'But it might explain it, yes?'

'It might.'

'So, you're saying Rhodes dumped his kids with a relative and dragged his wife out here, sat around doing nothing much for about a week, then calmly shot his wife in the face, set fire to the caravan, before turning the shotgun on himself?'

'Well, actually you're saying that. I'm simply agreeing that it could have gone that way.'

Green regarded him closely for a moment. Bliss gave nothing away. After a pause that went on a fraction too long for Bliss's liking, DS Green nodded. 'Fair enough. I guess we'll see.'

'I'm sure we will. It's early days for this particular investigation. And on that subject, I wonder if you would do me a professional courtesy, Sergeant. Once ID has been confirmed, and the crime scene report written up, would you contact me directly before anyone else?'

The tall, thin detective scratched the back of his neck. His cheeks were hollow and he looked in need of a good meal. But his eyes were sharp and intelligent. They flickered now.

'That's more of a favour than a courtesy, by my reckoning. But I suppose you must have your reasons. With officer involvement this has obviously got to be relayed to the very top, but I'll give you a heads-up. That's the best I can do. How long do you need?'

'As long as you can give us.'

Green nodded. 'Is there anything else I need to know, Inspector? You know, as a professional courtesy?'

Bliss smiled. They both knew he could use his seniority to push harder, but he didn't want to get under the detective's skin. Also, doing so would be treating Green as he himself was treated by Sykes. Bliss wasn't about to sink to that level.

'There's nothing going on here, Sergeant. We're not covering anything up, and we don't intend to. The fact is, we genuinely don't know if our own investigation prompted what happened here today. I admit that our being here right now must seem terribly coincidental, and I doubt you trust coincidences any more than I do. All I can tell you is it's possible that this tragedy and what we were about to discuss with Rhodes are linked. But now that Rhodes is dead, we may never know for certain. I won't be happy with that, but I can do nothing about it. Does that satisfy your curiosity at all?'

'I think so. For now. Like I said before, I'll call you when we have confirmation and give you as much time as possible with it before I have to take it to my boss.'

Bliss thanked him. He wrote his mobile number on the back of a card, which he then handed to the sergeant. Green glanced at it for a moment before popping the card inside his jacket pocket. There were handshakes all around, then Bliss and Chandler left him to it.

***

Shortly after six thirty, Bliss and Chandler sat in a fish and chip restaurant overlooking the Hunstanton seafront, wearily forking fuel into their mouths, faces pale from exposure to cold rain, yet tinged with red as a result of the driving wind whipping in off the North Sea. Bliss could still both smell and taste smoke. The greasy, uninspired food was not the only unpalatable offering they had to chew over.

'This sorry mess makes things doubly difficult,' Bliss said, munching on what was supposed to be a piece of cod but could have been almost anything covered in batter. He shook his head in exasperation. 'It was a tough enough job keeping a lid on both Weller and Alan Dean, but this is a far more difficult prospect. Someone is bound to piece this whole thing together once news of Rhodes's death leaks out.'

'All the more reason to take the case to someone else,' Chandler reasoned. She pushed her plate to one side, the food barely touched. She took a sip of Coke straight from the can.

Bliss nodded. An idea had just formed perfectly in his mind. 'I might just do that.'

'Really?' Chandler leaned forward. 'Thank God for that.'

'Yes. I might take it to Flynn.'

He saw a certain look appear in Chandler's eyes. The look that says the person they belong to has come to the conclusion that the person they are looking at has gone completely mad. Or at least has lost the plot.

'Think about it,' he said, raising a hand to forestall the inevitable complaint. 'First of all, do you buy this suicide/murder scenario?'

'It's possible. Sure, why not? Rhodes was starting to look a far more likely candidate than Flynn, that's for sure. It's possible that when you phoned he realised we were on to him and decided to take the easy way out.'

'Exactly. It is possible. In fact, it makes a lot of sense. It's also possible that it didn't go down that way at all, but that we're meant to believe it did. And you're forgetting, Penny, even if Rhodes did shoot his wife before turning the gun on himself, and even if he was also responsible for killing Weller and Dean, Flynn was still involved in some way.'

'So?'

'So we can kill two birds. I can now go to Flynn and tell him that I've been working on this off the record, and am now convinced that Clive Rhodes murdered Jodie Maybanks, and subsequently also murdered both Weller and Dean who covered for him at the time. I'll also speculate that, once he knew I was on to him, Rhodes took the ugly way out. The two benefits of that story are that, a: the finger gets pointed at someone other than Flynn himself, which will buy us some time, and b: he'd never imagine me going to him with this if I actually suspected him.'

Penny looked no happier. 'That's a bloody huge risk, Jimmy. I know what you've said about the whole inquiry being tucked away somewhere, but surely you must know somebody you can go to with it? Someone from your days with the Met, perhaps? Someone with clout who will see that what needs to be done is done.'

Bliss gave a crooked grin. 'There speaks someone who seems to have forgotten why I fell out with the Met in the first place.'

'No, I haven't. Who could forget something like that. Yes, so they thought you might have murdered your wife and they thought you might have almost killed another copper she'd been sleeping with. As a consequence you have a dark cloud hanging over your career, and closed records to all but the most senior officers. But you must have some friends down there. Someone senior who believed your side of the story.'

'No one I've kept in touch with.'

'At their request?' she asked, her gaze narrowing now. 'Or is that another example of you cutting yourself off.'

'If I did it was to keep the associated dirt off them.'

'All very noble, I'm sure.' She forced Bliss to meet her eyes. 'But if they were friends, or even just good, honest coppers, they'll open their doors to you.'

'I'm not so sure. And with something as big as this, I have to be.'

Chandler let go a long, loud sigh. Now she was frustrated with him, he could tell. Perhaps even angered by his dismissive attitude. Bliss stared out of the window into darkness broken up by multi-coloured lights on the promenade and, beyond those, the faint white glow from whatever vessels were heading out to sea or in to shore. When he spoke next, his voice was low and even.

'Penny, believe me, I'm not taking this lightly. I see what's happened to fellow officers and it makes me want to pull back for the sake of you and Bobby, as well as for my own safety, of course. But it's become unwieldy enough, in my mind. Involving someone else at this late stage just creates more cracks in what is already very thin ice. I think I can pull this off by going to Flynn. If he was tense, he'll relax. This could turn out to be a break. Besides, if you think about it, once he gets to hear about us being here, he'll wonder what we wanted with Rhodes, and he'll expect me to have answers.'

'But what will he do with it? Officially, I mean.'

'My guess is he'll ask me to run with it. Get me to point the finger more firmly at Rhodes. If he's done nothing wrong, it'll be the correct thing to do. If he's guilty of anything, and he can have me pin the whole sorry mess on Rhodes plus a few minor accomplices, he'll be laughing. Best bit for him is that it'll be me going to him with the story. He'll have bugger all to lose and everything to gain.'

'So when he tells you to carry on, you will. Only you'll be digging up the dirt on him, and not Rhodes.'

Bliss nodded. 'Something like that, yes. More like working on both of them at the same time. I'm not convinced either way as to who did what, though like you I'm favouring Rhodes right now.'

'But what about daily reports? What about case notes and records?'

He grinned. 'We're police officers. We'll be inventive.'

Chandler laughed, despite herself. She shook her head and sighed. 'Jimmy Bliss, you are one mad cockney bastard.'

'And you, Penny Chandler, are one lippy carrot-crunching DC.'

***

They arrived back in Peterborough a little after eight thirty, the gentle amber glow of the city sky in stark contrast to the depthless black night they'd left behind in Hunstanton. Bliss recalled being puzzled by the night when he first moved up from London, whose skies never seemed to be anything other than bright, no matter what the hour. The difference was that London is a city that doesn't know the meaning of sleep, whereas Peterborough staggers bleary-eyed through each and every day. Hunstanton and places of its ilk, on the other hand, seem to be in almost permanent slumber.

Chandler invited Bliss in for coffee when he dropped her off. He accepted readily, coffee meaning exactly that in their case. He liked Penny a lot, and her physical attractions were obvious, but he never really thought about her in that way. To do so would seem almost incestuous, such was their close relationship. Her flat, a modern featureless effort, overlooked the river Nene. It looked lived in, which was something Bliss appreciated. Small, a little cramped perhaps when two people moved around inside, her home was nonetheless welcoming.

They worked their way through their drinks while seated at the narrow dining table in the open-plan kitchen-diner, which afforded them a view of the river and the Thai restaurant and bar masquerading as a barge tied up by the town bridge. A low thrum of music drifted across to them, which Bliss found to be a pleasant backdrop.

'So, how are things going with Emily?' Chandler asked him.

Bliss gave a nod. 'Pretty good.' He told her about the walk over by Orton Mere, Sunday lunch, their evening at the cinema. 'It's early days, and we're taking things slowly.'

'And the moment of madness with Connie Rawlings?'

'Was just that. A moment.'

'I hope things work out for you and Emily.' Her look turned swiftly from warmth to concern. 'What about your illness, though? I've never heard of this...' Chandler shrugged.

'Ménière's Disease,' he reminded her. 'I'd never heard of it, either. And to be honest, I don't like to think about it too often. From what I gather it could get a lot worse, stay pretty much as it is now, or even burn itself out altogether. Hardly a definite prognosis. I could easily drive myself crazy thinking about the possibilities.'

'But you think you're fit for work?'

'Absolutely.' Bliss nodded firmly. 'My balance is out of whack and I feel rough and tired, but my mind is still sharp. Don't worry, I won't let this stupid bloody illness affect anything we do as a team.'

Chandler gave an easy grin. 'Fair enough. I trust you on that. Going back to Emily, what does she know about Hazel?'

'The basics. And thank you very much for telling her about me and my wife.'

'You're welcome. Emily was interested. I gave her just enough to want more.'

'I don't think she's ready for the full confession. I'm not quite sure how she'll take it.'

'You mean you think she might feel less of you?'

'Perhaps.'

'I don't think so,' Penny said, shaking her head. 'Giving that prick a beating was wrong, but who couldn't understand why you did it? Killing him would have been easy, but you didn't take that way out. You didn't cross that fine line, and if she's anything like me, Emily will focus on that rather than the hiding you gave that man.'

Bliss inclined his head. 'There's also the issue of me and Hazel being swingers. A lot of people can't get their heads around that.'

'True. I couldn't. Still can't, if I'm being completely truthful. But it's not the end of the world, either.'

'It was for Hazel.'

The silence that followed hung in the air between them. Bliss closed his eyes and willed himself not to weep. Guilt rose up within him as it always did, threatening to overwhelm his conscious mind. But he was pulled back from the brink by Penny.

'No,' she said adamantly. Chandler gave a firm shake of the head. 'It wasn't your lifestyle that got your wife killed. It was one man's warped mind. One man's inability to cope with rejection. I've told you before, Jimmy, if you can't get that straight in your head then you need to see someone about it. Someone who can help sort you out.'

Bliss smiled. 'I can't believe you're still trying to get me to see a bloody psychologist.'

'And why not? You're carrying too big a load, Jimmy. It's going to pull you under if you don't shed some weight.'

Chandler had taken Psychology in college, and occasionally she liked to play at it. Bliss drained his mug and stood. He fastened his jacket, tugged on his overcoat.

'Pen,' he said, looking down at her, 'you're a good friend, and you mean well, but among the vast number of things I'm not ready for in this life, seeing a shrink rates very high right now.'

Her shoulders slumped. Bliss could tell she was beaten. For the time being.

He had just stepped inside his front door when Penny called his home telephone.

'You weren't the only one to have a visitor earlier today,' she said without preamble.

'What do you mean?' He tossed his keys down on the kitchen counter and pulled out a stool to perch on.

'On my bedroom wall, right above the bed, was written three words: Leave. Me. Alone. I checked my front door lock and it looks as if it may have been picked. There are some scratches.'

'Have you checked the rest of the flat?' Bliss felt a bloom of panic unfurl across his chest.

'What rest? You were in the only other rooms.'

'Not the bathroom.'

'Okay, you got me there. But yes, I checked.'

'If it was Rhodes, he was a very busy boy today. Came all the way down from Hunstanton to do this to us, then drove back again. Plenty of time to do it, of course. But the question is: if he's been living on that caravan site all this time, how did he know prior to my call that we were on to him?'

'I was thinking the same thing. It points to Flynn again. I still think Rhodes has been responsible for most of what happened, but I also think Flynn has been protecting him. They were in it together, Jimmy. Still are.'

Bliss thought she might be right. 'We have to find out why. As for the message on your bedroom wall, are you okay? You want some backup for the night?'

'No. Thanks, but I think I'll be fine. As with your dogs, this was just a warning. And if it was Rhodes, he won't be popping by again any time soon.'

'That's an understatement. I wonder if Bobby's been warned off in any way.'

'Knowing Bobby he probably just shrugged it off.'

Bliss could well imagine that. 'I guess we'll find out in the morning. Have a good night, Pen. See you in my office first thing.'

'What about the evidence?'

'Evidence?'

'The writing on my wall. Do I get rid of it or leave it for forensics?'

'Leave it. For tonight. If you can bear to. We'll discuss it in the morning.'

'Okay. Jimmy, are you going to be all right? It must feel strange to be there without the Labs.'

He knew it would be. 'I'll be fine. I'm knackered and all I want to do now is sleep.'

'Sure. But will you?'

'Of course. Don't fuss.' He said goodnight and killed the line before she could question him further.

Two in the morning caught Bliss on the Internet, continuing the research on his disease. He'd applied for membership of the Ménière's Society, who were going to send him a welcome pack of information. He also signed up for a couple of online forums. The pages he read were of little comfort. Essentially, fellow sufferers ranged from people you'd never guess had anything wrong with them, to people whose entire lives were blighted by extreme vertigo and the resulting side effects.

What he saw on the web that night was infinitely more frightening than anything the Jodie Maybanks case had thrown at him.

THIRTY-THREE

Thursday morning. Rain fell in cold arcing sheets, and the wind that blew in from the north-east had teeth. Hail was forecast for later in the day, and the temperature was set to plummet and lay a film of ice upon the streets. Bliss had beaten it all, arriving at his desk before seven. After trying to wake himself with a cup of black coffee, he caught up with the e-mails waiting for him in his inbox, collected a few items of post from the central pigeonhole, and scratched a few notes in his diary. Then it was down to the serious business of concocting a string of convincing reports and case notes.

The notion of taking what they had to Flynn had fermented overnight, and by the time a feeble light crept into the furthest reaches of the sky, Bliss had made a firm decision. Detective Chief Superintendent Joseph Flynn was untouchable with the evidence they had, and the best way forward was to lull him even further. More to the point, Bliss needed to buy time and keep Sykes off his back.

Someone cleared their throat, and Bliss looked up to see constable Jerry Hopley standing on the threshold. Hopley's hands gripped his cap, twisting it anxiously. Bliss pushed himself back from his desk and said, 'Not with your partner in crime, PC Gascoigne, today? What is it this time? Someone reported me for exposing myself in Queensgate shopping centre?'

The fresh-faced officer gave a swift glance over his shoulder before stepping inside the room and closing the door behind him. A large man with a buzz cut that made him look a real bruiser, Hopley appeared curiously timid.

'Inspector Bliss, I have to tell you I wanted no part in what happened yesterday. I feel bad about it now, and I wanted to explain what went down.'

'You've got two minutes,' Bliss told him.

Hopley nodded. 'Gazza and I were sitting in the patrol car when his mobile went off. He checked the screen to see who was calling, and then he got out of the car and walked a few yards away. I assumed it was his girlfriend. Something personal.'

Bliss motioned for Hopley to take a seat, which he did. 'Go on,' Bliss prompted.

'A minute or so later Gazza jumps back in the car and speeds off, tells me we've had a tip-off. The next thing I know we're outside that house in Stanground and you are coming out of the door. I had no idea what was going on. You have to believe that.'

'I do.' He did. Bliss realised Hopley was taking a big risk being here. 'And afterwards, after I was pulled in? Did you ask Gascoigne where his information had come from?'

'Yes, sir. He's got a few more years in than I have, but I felt angry. I felt used. Gazza refused to tell me, though. He seemed to think it was all just a bit of a laugh. I thought it must be related to that bit of trouble you had with Sergeant Grealish.'

Bliss nodded. 'And you're telling me this why?'

'I felt bad about it when we were dragging you in. Now I feel even worse, of course.'

'Worse? Why?'

Hopley frowned, then put back his head and rolled his eyes. 'Oh, Christ. You don't know, do you?'

'Know what?' Bliss sat forward, looking hard at the officer. 'Hopley, what the hell is all this about?'

'Connie Rawlings was found murdered yesterday evening, sir. The girl that worked with her found Rawlings in the hallway of her home, stabbed twice through the chest. I'm sorry, sir. I thought you knew.'

Bliss felt as if he'd stepped into a vacuum, oxygen impossible to come by. He blinked and saw only tiny pinpoints of light dancing like motes of dust in the air before him. An ache swelled inside his chest and made its way down to the pit of his stomach. Twice he opened his mouth to speak, twice no sound emerged.

The door to Bliss's office flew open. Superintendent Sykes barged his way in, stopping in his tracks when he saw Bliss had company. 'Hopley,' Sykes said. 'Leave us. Now, please.'

The constable did so wordlessly, offering Bliss the faintest nod of sympathy. Sykes shut the door with an abrupt clatter. He turned to face Bliss, petty amusement twisting his features as though he were sucking on a lemon.

'I told you you'd fuck up, Bliss. I warned you. Your friend DCS Flynn won't save your skin this time.'

'I've only just heard.' Bliss could feel and hear blood rampaging through his temples. His throat felt choked with emotion. 'It's a hell of a shock.'

'A shock? No, trust me, Inspector, it's more than a shock. It's the end of your career.'

Bliss blinked at the man. 'How do you make that out?'

Sykes took a step closer, thin lips forming a satisfied grin. He put his hands behind his back, striking a familiar pose. 'You're a detective, Bliss. Figure it out. Yesterday morning you were caught consorting with a known prostitute, casting an unsavoury light upon you. Just a few hours later that same woman is murdered. Who do you think we ought to be looking at?'

'Me? You think I killed Connie?'

'It wouldn't be the first time you've been suspected of murder.'

Bliss jumped to his feet, rage roaring up inside him now. He moved swiftly around the desk. 'Do you mean my wife? Do you? Is that who you're referring to, you malignant piece of shit?'

'Take care, Inspector. Get a grip and remember who you are.' Despite the clarity of his words, Sykes had taken a step back towards the door. 'More importantly, remember who I am.'

'Did you mean my wife?' Bliss raised his own voice louder still, as if he'd not heard a word Sykes had said. His breath came in short gasping bursts. He felt veins popping out all over his body.

He didn't care that Sykes was a superior officer, didn't care that he could be overheard by anyone who might be sitting out in the main CID area. What Sykes had said was unforgivable.

The room grew silent. Bliss kept his eyes fixed on the odious reptile responsible for his fury, but Sykes could not meet his outraged glare. Eventually, Sykes said, 'We would not be carrying out our duty if we did not question you about the Rawlings woman, Inspector. We have to know whether you murdered her.'

'Why would I?' Bliss wanted to tear the man apart, but with his anger diminishing, his thoughts turned to Connie once more.

'To protect yourself, of course. SOCO found tissues and a condom, semen and trace on the whore's bed sheets. I know you banged her, Bliss. And now we have the evidence to prove it.'

Bliss slumped back onto his desk. He shook his head wearily, scarcely able to believe this new turn of events. 'Connie Rawlings had sex for a living, so those pieces of evidence could belong to anyone. But even if what you said was true, why would that lead to murder?'

'I would have thought that was obvious. To silence her.'

'That's nonsense.'

'Perhaps. But it is the basis of an investigation, and even if you're completely innocent, that will be one investigation too many for the service to accept.'

'*If* I'm innocent? You know damn well I didn't kill her.'

'I know nothing of the sort. Where were you between noon and two o'clock?'

Bliss expelled some air at last. The timing was crucial. It probably meant that the evidence found in Connie's bedroom was his, but at least he had an alibi for the time of death. Sykes had floundered with his questioning by providing the timeframe before asking Bliss to reveal his whereabouts. It was poor technique and typical of the man.

'I was with either Dunne and Chandler, or Chandler on her own,' Bliss finally responded. 'But with someone at all times during that period.'

Sykes grunted and nodded once. 'Of course. You wouldn't get your own hands dirty, would you, Inspector?'

'Oh, so now I paid someone to murder Connie Rawlings? Is that what you're suggesting?'

'It's certainly one of the questions any investigating team will ask.'

Bliss straightened. His felt a little giddy, but he resolved not to show weakness in front of this fool. 'Go away, Sykes,' he said. Bliss wanted no more part of this nonsense. 'Go away and come back only if you have an arrest warrant in your hand.'

'Are you refusing to help us with our inquiries, Inspector?'

'I'm refusing to help you, yes. Anything I have to say will be to a real policeman.'

This time, Sykes did not rise to the bait. He was relaxed now that Bliss no longer appeared threatening. 'Expect to hear from me later, Inspector Bliss. Expect that arrest any time soon.'

Meeting the repellent man's watery gaze, Bliss pursed his lips and nodded. 'I'll welcome it. It will be my chance to reveal you for the petty, vindictive little prick you really are, Sykes. I'll have you squirming on the hook, and then I'll gut you like a fish in public.'

'Over my dead body.'

'Be careful what you wish for there, Sykes. That's not the kind of thing you ought to be suggesting to a cold-blooded killer, is it?'

Bliss was in the canteen by eight. He caught a few looks from some of the uniforms, news of his dalliance with Connie Rawlings and her subsequent murder having probably filtered through the Thorpe Wood communication channels. Right now he couldn't give a toss about them or what they thought. He just felt exhausted and desperately sad.

He bought himself a full English breakfast, but pushed the plate to one side after only a couple of bites. Earlier he'd felt famished; now his appetite had been ruined. He was working his way through a mug of tea when Bobby Dunne joined him. The sergeant's own plate of food clattered onto the table, followed quickly by his cutlery.

'Have you heard what happened to Connie Rawlings?' Bliss asked him.

'Yeah. Bad news all round.'

'Particularly for her.'

'Of course.' Dunne peered at him. 'You going to be okay, boss?'

'I'll have to be. We've lost a potential witness, which is never a good thing. But more than that, I liked her. I really did. She was a decent woman.'

'I hear Sykes is gunning hard for you.'

'That wanker doesn't bother me one little bit.'

Dunne forked some food into his mouth. 'So he shouldn't. Piss-poor copper and an even worse bloke. How are the Labs?'

Bliss shook his head. 'No idea, Bobby. I'll call the vet in an hour or so. Speaking of the dogs, though, has any similar kind of warning come your way?'

'How d'you mean?'

'Penny had someone break into her flat yesterday and write a warning on her bedroom wall. The thing with Bonnie and Clyde was a warning to me. I wondered if they'd got to you, too.'

Dunne's forehead creased. He scratched the side of his face. 'Someone smashed the windows on my wife's motor yesterday morning. We thought it must just be local thugs, but I suppose it could have been the same thing as happened with you and Penny.'

'Sounds as if it could be. Big coincidence if not.'

'Bastard! Anyhow, I had that second chat with Hendry.' Dunne mopped his lips with a serviette and drank from his mug of tea before continuing. 'The man didn't falter. Eye contact was normal, body language gave nothing away, no nervous tics. Nothing. I laid it on a bit thick. You know, took him through the accident, how whoever was struck had been hurt, slight stress fractures, broken arm, maybe even some bleeding. He walked me through everything he and Weller did that night, how they'd scoured the area and found no sign. In my opinion, Hendry's involvement was minimal. No more than warning McAndrew off, under someone else's instructions.'

'Fair enough.' Bliss nodded as he processed Dunne's news. It wasn't a huge surprise. There was no reason why every officer involved in the case had to know about the murder. He couldn't even be certain that Weller and Dean had first-hand knowledge, though he remained convinced that Clive Rhodes had been in it up to his neck.

'How did you and Penny get on in good old Sunny Hunny?' Dunne asked.

Bliss glanced around. He leaned forward across the narrow table and lowered his voice to little more than a whisper. 'I'll go over the details with you up in my office a bit later. But Rhodes is dead. Probably suicide. It'll be all over this place before lunchtime once the guys over at Bridge Street Central are informed.'

Dunne put back his head and let out a low growl. 'This can't go on, boss. Weller and Dean were bad enough, but neither were serving officers. Rhodes was, so it's going to hit the fan. Big time.'

'I know. Don't worry. I've got it in hand.'

'Oh?' The big man's eyes asked the question.

Bliss shook his head. 'Not here.' He checked his watch. 'Look, meet me in my office in an hour. Nab Penny as soon as she gets in and get her up there, too.'

'Will do. Where are you off to?'

'I'm off to set a trap, Bobby. For a bloody huge rat.'

**

If DCS Flynn was surprised to find Bliss waiting for him when he arrived for work that morning, he disguised it well. Flynn's personal assistant had attempted to dissuade Bliss from hanging around in the small waiting area, insisting that her boss's diary was already full to overflowing. But Bliss had been equally insistent, and his authority prevailed. To her obvious annoyance, the DCS not only agreed to spare Bliss a few minutes, but also asked the PA to fetch them a coffee each.

Settled behind a huge teak desk, his crisp white shirt giving off an almost luminous glow, Flynn peered at Bliss over half-moon spectacles. 'What can I do for you, Inspector?' he asked, the edge of genuine curiosity apparent in his voice.

Bliss found himself watching Flynn as he would any suspect. It was an odd sensation, and in truth it made him feel a little queasy as the adrenaline surged through his system. This was the man who had welcomed him at a time when others remained wary of a reputation that carried the potential of creating more harm than good. A man who had continued to support him in the face of many grievances – some of which were genuine – raised by Superintendent Sykes. Bliss couldn't recall ever being so ill at ease with the demands of his job.

'A matter of immense delicacy has cropped up, sir,' Bliss told him. 'So sensitive, in fact, I thought it best to approach you directly rather than going through the usual channels.'

The eyes behind the glasses widened. 'Go on, Bliss. You've snared my interest.'

'Events relating to the Jodie Maybanks case have turned sour.' Bliss cleared his throat. 'Unbelievably so. To give you the broad strokes, I now believe that Jodie was murdered by a police officer, and that other officers were involved in covering it up. Two of those officers, both of whom are no longer serving, were murdered last week. The officer responsible for their murders and that of Jodie Maybanks killed himself and his wife yesterday.'

For almost thirty seconds, the only sound in the room was that of rain slapping against the windows. Bliss kept his eyes firmly fixed on Flynn's, and what he saw there very nearly caused him to gasp. It looked like relief. Relief tinged with excitement. DCS Flynn really was their man.

'Would you like to run that by me again?' Flynn eventually said. He pushed himself back into his seat. Too relaxed, Bliss thought. You should be leaning forward.

'A sergeant out of Bridge Street Central,' he said. 'Clive Rhodes. Let me tell you what I have.'

Bliss laid it out for Flynn exactly as planned. Where Flynn was suspected, Rhodes was put in the frame. The only part that didn't quite fit was the timing of the triple-nine call, as Flynn was quick to point out.

'I realise Rhodes was most likely not involved with that incident, sir,' he admitted. 'But I have a feeling that the accident may have been exactly that. There's also the chance that Rhodes had someone threaten Jodie Maybanks first. Warn her off. Ultimately, the result didn't satisfy him, and I suspect he murdered Jodie as soon as he came off duty later that same night.'

'And you came to this conclusion based on the fact that Rhodes was duty officer the night of an accident you can't prove ever happened, and that he may have known of the MisPer report regarding Jodie Maybanks.'

If Bliss hadn't known better, he would have sworn Flynn's incredulity was genuine. Shaking his head firmly, Bliss said, 'No, of course not, sir. Rhodes was never in the frame. In fact, no one was, we had no prime suspect. It's only subsequent events that point to him, having now reviewed every circumstance with the benefit of hindsight.'

Now Flynn did edge forward. He clasped his hands together on the desk, frowning at Bliss. 'So what exactly did you drive all the way to Hunstanton for? Just to ask Rhodes a few questions relating to Jodie Maybanks?'

'I realise that may strike you as a little unusual, but…'

'Unusual? Rather more than that, Bliss.'

'Sir, you know how it is when you're working a case. Particularly a case that's becoming bogged down. You get a feeling about a situation or some individual. Frankly, we had nothing and the case was winding down. Sergeant Rhodes was on our list of officers to question, and the more I thought about it the more I was uneasy about him taking sick leave and then immediately going on an unplanned holiday. Particularly when I put that together with the murders of Bernard Weller and Alan Dean. It seemed to me that Rhodes may have gone into hiding.'

'So when you drove up there to question him, you were thinking along the lines that Rhodes was involved in a significant way?'

'At that point, yes.'

'And now you're telling me that you knew about the murders of ex-officers, suspected a fellow serving officer of being involved with those murders and that of Jodie Maybanks, yet you reported none of this to Superintendent Sykes. That you deliberately withheld information germane to the case your team were working on.'

Bliss licked his lips and shook his head. 'That's not quite accurate, sir. The squad had been wound down when I put all the pieces together. Weller's death is still officially listed as an RTA, and Dean's name meant nothing to me at first, so there was no initial link between them. Like I said, it was only yesterday morning that I really saw the bigger picture. Even then it was still sketchy. It was just about my only lead, and I felt I had to act. I took an instinctive risk. Later, Rhodes killing his wife and then offing himself became the final piece of the puzzle.'

Flynn took a deep breath, exhaled through his nose. 'Your allegation against Rhodes is enormous, Bliss. The repercussions, if you're right, will have a huge impact on us all. If you're wrong, you'll be out on a limb I won't be able to rescue you from. That said, I've not heard anything to substantiate your belief. Conjecture and suspicion, yes. But evidence…?'

'That's why I'm here now, sir. I'm the first to acknowledge that what I have amounts to very little, certainly nothing to build a case on. But if I'm right, you won't want it sneaking up on you. If I'm wrong, it need go no further than these four walls.'

'What exactly are you asking for?'

'A few days. A week, maybe. Long enough to keep Sykes off my back while I firm up my suspicions. I know it was Rhodes, sir. And I know I can prove it if you give me enough time. What you do with any proof that I provide will be entirely up to you.'

Flynn ran a hand across his face. He appeared deeply troubled. Clearly he was weighing up his options. 'So at the moment, only you and I are aware of your suspicions?'

'Correct. DC Chandler was with me yesterday, but she knows only the official line. I have deliberately kept my own thoughts to myself.'

'And if you do get something on Rhodes you'll come straight to me, yes?'

'Of course.'

'And if you don't?'

'I'll close the book on it.'

'But what happens if anyone else gets wind of what you're up to?'

'Then, as you said earlier, I'm on my own. I just have to be careful.'

Flynn gave a curt nod. 'I'll give you two days. Officially you'll be working with the SIO over at Hunstanton, looking into Rhodes's background, assessing what might have driven him to the murder/suicide. I will inform Superintendent Sykes that you will be reporting directly to me. I will want daily reports from you, Bliss.'

'Yes, sir. Of course.' Bliss felt both elation at being given the time and space he needed, and a sense of anger and frustration at what Flynn thought he was getting away with. The temptation to throw it all in the man's face right now was almost irresistible, but Bliss knew he had to snap a lid on it. Despite the fact that he liked Flynn, he was determined to nail the murdering bastard.

'So, what's this I hear about your relationship with a prostitute?'

The question came out of nowhere, and Bliss felt his cheeks burn. He made light of it. 'Someone's idea of a joke. Connie Rawlings was the one who reported Jodie Maybanks missing back in nineteen ninety.'

'Yes, I read your report on that. So why the follow-up visit?'

Reminding himself that Flynn was probably more interested in potential links to himself than a genuine interest in the case, Bliss chose his words carefully. 'Well, as you will know, she gave up the name of Simon Palmer. We looked at him, but ruled him out. She also mentioned Jodie's dealer, but again we drew a blank. I wanted to see if she could think of anyone else Jodie may have been involved with.'

'She gave you Rhodes?' Flynn's gaze became rigid.

Bliss bought himself a moment by faking a coughing fit. He could tie this in quite neatly, but Flynn might know whether Rhodes had any dealings with Jodie Maybanks. The scenario was working out too well to push his luck and perhaps trigger any alarms.

'No, she didn't,' Bliss said, shaking his head. 'Palmer and the dealer were the only leads she was able to give me. I don't believe she was holding anything back, either.'

Flynn pushed himself back in his chair. 'And now I hear the poor woman has been murdered.'

'I just found that out myself, sir. I suspect Rhodes drove back here yesterday to take care of Connie Rawlings, tie up a loose end just in case. It all fits, sir. I just need to prove it.'

'Very well. And the murder of this Rawlings woman, are you clear on that?'

Bliss knew what he meant. 'I've made my feelings on the matter quite clear to Superintendent Sykes. I'm not going anywhere, so if he wants to take the matter further, I'll make myself available.'

'Very well. Perhaps it's a good thing that you'll be out of his hair for a couple of days. A cooling off period, eh? Now then, as DC Chandler was with you yesterday, how certain are you that she suspects nothing?'

'Absolutely positive, sir. I mean, she has all the information I have, but shares none of my suspicions. Chandler hasn't made that leap, and I've been careful not to lead her there.'

'Even so, you won't want to involve her in this any longer. As far as she is concerned, as far as anyone else is concerned, what happened with Rhodes and his wife is a terrible tragedy.'

'And the Jodie Maybanks inquiry?'

'Officially? Put it to bed, Bliss. Open unsolved, but no longer being actively investigated.'

Bliss had what he wanted. At any other time he would have felt victorious. Now he merely felt dirty and squalid. As he left the office, a tightening of his pectoral muscles caused his stomach to cramp. The spasm swiftly worked its way up to his head, and he was left with a nagging sensation that he might have missed something. Something potentially crucial. That something important had passed him by, something that had been said yet he'd not immediately grasped the significance of.

He let it go. Took a few deep breaths in the corridor outside Flynn's office. It would come to him provided he didn't focus on it. At least, he hoped it would. At this stage he needed every possible break he could get.

THIRTY-FOUR

'Paranoia creeping in?' Bobby Dunne asked, taking a final pull on his cigarette before tossing it away into the swirling river. The Nene was running high following all the recent rain, and its current was lively.

Bliss gave a tight smile. He'd decided to catch up with Chandler and Dunne somewhere other than his office, away from Thorpe Wood altogether, so the three of them were now gathered together on the deck of his boat, the *Mourinho*.

'Maybe a little,' he admitted, allowing a slight dip of the head. 'But we can't afford for a single word of what we're about to discuss to be overheard, and frankly we probably shouldn't even be seen huddled together from this point on. The situation is fragile right now.'

'I'm not sure I like where this conversation is headed,' Chandler told him, her eyes betraying both caution and strain. 'What exactly has happened, boss?'

'I went to see Flynn.'

He saw both his colleagues stiffen. Bliss held up a hand to forestall any immediate response. Then he told them what had been discussed, the arrangements that had been made. He spoke with a great deal more confidence than he actually felt.

'That was one hell of a risk you took,' Dunne said when Bliss was finished. The big man lit another cigarette, hands trembling slightly. Bliss wondered whether anger or fear had triggered the reaction. Perhaps even a measure of both.

'True,' he replied. 'But you'll be pleased to know that in doing so I managed to keep you two well away from the coal face. As far as Flynn is concerned, neither of you has the same sort of concerns

302

as me. You're both in the clear, and to be perfectly honest, right now I'll settle for that.'

'But doesn't that mean we can't help you, either?' Chandler asked.

'I'm afraid so.'

'Then I wish you hadn't settled. If Flynn truly believes you're going to be looking into the role Rhodes had, then you could have fought for some backup.'

'I got as much from Flynn as he was willing to give. The fact is, Pen, I went to him with this story to buy some time, not with any real expectation. Somehow I have to investigate Flynn himself while appearing to be working on Rhodes. That's hard enough for me to do, let alone two or even three of us. In my opinion, this was the only way forward. I had to make a judgement call.'

Chandler breathed a sigh, but made no remark. She would be annoyed, but in time she would see he was right. Bliss turned to Dunne. 'Bobby, you can help me just a little by using your personal knowledge to put together a list of people Flynn has worked with. Two columns: those still around, those no longer in the job. And asterisk any you recall who might have had a beef with Flynn.'

'I'll do my best, but I really don't know Flynn's colleagues that well. We never worked together that often – he's always been ahead of me on the rank ladder, and we're not exactly on the same social circuit.'

'Your best is all I ask.'

'And me?' Chandler demanded. 'Despite what you told Flynn, there must be something I can do to help.'

Bliss cast a glance upstream. One day he would take this boat and give it a run out. One day soon, perhaps. Maybe even sail it away and never come back. He didn't believe himself to be a stupid person, so the knowledge that he was hunting a man who might yet be responsible for murder caused more than a ripple of trepidation to course through his veins. But fear had to be dominated, conquered, and Bliss backed himself and his abilities. Without that inner belief he would be lost.

Where he felt vulnerable was in his responsibility for others. When he wasn't putting colleagues in harm's way, he was wrapping them in cotton wool. Only in considering his partners was he indecisive, and that led to mistakes. The task he had given Dunne was a simple one, but for Chandler he could give all or nothing.

'Let me think about it,' he said finally. 'Give me a bit of time.'

She nodded. 'I'm still not sure what we have to go on, exactly. Either of you want to run it by me?'

'What we have is a mess,' Dunne said flatly. 'A big fucking shitload of mess.'

Bliss couldn't argue with that. 'After I left Flynn's office I forced myself to take a step back, to try and see the whole case with a fresh eye. It's difficult, because there are now prejudices, but still it makes you question everything again.'

'And what conclusion did you arrive at?'

Bliss managed a choked laugh. 'None. Mainly because what we actually know amounts to very little. What we surmise comprises the vast majority of our case. And as for what we can prove… forget it. We do know that Rhodes cannot have been involved in the incident where Jodie Maybanks was run down. We also know that Flynn closed the book on that and the missing persons report lodged by Connie Rawlings, and that he was one of Jodie's regular customers.'

'So either of them could have murdered Jodie,' Chandler said.

'Or neither,' Bliss shot back.

'Neither? Who else is in the frame?'

Bliss rubbed a finger over his scar. 'You know, I've been kicking myself for not focusing on Clive Rhodes earlier. But there is someone we've never so much as suggested could be in the frame, and that's Hendry.'

'Hendry?' Dunne shook his head. 'Sorry, boss, but I'm not buying that. I've spoken to him twice now, and I'm telling you if he's guilty of anything then he's the best I've ever seen.'

'And I'm not doubting your ability, Bobby. But of all the officers other than Flynn who were involved in the two incidents,

Hendry is now the only one still alive. Maybe there's a reason for that.'

Now Chandler was shaking her head as well. 'I don't know, Jimmy. I'm not sure we should be thinking about anyone other than Rhodes and Flynn at this late stage in the proceedings. I realise we have no firm evidence against either of them, but I think we can all agree that our combined experience is telling us that those two are in it up to their necks. All we haven't been able to do as yet is apportion blame.'

Reluctantly, Bliss was forced to concede the point. 'All right. If I had to wager on it, this is how I think it went down: Flynn gets Jodie pregnant. They argue, he wants her to have an abortion, she threatens him with exposure. Flynn chases after her, accidentally knocks her down. He manages to force her into his car, but now her threats increase, so he takes her over by the lake, strangles her and buries her. With me so far?' He looked between them. They both nodded.

'Good. Now, I haven't come up with a good theory as to how Rhodes and Flynn end up involved together, except perhaps that Rhodes may have been paid to move Jodie's corpse and also take care of Weller and Dean. I'm sure now it was Rhodes who shoved me off the road, so I'm guessing he did the same to Weller.'

'So Flynn is responsible only for Jodie's murder?' Dunne said.

'Only? It's still murder. But yes, it's as likely as any other scenario.'

'We're still guessing. Still pissing in the wind. And I have to say, boss, I can't see you improving on that. I mean, say you're spot on and all that really took place exactly the way you said it did. Right now Flynn is sitting back thinking it's all over bar the shouting. I know you want justice for Jodie Maybanks, I know you don't want a guilty man to go about his business, especially if that business is being our boss. But we don't always get our man. We're not the fucking Mounties. And the truth is that there's no one left to finger Flynn. Even your witness, Connie Rawlings, the one who could have put Flynn and Jodie together, is now dead. So unless you come up with an eye witness who actually saw Flynn commit murder, you are never going to make a case against him.'

Bliss regarded Dunne thoughtfully. He'd never heard his colleague say so much in one go. And the problem was, what Bobby said had made perfect sense. He turned to Chandler.

'Pen? You agree with Bobby's assessment?'

She didn't need much time for reflection. 'I'm afraid I do.' She nodded emphatically. 'I'm sorry, Jimmy, but I don't see how you can get a result here.'

'This isn't just for Jodie Maybanks,' he reminded them both, feeling himself start to flounder. 'Are you forgetting about two fellow police officers? And how about Connie Rawlings? Doesn't she deserve some justice?'

'Since when did deserving justice ever mean you got it?' Dunne asked. 'None of us want to see Flynn get away with this, boss. But you're not being reasonable. You are not going to take Flynn down. But if you go hunting, one way or another, he might just take you down instead. Fight the battles you can win. Isn't that what you've always told us?'

Letting go a huge sigh, Bliss felt the set of his shoulders weaken. 'I know. You're right. You both are. I'm wearing blinkers on this one, and that's probably because I feel so betrayed. I thought Joe Flynn was one of us. One of the good guys.'

'So what now?' Chandler asked. 'Where do we go from here?'

'You two head back to Thorpe Wood. Sykes will be looking for me again, so fend him off as best you can. I'm going to stay here and think a few things through. I can't blunder into this anymore. I have to tread carefully now.'

'There's a first time for everything, I suppose,' Chandler said. Bliss could tell she was hurting as much as he was, but doing her best to hide it from him.

He smiled. Nodded. 'Maybe even a first time for you not to give me grief?'

'Oh, God no. I'd never go that far.'

They laughed, even Bobby Dunne, his huge shoulders juddering.

***

Bliss hung around for thirty minutes or so after Chandler and Dunne had left. Nothing was sitting right with him, and as usual he wondered if he was overlooking something obvious. The nagging sensation that something crucial had been said earlier in the day still dragged hooks in him. No matter which way he went, either focusing on his conversation with Flynn or trying to ignore it, the answer remained elusive. Frustration raged inside him, and Bliss was starting to feel bowed by the case.

When his mobile went off his first thought was to ignore it. When he saw Bobby Dunne's name on the screen he flipped the phone open and accepted the call.

'Make a note of this number and call it right away,' said Dunne. His voice carried a hint of regret. He read out a number.

'Who am I calling?' Bliss asked, memorising the digits.

'A reporter with the *Evening Telegraph*. She's running an item on you and wants your comments before going to print.'

Bliss checked his watch. He doubted there was time for it to be run today, but a story might be already written and awaiting the okay. 'Damn! I bet it's Sheryl Craig.'

'It is. She's the one who's given you a hard time in the past, right?'

'That's an understatement. Did she say what it was about?'

'Yeah. It's about the murder of Connie Rawlings. Your name features prominently. That's all I know.'

Bliss thanked Dunne, broke the connection and tapped in the number he'd been given. His hands were shaking. He'd considered the possibility of something leaking out to the press, but the timing could not have been worse.

'Sheryl Craig,' he heard.

'This is Detective Inspector Bliss. I understand you've been trying to get hold of me.' His voice was calm, the churning in his stomach anything but.

'Yes, thanks for calling me back. Inspector, I'm about to run a piece on the murder of a prostitute by the name of Connie Rawlings. Your name has come up, and in a very big way. I would like to add a bit of balance to the piece, so I thought I'd give you the opportunity of commenting.'

'I'd have to know what I'm commenting about.'

'Of course. Essentially, while the main item is about the murder, the background will reveal that you were arrested by your own colleagues yesterday morning for soliciting the services of Connie Rawlings, and that you are about to face an investigation into the murder itself.'

Bliss closed his eyes. This was much worse than he'd imagined. Someone inside Thorpe Wood had leaked everything. 'Are you running the story today?' he asked.

'That's the intention, yes.'

'Tell me, Sheryl, are you looking to print sensationalism or the truth?'

'I know we've had our disagreements, Inspector Bliss, but I resent the implication.'

'Well, I'm sorry if I've offended your sensibilities, but I'm sure it will come as no surprise to you that not everyone in your profession understands the meaning of integrity. I just need to know if you're one of those who does.'

There was a brief pause. Bliss could tell she was weighing up her options. He decided to add some leverage. 'Sheryl, if you run with what you have right now you'll very likely end my career. I have no doubt that I will be able to refute everything you print, but mud sticks and I'll be buried beneath a whole pile of it. The truth might not be as spectacular, but it will be factual and you won't have ruined someone's life. Plus… if you do this for me I will owe you one.'

That was the clincher.

'Where do you want to meet?' she asked him.

Bliss told her.

***

Like any other modern city centre, Peterborough's was awash with coffee bars. There were independents littered all over the place, plus the three main players: Starbucks, Costa, and Nero. Bliss chose Nero mainly because the coffee was his favourite, but also he hated the fact that Starbucks just a few doors away had taken over a beautiful old building that had once been the main branch of Lloyds Bank. Seeing fine institutions ransacked and replaced by a high-price coffee bar didn't sit well with him.

When he arrived, Sheryl Craig was already waiting for him, hunched over her drink. Bliss ordered himself a double shot of espresso and took it across to a narrow counter that ran along the spine of the bar. He pulled up a tall stool and plumped himself down next to Craig.

They exchanged subdued greetings and a few insincere pleasantries. But what they both wanted was to get right into it.

'I don't suppose there's any point in my asking for the name of your source, right?' Bliss asked. He took a sip from his tiny cup, the caffeine kicking right in.

The journalist merely smiled at him.

'I had to ask,' he said, his own smile barely thinning his lips. 'All right, then, Sheryl. Let me start by saying you've been sold a pup. I have no idea what the going rate for information is these days, but you didn't get your money's worth.'

'I didn't have to pay for this, Inspector. My source was only too eager to reveal all.'

Which told Bliss a lot. He'd been racking his brain for who might have done this to him. Sergeant Grealish, the uniform he'd fought with, was high on the list. PC Gascoigne was right up there with him. But either of those two pricks would have made sure they made a few quid as well, so that left just two names: Sykes and Flynn. It would suit the purposes of either man, but Bliss would lay odds on it being Sykes.

The huffing of the milk frother tore into Bliss's concentration, the loud voices of the counter staff piercing his ears like tiny razors. His nerves were frayed, and he felt sick. He took a moment to pull himself together.

'Tell you what, why don't you call me Jimmy,' Bliss told Craig. 'See me as a human being first.'

'Very well. Jimmy it is.'

'Good. So, tell me what you think you know.'

Craig knocked back some of her coffee. She referred to no notes as she spoke. 'I'm reliably informed that you were arrested yesterday morning for soliciting sexual favours from a prostitute posing as a masseuse. The woman's name was Connie Rawlings, and she was also arrested. Within hours of her release, Connie Rawlings was savagely murdered, stabbed to death in her own home. The word is that you are about to be investigated for that murder.'

The lack of notes told Bliss that Craig's story was already written and waiting to go to print. He had only once chance to rescue this. He finished his drink and took a breath.

'To begin with, neither I nor Connie Rawlings was arrested. That's the first error in your story, and can be easily verified if you choose to do so. What happened was this: having previously interviewed Connie regarding a case I am currently working on, I returned to ask her a few more questions yesterday morning. On leaving, I was… persuaded to accompany two fellow police officers back to Thorpe Wood. Now, it is true that I was interviewed and solicitation was the reason given, but I was released without charge the moment my reasons for being with Connie were made clear. Several minutes later, Connie was also released. It was a mistake. Pure and simple.'

Craig was nodding, trying to read his eyes all the while. 'This case Connie Rawlings was helping you with, that would be the Jodie Maybanks murder, right?'

Bliss had to think about that. By rights the journalist had no need to know, but he didn't think it could harm anyone now. He gave a nod. 'That's correct. The two of them worked the streets together.'

'You say you had already spoken to her. So what more did you think Rawlings could give you?'

'That I can't answer. It's still an ongoing investigation. I also think we're straying off course, here.'

Grinning, Craig nodded. 'Sorry. Old habits, and that. So, Inspector, what you're saying is that you did not pay Connie Rawlings to have sex with you. She was simply a witness, and you were in her home carrying out an interview.'

'That's about it, yes.'

'Then why would I be told otherwise?'

'Because it makes the second part of the story more believable. And the murder is the only part you are really interested in.'

'So you're telling me that someone has set you up. Using me as a way of getting to you, an attempt to ruin you.'

'The whole guilt by association thing, yes.'

The woman sat back and shook her head, golden curls dancing. 'Tell me why I should believe you, Inspector.'

'I'm not telling you that.' Bliss met her direct gaze. 'I'm asking you to check the facts before you run the story. I'm asking you not to ruin my career unless you are absolutely convinced of my guilt.'

Bliss saw in her eyes that she was wavering. Saw it long before she said, 'And if I do this for you, you'll owe me. That is what you said earlier?'

'It is. I did. And I will. Even though all I'm doing is asking you to do your job properly.'

If she felt rebuked, Sheryl Craig hid it well. 'What can you give me in return?' she asked.

'At the moment, nothing. But there's a reason why someone did this to me. That reason might be of interest to you at some point in the near future.'

'And if it isn't?'

'Then I'll still owe you. And I always pay my debts.'

She took a long, deep breath. 'Despite what you obviously think of me and people in my line of business, Jimmy, I do value integrity and I do report the truth where it can be found. Believe it or not, that you'll owe me is incidental, but I will call in that marker. We both know I couldn't run this story now without checking out your version. I trust your press officer at Thorpe Wood will be helpful?'

'Call and tell them you've heard a whisper about my being arrested and ask them to confirm or deny.'

Craig nodded. 'I'll do that. And what about the murder? Is it pure coincidence that Connie Rawlings was killed shortly after being interviewed in relation to the Jodie Maybanks case?'

'I told you before,' Bliss said with a thin smile. 'I can't discuss that with you right now. But keep your phone switched on and fully charged.'

THIRTY-FIVE

As he drove back to the other side of the city, Bliss tried to decide who had fed the story to Craig. He couldn't really figure out what Flynn would have to gain from such a move. In fact, officially linking the murder of Connie Rawlings with the Jodie Maybanks investigation would probably reignite an inquiry that had been all but extinguished. Sykes, on the other hand, was much more likely to have seized the opportunity to create a false impression of Bliss in the eyes of the public and influential senior officers.

Bliss decided it didn't matter right now. He and Sykes would butt heads again, but the immediate prime objective had to be nailing Flynn. Back at Thorpe Wood he felt curious eyes upon him as he made his way through the CID area, wagging tongues having done their work in his absence. Bliss had been at his desk for no more than a minute before Bobby Dunne came in and shut the door behind him. He wore a wide grin of excitement.

'You are going to love me, boss,' the DS said. 'You might even want to have my children.'

'That's an ugly thought I don't wish to dwell on, Bobby,' said Bliss. 'But I'm all ears, big man.'

'I've been sniffing round a couple of Flynn's old colleagues. One of them told me something that sent me digging into archives once more. This time I struck gold.'

'And? Don't fuck about, tell me.'

Dunne eased himself into a chair on the other side of the desk. 'Did you know Flynn was a big football fan?' he asked.

'Sort of. When I came for my first interview I noticed a photo of Goodison Park on one of his bookshelves. He said he'd been an Everton fan all his life.'

'That's right. But not only Everton. He's a member of the official England supporters' club. And guess where he was in the summer of nineteen ninety?'

Bliss didn't have to guess. The answer struck him immediately. 'Italy. He was watching England in the World Cup.'

'Spot on. One of the ex-cops I spoke to was actually there with him. They were together right from the opening game to the day after the semi-final defeat by the Germans. Including the Belgium game.'

Bliss licked his lips. Nodded eagerly. 'Okay. That obviously rules him out of the Jodie Maybanks murder, but it doesn't mean he didn't arrange for Rhodes or someone else to sort Jodie out while he was away. Perfect alibi, if you look at it from this fresh perspective.'

Dunne continued to grin. 'But you're forgetting my trip back to archives. See, this fresh information didn't gel right with everything else we had, so the one brain cell I still have started working overtime. I thought about the first piece of evidence that pointed us in the direction of Flynn. Those bloody records I dug out. So I went back, found half a dozen other cases where Flynn had signed off that same year. The signature on those half dozen all matched, but even to my untrained eye, the two we found didn't.'

Bliss let the new information sink in. 'Someone forged Flynn's name on those case reports. Someone wanted to lead us to him.'

'That's what I reckon, yes.'

'But why? Why Flynn of all people?'

'That I don't know. Maybe they just picked it out of thin air, not thinking it would ever come up. Who could have known back then where Flynn would be now?'

Bliss clicked his fingers. 'Or maybe... maybe they didn't just use his name for those reports. Bobby, what if it was Rhodes who was seeing Jodie Maybanks all along, only using Flynn's name? I realise that sounds wild, but just think about it for a moment. As soon as Jodie tells him about the pregnancy and makes her threats, Rhodes realises how much trouble he'll be in. In his mind, what better way of tying it all together neatly by apparently having Flynn sign the cases off.'

'It fits,' Dunne said, leaning forward now. 'It bloody well fits.'

But then something occurred to Bliss, and he frowned. 'Except for one thing. One major flaw. If Rhodes was on duty and Flynn was in Italy, who drove the car that ran Jodie Maybanks down that night?'

Dunne put back his head and exhaled his frustration. 'Fuck!'

'No, hold on,' Bliss said, raising a hand. 'That doesn't mean we're not right about this. It just means that someone else was more involved than we thought. Weller or Dean, maybe even Hendry.'

Bobby Dunne was shaking his head, rubbing the back of his neck with a meaty hand. 'So after all this, Flynn may be in the clear, completely innocent. Rhodes used his ID all the way through. Is that where we're heading with this now?'

'It's beginning to look possible.' Bliss could scarcely conceal his relief. Flynn's guilt had gnawed at him, but now he could see a way through. 'More than possible,' he added.

'The only problem is we can't confirm any of it. Not with all the major players now dead. Maybe that Rawlings woman could have picked Rhodes out as the man Jodie thought was Flynn, but now we'll never know.'

Bliss felt a smile spread slowly across his face. 'We do have one last card,' he said. 'On the day Connie was dragged in here, she told me about another brass who was good friends with Jodie. For the life of me I can't remember her name right now, but it'll come back to me. Connie even told me where I might find her.'

Dunne was looking at him oddly. The excitement had drained from his face, leaving narrowed eyes and a pained expression.

'When were you going to tell your partners about that little gem of information?' he asked.

'It had slipped my mind until now.'

'Slipped your mind? How convenient.'

'Bobby?' Bliss stared hard at his colleague. 'What the hell is wrong with you? You think I was keeping it from you and Penny? Deliberately so?'

Dunne closed his eyes and hung his head. It was as if someone had put a puncture in him. 'Ignore me,' he said without looking back up. 'I'm tired and I'm being a prick.'

'Forget it. What you've come up with has made my day, and may just have saved several reputations. I so wanted Flynn to be innocent, but I never thought we'd be able to clear his name completely. All I want to do now is hang it all on Rhodes. Then we can decide what to do with it.'

'You want me to interview this other brass?' Dunne asked.

'I still can't even recall her name. But sure, as soon as it comes to mind I'll call you. Take some mugshots over, include both Flynn and Rhodes.'

Dunne got to his feet. 'Fair enough. Sorry for throwing my toys out of the pram. I was feeling bloody good, and then deflated because I thought you'd kept me out of the loop.' He stuck out a hand. 'We okay, boss?'

Bliss took the offered hand and shook it firmly. 'We're better than okay, Bobby. You did great work today, my friend.'

For the first time in days, Bliss's thoughts were positive. On his own once more he reflected on how close he'd come to endangering his job by trying to investigate a senior officer. Despite his now apparent innocence, Flynn would never have forgiven him. Bliss was certain of that. A valuable ally would have been lost. And all for nothing.

His mind drifted back, fleeting glimpses of the past couple of days, snatches of conversations. Connie Rawlings. Penny. Bobby. Sykes and Flynn. Then out of nowhere something stuck, snagged in his mind and refused to loosen its grip. It was the snippet of conversation that had bothered him so much, the one he thought might be important. The one he believed might bring Flynn's guilt more into focus.

At first it felt good simply having managed to scratch the itch. The anomaly seemed little more than that – an innocuous remark made during an in-depth discussion. But the itch wouldn't let up, and Bliss felt his thoughts being dragged back to the conversation. Something else lay beneath the surface, another incongruity that was raising its head, begging to be noticed.

When it finally hit, disparate elements falling into place and forming something tangible, Bliss felt his mouth open, heard himself sucking in air. His insides seemed to drain away, replaced by something dull and heavy and insurmountable. He couldn't recall the last time he'd felt so emotional. Time and again he tried to deny the memory of that conversation, seeking to make sense of what he was now thinking. But there was no sense. The world had turned upside down and inside out. No sense. Only a terrible sense of outrage.

**

The Flag Fen Bronze Age site lay in the wetlands to the east of Fengate, and was a far more impressive sight than Bliss had expected. He'd noticed the brown road signs on many previous occasions, and was aware of the site's historical significance, but had never considered joining the many visitors it welcomed each day. He wished he had a better reason for being here now, but he knew he had to get this right, that he had to be absolutely certain of his suspicions this time.

At Reception he asked for Emily. It needed a flash of the warrant card to get the pale, bearded receptionist to take an interest, and the man eventually used a walkie-talkie to summon Emily from somewhere within the vast complex. When she arrived a few minutes later, she looked dishevelled, her hair tied up and clipped in several places to keep it off her shoulders and out of her face. She wore baggy jeans and boots beneath a thick, padded winter jacket. Bliss thought that beyond an uncertain frown, she looked pleased to see him.

He took Emily's arm and walked her outside, strolling alongside the visitors' centre. 'I take it this is business, not pleasure,' she said. She smiled, but Bliss could see the remains of uneasiness there.

'I'm afraid so,' he admitted. 'Not that it's not always a pleasure to see you, of course. I wish the circumstances were different, but I do need to talk to you about work.'

Emily nodded. 'Okay. Yours or mine?'

'A bit of both.'

'Ah. Our human remains.'

'I'm afraid so. Listen, do you happen to have completed your report? I told you my boss was being arsey about it.'

'I've been busy, Jimmy. With my own work. But it's just about there. I can have it done tonight if you need me to.'

Bliss shook his head. 'No, that's fine. You get it to me when you can. I just wanted to make sure that you hadn't mailed or faxed it in.'

'No. It's sitting on my laptop at home.' She narrowed her gaze. 'Why?'

'Why what?'

'If it's not urgent, why did you want to know if I'd already submitted it?'

'I needed to be sure that no one else had seen it. There's something I have to know. Something I need you to tell me.'

'About the burial sites? The poor girl herself?'

Bliss nodded. 'Yes, it's about Jodie. I need you to tell me everything that happened to her. And I mean everything.'

***

After thanking Emily and leaving her perhaps more confused than she had been upon being dragged away from her work to see him, Bliss spent the next couple of hours making calls and driving to three separate locations. First there was a trip to Werrington. This was followed by a drive out of the city to Whittlesey. Finally, after a short stop off to check on the Labs, he drove to a secluded location just a few miles from Stilton. Each additional piece of information he gleaned during those hours, each suspicion he confirmed, both convinced and saddened him more. The truth, at last, was unravelling. In the end, he'd been wrong. About everything and almost everyone.

Travelling back towards Thorpe Wood, Bliss received a call on his mobile. It was from Emily.

'Hey,' he said, delighted to hear from her, though his thoughts still lay elsewhere. 'How are you? Missing me already?'

'I *was* okay. In fact, I was feeling pretty good,' Emily replied. 'And yes, I was missing you. At the time that seemed like a good thing.' There was something in her voice that caught his attention.

'What's up?' he asked. 'You sound angry.'

'The *Evening Telegraph* is what's up.'

Bliss's heart seemed to suddenly lurch between no beats and far too many. 'What does it say?' he managed to ask.

She told him. It was everything Sheryl Craig had suggested would be in her original piece. Everything he'd expected not to see in print. Bliss felt the shadow of guilt press against him, its touch devastating. He'd acted foolishly, and now it was time to pay.

'Are you asking me if it's true?'

'I'm not really sure, Jimmy. I refuse to believe the man I spent time with is a murderer, but you know what they say about smoke and fire?'

'I had nothing to do with the murder of Connie Rawlings,' Bliss insisted, his voice cracking.

There was silence for a moment. When she spoke again, Emily's voice was even less certain. 'That sounds terribly specific, Jimmy.'

Bliss chewed on his lower lip. The easy thing, maybe even the kindest thing, would be to lie. But he liked Emily, and he thought maybe they had a shot at something. Yet he was unwilling to build that relationship on the foundation of deceit.

'There was something,' he heard himself say. His eyes focused on other vehicles flashing by, but his mind was anywhere but on his driving. 'Something stupid. It was brief and it was unthinking. It fulfilled a need. Nothing more.'

'It sounds cold. But the question now, and the answer that matters most of all, is when? When did this brief, unthinking need take place? Before or after you started seeing me?'

Again he could not tell her a lie. 'After.'

Another silence followed, one neither of them seemed to want to fill. In Bliss's heart he knew anything he might have to say would be crass and trite right now.

'Don't call me,' Emily finally said. And the phone was dead in his hands.

A familiar tone sounded. A missed call, but with a voice message left. Feeling numb on so many levels, Bliss thumbed a speed-dial number and listened to his message. It was from Sheryl Craig.

'I'm sorry, Bliss, but my paper ran the piece. I tried to get it stopped, but while I was confirming what you said, the decision to go to print was made by my editor. A detraction will run in later editions and in tomorrow's paper, of course. Please believe me when I say I tried.'

A retraction, he thought miserably.

Too fucking late.

Bliss could not believe how badly this day had turned out. He felt overwhelmed by everything that was happening both to him and around him. When he had calmed himself enough to think more rationally, Bliss placed a call to Bobby Dunne.

'The other brass, Jodie Maybanks's friend,' he said. 'Her name is Simone Jackson. I've arranged a meet. You want in?'

'Absolutely. You want me to let Penny know?'

'No need. Let's see what this woman has for us first.' He gave Dunne the place and time. When he ended the call he sat in his car for a few moments, thinking about Jodie Maybanks and Connie Rawlings. Connie had asked him to find Jodie's killer.

'This is for both of you,' he whispered to himself. Hoping they could both hear.

THIRTY-SIX

When the complex array of bridges, tunnels and roundabouts were completed at Norman's Cross in order to alleviate a traffic bottleneck on the A1, the developers left part of an access road behind. It went nowhere, dead-ending at a field, and was often used by police patrol cars and RAC or AA mechanics to rest up between calls. It was here that Bliss and Dunne met, the DS sliding into the passenger seat alongside Bliss in the pool car.

According to the Ford's dashboard clock, Simone Jackson was a few minutes late. Bobby Dunne glanced across at Bliss. 'You're quiet, boss. You think she might not show.'

Bliss shifted in his seat, facing his colleague. It had been a long time since he'd felt this way, so close to losing himself to rage. Part of him just wanted to give in to it and let the chips fall where they may, but he got a grip and steadied his breathing. 'She's not coming, Bobby.'

'What? Then why are we still here. Let's go pull her in?'

'No, I mean she never was coming. I've already spoken with her, as a matter of fact. Earlier today.'

Dunne turned, the Focus lurching as he moved. 'I don't understand. You said we were going to do this together.'

'I know what I said. I lied. It turns out that Simone knew Jodie very well. And fortunately for me, she also has a pretty good memory for faces. I showed her the mugshots and asked her to pick out Jodie's regular. I included one of Rhodes and one of Flynn. I also included one of yours. Can you guess which one she pointed at, Bobby?'

Dunne sat and stared at him. His chin jutted out, and a tic began to pulse in his cheek.

'Why did you do it, Bobby? And please,' Bliss put up a hand and shook his head, 'don't pretend you don't know what I'm talking about. Let's be adult about this. Tell me everything. Make me understand.'

Bobby Dunne's expression didn't alter in the slightest. By way of a response he dug his hand in his coat pocket, and a moment later took out an automatic pistol. He didn't point it at Bliss, choosing instead to rest it on his thigh, finger locked around the trigger. The threat was implicit.

'You going to use that on me now?' Bliss asked.

'It's just for a little protection while we work something out here.'

'I'm unarmed, Bobby.'

'Still… I feel better having this edge.'

'You'll need it. So go on then, Bobby. Tell me about it. Explain it to me if you can.'

Dunne nodded. 'I imagine you must feel very let down right now. But you know, I was only one of many coppers sticking it to Jodie Maybanks. According to her, though, I was the only one doing her bareback, without a condom that is. She told me she was in the club and that I was the father. She wanted money, I wanted her to get rid of it. That night in June nineteen ninety, we'd argued again about it and before storming off up the street she threatened to go to my bosses and the newspapers. I chased after her in the motor, and then she just walked out into the road in front of me. I clipped her, and could see she was hurt, but not too badly. Jodie was shocked and silent, though. I bundled her into the car. She was lucid enough to carry on screaming at me, and then she passed out. I had to be at work, and frankly I didn't have a clue what to do about the mess I'd got myself into. I was out of my depth. So I stopped and put her in the boot and then drove to Bridge Street to see Clive. He was about to end his shift, and because we'd done a bit of wheeling and dealing together and had become mates, I asked him to take care of Jodie for me.'

Dunne set his chin even more and shook his head. 'No, not to kill her. We were clear on that. He was to persuade Jodie to leave, even give her a bung if needed, and if I'm honest I didn't think too much about what form that persuasion might take. But Clive came to me the next day and told me that Jodie had gone berserk when she came round, making more wild threats, this time involving him as well. Then Clive admitted to strangling Jodie and burying her over by the lake.'

Bliss tried imagining each event as Dunne described it. He could see the logic, the panic, the mistakes, the way the situation had spiralled out of control. He could also see the heartless treatment of a young girl, the abuse and dismissal of her life as if it meant nothing.

'You want to put that gun away now?' Bliss asked. 'It's making me nervous.'

Dunne shook his head. 'No. Not just yet.'

'Okay. So tell me about the others, Bobby. How were they all involved?'

But Dunne wasn't having that. His fixed gaze narrowed. 'No. You tell me how you came to suspect me. What made you add my mugshot to the others?'

'All right. It was something you said. Actually, a couple of somethings, throwaway comments that meant nothing to me at the time, yet nagged at me somewhere in the back of my mind. Because I went to see Flynn after I'd spoken to you in the canteen, I thought it had to be some remark he had made. But when it finally came to me I realised it was when you asked me whether Chandler and I had enjoyed ourselves in Sunny Hunny.'

Dunne blinked a couple of times. Nodded. 'Ah. I shouldn't have known you were there, should I?'

'No'. Neither I nor Penny had seen you to tell you where we were going, and I doubted that anyone from Hunstanton had told you. I admit it didn't seem much to go on at first, just an oddity, a puzzle in need of solving at some point. But it got me running our discussion through the cogs, and that was when the clincher hit me. When you were talking about your interview with Hendry, you mentioned laying it on thick, telling him about the fractures and broken arm. I had to keep coming back to that, because you see, Bobby, I had no idea Jodie's arm had been broken that night. I couldn't recall Emily mentioning it, and it certainly wasn't ever discussed at briefing. So if there was no record of it, how could you have known?

'At first the answer appeared obvious: you were either wrong or you'd exaggerated the injuries to Hendry. But then I put that together with you somehow knowing where Penny and I spent our afternoon yesterday, and I became extremely curious. So I spoke with Emily. She confirmed that Jodie had broken her arm, and that the lack of healing meant she had died shortly afterwards. Emily also confirmed that she hadn't mentioned it before, nor had her report been completed.'

Dunne heaved a sigh heavy with resignation. 'I got a bit carried away telling you about Hendry. The Hunstanton slip was relatively minor, but knowing that arm was broken is impossible to talk my way out of.'

Bliss nodded. 'Yes. It's way too late for that. I didn't see the whole story right away, because I still couldn't completely accept your involvement. Not in something like that. So I put my mind to what you had been doing throughout the case. It was you who turned up the missing files in the first place, of course, and then again earlier today. Still there wasn't enough there to convince me of your involvement. I felt something had to be wrong, but didn't want to believe where it was headed.'

Bliss shifted slightly in his seat, eyes on the gun in Bobby's hand. He looked outside at the encroaching mist, wishing it would seep in and swallow them both up. His throat felt dry, but now that he had fashioned this meeting, he was determined to have his say. He glanced across at Dunne when he spoke.

'Coming back to your involvement with the investigation, I wondered about your interviews with Hendry, so I made a call to RAF Wittering. They told me Hendry was based in Germany and had been for the past four months. It seems to me that posting may have saved his life. But now there seemed to be no question about your involvement. Somehow you knew me and Penny had been to Hunstanton, you'd lied about interviewing Hendry, and you'd turned up the records that first pointed us at Flynn and then later away from him again. I went over it time and again. Only then did it occur to me that everything you'd said about either Flynn or Rhodes could just as easily have applied to you.

'So I went to see Simone Jackson on my own, and she fingered you right away when I showed her the photos. You'd used Flynn's name while you were seeing Jodie Maybanks. I guessed then that you must have forged the files supposedly completed by Flynn. I still don't understand that, Bobby. Why did you do that?'

Dunne heaved a sigh. Though resigned, he seemed curiously at peace. 'Clive had done a runner, and I thought the best thing I could do was keep your mind off him until I could track him down. I knew if you had time to think about it you'd see his absence from work as more than coincidence, so I had to make you look elsewhere while I put things together. If you'd collared Rhodes he would have coughed. I needed to protect myself. As you rightly guessed, when I was seeing Jodie I used Flynn's name – all us coppers used other names when we humping brasses. I didn't have much time to come up with a better plan, but in the end I really thought you'd dump the case once you thought Flynn might be responsible. I thought that would be the end of it. I couldn't believe it when you said you were going to carry on.'

'You took a hell of a risk.'

'Yeah. I called the play, and it came back to bite me.'

Bliss nodded. 'Tell me it wasn't you who took out Weller and Dean.'

'It wasn't. You believe what you want, but that was Clive. We'd used Weller, Hendry and Dean back in nineteen ninety, but all they knew at the time was that a colleague wanted those two cases buried. A while after, Clive, Bernie and Alan Dean spent some time together and it was then that Weller and Dean guessed what had happened. No details, of course, only that the two cases were linked and now a whore was missing. Clive decided to apply a little pressure, making them both realise that they might be in the frame, that it could look as if they'd covered up a murder.'

'You bought them off?'

'Dean, yes. Bernie refused to accept cash. Blood money, he called it. But it was agreed that everyone would keep quiet about it. They knew, or at least guessed, what might happen if they didn't. It was Alan Dean who panicked when the IKEA building was about to go up. Clive had told him where the body was buried, so Dean dug her up and moved her to Bretton Woods. Then it all hit the fan when those remains were found last week. We never discussed it, but it had to be Clive who took care of Bernie and Alan.'

His direct gaze flickered for a moment. 'I made sure he only warned you and Penny off. Clive was all for taking you two out as well, but I wouldn't let him.'

'So you were in contact, then?'

'Text only at first. Clive was scared. He knew if he spoke to me he'd cave.'

'Why did you put the block on me and Penny being killed, too?'

Dunne gave a shrug. 'I like you. You and Penny both. I didn't think we had to go that far with you two. I thought I could make it work. I still thought you'd back away from Flynn's supposed guilt.'

'And you almost did make it work. So in the end, Rhodes was responsible for all the murders.'

'Yes. It's the truth, Jimmy.'

'No,' Bliss snapped, shaking his head. 'Only my friends get to call me Jimmy. But that's not quite all, is it? Because Rhodes didn't shoot his wife, didn't commit suicide, did he, Bobby? I think you murdered them both.'

Dunne turned away for the first time, staring ahead through the windscreen. 'You think what you like.'

'I will. I think that once you realised the whole Flynn issue had got out of your control, you saw the chance to lay it all on Rhodes. But for that to work you had to get rid of him. And you couldn't know what he'd told his wife over the years, so you had to do her as well. I'm not saying it came easy to you, but I'm sure you did it.'

'What if I said it was to save you and Penny, not to make things easier for me? Would that make a difference?'

'Difference?'

'How you think of me.'

Bliss shook his head. 'No. You may not have murdered Jodie Maybanks, Weller or Dean, but you knew all along who did and you hid behind it.'

'Okay. You're right. It doesn't make any difference now, so yeah, I killed Clive and Chloe. He called me, and I instructed him to make the hit on you and Penny. I did that just to make him let his guard down, never intending for him to get that far. He let slip where he was staying, and I made sure I got to him before he got to you.'

Bliss put back his head. 'What a sorry fucking mess. I can't believe I was so wrong about you, Bobby. I would have bet my life on you being a straight copper.'

'You remember that it was Rhodes who started it all.'

'Yeah, and it was you who ended it. The irony is that Jodie's murder is about the only one you played no part in.'

Dunne shook his head. 'Jesus. All this over a fucking tart.'

Bliss pulled back his hand as far as the confines of the vehicle would allow, then slammed his fist into Dunne's cheekbone. The big man barely flinched, but he looked at Bliss as if he were a madman.

'You crazy fuck! I'm the one sitting here with a gun in my hand.'

Bliss hit him again, harder this time, feeling the blow bite deep into his knuckles. 'And that's for Connie Rawlings,' he said. 'Rhodes might have been the one who killed her, but he did it on your say so.'

Dunne dipped his head. 'You hit me again, Jimmy, and I'll fucking shoot you. I swear I will.'

'Fuck you, Bobby. Fuck you.'

Neither man spoke for a while, anger sitting like a physical wall between them. Then Dunne put back his head and swept a hand over his scalp. 'It could have all ended with Jodie if I'd only done the right thing.'

Bliss thought he heard genuine regret in the man's voice. Regret at the loss of colleagues. Or perhaps that was what Bliss wanted to hear. Even needed to.

'There's no good way out of this now,' said Dunne. He looked out into the night. 'Not for either of us. But you are the only one who knows the whole story. Penny still thinks it was Rhodes and Flynn. You're the only one standing between me and my freedom.'

Bliss's eyes dropped to the gun. 'You think it's going to end here, Bobby? Do you really believe it will be all over for you if you pull that trigger?'

Dunne raised the weapon, stared directly into Bliss's eyes. 'Yes,' he said. 'I do.'

Then Bobby Dunne aimed the automatic at Bliss's face and shot twice. Before the echo of the gunshots had died away, he put the barrel of the gun in his own mouth and pulled the trigger.

THIRTY-SEVEN

It looked like the fair and circus had come to town at the same time. The area was awash with the flickering lights from myriad emergency vehicles. Squad cars, unmarked Armed Response Vehicles, ambulances, CID saloons and SOCO vans. Dozens of police officers and detectives littered a small area around the Ford Focus pool car. Still more were thrashing through the fields and undergrowth nearby, scouring embankments and weaving their way through thickets. Away in the distance, the lights of the city sparkled like jewels.

Chandler sat on the drop-down step leading up into one of the ambulances, head in her hands, palms nursing moist eyes. 'Oh, Jimmy,' she said beneath her breath. 'You stupid, stupid bastard.'

DC Mia Strong stood by her side, one arm around her shoulders. 'Hey, come on,' he said. 'You have to stop those tears.'

'But the blood. Jimmy's face... covered in all that blood... The stupid fuckwit!'

A shadow fell across her line of vision, and the sole of a leather shoe scraped across gravel. 'I could have you for insubordination,' Bliss told her. The laugh he gave was fleeting and insincere. His head was swathed in bandages, dried blood caking his cheeks, trailing lines reaching down towards his chin.

The two female DCs looked up at him. Strong gave a faint smile, but Chandler shook her head, eyes flaring with anger. 'I can't believe you came out here on your own to challenge him. I mean, have you seen the size of Bobby Dunne? Forget the weapon he had, he'd snap you in half with his bare hands.'

Bliss gingerly raised a hand to his head. 'I don't think that's what he had in mind, do you?'

After receiving treatment from a paramedic, he had spent ten minutes or so explaining what had happened between him and Dunne. He knew he'd have to do it all over again for Sykes and DCS Flynn. The sequence of events was clear, despite the flood of adrenaline it had released.

When the two shots were fired into his face, Bliss's head had jerked back instinctively. Far enough that the damage from the expelled paper wad and unburned particles of gunpowder was limited, although it still caused several lacerations and burns across his face. The explosive sound was surprisingly loud in the small car. When Dunne fired into his own mouth and the back of his head failed to erupt in a shower of blood, brain matter and bone, the big man stared at the gun for several seconds, clearly trying to work out why his mouth and cheeks were cut to pieces and burned, but he was somehow still alive.

'The clip is filled with blanks,' Bliss told him. 'I didn't think they'd be quite that noisy or that bloody painful.'

'But how…? How could you have…?'

'In a way, you told me. Just like you told me everything else I needed to know.'

'I did?'

Bliss nodded. 'When I was certain about you, about what you had done, I knew I would need all the evidence I could lay my hands on. It's the one thing this fucking awful case has lacked all along. I got to thinking about the report sheets you produced. Things have changed a great deal in the past sixteen years or so, and all forms are very different these days, which meant that if you had forged them recently, you must have a supply of them. I thought you might even have the original files tucked away somewhere. I spent some time trying to figure out where you would hide them, and then I remembered the night I went to see Simon Palmer. You and I had that smooth brandy in your shed.

That's when you told me that you thought a man's shed could hide all their secrets.'

Dunne eased out a sigh, and turned his head away.

'I know,' Bliss said, nodding. 'The fucking irony, eh? Anyhow, I drove over to your place, got into your garden, picked my way into your shed and started removing slats from the ceiling. I found a box of old blank crime report forms, cartons of other forms, plus the original files from the two cases. I also found your gun.'

Dunne looked back at him, his eyes betraying bewilderment. 'Why didn't you just remove it and lock it away somewhere? Use the evidence you found to arrest me?'

Bliss had asked himself that same question several times. He wasn't sure the answer was good enough, but it was all he had.

'I needed you and me to be alone, Bobby. No Sykes, no Flynn, no brief, no fucking rules and regulations. I wanted to look in your eyes up close when you told me your story. I wanted to see the truth for myself. I guessed you might go and collect your gun once you knew we were supposed to be seeing Jodie's friend, because you knew she was the only one left who might recall what Joe Flynn looked like. And, of course, you no longer had Rhodes to do your dirty work for you. I had to leave the gun in place in order to make sure you came here tonight, but I obviously had to make sure it was safe. So, among other trips I made to various places, I paid a visit to the ARV crew who were over in Stilton on the practice ground, and obtained a clip of their light-load blanks.'

Bliss felt the pain of the cuts and abrasions on his face, the sting of the burns. He grinned through it. 'Not light enough, apparently. I was assured these would do little harm. I'll be having a word with them just as soon as I've recovered.'

Dunne was looking closely at him now. 'You're good, Bliss. Too fucking good for your own health. You're acting like you have the upper hand now, but I don't think you've thought this through properly. See, I don't need a gun to kill you. I could snap your neck right now without too much effort.'

'Yes, you could,' Bliss agreed. 'But you were wrong earlier when you said this would all be over. You see, the last thing I did before coming to meet you was put a letter on Penny's desk. In it I outlined your involvement, and where the evidence can be found. Killing me won't end it after all, Bobby.'

Dunne was silent for several seconds, then suddenly threw open his door and made a run for it. In the darkness and gathering mist, Bliss lost sight of him within seconds. By the time Bliss had reacted and scrambled out of the car, Dunne was gone. Bliss started to give chase anyway, but after just a few strides his head began to swim, the world started to turn, faster and faster, until his legs buckled and he fell to the ground, smacking his head on the road and opening up a deep laceration on his scalp. Cursing, he managed to force himself into a sitting position, and when his head had cleared and his vision had righted itself, placed a call to HQ and waited for the inevitable overkill of personnel to arrive.

When Chandler pulled up and emerged from her car, her immediate response was to forget herself and start slapping his arms, berating him for acting so foolishly. Now, as Mia left them alone by the ambulance, Penny swept both hands through her hair, shaking her head gently.

'I'm still in complete shock,' she told Bliss. 'Bobby Dunne a killer? It's crazy. Absurd.'

Bliss thought so, too. He'd known about it for hours, yet still he felt numb. 'I could have lived another two lifetimes and not guessed. He played us brilliantly, me in particular. I had no idea he could be that subtle.'

'He had a lot to protect,' Penny reminded him.

'He did. His whole life, in fact. You know, I thought he might pull the gun on me and take me out, but I never expected him to try and off himself. I can't believe he'd do that to his family.'

'It makes me wonder if we knew anything about him at all.'

Bliss looked up sharply as several officers in the distance congregated swiftly. One broke away from the group and started to move towards Bliss and Chandler. As he closed in on them and came forward into the soft glow of flickering lights, Bliss noticed that the uniform wore a look of utter anguish. Bliss felt a tug deep in his gut. This was not going to be good news.

***

The search party had come upon the result of DS Dunne's actions long before they realised he had been involved. On the southbound stretch of the A1(M), a long tailback of cars had caught the attention of several officers. In the middle lane beneath one of the bridges, what remained of Bobby Dunne after he had jumped directly in front of a heavy goods vehicle lay in bloody, ragged pieces, smeared across the road's surface.

Bliss had no desire to take one last look at the man who had been a good friend these past few years. He didn't want his last mental image of Bobby to be the stuff of nightmares. Memories of the man would be forever tainted, however. There was no escaping that fact. Instead he allowed Penny to drive him back to Thorpe Wood.

'Did you see the newspaper?' he asked Chandler as they hit the slip road heading towards the city.

She shook her head. 'No. I heard about it, though. The retraction is out there now, as well.'

'Too late for me and Emily, unfortunately.' He told Penny about the phone call.

'I'm sorry, boss. Maybe she just needs some time.'

'It didn't sound that way. It felt… definite. Like the end.'

'But she didn't actually say that. Telling you not to call her is not quite the same as ending it completely.'

'You think I *should* call? Despite what she said.'

Chandler stifled a laugh. 'You really don't know women at all, do you?'

'Maybe not. Fact is, recent events suggest I don't know anything about anyone.'

'Except me, I hope.'

Bliss smiled. Nodded. 'Yeah. There's always you to rely on, Penny.'

'That's a fact. Perhaps you ought to do it more often.'

'Perhaps. Maybe you could have kept Bobby alive.'

Chandler rolled her eyes. She pointed the car in the direction of HQ and put her foot down hard. 'Jesus, Jimmy. Are you going to take Bobby's death on now? You want another burden to carry?'

Bliss made no reply, but he did give weight to her question. It was in his nature to accept blame, even to seek it. He'd always seen it as taking responsibility for his actions. When it came to his wife's murder, he'd been responsible for agreeing to the wife swapping. In the case of the suicide marking the end of his previous murder case, his responsibility had been to agree to using the poor soul to entrap a killer. And now there was Bobby Dunne. Bliss had decided to challenge Bobby on his own, whereas Penny's presence may have prevented the man from escaping. I'm responsible for that, too, Bliss told himself. That his decisions had been merely part of a sequence of events made no difference to him. Penny was right – he did carry these burdens.

Bliss doubted he would ever be released from them.

THIRTY-EIGHT

Detective Chief Superintendent Flynn's office seemed a great deal smaller than Bliss remembered. Perhaps it was the presence of an extra person in the form of Sykes, who sat at the desk alongside Flynn. Bliss felt the gaze of both men upon him, and the atmosphere in the room was charged with tension and raw emotion. He'd just been asked a question, but it had somehow escaped his conscious thoughts.

'Sorry,' Bliss said, not looking up. 'Would you repeat that?'

It was Sykes who had spoken. As he did again now. 'One would think you'd be keen to pay attention, Inspector. This may be an unofficial enquiry, but you'd do well to give it your due regard as a formal one will follow in due course.'

'Yes. Sorry. My ears are still not quite right.' Bliss nodded absently. Truth was he felt as if only a part of him was here in the room with these two senior officers. And not the largest part, either. Inside he felt as if he had nothing left to give, nothing to offer this or any other proceedings. He had been allowed to clean himself up, have a couple of stiches where necessary, his bandages and plasters changed, but this attended only to the exterior.

'I asked you to tell us at what point you began to suspect Detective Sergeant Dunne was responsible for murder.'

'Just today. Prior to that we had pretty much decided that Rhodes had shot his wife and then killed himself.'

'This was the verdict of your entire team?' Sykes asked, leaning forward. His eyes sparkled intensely.

Bliss forced himself to get a grip. He couldn't afford to make such stupid errors. 'No. Sorry, I meant to say that *I* had decided Rhodes was guilty.'

'In other words, you left your team out of this crucial stage in the investigation. Effectively, you went your own way, on a lone crusade.' Sykes rammed home the allegation.

But Bliss had been expecting it and was prepared. 'That's true. But I had my reasons. Good reasons.'

'I'd be interested to hear them,' Flynn said, inserting himself into the grilling. Bliss looked up in time to see a flush of irritation pass across Sykes's cheeks. The interruption had not been welcomed.

Bliss cleared his throat. 'The fact is, it was only yesterday that I began to suspect Sergeant Rhodes. At that point it seemed to me that his calling in sick and then taking an unscheduled holiday was more than coincidental.'

'But why on earth would you even suspect a fellow officer?' Sykes demanded, forcing the attention back to his own line of questioning. 'From what I've seen of the case notes, this inquiry had made few advancements other than identifying the remains. How did you come to make that mental leap, Inspector?'

'Connie Rawlings had informed me that one of Jodie Maybanks's regulars was a uniform. At first this made little impression, because that sort of relationship is not exactly unheard of, but when I later learned of what happened to both Bernard Weller and Alan Dean, I checked back through records to see whether these men might be linked, and how. It was then that I also noted the name of Clive Rhodes featuring significantly.'

'That's all very well, but you haven't explained why you took it upon yourself to move the investigation further along,' Sykes snapped. 'Why you deliberately kept this information from your team, why you excluded them from your ongoing inquiries.'

'Give Inspector Bliss a chance,' Flynn cautioned. His voice was low, but the point was made.

'Thank you, sir,' Bliss said. 'As I was about to say, the moment I started taking Rhodes seriously as a suspect, I realised had a decision to make. To involve my team in the investigation of one of their colleagues, or make progress on my own and spare them that dilemma. Police officers investigating other police officers often become tainted by their actions, and it can make future relations between officers extremely difficult. I didn't want to put my team through that ordeal until I was certain of my facts. You may decide that I made the wrong decision, but it was made with the very best of intentions.'

Bliss swallowed, dropped his gaze. This was the point at which Flynn could decide to interject. The DCS was aware that Bliss was now lying to a senior officer, and if he wished to make that known and disassociate himself from the matter, then Bliss would face the prospect of losing his job.

'It was most certainly the wrong decision,' Sykes insisted. He looked across at his own superior, expecting a nod of agreement.

Instead, DCS Flynn spread his hands and said, 'I'm not so sure about that, Superintendent.'

'But surely keeping such vital information from your own team is a direct contravention of the rules,' Sykes argued. His cheeks were turning red.

'That may be strictly true, but I'm convinced by what I've heard here today that Inspector Bliss was thinking only of his squad. We all know what a quagmire it can be when you're investigating your own colleagues, and I believe the Inspector was simply determined not to have such an inquiry taint his team.'

Flynn had given him a way out, and Bliss took it. 'That's exactly it, sir. I wanted to keep fellow officers away from what was always going to be a difficult and delicate matter. I accept that I broke the rules, but I genuinely believed it was in the best interests of everyone around me.'

'Not for DS Dunne, as it turned out.' Sykes fixed him with a hard glare, his words dripping poison.

Bliss felt the blow, and it stung because he knew that if he'd handled matters differently, Bobby Dunne might still be alive. Even so, Bliss felt he had to retort.

'With respect, DS Dunne was not only a colleague, he was also a good friend. I held his work in the highest regard, and considered him a decent man. I regret the choice he made. That said, he brought his downfall upon himself.'

'I'm still not clear about the details of what happened between you and Dunne. Another flagrant breach of protocol seems to have left you and Dunne alone at a moment of heightened tension. You should never have confronted him on your own.'

'And I'll regret that for the rest of my life,' Bliss said. And he knew he would, despite what anyone else said.

'The precise details are for another day,' said Flynn. 'I'm sure Inspector Bliss needs some time to recover from this tragedy, not to mention his own physical wounds, after which we will expect a full report.'

'As the Inspector's direct line manager, I'm not sure I'm happy with that arrangement,' Sykes complained. 'It seems to me that we need a full debriefing now, while the information is fresh in the Inspector's mind.'

'And as the officer in command of the entire CID team, I think we need to have a little compassion.' This time Flynn turned his hardened gaze upon Sykes. 'Mistakes have been made, and they will be discussed more fully once we have all relevant information at our disposal. However, I have no desire to make what is already a terrible situation even worse. I think we need to take a step back and remember who actually solved this case.'

'It's a sorry mess. Yet again the name of this service will be ridiculed in the media. And need I remind you, sir, who was involved the last time that happened.'

Bliss decided he'd had enough. He was being discussed as if he was not even present in the room. 'Excuse me,' he said. 'But while I am normally the first person to shoulder blame, I would like to point out that it was DS Dunne who was responsible for this series of awful events, not me. I didn't murder anyone. I simply did my job.'

Before Sykes could respond, Flynn held up a hand. 'I think that will be all, Inspector. Now, here's what I would like you to do: remove yourself from the duty roster, and don't let me catch you here again until Monday morning. While you are off, I want you to compile a fully detailed report. In addition, obtain and collate all other outstanding reports from members of your team. Prepare for an internal inquiry, Inspector Bliss. Prepare your team for the same. Oh, and one last thing: you were previously offered the opportunity of undergoing counselling and therapy, an offer you declined. This time you have no option. Are we clear?'

Bliss could have hugged the man. Flynn was allowing him time to get his story straight, to consider every angle and make the final report work. The counselling and mention of an inquiry was a bone for Sykes, but the DCS was effectively providing Bliss with the opportunity of emerging relatively unscathed.

'We're clear, sir,' he said. Bliss glanced across at Sykes, who had been shaking his head for several minutes. Their eyes met. In that instant, Bliss knew his most bitter opponent was not about to let this go without a fight. Behind the scenes there would be mutterings of discontent, veiled accusations against both Bliss and Flynn. But it was a battle Sykes would not win.

***

A fine mist of rain enveloped the mourners. Grey skies carried darker threats, harbingers of the storm to come. In the shadow of a hulking medieval church whose bells tolled without regret, Bliss stood leaning against a cold granite headstone that had been erected more than a hundred years ago. He wondered if there was anyone around who still remembered the person buried here, whether their legacy had crossed the generations. He also questioned what he would leave behind other than a trail of misery.

Bliss watched as the group of mourners dispersed to go their separate ways. Only three people remained at the graveside, their heads bowed. Bliss slipped between the burial mounds and moved across to join them. When he stopped, only a couple of yards away, the three looked up to see who had joined them.

A woman, in her mid-sixties Bliss guessed, gave a puzzled frown. She forced her mouth into what passed as a smile of welcome.

'Hello,' she said. Her voice was cultured and refined, her black clothes immaculate and expensive looking. 'We haven't met before. Did you know my daughter?'

'Connie?' Bliss nodded. 'Yes, I did. Not well, and only recently, but I felt I should come to pay my respects.'

'Did you work with her?'

To either side of the woman stood a man, whom Bliss took to be her husband, and a woman about Connie's age. She looked a little like her, too. Bliss saw something flicker in her eyes. She knows, Bliss thought. She knows what Connie did for a living, but her parents don't.

'Uh, no I didn't. We met socially. I liked her very much.'

The woman nodded and glanced down into the open grave, rain now beating down on the lid of the coffin. 'I'm not surprised. Our daughter was a very special person.'

Bliss thought about Connie Rawlings, wondering what had driven her into the life she'd chosen. He remembered her smile, the way she had relaxed with him in her bed, opened up to him in a way she never would have with a client. Their collision had been a fleeting, yet welcome instalment in his life. Bliss hoped Connie Rawlings had felt the same.

In days to come there would be two more people to say goodbye to. He did not relish informing Allison Weller of her husband's past, but he had taken on that duty willingly. The woman deserved to hear the words from someone with whom she was familiar, not some faceless bureaucrat from HQ. Bliss would tell her of Bernie's role in the Jodie Maybanks case, but he would coat it with just enough sugar to make his words palatable.

How he would cope with facing Bobby Dunne's wife was another matter entirely.

***

'Another chain of guilt, Inspector Bliss?'

Doctor Karen Hardy regarded him thoughtfully, but with an uncommon empathy. He had just finished telling her about Hazel and then about Bobby Dunne, before describing in detail the conversation with Connie Rawlings's mother, and his thought process earlier that morning at the cemetery.

Bliss nodded. 'How can it be anything else? If I hadn't questioned Connie, she would still be alive.'

'But in your line of work you question many people. On a daily basis. Are you to be held accountable for any and all of their ordeals that come about as a result of your investigation?'

'No. I'm not saying that. But I ought to have realised that my contact with Connie had left her vulnerable.'

'Do you believe you can protect everyone, Inspector?'

'Please, call me Jimmy.'

Hardy smiled. 'Another time, perhaps. This is our first session, and I think we need to maintain a formal basis.'

Bliss regarded her thoughtfully. Hardy was attractive, somewhere in her late thirties, thick black hair cut short and curling into her neck, bracketing an interesting face. Her eyes sparkled whenever she spoke. Her office was muted, no grandiose certificates attesting to her competence adorning the walls. Bliss decided this was a woman he could open up to. Eventually.

'Fair enough,' he said. 'And no, I don't expect to be able to protect everyone. People fall through the cracks sometimes. I've been in this ugly business long enough to realise that. But this was different.'

'How so? Because it was personal?'

'Maybe.'

'Then you feel responsible only for those with whom you have a close association.'

'No, not exactly. It's just that it feels worse. It feels... so unnecessary. Avoidable.'

The therapist shook her head. 'Every second of every day we make decisions that affect not only our lives, but the lives of others. If you decide to take a different route to work and are involved in an accident that takes the life of another, is the death your fault because you chose to go that way?'

'That's just cause and effect. I have no control over that.'

'The problem for you, Inspector, is that you have control over very little in this life.'

Bliss said nothing.

'Eventually you will break under the weight of this burden, Inspector,' Dr Hardy insisted. 'You are intelligent enough to realise that. Yet still you continue. I wonder why that is.'

'You wonder, or are you asking me a question?'

'I'm not asking, because I don't think you'll tell me at this stage. You are defensive, and that's understandable.'

Bliss pulled his attention back. 'Yes. Right now I have other things on my mind. Like the fact that a good friend and close colleague turned out to be a cold-blooded killer, and then committed suicide rather than face his punishment. That his suicide could have been prevented if I had done my job properly. And that a fine woman was murdered because again I didn't do my job properly.'

'Let's not forget your wife, either. Because that's where all this began. Isn't that right, Inspector Bliss? Did you feel responsible for everyone and everything before you lost your wife?'

'Hazel made sense of my life. She was everything to me. I failed her. I wasn't there for her when she needed me most.'

'And ever since you've been trying to ensure that never happened again.'

Silence filled the void between them, but Hardy nodded as if he'd spoken anyway. 'That's a place to start, Inspector. I think we can build on that. But before we go down that road, we have to assess where you are right now. Other than these genuine sorrows already discussed, other than your work and what drives you on, tell me what else ails you.'

For a heartbeat, Bliss considered telling her about his illness. Instead he said, 'There's this woman I want to get to know better.'

'I see. And what's stopping you, exactly?'

'Only the fact that I slept with Connie Rawlings.'

Dr Hardy smiled. 'Now, that's a much more familiar problem. I think perhaps we can deal with that one here and now.'

Bliss thought of Emily, and decided therapy might not be such a bad option after all.

THE END

ACKNOWLEDGEMENTS

It's hard to know where to begin. However, since home is where both the heart and oven is, I think it best I start there. So, a huge debt of gratitude goes out to my long-suffering wife for graciously allowing me the time and space in which to write.

I'm also not sure where this book would have taken me were it not for the efforts of my own editor, Doug Watts at JBWB. My gratitude is also extended to my Bloodhound Books editor, Lesley Jones.

To my family, friends, and supporters, a big thank you goes out to you all.

To my mother and father, for having the good sense to bring me into the world. I miss you, dad.

To Betsy, Fred and Sarah at Bloodhound Books – thanks for taking a leap of faith with me and for getting it out there.

Finally, this book is dedicated to Ei and Lori – my wife and my daughter, who also happen to be my best friends.

Tony J Forder
Peterborough
April 2017

Printed in Great Britain
by Amazon